THE VAMPIRE CROWN

THE VAMPIRE CROWN

THE VAMPIRE DEBT: BOOK FIVE

USA TODAY BESTSELLING AUTHOR

ALI WINTERS

First Edition
Paperback ISBN-13: 978-1-945238-26-0
Hardcover ISBN-13: 978-1-945238-23-9

www.aliwinters.com
www.thevampiredebt.com

The Hunted series Omnibus

In The End duology

Sound of Silence

Light in Darkness

In The End Omnibus

Stand Alone Titles

Cast In Moonlight

Favor of the Gods

Shadow World
SUNFAL
Nightwich
CASTLE
Progsdale
Durford
Littlemire
Valeburn

MOUNTAINS
Sangate
Gloamfarrow
Windbury
Galeport
Murhelm
Crescent Isle
Stormvale
N

For all those who follow their hearts, even when the odds are stacked against you.

And for my readers.

CHAPTER ONE

ALARIC

Lavender eyes framed by snowy lashes watch me expectantly. The growing adoration welling within my chest drowns out the last of an unwelcome feeling from moments ago.

In a blink, it is forgotten altogether. And along with it, the reason and cause that it sprouted from.

It must have been nothing of consequence to be banished so easily.

A hint of blood lingers on my tongue from a recent feeding, but the burn of hunger denied for far too long remains. It is harsh. Demanding. Unyielding.

The taste is… *off*, somehow, though I cannot pinpoint how. Was the mortal's blood tainted by illness ravaging their body, or had they ingested poison, thinking it would end my life along with theirs? It's impossible to know without a body anywhere in sight.

Buzzing swarms inside my head, loud and

unintelligible, turning into a pounding ache. Poison is the most logical conclusion.

Though that, too, hardly matters. Other than mild irritation, it didn't work.

It doesn't matter.

Our queen is here.

The thought intrudes over all others.

"Alaric?"

Every moment leading up to this one is lost in a fog. The name settles on my bones, fitting like a well-worn glove. Instinctively, I know that is who I am.

"Was there something you wish to tell me?" My queen arches a sharp brow.

Yes.

"Yes," I echo the thought out loud. Then I pause, unsure what words should follow.

We stand in the receiving room of my personal quarters. She would not be here if I hadn't summoned her for an important matter.

My hesitation brings the answer forward. *It is time. We will do as she has always wanted. We will finally take our place at her side.*

"It is time. I am ready to take my place as your consort, as you have always wanted." Each word scrapes up my parched and raw throat. An insatiable need to feed again.

A shift lingers in the air. Large enough to shake the world, yet ambiguous, leaving no clear sign of what it was beyond a haze of unfamiliarity, settling like dust in a room, long forgotten.

Satisfaction curls the edges of my queen's mouth.

She is pleased. As any vampire ought to be, I am her loyal subject. After all, she is the force that shaped the world.

Why had I not complied with her wishes before now? *Surely, Rosalie—*

Perched on the mantel, Kharis croaks and beats their wings against the air.

The past is of no consequence. We will right wrongs and not dwell on what cannot be changed.

The demon's eyes blaze bright red.

Searing pain lances through my skull like molten silver. Need and instinct demanding my full attention. I try to speak, but the only sound that forms is a furious hiss.

Large eyes widen in alarm. "You must be starving, my love." She lifts a hand and snaps her fingers once.

I don't have time to muse on how she knew. The door opens, and two guards enter, half escorting and half dragging a human woman between them.

The mortal's face is blank, and each movement she makes has the jerky cadence of a sleepwalker. Her hair is styled similar to that of a courtier—not a strand out of place. It is the dress that gives her purpose away. Every inch is the color of sea foam, save for the low neckline. The fabric shimmers, nearly black at the top, melting into a rich burgundy halfway down the bodice to give it the appearance of spilled blood.

The lack of a single scar shows that this is her first offering. A gift from my queen and a symbol to all others of my importance to her.

The guards stop halfway inside the room and

release the woman. When she doesn't move on her own accord, the larger of the two shoves a hand against the human's back, causing her to stumble.

"Do you offer your blood willingly?" the other demands.

"Yes." The one-word answer is flat and emotionless, but she holds her head high.

The second guard makes a barely audible sound of derision as he thrusts a sharp object into the mortal's hand, squeezing her fingers to tighten her grip. She whimpers.

Immediately, the pungent tang of blood fills the room as it cuts into her palm. A dagger without a hilt. Thick drops patter to the floor.

Hunger transforms into a beast with claws, sinking into my chest and shredding its way up my throat.

The harder I try to remember what events happened that left me in such a starving and weak state, the more my mind feels as if something has bored holes into my mind, draining away memories.

It does not matter.

Only our queen matters...

The human approaches, stopping half an arm's length away. Her chest rises and falls with rapid, shallow breaths. She waits for my answer to an unspoken question. My gaze flickers from the mortal's wrist to her neck.

I must hesitate too long because she drags the blade across her wrist with a sharp inhale, then presses the metal point to her shoulder near her neck.

Blood wells up from each wound, spilling over in

macabre rivulets. I am moments from losing the tenuous grip on my control.

A tear spills over as the blade begins to sink in.

"Feed," Elizabeth says.

I turn from the mortal and give my queen my full attention.

Our wants are nothing if she is not pleased.

"You must be at your strongest if you are to rule beside me."

It is all the command I need.

I reach out and take the woman's arm and pull her closer. My fangs are buried in her wrist before the dagger clatters at our feet. The first pull of blood is painful as it fights to quench my vicious thirst.

It feels as if centuries have passed since I last fed. The blood lends me strength, quelling the sting. But rather than sating the hunger, the edges only dull while the need only increases, leaving me little more than a creature of instinct.

A single thought prevails as I drink.

More.

I release her wrist and pull the human in, then clamp down on the wound above her collarbone. She clings to me, her weak fingers curl into the lapels of my jacket and soft, unintelligible noises work free of her throat.

She wobbles and leans forward, supporting herself against me. She sighs. Her knees give out and I lower us, kneeling. After a moment, the flow of blood slows and her heartbeat becomes faint. I wrench my fangs from her flesh.

Before she falls, the two guards catch her by the

arms and haul her back several feet. She gasps. They release their grip, letting her crumple into a heap on the floor. The taller guard toes her in the ribs with his boot, giving her a hard shove. The motion rocks her body, but she is otherwise still. Not a single breath stirs within her chest.

After a silent command, the human's lifeless body is removed from the room. The only traces left behind are the reek of mortality and the blood she spilled. It soaks into the area rug, blending with the intricate design.

I don't think she was supposed to die.

Alone once more with my queen grants me a small comfort through the rising turmoil.

Humans are born to die. This is nothing new, the thought hisses from the shadows of my mind. *She chose this death.*

My stomach churns.

She was happy to die.

Still, it takes everything I have to keep my meal from revolting and coming back up. My mind is at war with some deep-rooted instinct that should have faded well over a century ago. My head aches with the bevy of contradictions that eat away at all I know.

She wanted to die.

Elizabeth bends at the waist, tilting my face up to meet her gaze. "Well done," she purrs. Her voice is low and seductive.

Hers.

We belong only to her... her prince.

The glowing ring around her lavender irises is so intense, it would force a mortal to avert their eyes. It's only when she holds me captive with her gaze that I can remember who I am, the reason I exist.

Her tongue darts out, licking a smear of blood from the corner of my mouth. "You will finally be the prince I have waited so long for you to become." It is not a hope she has, but a command.

We will not fail her.

"I will not fail you." The words leave my mouth with the same effortless ease as drawing breath in sleep.

Her mouth descends on mine. Fangs scrape over my tongue as she allows both sets to lengthen. The points tear at my flesh, as her bottom fangs pierce my lower lip.

I relish the sharp sting because it is from her.

She ends the kiss. By the time she releases me and allows me to straighten, the wounds she inflicted are already healing.

One corner of her mouth tilts up. My queen watches me, assessing. A long, elegant finger taps rhythmically on the elbow of her opposite arm crossed over her body.

Kharis croaks, the sound an unsettling mimic of the word *blood.* My queen's attention slides from me to her demon. She nods to them once. Then, without a word or glance, she turns and strides toward the door. The bird leaps from the fireplace mantle and perches on her shoulder.

Without a discernible sound or signal, the guards on the other side open the doors and allow her to pass without breaking her stride. With a resounding thud, they close behind her.

The silence rings in my ears. Loud. Nearly deafening. I can hardly think through the viscous cloud it creates in my head.

Do not displease her. The thought comes harsh and scraping across my mind.

She should never be displeased.

CHAPTER TWO

CLARA

WHEN STORIES END, EVIL IS DEFEATED, AND WE content ourselves in knowing the hero will live a peaceful life from that point on. But reality has no such endings or guarantees. We may think we have found our way out of the dark, only to stumble right back into it without warning.

Two eyes swirling with the blood-red and burnished gold of molten metal grow brighter, rooting me to where I stand.

Thick shadows along the edges of the cell, where no light ever touches, stretch out, expanding until the dark swallows up what little I can see in the dim light of this cell until those bright orbs are all that remain. The demon's breath washes over my face with every exhale—cold as winter wind, carrying the faint scent of wood smoke.

"Do not make the mistake of thinking it will be easy to take in my power, and there is a good chance you will not live long enough to make use of it—

regardless of how hard you train. I may be chained beneath this castle, but that does not make me weak."

That might as well be a promise of certain death. A fact that should frighten me, but I find it doesn't. After all, the likelihood I'll die anyway before this is over is practically guaranteed.

If making a deal with a demon doesn't kill me, there are a dozen other, more terrible ways that await their turn. Only this offers me a sliver of hope for success. Out of the limited options available to me, *this* might be the least horrible end I could choose. Still, I don't wish to die.

The demon's low growl sends a shiver vibrating over my skin as it rumbles through the dank cell. Their gaze narrows when I do not respond. "Do you understand?"

"Yes." The sound is little more than a dry rasp clawing its way up my throat. "I have no intention of going back on my word," I say softer than intended, though grateful my voice doesn't waver.

Neither of us attempts to fill the heavy silence that follows. In the quiet, I have the uncanny sensation Varin is taking my measure for how well they think I will bear their power. The longer it continues, the more uneasy I become until my body hums with a rush of nerves.

I can't help but imagine how this demon's magic might feel coursing through me.

Will it be like Alaric's when he healed me the night I returned to Windbury after Kitty's wedding? The way sparks of crimson ran over his hands, like veins of lightning, and the tingling sensation that swiftly transformed into blinding pain, stealing my breath. The scars on my left leg prickle with the phantom burn and the echo of that vicious cold.

Or will it be worse?

I suppress a shudder at the vivid clarity of the memory but find comfort in knowing that whatever pain will come, it *will* be worth it.

What is necessary in life is often the more difficult path. All anyone can do is make the best choice from the options before them and move forward with confidence in that decision.

This is my choice, so I will bear whatever lies ahead. It is the least I can do.

"Then let us begin." Varin lists their head to the side with a sharp cracking of joints.

I try to untangle my thoughts, to sort them in order of importance, but it's no use. I am already exhausted after the events of the past day. My heart is raw, with too many jagged emotions tangled together as they vie to dominate each other...

After everything, Alaric and I still ended up in this near-impossible position. And what I'm attempting, what I need to do, what I must face is so monumental...

It's all too much.

I squeeze my eyes shut and tamp down the urge to surrender to defeat.

If I want to survive this, if I want to have a shadow of a chance at breaking the curse, then I must find a way to stay strong. But the thought of pain makes me want to weep.

"How badly will it hurt?" The question slips out

before I can stop it. It exposes the weakness I must tamp down and smother.

"It is too late for such questions," they say evenly. There's a sharp edge to the whisper-soft gentleness of their voice.

There are many things I *should* have said—things I should have asked before now. The deal is already struck. There is no point in asking because the answer will change nothing.

Ice crawls down my spine. My throat constricts as instinct takes over. I take a step back. My heel catches on the uneven floor, causing me to stumble.

Varin's hand shoots out in a blur. The speed of the movement causes me to flinch and squeeze my eyes shut against the dizzying effect. Their bone-thin hand, hard as stone, catches me, long taloned fingers curling around my waist. Varin pulls me in until my feet dangle in the air, bringing our faces close together. The night-forged silver chains that bind them rattle.

The two burning coals of their eyes sear into me. A low growl reverberates in their throat. Uncertainty slithers through my veins, quickening my pulse until it's a frantic drumming inside my skull.

"Even if you run now, do not think you can break our bargain so easily. I may be a prisoner, but I am not entirely powerless." They show me exactly what they mean, each word a spell of its own.

Pressure builds and builds, nearly suffocating. Like invisible hands wrapping around my neck, squeezing… slowly killing me.

"*No.*" I mean to speak firmly, but I'm barely able to

summon the breath to make a small, pitiful sound, but it must be enough. The pressure lifts, and air floods into my lungs, leaving me gasping.

I tentatively press trembling fingers to my neck, expecting tenderness, but there's not a single trace that anything has happened at all.

"I wasn't running," I snap once I manage to catch my breath. I glare at Varin as I fight the impulse to lash out and end our agreement, leaving the wretched creature to rot here for another three hundred years. I allow the spiteful thought to simmer until reason prevails.

Varin sneers in a very human-like manner, and I'm struck by the familiarity of the moment. It snuffs out my remaining anger. How many times did I stand face to face with Alaric, believing him to be nothing more than a monster, undeserving of even an ounce of kindness?

If nothing else, I owe this demon some trust. After all, it is because of them that I was able to break the compulsion Elizabeth placed on Alaric. There is too much at stake for me to change my mind. And knowingly or not, they have revealed as much is true for them. Their desperation is not entirely hidden under the blanket of anger.

Spite and fear will not do either of us any favors.

After Mother was claimed, Father gave up on everything, and the responsibility for my family's survival was dumped onto my shoulders. There are three rules to making deals, and I learned each of them the hard way.

One: Never let them know how much you want or need what they have.

Two: Never begin by offering the most you're able to pay.

Three: Always be willing to walk away.

And I have broken each of them.

I have already agreed to give Varin everything they ask for without challenge, and now, there is little chance they will settle for less.

I press a palm to the side of their face—cool and smooth like polished bone—and just as when Varin healed me in my prison cell, I can sense the hum of their power under the surface. The chill of freshly tilled soil seeps into my palm. It's unsettling to the touch—too much like death. Somehow, I resist the urge to recoil.

The dank dungeon air seeps through my clothes, leaving the material unpleasantly damp against my skin as the demon's silence continues. Their gaze sparks with their ire.

"Varin," I say their name slowly and gently, calling them back from their thoughts.

They go completely and utterly still as stone beneath my touch. Only when I sense their full attention, waiting on me, do I lower my arm.

"I have no intention of backing out now."

The tension around their crimson eyes gradually softens while the demon scrutinizes me, searching for any hidden meaning behind my words. The glowing power from within their irises sinks below the surface, leaving them the warm color of embers burning too low to give off any warmth.

Varin exhales a long breath that ends in a rumble from deep within their chest. They curl inward, hunching their overly long spine as they lower me down. I'm unsteady for several seconds when my feet touch the stone. The long fingers around my waist slowly unfurl.

Brace yourself. Varin's voice reverberates inside my mind.

Before I can process the warning for what it is, pain lances through my hand like a knife, cutting bone deep and slowly dragging past my wrist, then up my arm.

I claw at the ring on my finger, trying to take it off in any way possible. It refuses to budge. It's almost as if the thing is fused to my skin. I clench my jaw until it aches, fighting for every lungful of air.

It is unbearable.

Gravity upends itself. My stomach tumbles, and I swear I am falling up. Without warning, the unseen force releases me, sending me crashing down.

I flutter my eyes open, not knowing when I'd shut them. The only thing separating my face from the ground is the forearm I managed to bring up to block my head from the impact. Fine dirt stirs beneath my labored breathing. A bead of sweat rolls down my cheek, to my arm, then to the dry stone that swallows it.

I lift my gaze to Varin's, expecting a reaction, but the emotionless mask I find tells me nothing. My eyes are gritty, and my throat is tight, stinging with the need for water to soothe it.

"If we continue, you will die." Emotions whirl in

their burning red eyes, flashing from one extreme to the next. Varin helps me to stand, then shifts, scuttling backward.

Every muscle screams in protest at the slightest movement. I push past the ache and stand. It takes several seconds to process what they said. "We've only just started," I protest, advancing on them. "It cannot end like this."

Varin's retreat comes to a forced end by the wall behind them. "You cannot even endure my power by proxy of the ring."

"Then we keep working until I can." I stumble on the next step but catch myself on the demon's outstretched arm. "I will bear your power, even if it kills me."

Averting their gaze, Varin turns and ambles into the nearest shadowy corner, where they curl up like a wounded animal.

It feels like a dismissal. And it sets off a flurry of emotions, the sharpest rising to the top. First, they lashed out with their power, thinking I tried to escape, and now they have given up—doing the very thing they assumed I tried to do.

My hands tighten into fists. Fingernails digging into the tender skin of my palms sting with my attempt to remain in control despite the heightened feelings and sensations from the oath bond. It may take a while to get used to it.

I set my jaw and say, "No."

Varin stiffens at the cutting edge of my voice and peers over their shoulder. Crimson power flares in their eyes for a heartbeat. "No?"

"I will not run like a coward and leave him to suffer. This… this cannot be his fate."

"Everyone believes fate has something magnificent planned for them if only they dare to grab it." Varin makes a derisive sound, but I don't think it's directed at me. "It is never so kind. Most mortals will die alone and forgotten, lost in their delusions while chasing great things that never belonged to them."

My stomach twists sickeningly. The thought of leaving Alaric to be slowly devoured by the curse, to be used until there's nothing left, is unbearable.

"Do not be foolish, Clara. I know you love him, but there is no shame in living…"

Fear crawls up my limbs, leaving me shivering with a numbing cold that seeps into the marrow of my bones. The meaning of what remains unspoken hangs in the air. Cold and cramped, closing in on me, trying to bury me under the weight of it. But I do not accept it. I refuse to.

"If fate does not favor me, then I will change it."

Varin cocks their head. "What makes you think fate is so easily altered?"

"I did not say I think it will be easy." As I speak, something Alaric once said comes to the surface of my memories.

Only now do I realize how deeply I took his words to heart. I have made decisions that could have cost my life—decisions that perhaps no one else would have made. But they were mine alone to make, and I don't regret a single one.

A wry smile pulls at the corners of my lips. "Fate is

only what will come to pass. What matters is the path I choose."

Several moments pass. I'm unsure what they will do, but as seconds stretch to agonizing minutes, I grow more convinced they will still send me away.

"Very well. Then we will continue until we succeed or until you die." There's a slight hint of amusement in Varin's voice.

A chill ripples over the surface of my skin as fire burns along my nerves like poison. Perspiration breaks out across my forehead, and my body feels as though it's turning to ice from the ground up. With no more warning than that, the three pale scars on my lower left leg prickle and sting like needles dipped in acid.

The force of it rips the air from my lungs. Varin traces them with the tips of taloned fingers, barely skimming the surface.

Sparks of red trail in the wake of their touch. The old wounds feel as if time is reversing and all healing is being undone. Slow and torturous… I barely manage to keep my knees from buckling and remain upright.

Between one moment and the next, the pain fades like the smoke from a spent match. Varin removes their hand, withdrawing their power with it.

I slump, going limp while I gasp and cough. Varin lowers me to the ground. I can't breathe, and no matter how hard I fight against its pull, unconsciousness steals over me.

It's dark. The smell of rotting wood and stale air. Beneath me, the ground is hard and cold and uneven. I don't know how long I was unconscious, but I'm thankful that I can at least remember where I am.

"You are awake." Varin's relief is nearly tangible.

Groaning, I lull my head to the side and find the demon's face startlingly close. They are curled up against my side. Their body radiates a mild warmth instead of their usual chill.

It takes effort to sit up. The exhaustion that is coiled within every inch of muscle and bone is so intense I could nearly weep. Not even the Otherworld-damned stone beneath me could stop me from sleeping right in this very spot for a full day if I let myself. Calling on the remaining dregs of strength, I compel my body to rise.

Varin echoes my movements and watches me closely. They take my hand with the ring and hold it palm up, humming thoughtfully.

Before I can figure out what they're about to do, Varin drags something sharp over my hand. I suck in a sharp gasp and struggle to pull away, but I am too weak, and they are too strong for my efforts to do any good.

A stone shard falls between us with a fragile clack. Already forgotten. A wave of nausea rolls over me at the sight of raw flesh through my blood.

Pins and needles race through my veins and down my arm. The sensation is more uncomfortable than painful. But the shrinking well of blood captures my full attention. I gape, not daring to blink as the muscle and skin knit back together. In seconds, it's gone without a trace.

It was nothing how I expected it to feel. Nothing like the first time Alaric healed me or even when Cassius healed me after I'd killed Alexander.

"You did well, Clara." The demon's mouth pulls back just enough to show the menacing points of their double rows of jagged teeth in what I think might be a smile.

A small thrill alights inside my chest.

This might actually work.

My celebration is cut short when the demon's head jerks up, a low growl issuing from their throat. I sway on my feet, feeling the further loss of the energy that small amount of healing took. On instinct, I swivel to face the same direction, though I cannot make out whatever they must have heard or sensed.

"Quickly now," Varin hisses lowly. There's a sense of urgency that wasn't there before as they push me toward the door.

CHAPTER THREE

CLARA

I hesitate, unsure if I'll be able to make it all the way back to my room in my current state, let alone escape the underground level before I'm discovered.

"Go," Varin hisses. "You must hurry." Their sharp tone makes it clear there's no time for questions.

Slipping out, I move as quickly as possible, using the wall for support. Much slower than I would like, I leave the way I came. It's not far from Varin's cell to the door, but by the time I reach it, a cold sweat has broken out across my brow.

I grasp the handle and use my weight to push through. The torch is still where I'd dropped it, but the fire has died down, leaving only lines of embers and the tiniest flickers of flames clinging to life.

A reverberating clang in the distance sends a bolt of panic up my spine.

Boots thud into the corridor. Two, maybe… three sets—it's hard to tell as the pounding of the guard's steps bounce off the walls and through the long passage, the sounds doubling over themselves. Voices speak in casual tones too low to make out what they're saying, punctuated by sharp laughter.

I close the door, gritting my teeth with the effort. It clicks as the lock engages. I hold my breath, listening for any change in their footsteps or speech. Thankfully, it seems to go unnoticed by the guards.

Demons and saints... After my first foray into these lower levels, I've become careless, forgetting that it is not entirely unguarded. It's a wonder I haven't encountered a guard any of the times I carelessly came and went. I will need to be vigilant more than ever because I cannot risk getting caught.

Gathering up the torch, I start up the dark, narrow steps—every passing minute craws by as slow as an hour. The unrelenting, weary ache has settled deep, taking root within every muscle, coupled with the dim flickering light only allowing me to see a few steps ahead. It gives the impression that the way before me is infinite.

The odds are stacked against me. More likely than not, the curse will kill Alaric before I find a way to break it. But as long as the bond we share through the oath remains, keeping us connected, it gives me hope. I know he is alive, so I will keep working to save him. That connection is the only thing preventing the frayed threads holding me together from snapping.

At the top of the stairs, I stop and prop myself against the wall to catch my breath. I lower my arm, no longer having the energy to hold the torch aloft. It slips from my fingers, clattering on the cold stones.

Tiny sparks scatter as the weak flame finally extinguishes.

A few sconces at the far end of the corridor illuminate the space between the armory where Cassius and I train and the spiral stairs leading to the main level. I want nothing more than to rest, but I force myself to keep going.

Using the wall for support, I concentrate on placing one foot in front of the other, refusing to think of the challenges that await me once I make it to the far end.

As I near the training room, the steady, unfamiliar gait of a man's leather boots descending the stairs breaks my focus.

Demon shit. Either the saints are working against me, or I am too far underground for them to aid me.

My thoughts race, looking for an excuse—any excuse—as to why I would be down here by myself.

When I left Cherno in my room, I hadn't told them where I was going. And as far as Cassius is aware, I only come down here when we train. Besides them, I can't think who else might come down to this abandoned part of the castle.

Regardless, whoever it is, whatever their reasons, it doesn't matter. I cannot allow anyone to suspect the truth of what I am up to. I lengthen my stride, forcing my tired legs to move faster. A tall figure comes into view just as I make it within a few feet of the old armory door.

I turn away from them, sniffling as I swipe the sweat from my face and hope that whoever it is believes I'm just a miserable human girl who hid away to cry. It's pathetic, but it's all I can come up with on such short notice.

"Clara?"

The sound of my name freezes me where I stand as I try to place the hesitant voice. Then it clicks, and I whirl to face him.

Lawrence stares at me with what I imagine is an identical expression to the one I give him. In a blink, he is before me, gray eyes wide as if he sees a ghost. Genuine worry has replaced the cool demeanor I'm used to. He grips my shoulders roughly.

"Where have you been? We've been looking for you all morning." He tears his gaze from my face and looks up and down the hall.

Arinah scurries from one of his shoulders to the other, their pink nose twitching long whiskers, then stills. I plead with my eyes for them to stay quiet and give a nearly imperceptible shake of my head.

The white and gold demon rat has no reason to keep anything from their vampire. But if I've learned anything from my encounters with demons, it's that they are capable of a lot more than I ever thought possible—including compassion.

Their red eyes narrow, and I tense, awaiting their decision. They scurry to settle between the collars of Lawrence's Jacket and shirt, leaving only their long pink tail visible. My back wilts as the tension releases my spine.

Finding no one around, Lawrence brings his attention back to me. "Why are you down here?"

I open my mouth to answer, then close it when I

realize I don't have an answer—I don't know what I can say, let alone what I *should* say.

He frowns and presses his lips into a thin line when I stay silent.

"Are you hurt?" he presses.

I shake my head and swallow against the dryness of my parched throat. "No."

Lawrence releases me with a heavy sigh. "Della and I have been searching for you everywhere since dawn."

That surprises me. I could understand Cassius or Della, but… *him?*

"Why? What happened?" Part of me doesn't want to know what more could have possibly gone so wrong that Mr. Harkstead voluntarily came looking for me. The question is already out there. It's too late to take it back.

"If you don't know…" He gives me a look that seems to ask if I've completely lost my wits. He takes in our surroundings as if only now noticing the slight scent of mold, cobwebs in every corner, and the complete lack of adornment. He gestures to my training clothes. "Then why are you down here, dressed like that?"

"I-I needed space to think." I grimace at the pathetic non-answer. Then, to keep him from insisting on more answers I can't give, I add, "Did something else happen?"

Lawrence's expression darkens. A muscle jumps along his jaw, and for a moment, I think he will see through my attempts at diversion.

"Something *else*?" Lawrence snatches my wrist and

drags me closer, then lowers his face to within inches of mine. "Why do I get the feeling there is a lot you are not saying?"

I wince at my careless tongue. There is no chance he will accept anything other than the straightforward truth. "I will tell you, but not here. It would be better if we were with the others. Then I will explain to everyone at the same time."

His nostrils flare. For a moment, I expect Lawrence to argue, but he surprises me when he doesn't. "Fine," he says through clenched teeth.

"Will you take me to my room first? Cherno is waiting for me to return."

Lawrence reaches up and pulls the white and gold demon rat from behind his neck, setting them down with a command to tell Cherno and the others to meet us in Cassius's rooms. Then he takes my arm in his, supporting me as we walk. By all appearances, we are on a leisurely stroll as he silently escorts me through the halls.

An unusual number of the gentry are out in the main areas. I keep my chin high and gaze downcast. The last thing I want right now is to draw unwanted attention.

I'm vaguely aware of servants rushing about as they speak in hushed whispers. They fall silent when they near us, but I catch enough words to understand the abrupt end of the Red Hunt has put everyone on edge.

With each step, Lawrence's impatience begins to show. He hurries us the rest of the way, only slowing when I struggle to keep up. I don't say a thing the entire way. I have a feeling he is one word from throwing me over his shoulder like a sack of grain.

With his help, we soon find ourselves alone in the parlor of Cassius's quarters. A fire crackles in the hearth, and the heat sends a shiver coursing through me. It's as if my body didn't realize how cold I was until I felt the contrast of the warm air.

"You might as well sit while we wait," Lawrence commands, his tone cutting. "Or better yet, lie down. You look like a demon's ass."

I do as he says and stretch out on the couch, propping myself up on the arm.

"I would demand that you explain exactly what the fuck happened, but something tells me you won't speak a word of it until you're good and ready," he says dryly, arching a brow as if daring me to contradict him.

Pressing my lips into a thin line, I don't speak, which only proves his point. I need to think over what I'm going to say and how… what I need to tell them is not something I want to repeat more than once.

Now that I'm not forced to run or fight, unease finds me, creeping in under my skin and settling along every nerve ending. It's the stillness of waiting, of doing nothing, that gets to me.

Even I know I cannot do everything I need to in a single day. I must rest, or I will be useless to Alaric.

Lawrence helps himself to a drink from an ornate liquor cabinet set against the wall. He throws the first glass back in a single gulp, then pours another, sipping this one as he paces the room.

His restlessness burrows beneath my skin until I can't stand it. I straighten up.

"Where is Cassius?"

Lawrence stops in the middle of the room. The crimson rings around his irises, flaring bright. "He sent us to find you because he is being watched." His eyes narrow. "Where is *Alaric*?"

I peer at my hands clasped in my lap and brush my thumb over the healed skin of my palm. Was it only last night that we irrevocably bound ourselves together? So much has changed since then, and the few moments we shared feel like a distant dream.

Slowly, I lift my head and find Lawrence studying me, his expression utterly unreadable. "I ruined everything," I blurt, my voice strangled by emotion. "If I'd done things differently..."

He pulls a handkerchief from his pocket and begins wiping my face.

I hadn't even noticed when I started crying.

With a sigh of exasperation that doesn't quite ring true, he drops down next to me and drapes an arm around my shoulders. "It's just like a human to think they have the power to affect everything."

"This isn't a joke. If it weren't for me, Alaric would be—"

"Alaric would be exactly where he is now. One way or another, Elizabeth would have found a way to drag him back here."

I shake my head. "You don't understand."

"I understand enough." He heaves another sigh. "There are many ways to reach the same end, and there is seldom a right or wrong decision when your hand is forced."

Pulling back, I meet his gaze and frown.

"Even if there had been one correct path," he continues, "You are flawed. No one learns by always making the right choices, and it would be unrealistic to expect anyone to do so."

"Perhaps you could wait to insult me until after I've had a chance to rest?"

He snorts. "That was not meant as an insult. Your flaws are what make you interesting. If humans weren't too busy shunning each other for their seeming imperfections, they would see how those very things are, in fact, great strengths."

"You won't think so favorably of me once you know everything."

"That would imply I ever had any fondness for you at all," he says flatly, then grimaces. "Well... I didn't. But you're like a weed once its roots take hold—nearly impossible to get rid of—and I am no gardener."

I send him a sidelong glance. "Is *that* supposed to be a compliment?"

Lawrence shrugs. And for a moment, my breath comes a little easier. His smile slips when his gaze drops to my hand. His fingers wrap around my wrist, gripping firmly but not painfully so. He lifts my hand in an unspoken question and leans in, searching for some physical mark to confirm his suspicion.

The skin has healed completely, leaving no trace or sign behind. Yet somehow, Lawrence manages to find the line, tracing a finger over the exact place

Alaric cut. The touch leaves a trail in its wake, like sparks of static.

His brows furrow. "You are oath—" he starts haltingly, but he doesn't get a chance to finish.

Della strides through the door with Cherno perched in one hand. "Still no sign of her, but I—" She stops abruptly, eyes narrowing as she takes in our proximity. "You found her."

CHAPTER FOUR

CLARA

Lawrence drops my wrist and stands.

Cherno leaps into the air and glides across the room. I stand and catch them in my cupped hands. Arinah's small form hops through like a whisper of fog, chittering angrily and solidifying on this side. The demon rat runs to Lawrence and climbs up to his shoulder.

Cassius bursts into the room, throwing the doors shut behind him as he storms toward me. "Where in the Otherworld have you been, Clara?"

I flinch and take an involuntary step back. Cherno scuttles up my arm and clings to my neck, pulling on a lock of hair as they tangle themselves in the strands.

"She looks like demons tormented her for a week," Della says coolly, attempting to hide the edge of worry in her tone. Not so long ago, I might have missed it.

While I am exhausted, both of their comments on

my appearance make me think I'm in worse shape than I thought.

"I found her near the old armory, hiding like a feral animal."

Cassius's posture goes rigid. He tilts his head and takes in my appearance. His expression only solidifies the other two vampires' remarks.

A headache is forming behind my eyes. I lower into the chair beside the fireplace and massage my temples.

"Are you injured?" Cassius moves dizzyingly fast and kneels at my feet, then takes my face in his warm hands. "What went wrong? Did Alaric find you? Why—"

I press my fingers against his mouth to silence the stream of questions. It seems to communicate my meaning well enough. He sits back on his heels and waits.

Now that they're all here, I can tell them what they want to know—at least as much as I am able. Hopefully, it will be enough to answer their more pressing questions.

My stomach twists with nerves. The series of events isn't overly complicated, but it feels like a monumental task. Putting it off or trying to avoid it won't make it easier. So, I take a fortifying breath, and then I tell them everything. From the moment Alaric woke me to the moment we oath bound ourselves to each other—skipping over the more intimate details that followed. When I get to the part where we made plans, their expressions send a wave of guilt crashing down on me. The words I don't say ring loud.

Alaric and I planned to leave without so much as a goodbye to any of them.

I thought merely uttering all of this aloud would undo me. I thought I might not even get them out between sobs. Instead, they fall from my lips, as hollow and empty as I feel. Finally, I tell them how Cherno came to me, telling me how Elizabeth cursed Alaric.

I stop there, allowing them to draw their own conclusions as to why Lawrence found me where he did. A thick silence settles over the room. It's nearly suffocating, bearing down, until it breaks with a shatter.

The scent of liquor fills the room, cloying and thick. Blood drips from Lawrence's clenched fist onto the wood floor, glittering atop the shards and mixing with the liquid of the spilled drink. He is furious.

"Did you not think it prudent to lead with this?" Lawrence grinds out each word. He stalks closer, stopping just over an arm's length away when Cassius makes a warning gesture. "Do you have any idea what this means for him, or is it simply that you do not care?"

"Of course I care." I did warn him that he would not think favorably of me once he knew.

Cool fingers brush my arm on my other side, startling me. Della's eyes shine with the tears I can't seem to summon.

I press the heel of my hand to my forehead. I can't think… I'm lost in a fog of overwhelm.

Cassius stands and moves to the fireplace. He

stares into the flames with one hand on his hip and the other braced against the mantle.

Between the warmth and soothing crackle of the fire, I allow myself to sink deeper into the plush cushions. Weariness settles in my bones, turning my muscles leaden. My eyelids flutter, and I struggle to keep them open. What sleep I managed in the past day was restless, and since then, I have pushed myself past my limits.

I'm somewhere between consciousness and dozing when a hand alights on my shoulder. I pull in a breath and peer up into Cassius's face.

"I'm sorry," he says. Though I can't think what he would need to apologize for. He must see the question on my face because he elaborates. "I do not want to see you suffer more than you already have." Wretchedness fills his features, darkens his gaze.

A tendril of dread wends through me, to my heart, wrapping around it, and squeezes. I try to swallow past the lump in my throat, but I still can't find my voice. His growing disquiet sets my nerves on edge, chasing away every last speck of exhaustion.

"What are you talking about?"

"I must ask something of you," he says, taking my hands and clasping them firmly between his own. "Don't answer right away. Think about it first."

"Cassius—"

"Promise me that you will consider my request before answering."

"I promise. Now, out with it. You're making me nervous."

"Leave with me—tomorrow night."

I am briefly stunned. What Cassius wants doesn't make sense. I don't understand what he means. I want to hope that it's the beginning of a plan, but my gut tells me otherwise.

"And go where?" I ask when I manage to find my voice.

"Sangate," he says simply. When I continue to stare at him in confusion, he goes on, "I was born there, but I haven't set foot in that city for a long time. There, I will be able to keep you safe."

His meaning slides into place like the harsh snap of a deadbolt. He wants me to abandon Alaric—forget about him as if I don't love him... as if I never did.

"No," I say in a tone that brooks no room for argument. Pulling my hands out of his grasp, I rise to my feet. I don't consider his request—I don't need to. My decision would have been the same either way. He likely expected as much.

"If Alaric is truly cursed, then he is as good as dead. It will eat away at his body and mind. It is only a matter of time before he succumbs." Each word is harsher than the last. More cutting. "Elizabeth did this to him, but she will blame you, and for that, she will make you pay."

I cannot fault him for anything he said, but I can fault him for the way he said it. True or not, his delivery leaves me stricken.

Cassius at least has the decency to look chagrined when he sees what his words have done to me. He reaches out, but I move out of reach before he can.

"No," I say firmly. "No, I will not leave this place— not with you. Not with anyone. Not without Alaric."

"Be reasonable—" he cuts himself off, seeming to realize his mistake immediately, and holds up both hands. "What I mean to say is there are others who care about you and don't want to see you come to any harm."

Across the room, Lawrence snorts. The sound is swiftly followed by a grunt, which I can only assume is caused by Della shoving her elbow into his ribs.

"I can't give up on him—I *won't*."

"There is nothing anyone can do to stop what she has put in motion."

"Nothing anyone *can* do, or nothing anyone is *willing* to do?" If Varin hadn't promised to help me break the curse, would I feel as I do now, or would I believe it as hopeless a cause as they do?

"Do not do this to yourself, Clara… please. Take what time you need to mourn, but do not doom yourself by clinging to the impossible."

"I will not stop until he is dead, and even then, if I have to wrest him from the Otherworld and bring him back, then I will."

Cassius leans back, one brow arched as he regards me with suspicion. "What exactly are you planning to do, little bird?"

"Everything," I whisper. I sigh, then drop back down into the chair. His eyes narrow at the nonanswer, but I am careful to give nothing away.

We are at a standstill, neither willing to concede.

"Haven't you ever lost someone you loved?" I ask.

Cassius wears a blank mask. After a moment, his answer comes in the barest shake of his head.

I close my eyes and take a breath. It is not the

response I expect. There's no reason for him to lie, and even if he did, there is no doubt in my mind that Della or Lawrence would have spoken up.

"When my mother was claimed, we assumed she had been killed—or would be sooner rather than later. I spent years in the shadow of regret, wishing I told her I loved her more. That we'd had more time together. I thought, if only I had gone with her into town that day, maybe she would still be with us—or that, even though I was a child, maybe there was something, *anything,* I could have done to prevent her from being claimed...."

Pity softens Cassius's expression. But that's not why I'm telling him any of this. This is about doing what I can, so even if I stand no chance of succeeding, even if all I do results in nothing, I will not live the rest of my life regretting that I stood back and let it all happen.

I hold my head high and set my jaw in determination. "Cursed or not, Alaric *is* still *alive.* And so long as he is, I will not stop trying. Even if it amounts to nothing, then I will know I did everything within my power to save him."

Cassius dips his chin in a deferential bow. Understanding and respecting my decision, even if he might not agree.

The soft rhythmic ticking of the clock counts the space of the silence between us. Della looks uncertainly between me and Cassius.

With all the words spoken in the last hour, I can find no victory nor answers as to what my next move will be. Though I suppose I can find some solace in the fading anger in Lawrence's expression. Until I have a solid plan in place, there is not much else to say.

"We should let you rest," Della says as if sensing as much.

"I'm not tired." The lie slips out before I can stop it —earning the pitying look I get. "I'm not sure I could sleep even if I wanted to," I amend.

"The dark circles under your eyes disagree," she says, not unkindly. "You've been through a lot recently, and last night…." She trails off, pressing her mouth into a tight line.

There is so much a simple look can convey. Sometimes, it can seem louder than any spoken word. Della doesn't allow me time for further protests. She leads Lawrence from the room with a promise to return later.

The room feels smaller with them gone and silent. I cradle my throbbing head in my hands.

"I will ready a bath for you," Cassius says after several long moments pass.

When I glance up, I find he has already left the room.

I don't want to fight with him. That he cares enough to speak his mind means a great deal to me. Especially when he is doing so out of concern for my well-being when so few people ever have.

Kitty loves me, and Father does too, in his own way… but they always pretended away whatever risks I took. They told themselves whatever they had to avoid feeling concerned because what I did benefited them. It seems cold, but I know it didn't come from a cruel place but one of complacency.

"Little bird?" Cassius's deep timbre breaks through my thoughts.

"I don't want to fight with you," I say, standing to face him.

The corners of his mouth tug but don't quite form a smile. "Neither do I." He motions to the bathing room. "Bathe, then rest. We can talk more after."

I nod and shuffle past.

He stops me with a hand on my arm. "You can come to me with anything. Whatever it is—I am here for you." There is an undertone that adds meaning to his words and makes it clear in the way he gazes at me that he isn't just talking about drawing a bath or other small gestures.

I find myself moved. My eyes prickle, growing hot as tears well up and blur his face. It's hard to know if it's exhaustion, the heightened emotions from the oath, the rarity of someone offering to help shoulder my burdens... or all of it.

My smile wavers, and I bite down on my bottom lip to avoid looking like I've gone mad.

"I don't know what I did to earn such kindness from you." My voice is raspy and raw. I clasp my hands in front of me and stare down at them. Gravity makes it impossible to hold back any longer. Several fat tears slither down my cheeks, dripping onto the dark wood floor at my feet.

Cassius's hand comes up to cup the back of my neck, pulling me in to press our foreheads together. "Kindness is not something you need to earn—it is something everyone deserves. Besides, we are friends." Then, in a conspiratorial whisper, he adds, "And what are friends for, if not to go along with schemes and fight beside you until the end?"

My breath hitches. Cassius won't always be with me. And there are things I cannot share with him. Yet, that doesn't mean I must shut him out of everything. It is still difficult to open up and confide in someone… difficult to depend on anyone other than myself.

A bubble of laughter rises up my throat that is half sob. I don't want to lie and hide everything from these vampires who have become my friends.

No… they are more than that. They have become a surrogate family. Despite all our differences, we have been through so much together. They are loyal, and if any of them were cursed, I would fight for them just as hard as I will fight for Alaric.

And I am so tired of doing everything on my own… of shutting the world out. What would it be like to put my trust in someone else for once?

"It will be different to have someone to scheme with," I say with a sniffle. It isn't exactly a promise, but it's the best I am able to do for now.

Cassius grins, fangs and all.

CHAPTER FIVE

CLARA

A BEAD OF SWEAT TRAILS DOWN MY TEMPLE. I FOCUS on keeping my breath even. A strand of hair slips out of place, dangling before my eye. The moment I move to swipe it out of the way, I know I made a mistake.

From across the room, fangs flash with Cassius's wicked grin. I blink, and he's before me. He grabs the staff, yanking it from my one-handed grip, simultaneously shoving me off balance. His foot sweeps my legs out from under me, and I'm falling.

The wooden pole flies across the room and clatters against the unforgiving stone floor. I remain suspended in midair, held aloft by a smirking Cassius. "Your eyes seem brighter today. If I didn't know better, I'd think you had something nefarious up your sleeve."

I groan at his ridiculous attempt at flirting and lightly push against his chest. He straightens and releases me, smirking. I collect the training weapon from where he flung it.

"I didn't expect you to want to train today," Cassius says casually, feeling me out. "It would have been understandable if you needed to take time… it hasn't even been a full day yet."

I glance at him from over my shoulder. He has been walking on eggshells with me since I woke up earlier this evening. Almost as if he is afraid that I will break if anyone speaks too loudly.

In truth, I do feel entirely too fragile for what is required of me. The only thing holding me together is their support and my deal with Varin. As soon as I found a minute alone without one of them hovering, I returned to the lower levels. Only to have Varin turn me away, saying magic shouldn't be rushed.

Lying around, wasting the precious little time I have dwelling on things, will not help me break the curse. But a demon's power will. So, I can't let myself fall apart yet.

It is part of why I want to train. I need to feel like I am something other than weak. I need to put this nervous energy to use.

"I am fine." I mean to say it with an air of nonchalance, though it comes out sharper than I intended. "Besides, I need to make sure I'm ready for anything."

He gestures for me to hand him the staff. "You did well today. It never ceases to amaze me how quickly you improve," he says as I near.

"Is it truly that much of a surprise?" Pulling my arm back, I deny him the training weapon and arch a brow. "I've been claimed, and now…." I don't finish. If I don't speak the words *oath bonded,* then I can pretend, for this brief moment, that things are as they were. I can pretend Elizabeth hadn't doomed the man I love.

"We've already trained longer than usual," Cassius says. Then, when I don't relinquish the staff, he reaches out and flicks my braid over my shoulder. Arrogance curls the corner of his lips. "Fine, one more round, but do try not to be disappointed when I win."

I snort. He may act overly confident, but every win he had on me today seemed to take him longer than usual. Then again, I'm never half as focused, and I have never had a demon's power to lend me strength. When he turns his back, I reach for another one of our practice weapons.

Once we are both in position, we each nod once to indicate when we are ready. As I watch him, looking for a tale-tell sign of an impending attack, an idea occurs to me.

For as long as he has trained me, it's always the same. I always react to his moves as he makes them, never anticipating them. But now I have added strength from Alaric and Varin. So, what if…

His arm shifts, barely noticeable, but I catch the movement. Then he's in motion, coming at me. Instead of head on, he changes course. The air stirs the fine, loose strands of my hair. In the space of two heartbeats, Cassius is nearly upon me.

It's a move he's only used once before. Attacking from behind. I sense him reaching for me, as clearly as if I'm watching from the sidelines. In my mind's eye, I see how everything will play out.

And then I act.

This time, I don't look for him, nor do I sidestep as he has forced me to practice until I could do it without thought.

I bring the staff into the defensive position to my front, then drop into a low crouch as I pivot. I kick out one foot for balance and feign going for an obvious strike.

Cassius corrects in the other direction to avoid it. I flick my wrist and catch his ankle enough to slow him. He recovers, but not quick enough. I release my grip on the staff and tackle him as I pull the practice dagger from where I hid it inside my boot.

He lands hard on his back with me crouching over him—a position that wouldn't usually give me an advantage with his strength and speed.

Cassius reaches out to dislodge me and turn the tables, only to stop short when he realizes it's the dull edge of the dagger pressing lightly against his neck.

We remain like this for several long moments. Our chests rising and falling with our labored breaths are the only sound in the room. I think we are both surprised that I have won.

"Well, aren't you clever?" His voice is low, but there is pride there, too. "I may have gloated too soon. It seems I underestimated how formidable you really are."

Gently, he guides my wrist away. Satisfaction fills my chest briefly as I let him up. A shadow passes over his face as he moves to sit. There and gone so fast, I might have dismissed it any other time. This is not the first time I have seen that look, though he tries to hide it. It's not displeasure, but something I can't read.

It's hard to be sure. I am positive he is keeping something from me.

On his feet, he faces me, beaming. However, now I can see the cracks in the edges of a careful mask. "Well done, Clara. This will be our last lesson."

I frown. "Why? I don't understand."

"You have known these techniques for a while, but now you have finally learned how to use them to win." Cassius squeezes my shoulder. "I will see you back at our quarters later. Della stopped by shortly after you ran out this evening. She was disappointed to find you were already gone."

He returns the practice weapons back to their rightful place.

I start to ask if something is bothering him, but I'm not sure what to say that won't be ridiculous. Without proof beyond catching a few odd looks, it would sound like an overactive imagination trying to create problems where there are none.

Before I can think of something, he continues. I stifle the urge to interrogate him. If something were wrong, he would tell me.

Wouldn't he?

"I hope she doesn't make a habit of inviting herself over. Because the next thing you know, she'll be moving in and evicting me." Cassius turns to me, dusting his hands off. He must see something on my face. Even though his carefree grin remains in place, there's a tightness around his eyes. "If you will excuse me, I must feed."

Cassius dips his head in a bow, then he strides out the door.

For a moment, I stay put, too stunned by his abrupt departure to move.

Demons and saints... that man is *up to something.* The way he filled every small silence with idle chatter, then ran off as if demons were chasing him, only fuels my suspicions.

I jog after Cassius, catching up to him as he steps into the main corridor. Even without looking back, it's obvious he knows I'm there. His pace is intentionally fast enough to keep me from catching up enough for us to walk side-by-side without drawing unwanted attention.

"Cassius," I say, pitched low enough to avoid drawing attention to us but loud enough that I know he hears. "Will you *please* wait for a moment?"

At first, I don't think he will. Another couple of steps and he stops to face me. "Oh, Clara. Forgive me. I was lost in thought."

And demons thrive in sunlight, I think irritably.

When I reach him, Cassius loops my arm through his and starts walking again. We don't speak as a small group of gentry, made up of lesser vampires, passes us. Three pale humans, their heads down and hands clasped behind their backs, trailing behind them.

I wait until we're alone and tug him to a stop. "Something is bothering you. I can tell."

"Only that I have nothing left to teach you."

An obvious deflection.

"No." I shake my head. "You're hiding something from me." If anyone were to look our way, they would think we are having a friendly chat about some inane topic with the way we're both grinning like idiots.

"What makes you think that?" It isn't quite denial laced with saccharine sincerity, but it also isn't an admission.

And there it is again, the flash of worry in his green eyes. The heightened urge to allow my temper to take control is doused.

"Please," I beseech, stepping closer. "I can tell something is worrying you." Laughter from around the corner echoes, soon joined by several chattering voices. "You said you would be there for me, so let me do the same for you."

Cassius drops the pretense. "You have enough to worry over as it is without adding to the burden."

He falls silent as the group of three lesser vampire women rounds the corner.

And among them is Alaric's ex-employee, Elise Holmwood. She is different from when I first met her, and it is somehow both subtle and very noticeable. Skin that has changed from a healthy peach has become the color of watered-down milk with the barest hint of blue and nearly transparent. Her red hair is done up in a fashionable style that appears an even more vivid shade than I remember. The powdery pink of her dress seems to exaggerate both.

Elise meets my gaze before I can avert my eyes. The placid features of her face contort into a promise of violence.

I doubt anything will come of it since she hasn't tried anything since our last encounter. And anyway, I prefer to wander the back halls whenever possible, where I can move about unnoticed and as unmemorable as every other human in this castle.

"Thank you for your concern, but it is a trifling matter," Cassius tells me once we are alone.

My smile falters. His is a shade too bright. I see through the lie. I don't think anyone has ever dismissed something as unimportant and meant it. He must realize I'm not fooled because his mouth presses into a thin line.

I nod. A silent agreement not to push further for the time being. He has his reasons for putting this subject off, and I will respect that.

Cassius's cool palm cups the side of my face. "We will talk later."

That is a promise I have every intention of holding him to.

For the second time, I watch him walk away. I remain where I am for a moment longer. Something builds in my chest. A feeling... one I cannot begin to describe or put a name to. It settles deep within my bones, tangled with a sense of importance.

A movement from the corner of my eye draws my attention to the open atrium on the second floor.

Elizabeth stands at the balustrade, looking down. Her golden hair is twisted and pulled to the side, cascading over one shoulder, and tied with a thick, black ribbon at the end. The golden strands are stark moonlight against her black dress.

The Voice stands a pace or two back and off to her right, appearing like winter personified.

But it's Alaric on her other side that steals the

breath from my lungs, and I cannot force myself to turn away.

He looks exactly as he did the last time we were together. The sensation in my chest expands. It's almost too much... too many emotions twisted up into an impossible knot.

I squeeze my eyes shut, swallowing the sensations threatening to overwhelm me.

Ever so faintly, I feel it—though I am not entirely sure if it is real or merely the product of longing—the soft, rhythmic echo of his heartbeat.

When I open my eyes again, both the sensation and Alaric are gone.

CHAPTER SIX

ALARIC

Nothing slows the passing of time to an achingly unrelenting pace quite like listening to nobles and gentry acting like spoiled children as they ask for endless favors.

It was the same as every other night since I arrived at Nightwich and accepted my place as consort. Yet today, I couldn't seem to recall any specifics from previous sessions or what to do without prompting from the Voice.

Ever since I woke as the last rays of light vanished, a sense of wrongness has followed at my heels like a shadow. It is a persistent itch inside my skull, plaguing me and setting the world askew.

My queen and I stroll leisurely through the halls—a much-needed reprieve after the past several hours. A strange, prickling sensation travels up the back of my neck. One I haven't felt since I was human. I glance furtively at the surroundings, alert for any sight or sound that is out of place, but can find nothing.

My stomach cramps painfully.

Hunger… endless hunger.

The need to feed has the urgency of having been neglected for far too long. I cannot recall the last time I fed. It couldn't have been more than a day or two at most from the dried blood spilled on the rug in my parlor. The harder I try to remember, the more difficult it is to hold on to anything.

It is a dark and sharp presence slithering through my mind, contorting parts of who I am. Squeezing. Suffocating. Cutting the shapes of my thoughts, of my past, of who I am into harsh facets with razor-like edges.

For perhaps the twentieth time today, Elizabeth sends a sidelong glance filled with concern in my direction. I thought nothing of it at first, however, now I wonder if I have displeased her.

"My prince?" Elizabeth's sweet voice pulls me from my thoughts and back to her. "Is there something on your mind?"

Kharis perches on a statue, with features worn down by time and weather before it was eventually brought inside. The high-pitched sound rings painfully in my ears. When the echoing resonance fades, my head is clearer.

"Nothing important, my queen. I found it tiresome having to listen to endless complaints from incapable nobles. They seemed pettier than usual."

She frowns, and… there's that look again.

"There's no need to fret over me when you've endured the same tedium," I add quickly.

She waves her hand apathetically. "I've had centuries to grow accustomed to it."

Elizabeth hums, seeming pleased. "I am glad you finally decided to embrace your role. You have settled in quite well."

That would explain the way she keeps glancing at me.

Does she think I am straining under the few simple duties I've taken on? I make a mental note to prove to her that I am more than capable.

"Thank you, my queen." I take one of her delicate hands in mine, bending at the waist to press a soft kiss against the cool skin of her knuckles.

She pouts, though there is an obvious teasing quality to it. "You needn't be so formal when no one else is around, my love…"

We are not what I would consider being alone. The Voice stands a few paces to my queen's side, as unmoving and pale as a sculpture carved from moonlight and ice.

When she took up the position, she surrendered whatever name she once had. Now, she is only the Queen's Voice, rarely speaking outside her duties. With her head held high, her bright pink eyes slide to mine, though she seems unbothered.

My queen moves closer, grabbing my cravat near the base of my throat and pulling my face to eye level. "Call me Elizabeth," she speaks each word slowly.

"Elizabeth." The name feels awkward on my tongue when I attempt to infuse my affection and loyalty into the sound. It comes out coarse, though she doesn't seem to notice.

Pleased, she releases me. "I could use some air. Would you care to escort me?"

Briefly, her voice doubles over on itself. One version is a sweet request for company, the other a sharp demand. It vanishes before I'm able to make sense of it. Not wishing to ruin a pleasant night, I put it out of my mind.

I offer my arm to Elizabeth and say, "I would be honored."

She settles her hand in the crook of my elbow, and we change course, heading toward the eastern wing of her floor where the expansive balcony overlooks the valley.

It is the second night of the full moon. Within an hour, it will be at its zenith. From her expansive balcony, we can see the entire valley cast in pale moonlight.

Elizabeth talks of the events leading up to my coronation—a ball to end each week. The first will be the smallest, held for the nobility, then becoming grander each week, inviting the gentry and other lesser vampires and even allowing a few chosen humans from the city for the main event.

I can't help but think how much Rosalie will love the spectacle. She will need to have new dresses made. I will stop by her quarters later to tell her—

Sharp pain pierces my head with a sudden throbbing at my temples that makes it impossible to remember how to find her room.

"Rosalie..."

Elizabeth abruptly stops talking and glances at me with one brow quirked. "Who? Ah, you mean your sister."

I nod. The headache surges, pounding ruthlessly. "It must be time for me to feed because I can't seem to think where she is."

"Yes," Elizabeth agrees, jaw tense. The warm red ring of her power lights up around her lavender irises. "It seems you forgot she remained back at the manor. It has only been a few days since we sent word of the coronation. I'm afraid she likely won't arrive until the day before." She releases a breath, relaxing her shoulders. "You should be more mindful that you don't go too long between feedings."

Rosalie always insists on traveling with me, teasing that it's for my protection rather than to satisfy her curiosity about how the world has changed with time.

Surely, I would have brought her with me? The sense of wrongness rears up again, frantically drumming through my veins. I force myself to release those contradicting thoughts—

Elizabeth wouldn't lie. There must have been a reason… even if I have forgotten what it was.

"I must have lost track of time," I say. "I will take care of it soon."

She hums. "See that you do. I cannot have my consort weak from starvation." Her tone shifts from concerned to venomous. "It would send the wrong message to the world."

I have been careless. My queen chose me to rule

beside her. Now, I must show that I am worthy of the position.

The corridor opens to an atrium overlooking the main hall below on the left. At the far end on the right, there are more winding hallways and another grand staircase that is heavily guarded.

Halfway, Elizabeth halts abruptly, slipping her hand from my arm. She approaches the balustrade and grips the polished surface. Small clouds of fine dust form around her fingertips as they press into the stone. It is the only indication of the fury underneath her calm exterior.

Who has earned such ire while lacking the sense to leave Nightwich immediately?

I stand at her side and follow her gaze to one of the more powerful courtiers below me.

Cassius Wellington cups the cheek of a mortal woman. The way he looks at her—it appears he's lost his wits and, through some unfortunate circumstance, has come to care for a creature so inferior to him.

Even when he was still human, love was a game. He would seduce the daughters of prominent men, promising them the world. Only to abandon them after they surrendered their bodies to him.

No. The human must only be another one of his games to pass the time.

Still, as a court member, such behavior is beneath him. He would do well to avoid intimacy with one publicly. Others might misunderstand, thinking him weak. And that weakness would reflect poorly on our queen. It's no wonder she is furious.

Cassius leaves, yet Elizabeth's focus doesn't follow him but stays locked on the human.

I frown. If his actions are not the cause of her ire but rather the woman, then why does she still live?

I glance at the Voice, hoping for a hint to better understand this peculiar situation.

She watches me with an unsettling expression. Her eyes, encircled by a ring of glowing crimson, bore into me. Then, the pink disappears beneath a cloud of white. In this state, she's as fragile as fog. It's over in the span of a breath, her irises returning to their brilliant hue as if it never happened.

Between this, the memory lapses, and numerous small details not adding up… It makes me wonder if I am losing my mind.

Wings beat against the air in a steady *thump, thump, thump.*

With my next breath, I've forgotten what I had been thinking a moment ago. It must not have been anything important.

Returning my focus to the mortal, I regard her from the back. She wears men's clothes that are tailored for ease of movement as well as to enhance her feminine figure.

Dressed like that, it's clear she isn't kitchen staff or a maid. And no guard would permit her entry if she were a mere stable hand. I cannot think of a single place within these walls where she could possibly belong.

The human turns as if she senses my scrutiny. There is nothing remarkable about her. She's neither a great beauty nor homely, yet she possesses an undeniable, captivating quality.

My mind quiets. The constant droning buzz I hadn't noticed before is gone. In its absence is a balm of peaceful quiet.

"Alaric?" Elizabeth says my name. "Do you know her?"

I examine the mortal's face. It is the kind that looks familiar, yet I have never set eyes on her before.

"No," I say. It takes more effort to drag my gaze to Elizabeth than I'd like to admit. "Should I?"

"Of course not," she says, then continues, this time without the hard edge in her tone, "It was the way you were looking at her that had me curious."

"Mr. Wellington seems rather fond of her." The observation has an unintended bitter thread along the edges.

Elizabeth purses her lips. "Any vampire that would give that weak mortal a second glance would be better off cursed," she says coolly, her voice piercing like a cutting winter wind.

It's unlike her to be so affected by the presence of a lowly mortal. Humans are below her notice. Their usefulness ends with menial labor and food.

"Such a disgrace to see him continue to allow that slayer to freely roam my halls," she mutters under her breath, so quietly that I'm unsure if she intended for me to hear or if she's even aware that she spoke aloud.

Kharis swoops through the air, circling us, and lands on her shoulder. The raven's eyes flash red.

By the moment you think of her again, she will have perished from old age. She is unworthy of even a second of your time. Do not let trifling matters ruin your mood," I soothe.

Elizabeth's nostrils flare with two calming breaths. When she releases her grip on the balustrade and takes a step back, a divot remains where each finger had pressed.

She turns her face toward me. The red ring around her iris sets off the violet shade of her eyes. "Yes, you are right."

I step into the center of the corridor and hold out my arm. "Shall we enjoy the evening while it lasts?"

The implied meaning within my question pleases her, and I am rewarded with a smile. I vow to put the human from my mind.

Our queen is all that matters. We must please her.

Pleasing my queen is all that matters.

The low, droning buzz gradually returns with every step that takes us further away. It is so subtle that by the time I notice, my awareness of it is already slipping away, and the mortal woman is easy to forget.

CHAPTER SEVEN

CLARA

DEFEAT SETTLES HEAVILY OVER MY SHOULDERS, FEELING a little too much like despair. I trudge all the way back to Cassius's quarters, willing my heart to remain whole.

Seeing Alaric's face and the way he looked at me as if I were a stranger— as if he hated me—hurts far worse than I could have imagined. It is a physical pain no armor can guard against.

The rage sizzling through my veins whispers in my ear that only revenge will quench its flames. It is the only thing keeping me going.

When Cherno told me he was cursed, I knew it was true because I had felt the change in our bond, but I know too little about it to use it to my advantage.

There's little solace in knowing that I can still sense him when he is close. And Elizabeth will do everything in her power to keep me as far away from him as possible.

If I cannot break the curse, it will kill him. The oath bond grants me a lifespan to equal his, so what does that mean for me? Will I die alongside him, or will my mortality resume with his death? I suppose it hardly matters because I will most likely die trying to do the impossible before the curse takes his life, anyway.

Cassius is nowhere to be found when I return to his chambers. Though I am glad to have time to process the emotions bombarding me, a small voice at the back of my mind worries that he is avoiding me.

A fire crackles in the hearth, sending embers up with each snap of the wood as the flames devour it. The doors to the bedroom are open wide. And the watery light of dawn seeps through the windows.

I'm not sure when Cassius managed to bring my belongings from my old room, but I'm thankful for his foresight. Quickly stripping out of my training clothes, I change into Alaric's shirt that I've claimed as my own.

For a moment, I stand at the foot of Cassius's bed and debate taking the top blanket and sleeping on the couch in the parlor. I don't want to take his bed—it feels brazen, considering... everything.

But the heavy blankets and thick mattress beckon irresistibly. In no time, I'm burrowed under layers of luxurious covers. When Cassius returns, I will gladly move. We need to talk anyway, so we might as well figure out more appropriate sleeping arrangements at the same time.

My eyelids have just closed when the flap of

leathery wings pulls my attention to the bat soaring through the wall. Spotting me, Cherno comes to land on my chest. We are connected through Alaric, and I imagine that their bond is as affected in a similar way as mine is.

"Clara…" they say, shifting uncertainly.

Their already large eyes widen, and I can't help but immediately be suspicious. Yet I'm not immune to it. I reach up and pet their soft head. I never thought I'd find such a creature so irresistibly cute—especially not a demon.

Once, I thought they were all the same. Bloodthirsty. Cruel. Evil. Cherno and Arinah and Asmod and even Varin have changed how I view demons. Victor's toad and Alexander's spider were every bit as horrible as their vampires. But I've discovered that the personalities of demons are as varied as humans.

It's not always easy to differentiate between the improbable and the impossible. Many things I once thought impossible have come to pass since the day I met Alaric. And I am counting on my chance to break this curse to be another one of those things.

"Yes?" I prompt.

"You are keeping things from the others."

It's not an accusation but a statement. Still, I cringe. I sit up, pulling my knees to my chest, giving them a place to perch.

"You're right." Then, thinking I ought to say something more, I add, "There are things I can't share with them yet."

Cherno makes a plaintive sound. They want to know more but aren't willing to make demands of me.

"I suppose you deserve to know more than anyone," I say casually.

Cherno's head lifts. Hope shines in their jewel-red eyes. Tiny claws tighten their grip on the blanket as they wait.

Swallowing the lump trying to form in my throat, I begin before the fear of judgment can settle in. "I meant it when I said I will do whatever I can to help Alaric. I hope you understand, and if not, all I can ask is that you not tell anyone."

They scrunch their little body, wariness clear. They offer no promise or agreement one way or the other.

"I have made a bargain with a demon," I whisper the words so quietly that Cherno leans in to hear. "In exchange for their help to break the curse, I will find a way to set them free."

"Who?" they demand in a low hiss.

"Varin." I mouth the demon's name. I'm suddenly unsure if I've ever spoken their name aloud outside their company.

The next thing I know, Cherno is clinging to my face with their leathery wings, tremors rolling through them. "Do you have any idea what you have done?"

Unable to speak, I nod. Cherno glowers skeptically. So, I blow a puff of air against their belly. They take the hint and drop back down to perch on my knee.

I tell them of every interaction I've had with Varin, going over the deal we made word for word until Cherno seems mollified.

Just as they are about to question me all over again, Asmod slithers into the room and quickly joins us. I flash Cherno a pleading look, then smile at the dark metallic-green snake. Their tongue flicks out to scent the air.

To my relief, Cherno lets the conversation drop, and they hop over to Asmod, greeting the emerald snake.

I settle back under the covers and listen to the crackling fire coming through the open door. There's the rustle of the bed curtains as the two demons work to untie the silken ropes. The light dims, and in seconds, the pull of sleep is too strong to ignore.

My bare feet pad silently on the thick carpet runner that stretches from one end of the great hall to the other. Inky, impenetrable shadows shroud every corner and alcove. Save for a few sconces that give off just enough light to see. All others have been extinguished.

No nobles or gentry mill about as usual. There's not even a hint of the human servants bustling through the back halls.

It is as if every living thing has simply vanished

without a trace. And the silence left behind sends a shiver crawling down my spine.

Outside, snow has piled up, crusting against the glass of the wrought iron windows. Beyond that, the night is pitch dark. It leaves me with the sense that I am alone in a castle entombed in ice.

I wrap my arms around my middle and rub my hands along the bare skin to chase away the chill. That draws my attention to my clothing for the first time.

I am unsettled to find myself in a diaphanous dress I have never seen before. The material is white and is as delicate as cobwebs. Elegant patterns are embroidered in strategic places to give it the appearance of frost, down to the hem, which is as uneven and tattered as torn moth wings.

Who changed my clothes... and when?

"I should have killed you the moment you arrived," a feminine voice hisses at my back.

Startled, I whirl. Elise glowers at me with smokey eyes that burn with hate. She's close enough that she could have wrapped her hands around my neck and snapped it before I could react.

Her hands ball into fists at her sides. "You are beneath me, *slayer*. You've always been beneath me." The words are clipped and sharp. "Each kill was nothing but luck—you're not even worthy of the title."

Part of me agrees with that last part. Even though I decided to use it to my advantage against Elizabeth and any other who seeks to cut me down—a slayer isn't who or what I am.

I open my mouth to speak, but in a blink, she has closed the distance, snarling inches in front of my face, a metallic odor on her breath. Nails filed into points, dig into my arms, piercing my skin. Rivulets of warm blood trickle down.

Heat slides over my right hand. Chancing a glimpse, I find my fingers gripping the night-forged dagger, plunged into her heart. Elise's blood stains my hands and arms and is splattered down my front.

Horrified, I recoil, jerking back. My heel catches, and I stumble back against the wall. The winter chill has seeped through the stone and mortar and stings my skin.

The blood is gone.

Elise is gone.

Then, each light is snuffed out one by one until only the single flickering candle across from me remains.

Shadowy figures stalk toward me from all sides. Their shapes morph from human to demon, then back, each impossible to look at directly.

A growl rumbles beside my ear and turns my blood to icy sludge. The final light extinguishes as if by the sound alone.

Taloned hands brush over me. Too many to count. They skim down my arms, my legs, curl around my shoulders, and dig into my waist. One tightens its grip, piercing my skin and muscles, and scrapes against my bones.

I can't move. I can't even scream.

The scent of my blood drives them wild. Their vicious claws pull me in all directions and into mouths with razor-sharp teeth that clamp down, ripping into me as they drink me dry.

I squint and blink until my eyes adjust. For a brief moment, I'm confused as I stare up into Della's face. She studies me with dark eyes, sharp as that of a hawk. Graceful and beautiful. Deadly. And seeing far more than anyone will ever know.

She arches a brow in wry skepticism. "What in the Otherworld have you done to those demons?"

My body is heavy, and my mind sluggish. I shift. And that's when I feel them. Cherno and Asmod have both curled up against me. Cherno is tangled in my hair, while Asmod has snuggled up in the crook of my neck, with the lower half of their long body wrapped around my arm.

Della walks around the bed, tying the curtains back.

After some effort, I untangle myself from Cherno and Asmod. The two of them turn accusing glares on Della before burrowing under the blankets, warmed by my body. I slide my legs off the edge of the bed, letting them dangle as my eyes adjust to the light.

"You still look like a demon's ass," she says, wrinkling her nose. "You bathed, at least. That's a start."

"A start to what?" I stand unsteadily on my feet as the last vestiges of my dream sluice off.

The details of my dream grow hazier with each passing second until I'm left with nothing more than an unsettling feeling.

Della ignores my question and crosses the room to my trunk. She digs through it, grabbing one of the first things that isn't a set of training clothes.

Behind thick pockets of gray clouds, the sky is a sickly blue with washed out golds as the sun sinks lower in the sky.

"Get dressed," Della orders, shoving a bundle into my arms.

"If this is your attempt at distracting me—"

"If I wanted to distract you, I'd set wild animals on you," she says, cutting me off. Crossing her arms, she waits for me to do as I'm told. "We are going into the city to fit you for dresses."

"I have—" I say, pausing in the middle of changing.

She snatches the shirt over my head before I can refuse, leaving me with no choice but to don the dress she selected.

"The queen is throwing a ball in three nights, the first of four leading up to the coronation, and you need something suitable for the occasion."

"No." I shake my head. Nothing about that is a good idea. "Even if Elizabeth doesn't kill me on sight, why would I take part in her victory celebration? My time is better spent trying to stop her."

Something unreadable passes over her face. "It would be better to have them and not need them than to find ourselves unprepared."

I try to object, but she will hear none of it, so I give in.

Less than a quarter hour later, we are sitting across from each other in a small carriage. Della's mouth quirks up on one side, gloating.

The interior is simple and elegant, with dark materials, polished brass, and cushioned seats covered in butter-soft suede.

The carriage rocks from side to side to the rhythm of the horses' hooves clomping rhythmically over the cobblestone road.

The drive into the city is relatively quick. So close to sunset, the main square is already bustling with activity. Citizens duck in and out of the shops, weaving around each other on the sidewalks and crossing the streets in the spaces between carriages and riders on horseback.

On nearly every corner are vendors with wheeled carts. They call out to anyone passing by, soliciting their wares, from flowers to hats to food made to eat while you stroll, and more than I can focus on.

There isn't time to take everything in before we come to a stop. The driver swings the door open and hands Della down. I'm surprised when he extends the same courtesy to me with a warm expression rather than the loathing I am used to.

When I hesitate, the driver reaches for my hand, making the decision for me. I mutter a thank you, and from the corner of my eye, I think I see his lips curl in an amused smile as he turns away.

Della loops her arm through mine and drags me into the dressmaker's shop. Exquisite dresses are draped over fitting forms across the front to lure customers in. On the wall behind the counter are cubicles stacked from floor to ceiling, each holding large rolls of fabric in an array of colors.

A woman emerges from behind a curtain at the back and strides forward to greet us. She wears a dress that appears simple at first glance, but the longer I look, the more the details stand out—fine embroidery and beading combined with a mixture of fabrics that come together in quiet elegance.

She wastes little time on small talk, ushering us into the back room. Tables with neat piles of fabric are along one wall. Opposite that are three mirrors set in a semicircle around a fitting block, with a dressing screen to the right. Situated along the center of the back is a table with measurements etched along the edges, a pair of scissors and a pincushion placed off to one side.

I feel like a living doll as the seamstress positions me and begins to work.

Della looks over the fabric samples, discussing the colors with the woman, who nods as she takes my measurements. The tape is barely in position before she drops one end and moves to another part of my body. I don't see how she can even read it, let alone remember any of the dozens of numbers without writing any of them down. Her fingers are swift and careful, pinning together a makeshift muslin dress.

Finally, she takes a step back to examine her work beside Della. They point and discuss draping and necklines, among other details, without a single word in my direction. Just as they had from the moment we entered the back room.

I shift in place, stiff from standing in one spot for

so long while keeping as still as humanly possible. It earns me a scowl from the seamstress. But after a few more adjustments and marks made with blue chalk, the woman looks to Della for approval.

The seamstress removes the mockup. I release a weary sigh as I'm allowed to get dressed.

CHAPTER EIGHT

CLARA

THE SEAMSTRESS IS ALREADY AT WORK WHEN I STEP OUT from behind the changing screen. Scissors cut through fabric, tracing the outline of pins.

Aching muscles and stiff back beg to move. "Is my part finished?" I ask Della. "I could use some air."

"I can have the first dress ready to be fitted in an hour," the seamstress interjects without looking up from her work.

Della nods. "Try not to wander too far." My stomach chooses that moment to growl, so she adds, "There is a patisserie across the street."

She presses a small purse heavy with money into my palm. I thank her, then hurry outside.

The cold air hits my face, waking me up. I welcome the cold sting of winter. Night has descended, blanketing the world. Above, the sky is clear, though the stars don't appear as bright, surrounded by the city's glow. The gas lamps are so numerous they manage to stop time, bathing the city in a perpetual sunset. It's just bright enough to keep the wild demons at bay.

This city is so different from the village where I grew up. I can't help but feel inadequate, surrounded by such elegance everywhere I look. Even the buildings with their pale stones and fresh paint are a striking difference.

A thought hidden in the recesses of my mind wonders if they can see the poor girl from the soot-coated town of Littlemire with threadbare clothing beneath the beautiful dress I wear now.

I weave through the throng as effortlessly as I did back home on market days. When I was here with Alaric, my nerves were strung so tight I couldn't see anything other than vampires.

But now things have changed.

I'm no longer afraid of them the way I used to be. Whether that's due to my increased strength or something else, I'm not sure.

When there is a gap between carriages, I hurry across the street, following the scent of delicacies. I'm salivating before I reach the other side.

Inside the patisserie, it is warm and fragrant, with the taste of melted sugar in the air. The large glass case, taking up nearly one entire wall, displays the most exquisite desserts I have ever seen. Round tables line the front windows, and booths fill the remaining spaces. Patrons, in groups, big and small, fill nearly every seat. Since I'm alone, I don't want to take up a table others could use, so I opt to walk around while I eat. I don't go far, keeping the dressmaker's storefront in sight so Della can find me.

I stop at a water fountain in the middle of the square. It's made of flawless black stone and is almost big enough to swim in. It's polished and buffed to a mirror finish.

The center is comprised of five levels, each depicting a scene. On the first is a woman lifting her hand for a bird to perch on. The second is the woman with a handsome man with pointed ears and a crown. War fills the third, two sides colliding in a tangle of chaos. The fourth shows the two lovers cling to each other as hands try to pry them apart. The final scene on the bottom-most level depicts the man weeping over the woman's fallen body, a sword through her chest.

"Do you know the story behind this fountain?" a warm male voice asks with an unmistakable sensual rumble.

His warm breath fans against the side of my cheek. It's so unexpected I nearly topple into the icy water as I turn.

Two strong arms encircle my waist. He pulls me in, preventing me from getting drenched by pressing me against his body. I gape up into familiar amber eyes glittering with mirth. The mischievous grin on Oliver Wolvrik's face is all the proof I need that he knew exactly what he was doing.

"What a coincidence running into you like this," he all but croons, still holding me aloft. "It's a pleasure to see you again, Miss Valmont."

I level a glare at him. "I very much doubt this is a coincidence."

Oliver wrinkles his freckled nose and shrugs, not

bothering to deny it as he sets me upright. I step back and smooth out my skirt.

Oliver clasps his hands at the small of his back as he gazes at the fountain. "Not many know this piece originally came from the fae lands. The story behind it is actually quite sad."

My mouth opens and closes a few times, but I'm unable to come up with a response to his strange ramblings. I stay quiet and glance around. If any vampires have noticed the wolf among them, no one seems to care.

"Oliver?"

"Oli," he corrects absently.

"What are you doing here?" I demand in a harsh whisper. "I thought you'd left…."

"I did, but I returned to see you, of course," he answers as if it's obvious. Then, seeing I'm not amused, his expression turns grave. It looks out of place on his youthful features. "There is something amiss—something big—but no one is talking about it. Nightwich has doubled the guard, and our… people haven't been able to get in." Oliver pauses. "I need you to tell me what you know."

I nod, and he moves close enough that anyone who sees us might mistake us for lovers.

In the absence of all rumors, it's clear Elizabeth wants to control every scrap of information that goes in and out of the castle. I take a moment to think. Even here, I must be as careful with my words as possible.

"He is cursed," I say, keeping my voice low and tucking a strand of hair behind my ear to hide my mouth. Oliver's eyes widen. "On the third night of the full moon, she will make him her consort." There's no need to speak names for him to understand.

Oliver's expression slips for a fraction of a moment before he schools his features. Other than a slight narrowing of his eyes, his face is a blank mask. Amber brown irises shine like sunlight through honey in the light of the gas lamps.

There are so many questions I want to ask. Why are his people coming and going? Is he upset because he and Alaric are friends? Or is there another reason? But I keep them to myself as he mulls over what I said and the unspoken details hidden among my words.

"This is worse than we thought," he says, more to himself than to me. One hand absentmindedly scratches the day-old layer of scruff along his jaw.

Enough time passes with the two of us staring at each other, that it begins to look strange. I place my hand on his forearm, drawing his attention, silently begging for him to explain.

"Knowing this, I'm surprised you found your way into town." He shakes his head and loops my arm through his, then walks with me as he continues talking. "Now that you're here, you should come with me."

I balk and plant my feet, refusing to be dragged away. "Where?" I shake my head. It doesn't matter. "You know I can't."

Oliver appears to be exercising his patience to the limit. Even if there is a compelling reason for me to go along with him, I expect more information than that before deciding.

Regardless of good intentions, I will not blindly follow anyone or let them make decisions for me that could take me further from what I must do.

He pulls me to stand before him, hooking an arm around my waist and cupping my cheek with his other hand. "You are in grave danger, Clara. With your vampire gone, you need to be somewhere out of *her* reach… he would want you to go somewhere safe."

That last part feels like a punch to the gut. Oliver might be right because I would want the same for him were our situations reversed. But I can no more abandon Alaric than he would abandon me.

"He's not gone." I can't give up on him. I'm not ready to. Not yet. There is still some sliver of hope left in me yet.

Oliver frowns and parts his lips to protest. But I don't give him the opportunity.

"Thank you, but I can't leave," I say, taking half a step back, separating us. "There are still some things I need to do."

Oliver's brow furrows. He grabs my hands, trapping them in his grip to keep me from walking away.

"Nothing good will come from remaining there. You can only stand by and watch him slowly wither away day by day. If he could get away, her influence would wane, but in the end, the curse would still kill him."

I give him a wan smile and manage to free one of my hands. "There is one thing I can do."

Oliver's fingers loosen as I turn, only to tighten painfully, squeezing my fingers against the ring I wear. He yanks me back to him, holding my hand up between us. The band shines like liquid moonlight.

"Where did you get this?"

"It was a gift," I say. It's at least partially true. Varin did give it to me.

"This is no mere trinket of affection, Clara."

"I didn't steal it, if that's what you're thinking."

His lip curls, and though nothing about him physically changes, I feel the truth of what he is for the first time. It roots me to where I stand. Amber flashes in his eyes. The force of his power increases, making it harder to keep eye contact.

I let out a gasping breath as it relinquishes its hold over me.

"I have never called you a thief. Now answer the question." His demeanor shifts. Eases. "Please. The last thing I want is to see you needlessly risk your life. Tell me what you've gotten yourself into—I might be able to help."

I have had more help in the last few months than ever before in my life. Friendships given freely, without the demand of payment to earn it first. Cassius, Della, and Lawrence have risked their lives once already, and now this man is asking for the knowledge to do the same.

But I have yet to form a plan beyond the deal with a demon, and until I figure out the best course of action, there's no point in getting anyone else involved.

"It will be fine," I say soothingly. "There is nothing I can ask of you. Unless you know how I can break the curse?"

He shakes his head. "No one has ever survived it, and those she has inflicted are taken faster than what you have previously witnessed." Oliver lowers my hand but does not release me.

He is no fool. If he hasn't fully guessed the meaning of the ring, he understands enough that I am tangled up in something dangerous. It was pure luck that Lawrence hadn't noticed it when he grabbed my hand after realizing Alaric and I were oath bonded.

"There has to be a way to save him..." I am desperate and so terrified I will fail.

The corner of Oliver's mouth twitches. "I will find out what I can. But promise me that you will undo whatever you agreed to," he says pointedly, squeezing the finger wearing the ring. "You are playing with demons, Clara. It won't end how you think it will."

I swallow thickly. He will help me regardless of my answer, but I feel the need to offer him something other than a lie in return. So, I exhale and decide on an honest compromise.

"It's too late to go back on the deal I made. And as of this moment, it's my only option, and I must make sure I'm ready. Will you accept my word that I will not do anything more until or unless there is no other choice?" Each word is careful and deliberate—honest and clear, but not so obvious that anyone passing by might understand.

Oliver accepts with a sharp nod, then says, "There is one other thing. If you should find your sanity and decide to take me up on my offer...."

I give him a warning look.

His familiar teasing smile slides back into place.

"There is a forest to the west of Nightwich, beyond the mountains—I will be there," he says with a wink.

"You would do well to make offers to those who aren't oath bonded to another man," Della snaps. She wrenches Oliver's wrist, forcing him to let go.

Panic rises, flooding my senses. All thoughts are momentarily drowned out by a rush of adrenaline. It takes me several seconds to realize she misunderstood his words. Which means she hadn't overheard anything except his teasing.

"He didn't mean it like that." I try to put myself between the two of them, but they are too focused on each other.

Oliver is a head and a half taller than Della, but one would think neither noticed with the way they face each other down. Each baring their teeth. Him growling, and her snarling.

They look ready to rip each other apart at one wrong move. I'm not sure I want to get between them.

"Do you have any idea who I am?"

Della snorts. "The stench of dog gave it away before your louche offer."

"You should be more careful who you choose to insult, *bloodsucker*."

"Men have a nasty habit of underestimating women, and you are no different. Make no mistake, if you keep it up, I will make you regret it."

"Bold words for someone half my size."

"Yet, I could still bring you to heal with little effort."

Passersby slow to watch with sidelong glances

while others stop completely to gape openly. Their fighting is calling too much attention to us.

"Will you two attempt to control yourselves?" I hiss. "You are causing a scene."

Neither listens to me at first, too caught up in their quarrel. But then Della reins in her temper with visible effort. She adopts a haughty air, somehow looking down her nose at him despite having to tilt her head up to meet his gaze.

Oliver's nose twitches, and he relaxes his posture, though he refuses to take his eyes off her. His curled lip takes on an amused quality.

With an exasperated huff, Della breaks eye contact with him and sets her full focus on me. Her cheeks are slightly flushed. It's hard to tell if it's from irritation or a blush for nearly getting into a brawling match with a man in the middle of the town square.

"The first dress is ready for you to try on," Della informs me, making a show of ignoring him as she leads me away.

"Clara," Oliver calls to me before we've taken more than a few steps.

Much to Della's irritation, I stop and glance back.

"I will let you know what I find. And my offer stands if you ever change your mind."

Della throws a deadly glare in his direction before hurrying me back to the dressmaker.

CHAPTER NINE

ALARIC

A sharp ache twists in my gut. It is constant. Plaguing me. Though it has only been three days since I last fed. Images of a human flicker through my memory in an infinite loop. Of her offering up her bleeding wrist. Of her legs so weak, she had to be held up by the queen's guards. Of her crumpled and lifeless body on the floor…

A darkness writhes through the hidden corners of my mind.

I nearly drained the human of all her blood. The offering had brought me closer to my queen… and yet not a single drop in the mortal's body had come close to sating my hunger or fueling my waning power.

Tonight was much the same. The human fainted, and I left, not staying long enough to see if they lived or died.

My lip curls, and I snarl at a passing servant carrying a gilded tea service. She whimpers and skitters back, bumping into the wall. The items on her tray clatter with her trembling.

The darkness, the monster that lives inside me, digs in with talons, planting visons of blood and death. Injecting its rancid poison.

Perhaps she could be of use... I could drink my fill—

The thought is there and gone before I pass her by. My mood sours further, just knowing it would be pointless to bother.

What is the point of feeding if it doesn't stop this agony that eats away at me from the inside?

Fluttering wings drag me back to the present. My stride falters before I come to a stop. I glance up and down the servant halls, realizing where I am for the first time since I returned from tonight's feeding.

That dark beast will weaken me until it can claim my body and mind for its own, pushing me out.

What in the Otherworld possessed me to come to this part of the castle?

But that question will have to wait.

A bat swoops around the corner and hones their trajectory on me. They flutter in circles above my head, chirping incessantly as if attempting to communicate. This demon must be new or incredibly weak or stupid to think I can understand them. They seem to have me confused with their true master.

I reach up and snatch the peculiar creature from the air, pinning their leathery wings to their side. They don't struggle against my grip. Only the same pattern of chirps.

"Leave me be, demon, unless you wish to die."

The bat stills and blinks up at me. Satisfied, I release them. They flap back the way they came, pausing to hover as if waiting... it seems the ridiculous thing expects me to follow. Though I have no intention of doing so. nevertheless, I find myself trailing after them.

If I cannot satisfy the incessant hunger, I may as well satisfy my curiosity.

They lead me back toward the main halls. I'm beginning to wonder if they thought the crown prince ought to deign to wander among lesser creatures. I frown because that assumption has a false ring to it.

I'm debating on whether to allow this creature to lead me around or not when the flickering light from sconces dances over two figures at the far end of the corridor.

One woman has wild hair the color of flames. Even from this distance, it's easy to see that she is a lesser vampire, despite how she attempts to hide it with a courtier's dress and fine jewelry. She is upset. Her face and neck grow splotchy with anger or barely controlled tears. With a hiss, she whirls and is gone, using the gift of vampire speed to flee whatever transpired between them.

A disgusting display of weakness.

The demon forgets all about me and wings their way toward the other... a mortal woman. She glances up and cups her hands, holding them out. The bat glides the remaining distance and all but collapses in her palms.

Did the demon intentionally bring me to this

woman, or have I misunderstood what they wanted? She is the one Elizabeth said was a slayer.

Every question that arises only brings more.

Holding the demon close to her face, she seems to examine them for injury. Finding none, she strokes the top of their head with a finger, then sets them on her shoulder… and the little beast clings to her in return.

Slayers have no more love for demons than they do for the vampires they kill. Yet the scene would suggest otherwise. She clearly feels affection toward them. Everything about her is a paradox. Inexplicable.

Narrowing my gaze, I inhale deeply, searching for some trace of magic in her. Though I sense none, she is far too peculiar to be fully human. I have never heard of a demon being so attached to a mortal… let alone to a slayer. It's possible she came to bear that title by chance.

Her presence mocks the crown, yet Elizabeth has graciously spared Cassius's little pet from punishment for her crimes.

Still, she is prey, even to a demon as small as that.

Large brown eyes turn on me. There is no trace of fear or hate in her gaze. Just as when I saw her from the upper mezzanine, I am drawn to her. It's as if there is an invisible thread connected to something inside me, urging me forward.

Before I realize I've taken a step, I find myself standing before her—wisps of loose hairs that have escaped her braid stir by the air whirling from my movements.

Up close, I still can't sense any trace of

enchantment—spell, charm, potion, or otherwise—on her.

Only her purely mortal scent. Something wild, like an untamed forest heated by the sun after a brief rainstorm and spice. Her dark brown eyes are flecked with gold. And she is... beautiful. I was wrong not to think so before. From the defiant tilt of her chin and her full lips to every curve and plain of her body.

A sense of calm envelops me, and there is silence in my mind. That persistent buzz, the dark monster that has been with me for as long as I have breathed, invading my every thought, has quieted, noticed only in this instant because of its damnable absence.

Her mouth parts, but she doesn't speak. The tip of her tongue darts out to wet her lips. I am drawn to the movement. It sparks a need to touch her. Taste her. Possess her.

We are alone in this hall, but anyone could turn the corner at any moment. While we do nothing but stand, staring at each other, I cannot help but sense that I have somehow crossed a line that would not please my queen. And I have never wanted anything more than to please her.

"You should leave Nightwich." The warning comes out harsher than intended, scratching up my raw throat.

Her long lashes flutter with rapid blinking. Whatever spell held her broke at the sound of my voice.

"And why is that?" she asks.

I can't look away from the beating pulse at her throat, beating just below the surface of her skin. I can almost hear the rush of blood in her veins. As tempting as the sweetest water to a man dying of thirst. As fragrant as the rarest wine.

I force my face into an expressionless mask. "It would be the wise thing to do." When she only arches a brow in question, I add, "Unless you wish to die."

"I can't," she says. But those two words sound more like *I don't want to.*

She must be insane. A thought I mean to express with a look of derision, except my gaze lands on the bite marks where her shoulder meets her neck. There is a web of pale scars, a single set of nearly unnoticeable bite marks among them, and two more recent sets of scars over top of them. She was attacked sometime around the first mark she received.

There is no mistaking that she is fully claimed. I should not want another vampire's human—especially not one Elizabeth loathes. Yet, I am uncertain that I could keep from claiming her as my own, right here and now, if she were not marked by another.

She shifts nearer. So close, the warmth of her is like a gentle caress. So close that if either of us leaned forward, what little space remains between us would vanish. Her scent is overwhelming and intoxicating.

It would be too easy to reach out and wrap my arms around her. I can almost feel her body pressed against my own… feel her skin beneath my lips as my fangs sink into her flesh. I swallow and take half a step back.

"Why is that?" I throw her earlier question back at her.

Everything about her is intriguing, from her lack of fear to the mysterious, inhuman qualities she possesses.

She steps into me, pressing her chest to mine. Her palms pressed against my chest, fingers splayed as she lifts up on her toes, bringing her mouth so close to mine that I can taste her. My eyes slide shut.

"Because you are here," she whispers.

It's the strangeness of the answer that brings clarity crashing down again.

She stands back, watching me carefully. It takes a moment to realize her closeness was all in my head.

However, there must be something more at play. Though it's impossible to tell if it's a charm, spelled perfume, or some natural ability.

"What are you?" I demand, infusing every ounce of power I possess into my voice, compelling her to answer. I tower over her in a way meant to intimidate, to show how little effort it would take to end her life. Though it is to no avail. She is entirely unfazed by my posturing.

"I—" she starts, only to be interrupted by the demon on her shoulder. Pausing, she darts a glance at the bat from the corner of her eye, then she continues, "I am human."

"Lies." It's more snarl than word.

Hurt, not fear, shadows her large, brown eyes. She does not cower or tremble in fear but presses her lips into a thin line and glares. "I am not lying."

I scoff.

"What proof do you need?" She tilts her head to

the side, exposing her neck. "Would feeding on me be enough to make you believe?"

The bat lets out a series of chirps and scrambles to cover her exposed jugular with their wings and body.

Instead of heeding the demon's warning, she removes them, plucking the demon off to expose her vulnerable flesh. Their tiny claws leave behind hairline scratches that cause the smallest beads of blood to well up.

I retreat two steps, needing space before I fall into the grasp of the unknown power she possesses.

My chest rises and falls with heavy breaths. *Fear?*

Absurd. I can't possibly be afraid of a mere mortal woman. Except, what else could it be?

"Leave Nightwich, or you will die here—and it will not be a good death," I warn.

The corner of her mouth ticks up. Unbelievable. She is either too naive to be afraid, or her status as slayer has allowed her more courage than wisdom.

I turn and walk away, not giving her the opportunity to say another word or continue this game she is playing with me.

I do not look back. Not even when the erratic flight of leathery wings trails behind me.

CHAPTER TEN

CLARA

Talons clack a slow, steady rhythm against dry stone. It instantly puts me on edge. Self-preservation keeps my feet planted within arm's reach of the door.

Squinting into the dark cell, I can't see any hint of Varin, despite the fact that they can almost fill half the space with their full size.

The tap, tap, tapping stops abruptly.

I hold my breath, slowly reaching for the door. The sound of my pulse racing nearly drowns out the quiet tinkle of metal chains.

Just as my fingers brush over the cool metal of the handle, hot breath fans over the side of my face. A low growl freezes my blood. They crossed the distance without sound. Shadow passing through shadow. I hadn't sensed any sign of their approach.

"And to what do I owe the pleasure of your company at such a late hour?" The question is casual, but there is a coldness underneath that keeps me alert.

It takes more courage than I'd like to admit to respond. "We need to train."

After two nights' sleep and heartier meals, I feel refreshed and stronger. I wonder how much of my enhanced abilities are from the bond with Alaric and how much is thanks to Varin. Though I suppose I'll find out soon enough by the demon's reaction to how well I do.

Varin chuckles humorlessly as they move back, letting the cover of shadows slip off them like droplets of water. The effect makes my eyes itch.

It should have been impossible for a demon their size to go unseen in any corner of space this small. Let alone keep from making noise with their chains.

"I had begun to wonder if you intended to return or if you mistakenly believed you were strong enough to handle the full force of what you bargained for."

So that is why they are upset—because I didn't return when they wanted me to... even though they sent me away when I did try. "Of course, I was going to come back. I'm here now, aren't I?"

They snort. "Have you forgotten that I can sense your presence?"

"No, I didn't—"

"You left the grounds as soon as you woke, and when you finally returned, you dallied. I'm curious what was so important that you neglected your responsibilities."

I could tell them I left with Della because she wanted to help. Or how seeing the way Alaric looked at me had crushed my spirit. But no matter what, everything that happened sounds like nothing more than weak excuses.

"I will do my best to keep anything from interfering again."

Varin is silent for a long stretch before they return to crouch in the darkest corner. Only the faint outline of their shape and the dim, red glow of their eyes are visible through the shadows they pull toward them.

"I saw a friend in the city earlier," I say, wanting to ease the tension. "He is searching for a way to break the curse."

Varin raises their head at that. "So, that is where you ran off to." They shift, rattling the silver chains that bind them. "You were looking for a way out of our bargain."

I blink in confusion. Once their meaning sinks in, I realize they have misunderstood. "No," I say firmly.

Trust is a delicate thing. The more often it's broken, the harder it is to grow. Only those who know little of betrayal spend trust like an overabundance of coin. Words are only the soil in which it's planted. It needs the sunlight and water of action.

"I made a deal with you, and even if I found another way to save Alaric, I will still hold up my end."

Gradually, I inch closer, only stopping when I'm well within reach. This makes my promise to Oliver harder to keep, but not impossible.

"Seeing him was unexpected. I was only in the city because Della dragged me there to have dresses made."

Varin leans forward, setting their hands on either side of me. Gravel jumps over the ground around my feet as their taloned fingers dig into the stone. "You waste your time buying pretty dresses for a victory that is not yet in your grasp? I have to question if you truly want my powers to save your vampire or if there is another motive behind it."

I gape at the mercurial creature. Hurt and irritation spark, quickly growing into anger, strengthened by the bond. Not used to the heightened emotions it creates, it slips from my unpracticed grasp. "Did you forget the reason *you* wanted to bargain with me?" I snap.

Varin growls in warning at my impudence, but I hold my ground.

"I don't give two demon shits about dresses or any reason I might need them. If my friends want to help, I am in no position to turn them down, especially when I haven't a clue where to begin. And in case you forgot, I am a human in a castle filled with vampires— many of whom would like to see me dead. I don't have the luxury of freedom. I must watch for guards and sneak around and make sure I am never in a place that is too empty or too crowded." When I finish venting my frustrations, my breathing is ragged.

Losing my temper wasn't part of my plan, but there must be a limit to accusations. With every passing second, the curse is gradually eating away at Alaric.

"Let us stop this. We can't afford to waste time arguing," I say after what feels like minutes have passed, earning a glare as if I wasn't already aware that I'm responsible for letting most of the day pass without training. "I'm here now."

"Very well." Varin seems to grow smaller, hunching in on themselves.

I breathe a sigh of relief at having escaped unscathed, but it's a moment too soon.

Varin pounces. Their massive body crashes into mine. We fall together. The impact of their weight forces the air from my lungs in a painful whoosh. My head hits the stone floor with a resounding *thunk*.

The demon's weight presses down, seeming to increase, keeping me from drawing half a breath until I am dizzy. No amount of struggling helps, and my strength rapidly wanes. I'm unable to crawl out from under them.

Focus, Varin hisses in my mind.

I cannot breathe, let alone think beyond the primal urge screaming at me to survive, to claw my way out from under them.

Two blazing orbs of red hover above me, going in and out of focus. Then their weight shifts, just enough for me to draw in a deep breath. My lungs ache. The slight relief it brings doesn't last long.

A taloned finger drags over my shoulder, leaving a shallow scratch trailing in its wake. The point comes to rest on the tender scar above my heart. Varin snarls, pressing down, piercing through skin, sinking into my flesh agonizingly slow. Further and further until the point connects with bone. I am delirious with the paralyzing pain.

Something cracks, gives way. I break out in a cold

sweat, freezing on the inside, burning up on the outside. A wave of nausea rolls through me.

Varin makes a growl of satisfaction and scrapes the surface of my heart. I can feel every thump as it fights to keep going.

I can feel the space between beats grow longer and further away until it's so distant it doesn't sound like it's in my chest anymore. Then, between one moment and the next, that stretches on far too long.

I think I might be dying.

Varin's power retreats lightning fast, ripping out and leaving a void behind as if it took something vital with it, and leaving something else, something foreign in its place.

The first beat is like being struck by a boulder. It beats again and again and again. The pace picks up, quickening until it's racing, pounding inside my chest as if demons have chased me for miles. It's no longer the eerie echo as if I clasped it in my hand.

My back arches off the ground as I draw in a deep breath. The air is hot. Stifling. Or maybe it is that I am too cold. I sit up, coughing violently, and clutch at my wound.

Except...

There is no blood... no hole.

I turn to Varin. The demon is precisely where they were. Instead of idly scratching at the stone, they are oddly still, observing my every movement and reaction.

Glad as I am to be alive, I am furious.

I don't need to ask if they nearly killed me. The

guilt of dragging me within a hair's breadth of dying is written in their posture.

This time, I don't attempt to control my temper. I use them to pull myself up on shaking legs. I face them down as if *I* were the demon, and they were my prey.

"I gave you my word, and still you don't believe me," I say, enunciating each syllable as the hold on my emotions slips. "Even after I explained what happened, you punished me. And for what? Coming here a few hours later than you wanted me to? Tell me, why shouldn't I leave and never return?"

Varin lowers their head to the floor, their taloned hands coming up beside their face. The look of contrition is unmistakable. "Because you now possess a direct portion of my power. I can't take it back, even if I wanted to."

A gift... given in good faith.

Demon shit.

I sigh.

"I should have warned you what would happen, and..." Varin trails off, angling their face away. "I was not as careful as I ought to have been. For that, I am sorry."

Empathy worms its way beneath my simmering ire. Forgiveness is inevitable.

Even without their gift, I can't let them off the hook without consequence. Just as they would not give me a free pass for my recklessness. We must keep each other in check.

"I will return as soon as I can. However, if you ever risk my life again because you are upset, then I will let you rot down here for another three hundred years." The words come without thought and hold the promise of suffering that I have only ever heard from vampires and demons.

I hate how much self-control it takes to keep my emotions steady, preventing them from seeping out. Then I slip out of the cell, closing the door quietly behind me, and then make my way to the upper levels of Nightwich.

Perched on a stool in the back corner of the kitchen, out of the way of the staff, I gaze out through the doorway, propped open for the winter air to offer a reprieve from the stifling air heated by several fires and ovens. I am so consumed by my thoughts that I barely taste my meal.

Moonlight reflects off the barren mountains bordering the western side of the castle. There is, what I estimate to be a field, stretching for roughly five miles between here and the jagged terrain of the foothills, speckled with sparse clusters of gnarled and twisted trees.

A patch of land peeks out from a gap. I squint and try to make out whatever it is. The longer I focus, the more similar spots appear until I can follow a path meandering into the mountains.

I frown. How could I have missed something so obvious before? It makes me think of Oliver. It would be too much of a coincidence if that path led directly to his pack.

Scoffing, I shake away my wild imagination. Oliver said it would be safe there, and a clear route from the backdoor of this castle would be anything other than safe.

As brief as that imaginative diversion was, it did help me to regain much-needed control over my emotions. Though it will still be some time before I am ready to forgive Varin fully, but almost three days have passed since Alaric was cursed, and I have made no headway. Allowing petty grudges to get in the way will only hurt him.

I take the pair of kid leather gloves I grabbed from my trunk before coming to the kitchens and pull them on, hiding the band that connects me to Varin. Then I stand and weave between gold platers, piled with food as a bevy of servants take them to their destinations. There are still several hours before dawn that the demon and I can put to use.

CHAPTER ELEVEN

CLARA

Cherno follows me through the main corridor. They circle my head several times before landing on my shoulder. Then, as if I wasn't already aware of the demon's presence, they yank on a lock of hair.

I turn a glare on them. "Are you trying to rip it out of my scalp?"

"Clara, please, find another way," the tiny demon pleads. "Alaric wouldn't want—"

"I had to take the chance… besides, it's already done. It's too late to do anything about it now," I say, turning a corner.

Most of the courtiers and guards ignore my presence. Only a few deign to send a passing glance in my direction. For the most part, humans are beneath their notice. To do so would imply humans have some semblance of importance to the vampire court, rather than something easily disposed of at their whims, allowed to live by the grace bestowed upon us.

By now, the way I head is so deeply ingrained that

my feet take me there by habit. When we first arrived, the halls felt labyrinthine. It's a wonder I never became hopelessly lost when there is always another corridor I've never noticed before, seeming to appear from thin air.

After what happened between Varin and me earlier, more training is one of the last things I want to do tonight, but just thinking of Alaric gets my feet moving and spurs me to do what is needed.

Careful to keep my pace leisurely, I pause occasionally, using the excuse of admiring paintings or suits of armor to check if I am being followed. The last thing I need is someone tailing me to the lower levels.

A handful of turns later, things are quiet. It's the kind of quiet that will allow me to slip easily into the concealed stairwell without bringing a vampire with ill intentions down on me. Cherno shifts and tugs on my hair again.

"I wouldn't be doing this if there was anything else I could do."

Cherno grumbles, then wilts, draping themselves over my shoulder. "Be careful."

"I will." I can't help but smile as I reach to pet between their two large, pointed ears. "Besides, I have you with me. I couldn't ask for a better escort."

They chirp in what sounds like determined agreement.

I'm unsure how much of their worries are solely Cherno's or if they voice my own, so I don't have to. I push the thought away.

No. I did what I had to. Alaric sacrificed himself to

Elizabeth, giving in to a fate he never wanted. And he did it for my sake. I cannot turn my back on him and walk away. Reaffirming my decision strengthens my resolve to see this through.

A final turn and the stairwell leading down to the lower levels comes into view. As far as I've seen, no one else has noticed the darkened gap between the wall and the spiral staircase leading to the mezzanine on the second floor. But if one bothers to look past the shadows shrouding the corner, it is as plain as day.

Halfway there, I slow my pace when the pounding steady of heavy footsteps thud behind me. I throw a glance over my shoulder. Two guards are striding down the hall. They are not merely patrolling—they are on a mission. I move off to the side, press my back against the wall, then wait for them to pass.

Except their gazes narrow in on me.

It seems I am not that lucky.

"Go to Cassius's room and wait for me there," I murmur to Cherno.

Without argument, the demon lifts off into the air and flies in an aimless pattern. They wait and watch, memorizing these specific guards in case something happens.

Instead of continuing on as I hoped, they stop before me, blocking any hope of escape. Neither bothers giving any of their attention to the demon darting up and down the corridor.

"This the one?" the larger of the guards asks his companion.

She nods sharply and grunts. They grab me by my

upper arms and practically drag me along with all the consideration of an inanimate object. At least they are taking me in the opposite direction of the dungeons.

"I am perfectly capable of walking on my own," I say.

That only earns me an irritated growl in response. I do my best not to struggle against them. By the time we make it to the second floor, I have a pretty good idea where they are taking me. Any relief I felt is short-lived.

"I'll go willingly," I say again.

They share a look over my head and stop after a few more paces. I expect a threat to remain silent and am surprised when they release me instead.

"Don't even think about running, or I will cut you off at the ankles," the woman warns.

Her companion only bares his fangs before taking up position a few steps behind me. He draws his sword with a ring of metal against metal, and when he shoves me forward, I barely avoid stumbling. Not giving him the satisfaction of getting under my skin, I march obediently behind the first guard.

Any time I fall more than two strides behind, the oaf at my back prods me with his sword.

We climb to the second level, past the hall to the courtiers' wing, and past the third, where Alaric's quarters are located. The stairs finally come to an end on the fourth level.

No one could set foot on this landing without knowing this wing belongs to the queen. The opulence is so overdone it borders on garish.

A thick carpet runs the length of the hall to the

only set of doors on this floor. They are bleached white with a tree carved into the wood. The least subtle touch is the chandelier right outside. Hanging crystals throw lacy patterns of light onto the etched leaves, giving the illusion of a light breeze blowing through the branches.

Between standing candelabras, tapestries cover the walls, and strands of what looks like silver or gold stitching are woven throughout. It's hard to tell in the flickering light.

The vampire leading me steps to the side and bows just as one door opens. At first, I think it's part of Elizabeth's show until I am ensnared by deep pools of midnight.

My heart leaps into my throat at the sight of Alaric's face. I can see the question in his eyes. It takes everything in me not to go to him. I reach for our bond and imagine myself pulling on a rope with him tied to the other end.

The barest hint of a frown takes shape, then it's gone, and he's striding down the hall without a second glance. As if we were strangers. A hollow pit opens in my chest. I don't know if it will ever stop hurting when he looks at me like that.

Once again, I'm shoved roughly from behind. I grit my teeth. This time, I am thankful for that guard's ability to irritate me. If I'm to face Elizabeth, it is better to be made sharp by anger than dulled by heartache.

I don't wait to be announced before entering. The horrified look on the first guard's face is worth it as I storm inside. I'm sure she will have a thing or two to say to her companion for not holding me back.

Elizabeth's face twitches at my blatant disregard for protocol before she can stop it. The last sign of ire. She has a game to play and will not be caught off guard again.

The parlor alone is easily twice the size of Alaric's entire chambers. There is an excess of silks and suedes and brocade with shimmering threading. Each piece of furniture is a piece of art with detailed engravings.

Elizabeth's hair is down, blonde waves cascade over one shoulder, obscuring the front of her pale lavender gown embroidered with rose gold accents.

Not wanting to push my luck too far, I stop halfway in.

She sits at a small table against a wall, another chair opposite her, and tea service for two.

The hair on the back of my neck rises at the similarity of this scene to the last time she wanted to 'chat' with me. If I weren't already suspicious, this would certainly do the trick.

"Come. Sit." Elizabeth waves a dismissive hand toward the chair across from her. "There is something I would like to speak with you about."

I resist scoffing. Civil conversations with her are as probable as my ability to break Alaric's curse with a kiss.

Tentatively, I walk over and take a seat.

I assess the situation. She gives the appearance of mutual respect by having me sit at the same level to lure me into a false sense of security. I wonder how often she plays this game.

Elizabeth regards me placidly, but her expression cannot hide the cold loathing behind her eyes. She lets the silence drag on, waiting to see who will break it first.

It makes no difference to me. The sooner we begin, the sooner I can leave, and giving this to her will be to my advantage. The more hollow victories I give her, the more likely she is to underestimate me.

Without knowing her intentions, I don't want to give her so much as a word to use against me. I opt for empty praise. "This room is quite beautiful."

Elizabeth's smile matches my sincerity. She hums in agreement as she pours the tea, first filling my cup and then her own.

I accept the cup and set it down, clasping my hands in my lap. The skin around the corner of her eyes tightens slightly, but unlike last time, she doesn't force me to drink. I continue pretending to admire the room, waiting for her to begin.

She sips her tea delicately as if we are friends and sitting together is an everyday occurrence. Finally, she sets her empty cup down on the saucer with a gentle clatter. "I'm sure you must be feeling uncertain of your future and what will become of you."

I swallow, then slowly nod. Confused. Because that is not what I expected her to say.

"Once Alaric is crowned, he will no longer have use for you," she speaks sweetly, her tone oozing with concern. "I doubt he would have bothered to claim you if he knew how inconvenient you would become.

However, I am prepared to give you more riches than you could dream of having."

Elizabeth looks at me expectantly. If she thinks I will agree and say that, *yes, I am an inconvenience,* then she will be disappointed.

"I don't understand," I say, unable to resist nettling her.

The false smile of her mask strains at the corners. "I will allow you to return home to your family. You will have no problem finding a husband and living out the rest of your mortal life." She pauses, ready to deliver the sting of her offer. "All you must do in exchange is sever the oath bond."

My heart thuds against my chest. I inhale sharply. Then fear comes upon me like a beast sneaking up from behind. She is asking for the impossible as though it were as simple as cutting a thread.

...only death can break the bond.

How casually she asks me to die so she can save face. I'm unsure if she is threatening me or attempting to trick me into doing her dirty work for her.

"The oath cannot be broken."

Her brows rise. "Oh? Do you think a human would know more about such things than I, when I am the one who created the ability to form the bond?"

I shake my head. "That's not..." I stop to choose my next words carefully. I will not tremble before her. I will give her a threat for a threat. "What I meant was, Mr. Hughes once told me it was unbreakable."

One of her guards will have discovered his body by now, and I have no doubt she knows I'm responsible. What I don't say is that I already know the parts she is leaving out. Only death can sever it. Elizabeth would have me agree to what she wants, then force me to end my life to keep my word.

"Try to see it from my perspective," she continues. "How would it look if the court learned that my consort shared such a rare bond with a human?" She heaves a dramatic sigh. "You never should have bound yourself to him in the first place, but it can be undone." Elizabeth takes a vial from somewhere I don't see and places it on the table between us. "All you need to do is drink this."

Under my cream-colored kid leather gloves, the night-forget ring cools unnaturally. A warning from Varin, one I don't need but appreciate all the same.

"What is it?" I ask, knowing full well it holds death.

"It is an incredibly rare potion that will unravel the magic of the oath bond, nothing more. The ingredients are almost impossible for most to get ahold of."

I can't help but notice every evasion of the truth. Every lie is hidden behind carefully crafted words. Twice, she has handed me a bottle of poison. The first time would have killed me if Varin hadn't interfered. I can't help but wonder if she really thought the same tactic would work a second time.

"You understand why I hesitate?"

Elizabeth tsks. "I don't ask this for my sake, but for Alaric's. He is suffering, and the longer you remain bound, the worse it will become… I am afraid it may even kill him."

For her to even suggest that I am the one at fault for him being cursed makes my blood boil. But it allows me the opportunity to make her believe I am playing right into her hands.

With one finger, I trace the delicate cutwork of my glove on the back of my hand as if in thought. I glance up through my lashes. "Alaric is cursed, isn't he?"

"Aren't you quite the observant one?" Elizabeth's eyes narrow. "How did you know?"

Demon shit. I slipped up.

"It is the only thing I know of that could kill a vampire." It is a lie, of course. We both know that.

Sniffling, she nods—a lie to match. Once, the shimmer in her eyes might have fooled me. "If you care for my prince at all, even a fraction as much as I love him, then I implore you to do this for him."

Wavering between disgust and shock, it is all I can do to keep my face schooled in a mask of indifference. Every word out of her mouth is deceitful. Somehow, it seemed to slip out unintentionally. Still, I was not prepared to hear her say she loved Alaric outright. And it's the only part of this conversation I can't tell if that was genuine or by calculated design.

"Of course, it will only work if you are willing. You cannot be forced or compelled in any way. However, think of the consequences. Because of your actions, Alaric is suffering and will continue to if you refuse."

As Elizabeth's words sink in, I understand something I doubt she meant to reveal. She can't kill me—at least not outright. She would have commanded me, forced it down my throat, or more likely, she would have simply ripped my throat out the minute I came into this room instead of bothering with this farce.

A wave of calm slides over me. Elizabeth wanted to use my heart against me by twisting the truth and shifting the blame. But all she succeeded in doing was showing me her hand.

I reach for the vial and take it, turning it over. The amber glass is warm from the contents. Slowly, I get to my feet.

"May I have some time to think it over?" I ask. Though I have already made my choice, I need her to believe I've fallen for at least part of the demon shit she spewed.

And if the ingredients are as rare as she claimed? Well, then, I am more than happy to make them even rarer.

"Take the time you need," she says, then dismisses me. As I reach for the door, she calls out. "And, Clara?"

I halt and peer over my shoulder.

"Try not to take too long."

CHAPTER TWELVE

CLARA

I exit the queen's chambers and am glad when the two guards remain posted at the door rather than follow. As soon as my back is to them, I slip the vial down the front of my shirt. The fewer who know about it, the better. I don't want it to fall into the wrong hands, especially without knowing what it is yet.

The castle's activity continues to wane as dawn draws near. Besides an occasional sentry stationed in the usual places, I don't pass more than a handful of vampires and servants until I reach the main floor.

Any plans I had to train with Varin have gone up in smoke. I'm too distracted and would only end up seriously injured. I go over every word of the conversation with Elizabeth.

Her parting words were a threat. At first, I assumed it was directed more toward me than Alaric. But now, I'm not so sure. It could mean one of two things—if I take too long, she will find a way to force my hand. Or she will be happy enough to take it out on him.

I rub my temples and set those questions aside. While I would prefer to narrow it down to better anticipate Elizabeth's next move.

I know her well enough to regard every word out of her mouth as a deception but not well enough to guess how cunning she is or which of us has fooled the other into believing our act.

A figure steps out, blocking my way. I flinch, barely managing to avoid a collision and back up. Elise fixes me with a look of pure hate, baring her fangs. It's a weak attempt at intimidation.

Once, she nearly killed me. Now, she's as bothersome as an insect buzzing around your head in the summer.

Elise is a vampire. She doesn't see me as a threat. Despite the fact that I only have a fraction of her strength and speed, I could pull the dagger hidden in my boot and bury it in her chest before she would think to strike.

She is someone who is used to scheming to get what she wants, so she only considers her next move —not how I might react. She lacks instinct for confrontations because she's never had to fight to survive.

Tittering from two vampires off to the side draws the attention of several others in the hall. Splotches of red stain Elise's pale face, and I don't know if she is about to burst into tears or throw a tantrum.

I don't react, waiting for her to make a move or explain. Elise takes a step closer, keeping too much distance to have an effect. Her chest rises and falls with quick, shallow breaths, and the way she holds herself gives her away.

She is afraid *of me*, I realize.

The laughter in the background dies off. Those who've stopped to watch have come to the same conclusion. Some throw looks of disgust our way. Others walk away. Elise smiles, but it's not me they are looking at.

"You might have convinced yourself that you mean something to him," Elise says, pitched low so only I hear. "But you are nothing more than a mouse the cat plays with before it feasts."

She shoves past, bumping my shoulder with hers. I twist, dispelling the force of it to keep my balance. Unprepared for my reaction, her steps falter. She balls her hands into fists at her sides, then storms off, not looking back.

I make it to Cassius's quarters without further incident. I expect Cherno to swoop toward me when I enter the parlor, only to find it empty. A fire burns in the bedroom fireplace, warming the air for someone who isn't there.

After checking the rest of the rooms and finding them all empty, I remove the small bottle from my top and hold it up to the light to examine it. The liquid is dark and thick but far less so than blood. At least Elizabeth didn't attempt the exact same trick as last time.

Opening my trunk, I shove it down in the corner, under layers of clothes. That should keep it safe until I decide what to do with it. Then I sit on the foot of the bed, legs crossed, and eye the hidden vial of poison—because I can't think of what else it might be.

However rare the ingredients and magic involved, there would be a tale or myth connected closely with any mention of the bond. The fact that Elizabeth claims to know of it when no one else does *and* came to possess something so rare in less than the span of two full days is suspicious all on its own.

The clock tower chimes an early hour, and the sky changes from inky black to a wintery gray. It's the kind that seems to drain every trace of color from the world.

Briefly, I wonder if Cherno is still with Alaric. As if summoned by my thoughts, a plume of grey passes through the wall, taking the form of a bat. The demon spots me and alters their course. They land ungracefully on my head, tangling themselves in my hair.

"Where have you been?" I reach up and work to free the little menace.

"I thought she might have had you tossed in the dungeon again," Cherno chirps.

Several strands fall over my eyes as I finally free them. I hold them at eye level. "Not this time," I say.

Then I tell the demon almost everything. I leave out any mention of the vial. It's one more secret I need to keep to myself for now. I can't risk having it destroyed just yet.

If there's no other way... I push away the thought.

Elizabeth has gone to great lengths to get Alaric right where she has him. I doubt there's a limit to what Elizabeth is willing to do to keep him there.

I stand on the edge of a precipice, looking down over the sharp drop. It's too dark to see more than dead grass under my feet and a body of water beyond the cliff. The wind howls like a harmony of demons descending on their prey.

Ripples form on a mirrored surface below. From this vantage, it's impossible to tell if the water is deep or shallow. I step back, not wanting to find out and bump up against a warm body. A growl sets shivers skating over my skin.

My movements are sluggish as I turn. I don't feel entirely in control of my body. And that is the most terrifying part.

A hand presses against the base of my throat, sliding up, fingers tightening until I can barely breathe. Deep blue eyes with a dim ring of demonic power trap me more than his grip.

"Why are you here?" Alaric snarls. The words echo, lingering.

His hold constricts slightly. I gasp. My fingers curl into the fabric of his sleeves to steady myself. It seems to startle him, and his hand relaxes as his gaze travels from my touch to my face.

My pulse hammers in my ears as I lean into him. He is all I can think about. Not the dangers ahead or how to stop the curse from killing him, only how much my heart aches for missing him.

Alaric's expression is unreadable, but his lips part as the space between us dwindles. Only when his body is flush against mine do we go still.

Each breath comes a little quicker with the adrenaline brought on by the uncertainty of what he'll do next. He's just as likely to kiss me as he is to threaten me.

"You are a spell that has ensnared me," he says, "And I find I am unable to escape its enchantment."

He searches my face, looking for answers I do not have. His palm cups my cheek, and my eyes grow too heavy to keep open. I feel his mouth trail down my neck, and the sharp points of his fangs drag over my skin.

Heaviness weighs down my limbs and slows my thoughts. I can't seem to make myself move… I'm not sure I want to.

Then his warm breath fans over my lips. "Perhaps the next time I find you, I will break this spell of yours, little nightmare."

Then his hand drops away.

At first, I think he steps back. I force my eyes open and find that I'm the one moving.

Falling.

I reach for him. Open my mouth to call his name.

Icy black water swallows me up. It fills my nose and mouth, pouring into my lungs… burning. The harder I fight to make it to the surface, the faster it drags me down, down, down.

Air sears my throat as I gasp, struggle to sit up, and fail. A heavy weight settles on my chest, and panic seeps in.

"I said you would be too heavy," Cherno says, their voice sluggish with sleep.

"Forrrgivvve me." The mass on top of me shifts. Smooth scales unravel, sliding off.

As soon as they've removed enough of their weight, I bolt up and yank open the bed curtain to let in some light. Cassius must have found me sleeping and closed them.

"Demon shit," I hiss, squinting from the harsh light of the sun streaming through the windows. I have slept almost all morning, though it feels like only minutes have passed.

I glower at the jewel-green snake, who had apparently joined me at some point. Their body coils, giving the appearance of shoulders on either side of their lowered head.

"Were you trying to—" I start, stopping abruptly when something about this situation strikes me as unusual. I grab the snake and bring their face to eye level. "Did you… just speak?"

Ruby eyes blink innocently. They pull their body up and curve it in a shrugging gesture. My experience with demons is more than most, yet I have only scratched the surface.

Can all demons talk to anyone they want but prefer not to? "Why haven't you spoken before?"

Instead of answering, Asmod looks to Cherno.

I couldn't always understand Cherno. It wasn't until Alaric used his powers on me that I partially understood the demon and only fully after the first mark.

Was it my connection to him? If so, then that means…

That means Cassius has been keeping things from me.

I take three slow breaths, trying to keep my irritation from getting the best of me. Then I climb out of bed and storm into the parlor.

I find him sleeping with his hands folded over his stomach and one leg draped over the back of the couch. His peaceful countenance irritates me. I grab his booted heel and fling his leg, sending him toppling to the floor.

He groans, rolling to his back, and props himself up on his elbows, looking mildly confused. "Well, good morning to you as well, my lady," he drawls.

"I think it's time we have that talk." My hands ball into fists at my side, fighting the urge to wring his neck.

Cassius is on his feet in an instant. His mouth curls into a wicked smile right before he wraps an arm around my waist, pressing me against the front of him, hand tangling in my hair. "You see, little bird, when a man and a woman—"

I stomp down on his foot. He grunts and releases me, then drops onto the couch with a pout.

"Don't," I warn. "I am going to ask you questions, and you are going to give me straight answers."

His expression shutters. We both know I could do nothing to stop him if he left. Perhaps it's my anger or knowing I deserve to understand what's happening. Either way, he stays put.

"How is it possible that we have a connection?" I demand.

Cassius relaxes back against the cushion, arms crossed, and studies me. "How did you find out?"

"I can't think of another reason why Asmod can speak to me."

He turns his head and hisses at the snake. "What part of 'keep your fucking mouth shut' was difficult to understand?"

I shift to block his view of the demon. "This is between you and me. Leave them out of it."

Cassius rubs his hands over his face and gives me his full attention. "You already know the answer to that."

I am about to snap at him when I realize *he is right*. Despite the warmth from the fire, I shiver. My legs give out, and I sink to my knees.

How could I have forgotten something so important?

CHAPTER THIRTEEN

CLARA

"You are a bastard, Cassius. You should have told her."

"She will find out after she heals."

The hazy snippet of a distant conversation replays again and again.

Cassius kneels before me and takes my face in his hands, forcing me to look him in the eye. "I assure you, it's nothing like your connection with Alaric," he says, misunderstanding my reaction. "We are not quite so tangled up... at least, that is what the witch claimed."

"Your lives are now tied together. Magic demands a price, and that was the price offered to save your life."

I remember asking him to explain, but each time he would deflect until the chaos of everything else took over my every thought.

"Tell me how," I say, my voice little more than a rasp.

Sitting back on his heels, Cassius finally relents.

"Did you think she would give you the opportunity to take my life without my consent?"

My stomach churns. I'm completely horrified.

"If you sacrificed me, I would have slipped quietly into the Otherworld. But then you decided to forfeit your own instead." He shakes his head. "I was meant to be the sacrifice. Della and Lawrence were subdued to keep them from interfering."

"How could you think I would do that to you?" Does he think I'm so selfish that I could kill him without a second thought? Tears slide down my cheeks.

"What good it would do to break the compulsion if you weren't there to welcome him back?" Cassius smirks as if to make light of it all. "You left me with no other choice but to give you some of my years."

I lurch forward and grab the collar of his shirt, eager to know everything all at once. "What does that mean?"

This is no simple explanation—I need more than a few simple words.

"Did you forget? Vampires are immortal. What is fifty or sixty years in the span of eternity?" He pries my hands loose and clasps them in his. "It's those years that connect you to Asmod in the same way I am."

The fact that we are connected seems far less important now compared to what he offered to do.

"Why...?" I don't finish the question because I already know the answer.

He loves me.

And though I do love him. He loves me in a way I

can't return—not in the same way. My heart belongs to Alaric. And I could no sooner change that than I could stop the sun from setting. Maybe, in another life, things would have been different. My chest squeezes painfully because there is no easy answer.

"There's no need to cry, little bird," Cassius says, pulling me into his side. "Perhaps you'll understand if I explain."

I doubt it. The expression I give him says as much.

"At first, I wanted to possess you, as one would a caged bird. I wanted to know what it felt like for someone to look at me the way you look at him. In my attempts to capture you for myself, I became that bird, trapped in a cage, with the door open but unable to fly away. However true my feelings are now, they grew from the seeds of selfish desire. I would not wish you to give your heart to someone like that."

When I shift to pull away, his arms tighten to keep me there. "Cassius—"

"Of course," he continues, not even attempting to disguise the devilish smile in his voice. "Should you find yourself no longer able to resist me despite everything, I would not object to being on the receiving end of your affections."

Irritation simmers below the surface as I stare down the door to Cassius's quarters. After finally explaining everything, he simply got up and mumbled something about needing to feed, then left me sitting on the parlor floor.

I still don't know what to say or think or do after everything he said.

It was only when the shock wore off that small details began gnawing at me. I cannot help feeling that Cassius is *still* not telling me everything. He was a little too flippant.

For two hours, I'd waited for him to return, eventually choosing to face my own demon—a decision I now regret. I was distracted the entire time, and Varin used it against me, and now every inch of my body aches.

Now, here I stand, too much of a coward to walk through the doors. How can I go inside and demand more, knowing how he feels and what he would have done? I lean against the opposite wall with my arms folded over my chest.

Perhaps it's unfair to be angry with Cassius for holding back when I am keeping secrets of my own. Is it any different just because I've convinced myself that my reason for keeping things from my friends is to keep them safe?

Others caring about what happens to me is nothing like I imagined. I want to be more open and confide in them, but how can I burden them? How can I justify putting their lives at risk?

No matter what I do, the chances I will live to see the end are slim. I may have enhanced abilities from my bond with Alaric and a demon willing to let me borrow their powers... but Elizabeth is a vampire with an army at her back.

"I must know what that door has done to offend you so," Lawrence drawls.

My thoughts are too at odds with his teasing for me to respond. Not capable of anything more constructive, I turn and walk in the opposite direction. I move slow to avoid limping. It feels like I was trampled by a harmony of demons.

Not getting the hint—or maybe choosing to ignore it—Lawrence catches up and effortlessly keeps pace.

"You look exhausted."

I send him a sidelong glance. "I'm rested enough." After a pause, I add, "Unless that's your *nice* way of saying I look like a demon's ass?"

He snorts.

"Thank you for your concern, however, it's unwarranted."

"Mentally and emotionally," he says, far too gently. "There is more than one way to wear yourself down."

That strikes a chord... and I hate it. If given a choice, I would much rather deal with his thinly veiled insults than his genuine worry.

Much to my surprise, Lawrence doesn't comment on my aimless and wandering route, and no matter how silent I am or how hard I try to ignore him, he doesn't leave my side.

After a while, we end up in a part of the castle I am unfamiliar with. My stride slows.

Neither of us speaks more than a few words here and there. I pointedly ignore the awkwardness between us, focusing on memorizing the twists and turns.

"I owe you an apology," Lawrence says, clearing his throat.

His words make me jolt more than the abrupt breaking of the strained silence. I stop and gape at his back.

With an exasperated sigh, he turns before continuing. He doesn't even attempt to hide the roll of his eyes at my reaction. "I lost my temper and shouldn't have taken it out on you when it was not your fault."

The look on his face doesn't quite match what he's saying. I regard him with suspicion.

"Della put you up to this, didn't she?" I say slowly.

He sniffs and looks away. "Some might call it twisting my arm." Lawrence pins me with a glare. "Della isn't usually so outspoken. It seems she picked up a few habits from you. I just hope she doesn't start scheming, or the Otherworld only knows what else." After a pause, he adds, "I wouldn't say anything if it wasn't sincere."

Lawrence is walking again before I finish processing it all. I hurry to catch up, matching his stride.

"Thank you."

He darts a glance at me from the corner of his eye but doesn't respond. The corner of his mouth twitches up. It would have been impossible to catch if I wasn't looking.

He leads the way. This time, the quiet that falls between us is easy. I'm not sure we would call ourselves friends, but it's more than a superficial acquaintance. I don't think there's a term for reluctant, almost friends.

Lawrence pulls me aside, caging me in with his hands planted against the wall. Then, he slowly leans forward.

"What are you doing?"

Bringing his mouth close to my ear. "I can see the gears in your head turning. If you have a plan, let us know," he whispers.

"I… what?"

He leans back, giving me a mischievous grin, pleased to catch me off guard.

"Not yet," I say begrudgingly, refusing to acknowledge his teasing.

That earns me the sort of disappointed expression one might give a child. The more I get to know this man, the more peculiar he becomes.

Lawrence shrugs, then loops my arm through his and proceeds to half-drag me down the hall.

"What are you up to now?"

"I'm helping," he says with that grin I don't trust.

Moments later, we come to an abrupt stop before a set of double doors engraved with elegant curves and twisting ivy.

Voices float to us from down the hall, but before they round the corner, Lawrence leads me inside.

It is the most beautiful library I have ever seen, larger than I could have imagined—and that is only what I can see from where I stand.

There are four stories of shelves up the walls. Wrought iron stairs, designed with the same wild vines that match the door, lead to each of the higher levels. Freestanding bookcases are arranged in long rows with rolling ladders connected to each. As I move further in, I notice alcoves at the end of several aisles along the inner wall.

Even if I had three lifetimes to do nothing but read, I wouldn't be able to make it through more than a fraction of the books here.

"I often find that when I'm stuck, reading is the best way to free the mind," Lawrence says in a conspiratorial whisper.

It is tempting... How long has it been since I've allowed myself such a simple pleasure?

"I can't." I shake my head.

Lawrence grabs my face, pressing in on my cheeks hard enough to make my face look ridiculous. "For the next few hours, read whatever grabs your imagination and put your worries aside. After that, you can put the weight of the world upon your shoulders again. It might surprise you what a good book can do for you." I open my mouth to protest, but he pinches my lips shut between his forefinger and thumb. "Tomorrow, we will help you come up with a strategy together."

Lawrence takes my shoulders, spins me around, and gives me a gentle push forward. The doors click shut behind him before I can even turn back.

Two hours, I decide. Then, I will begin planning in earnest.

I wander up and down the aisles of shelves, looking for a place to settle. Near the entrance is a cold fireplace with a few chairs nearby and too few candles to read by. On the far end, a warm glow dances across the rows of spines, making the gilded details gleam. I'm drawn toward it before I think twice.

When I turn the corner, I'm pleased to find no one in sight. An unoccupied cozy chair is beside the crackling fireplace, and several sconces are lit, spilling their light into recesses. It almost feels as if this space was prepared specifically for me.

Taking my time, I scan the countless titles, weaving in and out of the alcoves until I've created a small tower of books. I sit before the fire, surrounded by a circle of colorful tomes, as I flip through several before deciding where to start.

Before long, I am lost inside the worlds hidden between the pages as they come to life in my mind's eye. The unfamiliar settings pull me in and hold me in their grasp.

When I close the third book, the fire has died down. More time has passed than I intended to spend here. As much as I've enjoyed this break and would love to stay and continue reading the others in my stack, I am no closer to a free mind, able to come up with a solution to everything.

Perhaps there is no satisfying solution or even an unsatisfying solution. Perhaps there is no solution at all. That doesn't keep guilt from rearing its ugly head, whispering how I will fail if I continue to be selfish.

Regretfully, I return each book to its rightful place. But as I turn to leave, a book near the end catches my attention. It's worn and faded, looking much older than those surrounding it. Setting the stack I've collected on the floor, I reach for the ancient volume, pushing up on my toes to pull it down.

Carefully, I lift the cover and turn the pages. Exquisitely detailed painted images adorn nearly every page, surrounded by the words of a language I don't know. From what I can tell, it's a collection of fairy tales.

"Next time," I murmur the promise to the book.

I stretch, struggling to balance and maneuver the book back into its narrow space. It was a lot easier to remove. The sconce at the end of the aisle sputters out, drenching the aisle in shadow.

"Demon shit."

The book is plucked from my hand and slid into place before I can lower my arm. A solid, warm, and distinctly male body is flush against my back.

I go utterly still, too stunned to react.

CHAPTER FOURTEEN

CLARA

"Are you following me in the hopes of adding my name to your list of kills, little slayer?" Alaric's voice is a low rumble.

The sound sets my heart thundering with a myriad of emotions. I turn to face him, with anger across his features. He shifts to the side, forcing me to back up into the corner, making sure I am well and truly trapped. Black veins slither up his neck from under his collar, receding before I can decide if it was real or a trick of the dim, flickering light.

"I would never—" I stop abruptly, realizing the lie I almost spoke. Swallowing the lump in my throat, I try again. "I would never intentionally hurt you."

Alaric scoffs. One of his hands finds the decorative cuff of my sleeve and idly rubs the material between two fingers. His anger shifts to mild annoyance.

"Who are you?" he asks. The faint scent of liquor is on his breath, and his eyes have a glassy sheen.

It's tempting, so tempting, to tell him everything—

our history, our connection, what Elizabeth is doing to him. Though the words are on the tip of my tongue, I swallow them down. I'm afraid it will do more harm than good. The curse's hold is too strong.

"Clara Valmont," I say as if I believe he wanted my name.

The movement of his hand stills, and he fixes me with an expression I assume is meant to portray how little regard he has for such an answer. Except, the longer he studies me, the more intense his gaze becomes.

"No," he says.

I frown. *Does he think I'm lying?*

I bite down on my bottom lip. There is an air about this moment reminiscent of my first days at Windbury.

"That name does not suit you. It's far too ordinary for what you are." Alaric's lip curls, though it doesn't hold the promise of violence he intends. But something else entirely. Heated. Intense. Consuming. It makes the blood in my veins race and sets my heart fluttering.

Demons take me...

"It doesn't?" I ask, little more than a breath. "Then what does?"

He considers for a moment, then says, "Nightmare." He tastes the word on his tongue, then hums in approval. "Yes. That is more fitting."

My heart stumbles a beat. It cannot be a coincidence for him to call me that. "Why is that?"

I am unsettled by the way his gaze heats—equal amounts of loathing and desire.

"You are everywhere I look. You are in my dreams. It seems there is nowhere you cannot find me… How is it that my little nightmare has come to haunt me even when I am awake?"

This small, secluded corner of the library has taken on a hazy feel. Our voices are quiet, as soft as the intangible whispering of dreams.

For the first time in days, I feel the spark of hope relight. To him, I am a stranger he has been told to hate. Yet, there are parts of the man I know buried under the lie, peeking through. Parts of the man who still knows me on some level.

Alaric cups the back of my neck, slowly weaving his fingers into my hair. His grip is firm, and I let him tilt my head back. "I thought to rid myself of you the next time I found you."

"And now?"

He presses his body against mine, wrapping himself around me in a way that is both intimate and seeking comfort. He buries his face in the crook of my neck. I don't hesitate to return the embrace.

"Do not worry, my captivating little nightmare. I have no intention of ending your life tonight."

"I appreciate that. I would be quite cross with you if you did."

He chuckles lightly.

My heart squeezes, and I breathe him in, giving myself this moment to soak him in, wishing it could last forever but knowing it can't. He is in my arms, and still, I miss him—the parts that have been stolen. All of him. Even his actions and words show how keenly he feels their absence.

I thought my hate for Elizabeth was as deep as humanly possible, but I was wrong. It has become an infinite well.

After a while, he straightens and rests his forehead against mine. "Are you real? Is this moment real?" he asks. The question is so quiet I barely hear. He doesn't wait for an answer. "Lately, nothing has felt real. It is like the world has been painted in a strange light… the hour before nightfall as one season slips into the next. When everything is bathed in that odd golden glow, and the sky is a mix of blood and bruises."

The taste of tears rises at the back of my throat. I have to swallow twice to find my voice. "Yes." I nod. "I am real… *This* is real."

He closes his eyes, and for a while, our mingling breaths are the only sound. A lock of tousled hair falls forward as he leans a little closer. I reach up to brush it away, pausing mid-swipe when his fingers wrap around my wrist. The moment stretches on. His gaze flicks to my mouth in such a way my nerve endings tingle in anticipation.

I lower my arm, and he lets go. Alaric moves in as if he will kiss me, only to stop shy. I intended to defer to him, but my lips find his before I can stop myself.

At first, Alaric makes no move to kiss me back or pull away. But with a soft sigh, he leans into it, mouth moving against mine. Tentative and uncertain. It's slow and gentle, passionate and filled with need, yet restrained. A secret stolen in the shadows. Something he is almost afraid to allow himself. His tongue brushes over my bottom lip, seeking access, and I grant it. He tastes of wine and warm caramel.

The bond we share trickles past the curse's barriers whenever we are close, and I want to tell him, without words, how much I love and admire him, but sensing he needs a gentle hand to find his way back. I refrain.

Alaric trails kisses along my jaw and down my neck, nipping at my skin as he goes. Each scrape of his fangs sends a thrill along my spine. He tugs aside the collar of my top, but when his tongue sweeps over the scars there, he stills.

He pulls back to look me in the eye. "I was told Mr. Wellington marked you, but I didn't believe it because you do not treat him as his claimed."

I shake my head. "He has no claim on me—other than that of a temporary guardian."

The question of who *does* hangs unspoken in the air between us. When I don't answer, Alaric's curiosity turns to suspicion of what he thinks I might be hiding. The drink in his system must be keeping him relaxed because he dismisses the issue entirely.

"Strange," he murmurs, almost to himself. "You are nothing more than an ordinary human."

"That's right," I say.

I wait for him to continue, wondering where exactly his thoughts are tonight, but his eyes are unfocused as he reaches up to play with a lock of hair.

"Mortals do not possess magic." He heaves a sigh that makes my lips twitch from fighting a smile. Eventually, he continues, "But I think you must. How else could you have me so completely under your thrall?"

"I think you might be drunk," I offer.

Alaric stills, then his eyes focus as he meets my gaze. His hand lowers, falling down to his side. "I'm not drunk…" He glares. Though he clearly intends for it to intimidate, I can't help but find it endearing. Then, haughtily, he adds, "I am the crown prince."

A laugh bursts free from my throat. I clap my hand over my mouth to stifle it. Alaric seems to realize what he said and smirks.

From the far end of the library, a click and the rattle of a metal latch echoes back to where we hide among darkened shelves. At the sound, Alaric steps back, putting distance between us. I can't help but hate whoever it is.

The steady stride of a single set of footsteps moves closer without hesitation as if they know exactly where we are. We both smooth our hands over our clothes, taking a moment to gather ourselves. Alaric dons a mask of indifference, the same one he uses to hide his pain. Seeing it is a sharp knife.

And as if the last several minutes have been nothing more than a figment of my imagination, he walks away without a second glance.

A feminine voice greets him. They speak in low tones, and then his footfalls grow further and further away.

I stare at the shelves of books across from me. Their magic has drained away, and the stories within no longer interest me.

Before sorrow can root itself in place, I remind myself of the woman, the monster, who is responsible for the torment he's living with. Elizabeth has hidden among humans and vampires, and demons for too long. I have only seen a fraction of Alaric's pain. How many others have suffered at her hands? A new level of fury rises within me. I welcome it, fanning the flames. Suddenly, there is no sacrifice I can make that isn't worth it to destroy her.

Determination alone will not be all it takes. I might fail, but I must still try.

Even if that means surrendering everything I am.

My body.

My heart.

My soul.

And if I cannot defeat this monster as I am, then I will become something for monsters to fear.

Squaring my shoulders, I step out of the alcove and come face to face with bright pink eyes and skin so pale, even in this light, it almost appears to have a hint of blue.

She blocks my way. I glance around to see if Elizabeth is nearby. Tension eases from my shoulders when I don't spot her.

"Good evening, Lady Valmont," the Voice says.

I am not entirely sure if she is mocking me by calling me lady. It's not veiled insults that unsettle me so much as being unable to read her intent.

"Hello," I offer halfheartedly. My lack of decorum goes unnoticed. When the silence drags out, I make to go around her.

A slender hand wraps around my wrist, halting me. "You ought to take care, my lady."

I slowly drag my gaze to hers. "What do you mean?"

The expression makes it clear she thinks I'm an

idiot for asking. "Only that you would do well to consider each move you make ahead of time."

I stare blankly, not understanding what she means, and wait for her to explain.

She heaves an exasperated sigh. "It would be better to lose yourself in the bowels of the Otherworld than to remain here out of stubbornness. There are faster ways to die than stoking the queen's ire."

I set my jaw and narrow my eyes. "I have no plans to run away and leave him as he is," I say through clenched teeth. "I owe him."

"Then you are as foolish as she says." Then, more quietly, she adds, "What is it you think you owe him?"

"My life."

Those two words hang in the air between us. Her bright pink eyes bore into me, searching for weaknesses. I know I have weaknesses, but so does Elizabeth.

I hold steady under her scrutiny. When she relents, she gives no clue to the conclusion she comes to.

"You are walking an icy path. If you wish to live, take care to waste no foothold given to you."

With the queen's message delivered, the Voice leaves me to ponder over her vaguely threatening parting words. I have no intention of waiting for Elizabeth to make her move. Too many have suffered under her rule.

If the Voice means to keep me away from Alaric by assuming I will run to save my skin, then she is sorely mistaken.

CHAPTER FIFTEEN

ALARIC

BACK WITHIN THE SOLITUDE OF MY CHAMBERS, AN incessant buzzing fills my head. I press the heel of my hand to my temple, trying to shake off the persisting intoxication.

In the solitude of my quarters, There were several occasions when I consumed far more and was not affected to this degree.

Is it because of that woman... that slayer?

No.

That is impossible. Regardless, she has somehow found a way to use magic without possessing any. The scent of her skin lingers on my clothes. It should repulse me, and it's vexing that it does not. I will my senses to return.

First things first—I must rid myself of all remaining traces of her. I grab for the closest items, not caring if they clash, and toss them on the settee beside the wardrobe, then begin to undress.

Searing pain lances from my ribs, working its way

up my chest. It's as if I am being flayed open by a wild demon's poisoned talons. The unexpected shock of it brings me to my knees. I gasp uselessly for air as I struggle to remove my shirt.

The dark presence inside my mind forces its way to the surface. Black veins web over my skin, writhing, extending out from the concentrated cluster just below my heart. They stretch and recede in a rhythmic pulsing, spreading over more and more of my flesh.

The desire to feed and destroy is blinding. My fangs descend unbidden, slicing the skin inside my mouth. The taste of blood coats my tongue as I bite back howls of agony. I grit my teeth against the force of it, willing it back down until I can think again.

When I surface again, it's to the sound of firm knocking demanding my attention.

Dragging myself to my feet, I quickly finish changing. On my way to answer the door, I snatch up the human-tainted shirt and lob it into the fire. The material goes up like dry parchment.

My brow furrows as I watch it burn to ash. There's an overwhelming sense that I'm on the verge of remembering something. Something important....

The knocking begins again, the incessant sound severing my tenuous hold on the thought, letting it slip away.

I throw open the door and find one of the queen's guards, one I don't recognize. His face turns from annoyance to a weak attempt at hiding his fear confronted by my ire.

"Her Majesty requests your presence," he says.

Grabbing a waistcoat and jacket, I pull them on as I walk out, striding past the guard. He stammers something unintelligible, closes my door, and scrambles to follow. He trails me the entire way to Elizabeth's chambers as if there's a possibility that I might get lost.

Every door within is open, allowing an unobstructed view of her standing before the expansive windows of her bedroom. Elizabeth wears a silk delphinium-blue robe embroidered with black filigree. It covers her from the neck down but shows every plane and curve of her body, tied in such a way as to seduce.

I stride forward and stop halfway in the room. The powdery scent of lavender oil is thick in the air.

She continues to stare out on the valley to the east. She takes a drink. Elizabeth sets the empty cup and matching saucer down on the oval side table to her left. It makes a musical but hollow sound, betraying the fact that it is not made of porcelain as it appears.

I remain silent. Patient.

Finally, she turns to me with a warm and expectant smile.

Perhaps it is the cold moonlight, but I cannot shake the wrongness of this place, of this moment. A distance I can't cross, a sensation akin to reliving another man's memories.

Elizabeth's expression strains at the edges. She sighs wistfully.

"Come," she says. "I wish to speak with you about the upcoming coronation."

Dutifully following her into the bathing chamber,

I'm hit by a wall of humidity rising from a tub that's almost large enough to swim in. Two of the room's walls are little more than frosted glass with decorative wrought iron to hold the panes in place, creating the look of a garden made of cold metal.

Elizabeth glides up the three steps to the edge of the water. "Help me with this," she says over her shoulder, though I don't need to be told.

I'm already in motion. My duties were clear when she dismissed every servant whose job it is to wait on her hand and foot before my arrival.

I take the corners of her robe and set it to the side as she slips out of it and sinks into the water.

The pain that overtook me in my rooms has ebbed to a deep ache. I gaze through a circular area of clear glass at the endless night beyond.

The tangled web of black veins is a warning of some kind... but what exactly? Though they have receded, they haven't disappeared. I still feel them now, dormant.

I am not sure what to make of it. It feels both like a poison slowly working through me and like a living creature burrowed beneath my skin.

Could it be the root of all that has felt off these last several days? That only raises more questions. Had I fed from a human with poisoned blood? Or had that slayer done something to me, and her kiss nothing more than a distraction?

Thoughts whisper of her deceitful nature, even though she seems to be the only thing that can put me at ease. Just her presence can quiet the unceasing drone in my mind, dulling the pain and offering relief.

"What do you think, my love?" Elizabeth croons.

The question shatters through my tangled musings, and I realize I haven't listened to a word she's spoken this entire time.

I clear my throat. "I have no head for these things. All that matters is what makes you happy—that is the only thing that will please me."

Elizabeth regards me steadily. Reaching up, she plucks the long pin from her hair. Her long tresses spill down her back into the water. I reach for the bronze pitcher and scoop up water to wet the rest of her hair. She sighs as I massage soap into her hair.

After a while, she resumes going over the details of the coronation and the extravagant masquerades she plans to throw leading up to it.

I am careful to avoid getting lost in thought again. My queen would not tolerate it a second time. Thankfully, she does not ask for my input again.

When I fetch her towel, those lavender eyes bore into me. "Is there something on your mind? You seem… *distracted* as of late."

I bow my head, hoping she doesn't catch my wince. Sometimes I could swear she can see through me. See the void that has formed within. See that I am not whole as I must have been at one time.

"Forgive me, my queen," I murmur. "I must be missing my sister more than expected."

Elizabeth's gaze slides toward the raven perched in the corner, silent and unmoving since they followed us inside. Kharis croaks, the sound ricocheting off the walls.

Pain throbs behind my temples. I barely keep it from showing.

Elizabeth's lips are pressed into a straight line. As the drumming ache fades, her harsh glare softens the longer she watches me.

I'm glad my presence can ease her mind.

I help her out of the bath and drape the robe over her slender shoulders.

Elizabeth strides into the bedroom, halting abruptly a few paces in, then turns back to me. Her pale eyelashes flutter as she drops her gaze. She almost appears sad. "I did not want to tell you this. However, you deserve to know." She pauses, drawing the moment out. "I received word earlier today that Rosalie was murdered some time ago."

Everything seems to stop for a painful moment.

The sorrow on her face and the emotionless way she delivered the news don't fit together. They are cold and sound as if they come from someone else. Someone who doesn't understand… who doesn't care.

I couldn't have heard correctly. It doesn't make sense.

But then the meaning comes barreling into me like a violent wave. I wait for the world to crash down around me. To crack open my chest and shatter my heart into so many pieces, that nothing and no one could repair it, even if they had an eternity to try.

I wait for the pain.

But it doesn't come.

It hurts. Of course, it hurts.

What I don't expect is to find the sharp edge of loss, worn and softened by time and acceptance. I don't understand how I could accept it at all.

Rosalie. Who everyone loved. Who was kind to everyone she met… even those undeserving of it.

Who would have dared to hurt her, and why?

"How?" I can barely make myself speak the word. I both want to know the answer and dread hearing it. What good will it do? If Rosalie is gone, nothing can bring her back from the grasp of the Otherworld.

Elizabeth waves a hand dismissively as she disappears behind a changing screen. "It was that horrible woman," she says. Fabric rustles as she changes. Then, a moment later, she adds, "The one Cassius claimed."

That takes me aback. I know of only one mortal connected to Cassius… Miss Valmont. She *is* claimed, though not by him.

Though what other mortal could it be?

Then I think of what my nightmare said in the library. How she hesitated when I asked if she intended to kill me—she would never *intentionally* hurt me. Which is not the same as never. That careful wording was no mistake, and she is the only known slayer currently living. She must have learned that Rosalie is—*was*—my sister after the fact. Nothing else makes sense.

It doesn't matter that she is an enigma of conflicting elements, or that she is the only thing that has quieted my mind, or that I can only seem to breathe when she's close enough to touch.

I want her to admit what she's done.
I want to make her pay.

CHAPTER SIXTEEN

CLARA

The sky is a thick and heavy, endless gray that seems like it will last forever. It makes it difficult to remember the feel of the sun's warmth on my face. I stroke a black mare's neck and feed her another one of the sugar cubes I snagged from the kitchen.

The days since first arriving have grown quieter. There was rarely a time without clusters of vampires almost everywhere I turned. Now it's mostly the bustle of human servants preparing for the coronation and all the celebrations leading up to it, on top of their usual duties.

I spent most of the day tossing and turning, unable to quiet my thoughts long enough to fall asleep, unable to stop going over what happened with Alaric in the library.

When I finally gave up on sleeping, I walked through the servants' halls. It didn't take long to grow tired of the cramped, dreary corridors. I soon found myself outside and eventually ended up at the stables.

In the farthest stall, away from all the others, was a black mare. My heart went out to the mare. Isolated. Alone.

She poked her head out as I approached. We watched each other for a while. I expected her to have a mean disposition to be separated as she is. Perhaps I felt sorry for her, or perhaps what I felt was more along the lines of a shared kinship. Whatever it was, I decided it wouldn't hurt to grab a peace offering from the kitchens before approaching her. She turned out to be one of the most docile creatures I've ever met.

The stable hands ignore me, as they have since I arrived, and finish their work, then disappear. It would be easy to ride out of here and never look back...

I briefly wonder if this sweet mare would have been one of the horses Alaric and I would have taken if our plan to run away had worked.

A shiver sweeps through me as the air takes on the added chill of night sets in. I give the mare the last sugar cube. She bumps my hip when I don't continue to pull more from my pocket.

"Next time," I promise. "I'll bring you all sorts of treats." I let myself out and wrap my arms around my middle as I make my way toward the main castle.

I don't get far when someone grabs my hair and wrenches my head back. The force of it knocks me off balance. I'm rammed against the exterior wall of the stable before I can right myself.

"Shouldn't you be with the pigs?" Elise snarls. "It's where you belong." The desperation to regain a silver of pride shows in her eyes.

I don't have the patience for this, and I refuse to coddle her need to appear bigger than someone else. Shoving her back with my arm, I push past her. "Leave me alone before you embarrass yourself more than you already have."

It's probably not the best thing to say, but I am tired of her attempts to use me as a way to establish the strength she wants but doesn't have. There are more important things to deal with than status.

Elise moves with vampire speed to block my path. Her mouth curls in a cold, vicious smile. "There's no one to protect you anymore. He finally realized he doesn't need or want you when he could have a *vampire*." She spits each word like a knife, intending to wound me.

I suck in a sharp breath and hold it. My vision narrows. Elise laughs, shoving me back against the wall with both hands.

It's not what she said that stunned me or how she hinted it could be her instead of Elizabeth—even if the glee on her face tells me she believes it was—it's Alaric standing several yards away.

He stopped striding toward me the moment our gaze met. Now, he looks from me to Elise as if he hadn't noticed her before. When she finally realizes I'm no longer paying attention to her, she turns to see what, or who has my attention.

I thought I'd seen every emotion on his perfect features. Turns out, I hadn't. The murderous gleam in his eye sends a shiver over me.

Demons and saints, I wish things would go how I want them to. Just once.

Alaric approaches. It makes me feel like a bird with a broken wing and him a beast circling before he makes the kill.

Again, he stops, this time within arm's reach.

Elise swivels her head back to me with a snarl. "It appears *no one* will care if I cut your life short."

Her voice is distant. Muffled by the roaring of blood in my ears.

"Let her go. She is not yours to punish."

Either Elise is too intent on what she's doing to hear him or too arrogant to heed the warning.

Black veins writhe up from his collar like living things, crawling over his jaw and up the side of his face. His gaze snaps to her when she doesn't do as commanded.

No... no, no, no, no, no.

"I said to fucking let her go."

Everything happens too fast for me to track. He moves, and her head jerks to the side with a sickening crack. Elise crumples to the ground in a heap. Her neck is twisted in a way that isn't right. Isn't natural.

"Her death belongs to me," he snarls down at her.

Alaric drags me behind him, away from Elise. Away from her body. My mind is still struggling to catch up with what just happened when we finally stop. I don't know where he's taken me, but I do know I should be, at least, a little afraid of him. Killing Elise is entirely unlike him.

Again, I find myself cornered. We are more isolated than before. This is a remote corner of the castle, so it's unlikely anyone will pass by. And if they did, they probably wouldn't notice us within the shadows.

"What are you doing?" I ask, hating how breathless I sound.

My mind is whirling. I press my palms against Alaric's chest to keep him from coming closer, but he grabs my wrists and pins them above my head. A shudder rolls through my body.

"Slayer," he growls more than speaks the word, ignoring my question.

The way he spits the title is a knife to the gut. Though I claim it only to use as a weapon, I hate it. It sounds intentional… spiteful… heartless. As though I want to rid the world of vampires. That isn't who I am. Once, it might have been. Once, it was what I thought I wanted. But not for a long time.

Alaric showed me the world for what it is through eyes not clouded by fear. Not all monsters are beasts of nightmares. Some hide behind friendly faces, waiting for their prey to lower their guard. Oftentimes, the worst monster of all wears the most beautiful mask.

But for Alaric, I was his monster, and instead of cruelty, he showed me love and mercy.

I never set out to kill any of them—except for the one who least deserved it, and there will never be a day when I don't regret that. The others were self-defense. It had nothing to do with them being vampires. They would have kept hunting me as long as I lived.

"Tell me, *slayer*, how is it you came to earn such an infamous title and avoid punishment?"

I don't know if he actually wants me to answer.

"Did you kill Rosalie?" he demands.

I squeeze my eyes shut, realizing just how much Elizabeth stole from him. Not just me or our history, but everything.

"Yes," I admit softly.

"Why?" There is so much pain in that small word.

There is no reason or excuse I can give him, so I offer the only thing I can. "I am sorry, Alaric."

He winces at his name.

"I'm sorry. I'm sorry. I'm sorry." It's all I can say—the only words my mouth is capable of forming. And I cannot stop it.

I want to tell him how I would give anything to undo my actions that day. That I didn't know I would hurt him. I didn't know I would love him so deeply. But every time I open my mouth, the same two words fall from my lips. "I'm sorry."

I don't stop until he releases my wrists and turns his face away. My breaths come in broken gasps. It's then I realize my cheeks are streaked with trails of salty tears. Using my sleeves, I swipe at my face while attempting to regain my composure.

He shifts, and though he's closer than before, his chest pressed to mine and his demeanor more relaxed. All trace of threat has fled him. "Slayer." He scoffs. "You're not much of one."

I shake my head. "I'm not," I agree.

"How many vampires have you killed? More than three?" When I don't answer, he says, "That is what I thought."

"The others all wanted me dead." The words are

out before I can stop them. "I suppose you will say I should have let them?"

I am not entirely sure why I ask that. Maybe it's because I'm angry with myself. Maybe I don't want him to think I'm horrible, though he, more than anyone, has reason to. Maybe it's both.

He takes no offense to my harsh tone or to even notice it. Alaric seems to debate silently for a moment, treating it as a genuine question. His gaze settles on mine, clear and sharp. "No," he responds simply.

That is… unexpected. I thought he might have said yes or nothing at all.

"Do you think your mortal tears will save you from the consequences of your crimes?"

"No."

"Then why were you crying?"

"Because I took someone you love away from you. I hurt you… and I will regret that for the rest of my life."

Alaric's brows furrow, then his features soften. Hope doesn't have time to settle. the corners of his lips curl. Alaric's mouth part as if he will condemn me. Then he dips his head, pressing his mouth to the crook of my neck. His hands hold me against him by my waist.

Seconds pass with us like this, not moving.

Something is wrong.

I cautiously lift my hands and push against his shoulders until I can look him in the eye. Alaric's face is pale, and his pupils have dilated, nearly swallowing up his midnight irises. Black lines pulse up both sides of his neck, seeping up toward his eyes.

"What's happening?" I hold him firmer and bring him to eye level. "Tell me how to help."

He blinks. His confusion is a momentary distraction from the pain. Again, he opens his mouth as if to speak, but the strain transforms it into a pain-filled gasp. His gaze locks onto my neck, telling me what I need to know.

"You need to feed."

I'm unsure how much of his expression is agony from the curse or hating that I am his only option. If I leave it to him, who knows how long he will remain locked in indecision.

He doesn't fight me as I guide his mouth to the crook of my neck. Shallow bursts of warm breath wash over my skin. When he finally gives in, fangs piercing, he is careful to avoid causing me pain.

Each swallow is a light tug, both physical and on the bond that connects us. It ignites my blood, dulling all thoughts other than him. His touch. His mouth. I cling to him. I don't know if it's real or imagined, but I can sense the slightest echo of his heartbeat.

His lips are on mine as he grabs my upper thighs and lifts me, pinning me to the wall with his hips. There's no trace of blood on his tongue as he claims my mouth. There is only him and desire demanding to be satiated.

I need him—all of him—his words, his laugh, his heart. Our bond drives us both into a frenzied desperation, longing to be whole.

The press of fangs scrapes my bottom lip, drawing the smallest drops of blood. I moan against him as he grinds his arousal against me.

He pulls back, leaving me gasping, head reeling. Our hands are on each other, poised to remove each other's clothes in any way we can. But that small distance is enough to form a fissure in the spell.

"Little nightmare…" His eyes slide down, stopping in the space between us. "What have you done?"

My gaze follows his to the undulating shadows that rise off him, stretching out toward me.

I inhale in a sharp breath and release my grip on our bond. The swirling wisps vanish like a puff of smoke in a breeze.

Alaric looks at me with a mix of horror and fear. On some level, he knows, but because of the curse, he doesn't understand. I want to tell him. He needs… no, he deserves to know.

Before I can find my voice, he lowers me to my feet and takes several steps back. I'm not even sure he realizes the black veins and his pain have faded. I reach for him. Alaric only shakes his head, then turns and walks away.

I remain rooted to the spot for several minutes. Shivering from the loss of his warmth. From the emotions that his touch stirs in me.

Large fluffy snowflakes drift lazily down from the endless gray above in the time we lose ourselves in the spell caused by a mix of the curse and our bond.

Keeping any part of the truth from him is no longer an option. I don't know when or how I will tell him, but I have to.

I can't imagine what it would be like to be in his place. How devastating to find out everything you think is true is actually a lie, to know the horrible things someone you trust has done to you, to find out that you are irrevocably tied to the one you thought you should hate.

I slide down the stone wall and crouch with my face buried in my hands, and cry for him. When I run out of tears, I straighten and compose myself before going back inside. I might not be able to share everything with my friends, but in this, I can enlist their help.

No one pays any attention to me as I slip through the kitchen. Just as I reach the doorway, a young woman carrying a tray turns into me. There isn't enough time or space to move out of the way. Hot tea sloshes from the pot, and a teacup topples to the ground, shattering.

She falls to her knees and franticly gathers the broken porcelain shards. Breaking a dish isn't uncommon for a kitchen this size. She appears to be about my age, and from the terrified look on her face, I think she must be new.

I help her quickly clean up the mess, feeling terrible for not watching where I was going. "I'm sorry," I say. "Blame me, if anyone gets—"

Her hand grips my wrist, and I meet her large, honey-colored gaze. "Lady Valmont?" she asks, then glances around before leaning in, whispering a harsh warning. "You must get ready."

"Ready?" I frown. "Ready for what?"

Instead of answering, she stands, then with a

pointed look, the woman dips her head and hurries away, plunking the tray down where she picked it up a moment before. Then she's dashing out through the back as if a harmony of demons were on her tail.

154

CHAPTER SEVENTEEN

CLARA

A teapot with gilded roses on twisted vines with a matching cup is set out on a side table, waiting for me when I return to Cassius's rooms. I boil the water, then add a few spoonfuls of dried tea leaves and let it steep. As it does, it releases a beautiful, soothing fragrance.

Desperate for warmth, I down the first cup in three gulps, nearly scalding my tongue. The second cup, I take my time and sip slowly. The scent of jasmine and rose is delicate and light.

I still prefer not to add anything to my teas. Sugar is far too sweet, and milk overwhelms the beautiful subtle details of the flavor. This blend is far better than the nettle and dandelion mixtures I used to make for Kitty and me. They were always bitter with the extras I added to make them last longer.

With my nerves settled, I make myself comfortable on the chaise. After spending several hours training on my own in the old armory, my muscles are a little sore.

Though I'd initially intended on visiting Varin, but the sound of guards put an end to that plan. I'd waited, listening for them to leave for almost an hour before giving up. Much to my annoyance, it seemed they fully intended to make the most of that portion of their rounds.

Asmod and Cherno make themselves comfortable with me as their personal pillow. I wonder if all vampires put up with overly affectionate demons or if I'm just lucky. I flick a glance toward them and find I don't mind all that much. Asmod coils a little tighter around my arm.

Stretched out, I turn my head to watch the clock. Each minute passes achingly slow. I have no idea when Cassius will return, but with the night half over, I'm counting on Lawrence to show up for our promised discussion any moment now.

No matter how many times I go over the encounter with that odd serving girl and her odd warning. I can't figure out what she meant by it. Normally, I would brush it off as something as simple as a mistaken identity—except she knew my name.

Could she have been alerting me that Elizabeth found a way around whatever has prevented her from killing me so far?

The crackling fire is hypnotizing, and strangely enough, the rhythmic breathing of the two demons is relaxing. Soon, I'm able to put everything from my mind until I can go over it all with my friends. I watch the dancing flames gradually consume the wood logs, my eyes growing heavier and taking longer to open with every blink.

Something startles me. A noise, I think.

I sit bolt upright and glance around. The two demons tumble onto my lap. The fire in the hearth burns low, and according to the clock, I slept through the remainder of the night. A jacket that wasn't there before is slung over a nearby chair, and the tea has been taken away.

Pressing a hand to my head, I shake off the lethargy muddling my thoughts. I must have been far more exhausted than I realized. Cassius was here. Why didn't he wake me?

In the distance, beyond the doors, the muffled sound of marching echoes through the halls. Cherno meets my questioning gaze, then wordlessly takes to the air, disappearing through the door like a wisp of fog.

"Maybe you should go find Cassius," I say to the demon snake in a low whisper. There's not a logical reason to keep my voice down, but there's been a shift in the mood that has penetrated every corner of Nightwich.

Asmod looks from me to the door a few times. They look worried... It's a thought that strikes me as odd, given that... I don't think snakes have facial expressions. I suppose it's possible demon snakes may be different. I nod reassuringly, and they, too, disappear through the closed door.

The shouting fades.

A moment later, Cherno returns.

"The castle is under siege," they say, winging their way over to me.

Who would dare attack? Though, a better question might be, *who* would have the force and ability to?

I snatch them from the air and run into the bedroom, throwing the curtains wide. The sun has crested over the horizon, bathing the world in washed-out blues and watery grays.

Besides small clusters of guards jogging through the open courtyard, the castle grounds are the same as they always are. I glance at Cherno.

"I overheard the queen's general telling her," they say quietly. They shift in my cupped hands and peer up at me. "They would not have made the report if it wasn't happening."

"You're right." I worry my bottom lip between my teeth, considering. Finally, I decide to see what I can learn. Elizabeth is the last one I would ever worry about, but there are others in this place I care for and do not want to see hurt.

I set the demon down and hurriedly change into something that will draw less attention. Stopping before the door to the hall, I motion for Cherno to stay here.

"It might be dangerous," they warn.

"I'm only going to have a look to see what I can find out. I can blend in easier alone." At their pout, I add, "I promise to be safe."

With that, I hurry out before they can find another reason to protest. The halls are eerily quiet now. I walk quickly, keeping my head down, and try to appear as nothing more than another servant sent on an errand.

I slow as I reach the landing of the main corridor. Three guards are ordering a boisterous group of nobles and gentry away, ignoring those who are clearly of lower status. The courtiers are affronted. One even tries to argue but is quickly put in his place.

Cherno was right after all… It appears the castle is being locked down.

Is Elizabeth trying to save face by attempting to keep it under wraps, or is she trying to protect those who matter most, using those she deems beneath her as fodder for whatever fallout happens? Or both?

A woman dressed in umber breeches and a dark red jacket that appears almost black stands against the wall, halfway down the corridor to the left. She watches me with the demeanor of any other guard. Her livery is wrong. It lacks the gold embellishments along the collar and sleeves, replaced by dull yellow stitching.

I dip my chin and walk toward her before I think better of it. My footsteps falter, but I keep going. It would be more suspicious to turn back now. This might get me killed if I'm not careful. The best I can hope for is to make her think I am nothing more than another skittish human servant who believes she is just another guard.

I make the mistake of meeting her eye when I pass. Her face is unexpectedly familiar. My pace slows a little too much. She cocks her head to the side. My hesitation is enough for her to recognize me. The woman stalks forward, gripping my upper arms.

Wolves—the wolves are here.

She was one of the two betas who accompanied Oliver when he came to Windbury to discuss the demon infestation of the Shade forest.

"Miss Valmont?" she says my name as if there's a chance she is mistaken.

"It's you…" I say, surprise freezing my tongue.

Her eyes narrow on me, then dart behind me—probably to see if I'm being followed. "You shouldn't be out here right now."

What are they doing here? Is Oliver here, too? I glance up and down the hall for any trace of him—as if I could have walked right past him without noticing.

My heart thuds against my ribs. In the city, I told Oliver that Elizabeth cursed Alaric.

Oliver said he will search for a way to help me break the curse, but if that is the case, wouldn't he have sent word, rather than staging a covert siege? He wouldn't have come to kill Alaric… *would he?*

I bite down hard on the tip of my tongue, angry with myself for not thinking through things more thoroughly before trusting him.

Hope is a dangerous thing.

A sliver too much, and you throw caution to the wind and trust those you shouldn't.

"You should go back to your room until tonight." She begins guiding me back toward the stairs.

I plant my feet and refuse to be moved. Not if Alaric is in danger. "Where is Oliver?" I demand in a harsh whisper, not wanting to attract unwanted attention.

The beta's gaze darts toward the mezzanine on the

third level before returning to me. "He doesn't have time for you."

We stare each other down, neither wanting to yield. The flickering light of a nearby sconce sets off the amber flecks in her dark brown eyes. Her long, curly, black hair has been pulled back in a tight braid to match the other female guards.

She releases her grip on me when the quickened thud of several guards passes over our heads. No doubt reinforcements to protect Elizabeth, and likely Alaric as well. I hate feeling any gratitude toward her for the possibility of keeping him safe.

A door opens further down the hall, causing us to mutually break our silent battle of wills. At first, no one appears, then a man's head peeks out. When his gaze lands on us, he emerges. The incorrect livery is a tale-tell sign he is with her.

"Your uniforms are wrong," I whisper to her. "They give you away."

The beta frowns at me, unable to respond before her companion reaches us. I'm not entirely surprised that the other beta is also part of this operation.

"Time to—" he starts but cuts himself off when he notices me. He blinks and then gives me a smile reminiscent of Oliver's flirtatious one. I wonder if they are related and how I missed the similarities before. "Miss Valmont, how fortuitous it is that we should cross paths," he says. "Sadly, I'm afraid we must be on our way. However, you are invited to join us if you'd like."

"I can't," I say, oversimplifying the situation. The truth is that I refuse to leave Alaric.

The woman pinches his chin between her thumb and forefinger, demanding his undivided attention. "Hunt, did we get what we came for?" she asks pointedly. I can hardly blame her for her ambiguity.

He shakes his head. "No one has been able to get close enough—" A devious grin spreads over his mouth. Hunt doesn't seem to have such reservations. "But we did capture the pawn. He will make excellent bait."

Pawn.

A burst of adrenaline releases, and I can barely keep my body from trembling. There's only one person he could mean—Alaric.

My pulse roars in my ears. I grab his arm with more force than intended—probably with more force than a human should possess, even oath bonded. He stumbles back a half step. I move with him and we nearly collide.

"I'm going with you," I say before he can question my demon-granted gifts. "There's something I need to get first."

The woman huffs but doesn't argue, which makes me think the invitation came from Oliver rather than this man.

"All right, but hurry. We will wait as long as we can. Meet us on the western border near the foothills. If you aren't there an hour before sunset, we will have to leave without you."

I give a sharp nod, then turn and run back up the stairs. I'm out of breath when I get there, less from the exertion and more from nerves.

Cassius whirls to face me as I barge through the

doors. With the dizzying speed that only vampires are capable of, he's before me in a blink. I don't think I will ever get used to it.

"Clara, where have you been?" he demands. "It isn't safe outside these quarters for you right now. A band of humans have attacked. We don't know how they infiltrated the grounds—" he shakes his head and starts again. "There's something off about it though. They're too strong."

"Humans?" I furrow my brows and shake my head.

Cassius gathers me up in a hug. "You're safe now. No one will attack you here."

Oliver wouldn't use humans like that. At least, I don't think he would. Unless…

I push out of his hold. "No," I say, then lower my voice to the barest whisper. "Wolves are here."

He opens his mouth to argue and stops, considering for a moment. His lip curls like he caught the scent of something foul. With a snort, he says, "They must be disguising their scent. Regardless, I will kill anyone who attempts to come here."

"Cassius, listen to me," I say sharply. Immediately, he gives me his full attention. "There's not much time. They are leaving, and I need to go with them."

To his credit, he accepts my decision with a silent dip of his chin and doesn't try to talk me out of it. I suppose at this point, he understands my reasons.

I back up and head toward the bedroom, pausing before the doors to glance back at him. The last time I tried to leave the castle grounds without him, he warned me of the repercussions. When I go this time, there's still a chance Elizabeth will strike out at Cassius. "You can come with me."

"I am afraid I cannot," he says with a regretful sigh. "But you should take these two."

Cherno and Asmod perk up. I hold my hand up before they can get used to the idea. "They should stay with you. That way, if you need to get a message to me, you can send Cherno." The lie slips out effortlessly. They will be safer with him.

"Where exactly are they taking you?"

That is an excellent question. Other than meeting near the foothills, I didn't think to ask where we should go from there. But I have an idea.

"West," I say. "The forest on the other side of the mountains."

His face falls in the way an adult will look at a child with pity, knowing they must deliver news that will hurt.

But that is all the time I can spare.

I slip into the bedroom and go directly to my trunk. There is no time to change, and it would be too suspicious if I packed. I reach under layers of clothes for the hidden vial and quickly shove it into my pocket.

Then I rise and pull the night-forged dagger from my boot, then return to the other room.

"You're not taking anything?"

"No." I make a show of slipping the dagger back into place.

We share a look. Warnings to be careful. Wishes to be safe. And underneath it all, worry.

CHAPTER EIGHTEEN

CLARA

In the few minutes I spent with Cassius, chaos broke out in the main corridors. Servants scurry from one place to another in clotted groups.

I effortlessly meld into the back of a passing cluster, going in the right direction. As if by an unseen cue, screams erupt from around the corner, accompanied by snarls and horrible wet sounds. It takes a moment to process the sight of the monster that emerges a moment later.

A man dressed in the finest clothes, rings with glittering gems on his fingers, glistening red lips, and a decapitated head gripped by the hair in one fist. Burning red eyes zero in on our group.

He flings the head off to the side and stalks forward, relishing in the terror his approach inspires in any human who lays eyes on him.

The way swarms of humans stick together reminds me of a school of fish—using the whole in the hope that others will fall to the predator and give them a chance to escape.

I glance up, and it is the same horror on the two mezzanine levels overhead. A body tumbles over a balustrade. It's impossible to tell if they were pushed or thrown. Witnesses yell and shriek. I shudder at the sickening sound the body makes as it hits the stone floor.

That sets everyone into a panic. I'm shoved from every direction, as the mass of people begin to fight each other, using whoever they can as a shield.

Cassius's warning was more accurate than he realized.

Are the Vampires going after the humans because the wolves hid their scent? If so, I need to believe this is an unintended consequence.

I will never make it to Varin's cell this way.

The vampire grabs a man from the front and tears into his throat. His scream is drowned out by wet gurgling.

Wanting to avoid the gruesome sight, I turn to glance behind, looking for a way out. Another vampire is heading this way. If he reaches us, we will be trapped, and no one will survive.

Demon shit.

Indecision stays my hand. I want to stay and fight —but even if I remain, I don't think I could save anyone, most likely not even myself. My stomach rebels, knowing I have to abandon them.

I use all the strength I can muster to push past panicked arms and bodies shoving and bumping into me and inch closer to the wall. With stone at my back, it will be far easier to escape this tangled mass of bodies without fighting against the frightened push and pull from all angles.

Slipping away, I run for the stairs, taking them two at a time. I'm halfway up when the screaming grows more frantic even as it dies down.

I don't look back. I can't because I have to get out while I still can.

The silver ring on my finger burns, warning that Varin intends to hold me to our bargain. With a hiss of pain, I use my teeth to tug my glove off. I let it drop to the floor and begin prying at the ring, trying to remove it before the metal sears into my flesh. It doesn't so much as budge.

I'm not sure I will even be able to get near the hidden passage I usually take. It might be too heavily guarded or more of the same massacre from below. So I go up to the only other way I know.

The third floor is empty of all inhabitants. Fear and suspicion quickly temper any relief. It's quiet. The din of the bloodbath fades as I continue to distance myself from it. The silence is eerie, with the heaviness of a graveyard.

With each step I take, I pick up speed until I'm running. The doors to Alaric's rooms are wide open. I glance within as I pass. Furniture is upended and everything else not nailed down is in disarray. I don't let myself think about what condition he might be in —I will find out soon enough.

I don't bother checking to see if anyone else is nearby as I trip the hidden latch and slip into the musty passage. I wait at the top, letting my eyes adjust while I catch my breath and make sure no one tries to follow me through.

The door slides shut, muffling the sounds of death and surrounding me with a silence that is almost deafening beneath the rapid drumming of my heart.

I cover my mouth with my hands and smother a scream. Tears fall freely, and I do nothing to stop them, only swiping them away when they blur the way ahead. They are for everyone who has, or will, die today… for those I cannot save.

Humans and vampires. There is not a single life in this castle that has gone unscathed by Elizabeth's brutality.

I press my hand to the damp stone and use it to keep myself steady as I venture to the lower levels. It seems like a lifetime ago that I first took this passage.

Twice, I almost miss the next narrow step, though I make it down without falling. I ball my hands into fists and close my eyes, taking a deep breath. If I become careless, I will not make it out of here alive.

I crack open the door at the bottom of the landing and strain to listen for any stomping boots or voices before carefully peering out. When there's no sign of anyone around, I inch out, then race to Varin's cell, slipping inside.

Varin hunches in the center, night-forged silver manacles bright even shrouded by shadows, are pulled taught.

"For a moment, I thought you intended to flee without me." A statement and accusation. I say nothing to that. They are not entirely wrong. "Give me your hand."

I comply. Varin taps the band with a talon. At first, nothing happens. Then a hairline fissure forms and spreads. With my next breath, it shatters, falling like music to the ground.

"The ring has served its purpose," the demon explains at my bewildered expression. "Now, you must free me from these binds so I can possess you."

A shudder rolls through me. "Am I strong enough?"

"You either are or you are not." Varin tilts their head up, scenting the air. "We must hurry. No human within these walls will live to see nightfall."

The fear of dying before I even begin terrifies me to the marrow. I take a step back. "I will come back for you…"

From deep in their throat, a low growl rumbles forth. "Do you think to break our bargain? Have I not held up my end, giving you strength and power beyond your mortal capabilities?"

"I'll come back," I say again. The promise sounds weak even to my ears.

The embers of their irises blaze bright enough to pierce the dark. "We have a bargain." Venom laces their tone.

Elizabeth still lives, and there's no doubt in my mind that she will come for Alaric. If I ran now and found a way to escape with Alaric, could I forgive myself for betraying Varin?

I swallow a lump in my throat and force myself to move forward.

"I will keep my word," I say, gripping one of their taloned fingers. The gesture makes me feel a little childish since their palm is the length of my torso, but were I in their place, I would need the reassurance. "Forgive me?"

The demon's posture relaxes so slightly I almost miss it. I let fear get the better of me, and that momentary lapse caused me to be cruel. Varin believed I would abandon them when they have spent weeks waiting for me to fulfill the promise of freedom. No one deserves that, not even a demon.

"If I die, what will become of you?"

Varin is still, then quiet and resigned. "I have lived in these chains for too long," they say. Their other hand wraps around my middle and pulls me close. "Rest assured, I will do everything in my power to keep you alive."

The screams grow louder as the fray spreads throughout more of the castle. We both turn toward the sounds as though we could see through the door and walls to the slaughter. I look away first. The demon's skeletal face is frozen in an expression of horrified dismay.

"Then let's begin." I lift my chin and square my shoulders in an effort to at least appear brave, even if I'm terrified. "If I am to die, I might as well do so while stealing Elizabeth's prisoner."

Varin snorts, unable to stifle their amusement. "I may come to regret possessing you."

We went over each step as we came to it, neither bothering to speak about this part. After all, there was no point worrying about it if I was not prepared.

I press a palm to their face, right above the two

slits of their nostrils. "Wait," I say. "Will I be aware of what's happening?"

There's a heavy pause. The sense of urgency grows tighter by the second, and I know they feel it too. I'm relieved when the tension releases from their form.

"Think of it as both of us inhabiting your body. We will each have some control."

If that was meant to be comforting, it did not work. Though it is slightly better than I might have expected. I nod.

Going to each manacle, I use my dagger to break the locks. They fall away, one by one, leaving behind a band of grey scarring on Varin's shining black, shell-like skin. My heart lurches at the pain they must have suffered for three hundred years.

Their form wavers, and they look as though they might dissipate with the slightest provocation. I realize my life is not the only one in danger if this does not work. A fact they intentionally left out when I asked only about myself.

"Prepare yourself, Clara. You must stay strong, for this will not be easy." They glide forward, pausing before me. "I chose you, not only because you have been touched by many demons, but because you are strong—" They press a talon to my temple, then to the scar over my heart, saying, "—here, and here."

Agony swallows any peace those words might have given as they plunge forward. Their smoky body collides into mine with all the resistance of fog. But unlike previous times when they have ended up behind me, now they do not pass through, remaining within.

I collapse to my knees, unable to draw a single breath. My body feels too small, too full—as if I will be forced out if I cannot cling to it.

My blood grows molten hot. Burning. Turning to acid in my veins. It will devour me from the inside. The shadows fade as though a lantern has been lit, even as darkness edges in on the corners of my vision. My hold weakens.

I will not make it.

I assumed Varin would die if I did. Now I wonder if they would simply become the only inhabitant of my body. A primal fear winds around me like a rope of thorns piercing my skin.

I claw at my bones and scream but the sound is trapped within my mind. I don't have the strength to fight much longer.

Keep fighting, Clara. Varin's stained voice calls from inside my head.

A sensation, like the demon's hands, wraps around my wrists. Both from within and outside of me. The sharp points pin me down. I lean into them, needing the demon's help and seeking any sliver of comfort I can find. As I do, Varin mirrors the gesture, and the force of their presence gradually relaxes.

There is a sharp snap, and the remaining pressure releases its hold. I gasp for air, pulling as much of it into my lungs as possible. It tastes like thick smoke, singeing my lungs.

Rolling to my side is an effort I am not entirely sure is my own doing. Every motion and twitch of muscle sends new waves of sharp pain shooting through me. I wipe my mouth with the back of my hand, then manage to push myself up to sit. My limbs are heavy, and my movements clumsy. The stone floor is like hot coals under my palms.

Am I that cold?

My gaze settles on a smear of blood, bright against my ghostly pale hand. For a brief moment, I wonder if I was dead long enough for my body to cool or just very close.

We are alive. Varin's voice brushes weakly along the inside of my mind.

Yes, I agree, getting to my feet. I stumble and trip, catching myself on the wall. Nothing wants to work right. It's as if it's been weeks since I so much as twitched a muscle.

"Alaric," I rasp. Then regret speaking as I succumb to another coughing fit.

How long have I been unconscious? I hurl the panicked question toward the demon.

Varin hesitates, and I can actually feel it. *Nearly half an hour,* they eventually reply.

Not as long as I feared, though I worry that it's more than can be spared.

CHAPTER NINETEEN

CLARA

EACH STEP IS LIKE LEARNING TO WALK AGAIN. YET somehow, I find my way out of the cell and down the hall, only stopping to think about our exit once I get to the door that will take us past the old armory.

The energy it will take to backtrack and then make it out might be more than I have left. The wrong choice will lead to certain death. Fatigue gives hopelessness weight, pressing down on me.

Demons and saints... how in the Otherworld did everything go so fucking wrong?

I am with you now, Varin croons. *I have not spent centuries in this purgatory without learning a thing or two.*

It's surreal to see and feel my body move without my thought or will. Going through the doorway sends a jolt through me—the stride and pace are all wrong. I attempt to adjust. It doesn't work, and I fall up the stairs, banging my knee on a stone step.

Varin growls and I growl right back, demanding control of my body. It takes the entire way up for us to find a rhythm that works well enough to keep from stumbling and tripping. Varin's senses are keen, whispering when to stop and when to go, and where to turn to bypass clusters of humans and vampires.

The castle has quieted down in the main halls. Here, I gladly surrender to Varin. The death left in the wake of everything is an image I will never be rid of.

We move silently, weaving around the dead, avoiding the carnage as best we can. The scent of blood is overwhelming. I think I might be sick.

I nearly weep with relief when I feel the winter air on my face. Ahead, the monumental profiles of the mountains loom, casting their shadows over the land.

I take one step and then another until I am running. Varin turns my head toward the stables off to the right, and then with a jerk, my body follows suit.

My stomach lurches and twists at the thought of riding while running for my life. I doubt I'd be so lucky as to avoid breaking my neck the second time, especially when my body is no longer entirely my own.

Changing my direction, I make to run for the mountains.

What are you doing? You cannot outrun vampires, you fool. Get a mount! The force of the demon's command brings a wave of nausea rolling through me. Beads of sweat break out across my forehead and the back of my neck. Loose wisps of hair cling to my damp skin. When it passes, it leaves me feeling cold and clammy all over.

"I–I cannot—" I pant between shallow breaths. *I am not skilled enough to ride in this condition.*

I will help. This time, Varin's words are quieter, sparing me from the ill effects.

There's no time to argue. Unease tingles down my spine at the prospect of being controlled... what if they refuse to let go after? But to rely on my lack of riding skill is the more immediate danger.

The barn is thick with the aromatic scent of warm grains and oats. At the front are the favored horses. The space outside their stalls has the most elegant tack. Their restlessness is discomforting. I pass them all and stop before the black horse at the end. She is the only one facing away and utterly unalarmed.

She is small and appears lethargic. We will need a steed that can run.

Gently, I slide open the stall. I smile when she notices me and walks over. The mare pauses just out of arm's reach. Her nostrils flare, probably sensing Varin's presence inside me.

"It's all right," I say in low, even tones and advance half a step at a time. "I am still me."

She eyes me and snorts, but extends her muzzle, inhaling.

"There is a demon with me, but they are a good demon. You two will like each other." I am rambling now because I'm not sure what else to do.

You are aware that this is nothing more than an average horse? They are stupid beasts, incapable of understanding speech beyond basic commands. Utter nonsense would have the same effect in that tone.

Whether or not she understands or senses my

intentions, she presses her velvety nose into my hand. I stroke her neck, continuing to murmur before I attempt to saddle her.

"Ignore them," I say, partially to the animal and partially to nettle Varin. "They are cranky because they've been trapped for a long time."

She bobs her head, and I smirk. It was perfect timing, though it still looks like she agrees with me.

Maybe she is more intelligent than you give her credit for, I tease inwardly.

You're wasting time with this nag.

I fight the pull of Varin trying to steer me away. *If we must ride, then this is the horse we will take.* Then, aloud, I address her. "How long has it been since they let you out? Would you like to go on an adventure?"

Can it even move faster than a walk? Varin quips. The phantom prickle of talons along my scalp makes my eye twitch. If only they had turned into a bat or another small creature, I could have stuffed them in a saddlebag until they decided to be halfway pleasant.

Don't mistake her small stature and calm demeanor for weakness.

I step back and reach for the harness on the other side of the stall. When I try to slip it on, she lifts her head. The wasted seconds ticking by leave slivers of apprehension behind, building upon the ones that came before. Each one is a reminder that time is a luxury we don't have. If we aren't already too late.

However, considering this animal will have my life in her hands—hooves—soon, I don't want to risk upsetting her.

Varin is doing the mental equivalent of pacing,

grumbling about stupid animals. With a bit of coaxing, I'm able to get her ready without too much effort.

Just as I lead her out of the stable, a woman's scream tears through the courtyard, cutting off abruptly.

Damn Elizabeth to the Otherworld.

I mount the mare with Varin's unexpected help. The movement causes her to prance sideways. Then when I am firmly in place, she bobs her head and swishes her tail.

I have precious little knowledge about horses, but I choose to interpret that to mean she is not entirely thrilled with this development.

"Sorry, girl," I murmur, reaching to pat her shoulder. It seems to help a bit.

We do not have time for such foolishness, Varin snarls. *Unless you want the three of us to die together, hand over control.*

I wince from the harshness of their demand, scraping against the inside of my skull. I'm not sure if this is something I could ever get used to... or, for that matter, want to get used to.

Be gentle with her, please. I plead.

Then, with my next breath, I surrender to Varin's will.

All at once, it is a dizzying nightmare to feel my body move outside my control. They issue silent commands with small movements of my hands on the reins or my thighs squeezing. Varin shifts my weight and urges the horse into a run, ignoring the pleas I throw at them.

She moves fast, swerving around obstacles with grace. I don't know how much of it is the demon's skill and what is purely the mare, but if such a thing were possible, I would almost believe she was born with the heart of wind.

Is this the extent of your plan? Varin's question has a bite to it.

You can't read my mind?

The demon growls, but I press my lips tight to keep it from escaping and scaring the horse. *No. Thank the saints. I cannot begin to fathom what thoughts flit through mortal minds. You probably spend an extraordinary amount of time thinking about cheese or your feet or some other inane thing.*

Feet? Unable to help myself, I laugh. They have been locked up for far too long. I am relieved that some parts of myself remain under my control.

Wolves abducted Alaric, I tell Varin.

My head swivels to glance over my shoulder. And I get the impression Varin was trying to look at me. We've covered more ground than I expected.

They said they were convening at the foothills, and I intend to go with them.

Varin is silent for several minutes before they adjust our course. *If they intend to kill him, you will not be able to stop it.*

I am unprepared for the gentleness of their warning. Rather than the intended effect, it sets my nerves humming.

Oliver won't let that happen, I respond firmly.

The demon doesn't argue, but their heaved sigh of forced patience is tangible.

It is late in the afternoon when we catch sight of them. Varin eases the mare to a trot, letting her cool down.

A wolf lopes to meet us partway. It's twice the size of any I've seen before. It leaps, transforming into a man far enough back to avoid spooking the horse.

Regaining control of my body is a struggle, though not as difficult as I feared. Varin and I will need to come to an agreement on how to deal with this situation. Endlessly wrestling for dominance could cause problems.

On another day, witnessing a wolf change into a man before my eyes might have troubled me. Yet, after allowing a demon to possess me, I am unfazed.

Varin signals for the horse to slow, but she shakes it off, trotting up to Oliver.

"I'm glad you decided to join us after all." He strokes the horse's neck with a suspiciously wide grin as he attempts to slyly pull a cube of sugar from his pocket.

Well, I suppose that explains why she had no qualms about approaching a wolf. She is an animal ruled by her appetite. It's a silly thing, nevertheless, it only further endears her to me.

"You know why I am here," I say flatly.

He is rather dim-witted. Are you sure he's the one in charge?

Oliver scrunches up his nose at my unwillingness to play this game. He throws a lazy glance over his shoulder. There are perhaps a dozen of his people standing at a safe distance. Waiting. Watching. There could be twice as many out of sight.

Four of them cluster close together around a fifth figure. Instinctively, I know it's Alaric in the center.

I don't take my eyes off him as I ask, "May I see him?"

Oliver rubs his chin. "I am not sure that would be a good idea."

"I don't know what you're planning, but he has suffered enough." A sliver of Varin's viciousness permeates my tone, lending power to my warning. "I will not allow you or anyone else to harm him."

Oliver is visibly taken aback, though he recovers quickly. I am no longer the powerless human he met stumbling through the woods.

"Come," he says, jerking his chin toward the others. "I will introduce you."

I hand him the reins at his request and relax in the saddle as he leads the way. I lean forward and pet my stolen mare. She exceeded my expectations, and by the way Varin's remarks have shifted to Oliver, I would say the demon is also impressed.

She deserves a name, but a name worthy of her.

Is that one always *like that?*

Varin's question catches me off guard. *Who, Oliver?*

If that is what you call him.

Such a temperamental demon. *As far as I have witnessed, yes,* I respond silently. Though I infuse my words with a laugh, I can't help but wonder why they are in such a foul mood.

I never stopped to consider how Varin would feel once unchained and free of their cell. I suppose I expected joy or wonder or a dozen other emotions, not irritation. There's no way to know for sure without asking. I can't help but think, if I'd been a prisoner for that long, finally having my freedom in a sudden and unexpected way might be overwhelming.

Oliver gestures to his pack. A casual flick of his wrist summons the wolves to gather close, moving as if given a series of commands. They approach in groups of twos and threes, though a handful step up alone. The first two I recognize.

"You've already met my betas." He arches a brow.

"Not formally."

He cringes slightly, though, by their reaction, they find his previous lack of etiquette more amusing than insulting. "This is Adalynd and Hunt, the betas of the Shade pack."

Our introduction is brief. After that, a bevy of names and faces follow in a matter of moments. A race with the sun. Not a single member is treated as more or less important than another. And I like that.

Among all the new faces is the woman from the kitchens who collided with me. Her name turns out to be Calla, and she is among the group of younger warriors.

Is this what she meant by *telling me to be ready*? She'd intentionally bumped into me, and I'd believed her act. At my recognition, Calla smirks and gives me a one-shouldered shrug. I am glad to see she made it out in one piece.

In between, Oliver explains that the pack doesn't usually travel with outsiders and that knowing me will reduce their tensions.

"Do not look so worried, Miss Valmont," Oliver says, unable to keep that he knows precisely what he did from showing on his face. "We do not expect you to remember everyone… not today, anyway."

The glower I give him is wiped away with his next gesture. The wolves surrounding Alaric drag him forward. His hands are chained behind his back and other than his clothes being in slight disarray, he appears to be well.

I'm quickly introduced to the guards.

"Pleased to meet you," I murmur, barely paying them any attention because I can't make myself look away from their vampire prisoner.

Alaric's head snaps up at the sound of my voice, surprise quickly morphing into fury. "Was she right about you, after all, little nightmare?"

I bite down on my tongue in case Varin gets the idea to respond.

Alaric sneers, showing just enough fang that no one could possibly mistake him for anything other than what he is. "How fitting," he bites out. "A mare of night for a nightmare."

CHAPTER TWENTY

CLARA

It turns out wolves—at least these particular wolves—love animals. My stolen horse stands serenely between Adalynd and Hunt as if she doesn't have a care in the world while they argue over who gets to take charge. In the last several minutes, the two betas have gone from perfectly calm and rational to looking like they might brawl at any moment.

In that time, I've settled on a name for her. Nyx. It is everything she is. Short and sweet. Sharp and graceful. And made of the darkest night.

Oliver pinches the bridge of his nose and mutters something under his breath. He looks to me with a mildly embarrassed flush coloring the tips of his ears. "I can tell them to back off if you'd rather the horse stay with you."

I shake my head. "That's all right. They both seem… eager to care for her," I say slowly.

"Marvelous idea, Miss Valmont," Oliver says, and before I can ask what he's talking about, he calls out to them, "Both of you will lead the horse or neither of you will."

Adalynd and Hunt halt their bickering abruptly. They glare at each other a moment longer, then seem happy enough with the outcome.

Oliver issues a few short commands, and within minutes, the pack is organized and prepared to march. We begin the trek west.

I watch the guards in charge of Alaric. While Oliver has always been kind, I don't know what his pack is like. I stay out of their way but remain close enough to monitor how they treat him, which places me at the tail end of the procession.

Oliver walks beside me. I'm unsure if this is the position he usually takes or if he would typically be leading. For the first hour, I'm silent, grateful he doesn't try to fill the space with small talk.

I don't ask where we are going. It doesn't feel important at the moment. I'm content knowing Alaric is safe, even if he's a prisoner. Later, I will do whatever I can to free him, though I suspect it won't be easy.

Every few strides, I will stumble or misstep. Twice, Oliver has caught me by the elbow to keep me from falling. He throws glances of gentle understanding and pity, which I do my best to ignore. I'd rather he assumes I'm exhausted than know the truth.

One of my feet steps forward a little too far, throwing off my stride. A branch snaps underfoot, and several of the closer pack members send less than subtle looks in my direction—including Alaric.

I clench my jaw, feeling heat crawl up my face. *Keep this up, and I'll end up breaking my neck. I very much doubt you can do much if that happens.* I grind out inwardly toward the cursed demon.

Varin only snarls in response.

"We will stop at the lake ahead," Oliver announces several hours in. Then addressing me, he says, "We will arrive at the Keep right around nightfall."

The pack brightens at the announcement. Voices and steps become lighter as the tension sluffs off with each mile we gain.

A tri-color brown wolf leaps out from a thicket, barreling toward us. He changes into his human form in the last few yards without missing a beat, heading directly toward Oliver. He's young and lean with long limbs, and his golden hair is as wild as his eyes. Unlike the rest of the pack, he only carries a small satchel.

"What did you see, Daniel?" Oliver asks as he hands him a water skin.

The young man shakes his head, refusing, though he can clearly use it. "A harmony of demons is bearing down on us."

Oliver's gaze snaps to me, quickly flicking down to my hand. Questions take form in his light brown and amber eyes when he notices the missing ring.

Demon shit.

Mournful howls fill the air in a faint, ghostly song. Oliver lifts his head and inhales. I mimic the gesture, wondering what he senses, but all I notice is the way the air smells like snow.

"Fuck," he mutters.

The entire pack has gone quiet and still. Every head angles toward the approaching demons, listening. There is a moment of absolute silence.

"If you get separated, meet back at the Keep!" Oliver shouts.

And then everything descends into mayhem. Wolves of all colors appear where humans stood seconds before. They race toward the tree line to the south, colliding with the demons as they break through. The weak light is rapidly diminished by the masses of dark shapes.

Branches crack and splinter. I throw my arm up to shield my face. The lesser demons are so tightly packed together, they look like a cloud of thick smoke.

Oliver shifts and uses the side of his body to push me toward the nearest tree. "Stay down," he says. His voice is an unnaturally deep rumble, half human, half animal.

Pressed against the rough bark, I search franticly for Alaric. My eyes alight on him with half the pack between us. They have forced him to his knees, his wrists still bound, with only one guard to keep the demons from ripping him apart.

They don't need anyone else to worry about, but I can't sit back and do nothing. I can't watch as they all risk their lives. I draw the dagger from my boot and go after any that make it past the front line, protecting their backs.

I slash at a demon leaping for a wolf preoccupied with another. The blade's edge pierces the bark-like shell of a lesser demon's skin with no more resistance than water. I bring the weapon down between another's shoulders as they throw back their head, dislocating their jaw, preparing to deliver a fatal bite to a wounded wolf.

One after another, I move, spinning and slashing, drawing on everything I've learned in training. Varin doesn't interfere, only lending me strength and speed through their power. The mass of lesser demons is driven to retreat, and the fighting ebbs.

Varin's warning prickles over my skin, causing the hair on the back of my neck to rise. They turn my gaze toward the thickest cluster of dark between a copse of trees.

Silently, as the night sweeps across the sky, a higher demon emerges, clawing their way from the shadows. No one seems to notice for a long second. Not until they lunge for the only pack member still in human form—the one guarding Alaric.

Their long arm thrusts out and swats at a wolf, the taloned fingers slicing over ribs and sending them into a tree. Their body hits hard, then crumples to the ground.

Without slowing, the demon lumbers on, intent on reaching the prey within their sights. Gnarled taloned claws slice the air and drive into the guard's side. His blood is bright and harsh against the desaturated colors of winter.

Alaric is defenseless, and the demon will kill him if they are not stopped. Everyone close enough to help is locked in their own battle or too wounded to fight anymore.

My feet move before I can stop to think. Instinct

and fear and desperation drive me forward. The need to reach him is too strong for Varin's attempts to keep me where it's relatively safe. They quickly stop fighting against my efforts. I draw on the borrowed strength and speed to weave through the fray.

The tide of a battle nearly won has turned. The air grows thick with the stench of blood. It's strong, making my stomach churn, but I don't dare stop.

Alaric is up and running. He strains against the ropes binding him. Unable to break them, it slows him down. The higher demon's eyes shine with malicious glee as they stalk toward him.

Varin is shouting at me, but between the pulse roaring in my ears and the commotion of battle, I can't understand them. I slowly gain, but I'm afraid I won't reach him in time.

The demon dives for Alaric. Their massive, clawed hand shoves him from behind, sending him sprawling in the dirt near the foot of a bridge that spans a wide ravine above a rushing river.

No.

There is a sound, horrible and desperate. The demon halts mid-motion, swiveling to face me. And I think the sound came from me.

Alaric rolls to his back and sits up. The demon doesn't notice because their attention is now on me. Once, I thought Varin's grin was a sinister thing. But I was wrong because the way this demon looks at me now chills me to the bone.

"Yoooouuu…" they growl. "I willlll gut yooouuu thisss timmmme and ssstring your innardsss in the trreees for decorrrationnnn."

The distraction gives Alaric the opportunity to get to his feet. He runs, but the thudding of his steps draws the demon's attention back to him.

The demon's jaw opens unnaturally wide, and they let out an earsplitting screech that could shatter glass. They turn the sound on me, furious that I let their prey escape. For a moment, the demon seems torn between chasing Alaric or coming at me for revenge.

Alaric is halfway across the ravine when the demon moves. They feign as if they will attack me, only to twist, swiveling. They strike out, talons slicing through the ropes like cobwebs.

For a brief moment, the bridge seems to hover. Then time speeds back up, and it collapses. I can only watch in horror as Alaric falls, disappearing beyond the cliff's edge.

Then the demon sets their sights on me. Long twisted limbs eat up the distance with quick jerky movements at painful angles. I reduce my speed and prepare to attack.

Everything seems to stall, slowing to a crawl. The cacophony of fighting fades to a dull roar in the distance. I keep my gaze locked on the demon, judging the length of each stride, the speed, the way they move. I search for a weak point and prepare to strike.

My body drops to the ground, rolling without my permission. The air is knocked out of me from protruding roots and broken tree limbs digging into my ribs. The demon's talons slash at where I stood seconds before, carving deep grooves into the winter-hardened ground.

Stupid human, Varin hisses.

Anger flares from within. Mine and theirs.

I knew what I was doing!

I grit my teeth. This is not the time to argue. The demon skids as they change trajectory. I get to my feet and run for the fallen bridge. Hot, putrid breath surrounds me as I near the cliff's edge.

And then I jump.

My fingers tighten around the hilt of the dagger.

The river comes rushing up to swallow me whole before I draw a full breath. Ice cold water cracks over me—the contact a sharp strike that smothers every inch of my body with stinging pins and needles. My muscles seize from the burning cold.

The river carries me in its current, pilling me in every direction until I don't know which way is up, shoving me into large rocks protruding from the riverbed, only to drag my body to the next. Slowly, the ache in my muscles lessens as I go numb, and the fire in my lungs becomes more demanding.

I am going to drown. The thought comes as it spits me out with a whirling rush of water gurgling in my ears into an endless, dark abyss. Disoriented.

My legs and arms begin to move in rhythm to right myself until my head breaks the surface. I gasp and sputter for air. Feeling returns to my body, soaking outward to my limbs. Varin is oddly silent.

I twist in a circle. The lake stretches wide, lapping against the shore. Beyond that, the trees are thick, melting into the shadows of night. But wherever I look, I find no sign of Alaric anywhere. He must still be in the water.

Thrashing and screeching echoes from the ravine. I crane my neck to look, squinting into the last scraps of the dwindling sunset's light. A dark form rises up, the higher demon still pursuing both revenge and prey.

We need to get out of this water. Varin's voice is urgent.

I need to find Alaric.

I take several deep breaths, then exhale and submerge myself once more. Thick weeds sway in the murky water, reaching up from the silt-clouded depths. I still haven't found Alaric when the need to breathe forces me back to the surface.

We must go.

I ignore them and sink once more. *Where is he?*

A flash of white leaps out from the underwater forest of weeds. I swim toward it. The long, lacy greenery tangle around my limbs as I struggle to make my way toward Alaric.

His eyes are closed as if he's sleeping, trapped within like a fairytale prince, cursed to sleep, locked in a moment of time.

I press a palm to his face. Alaric's eyes twitch under his lids. My dagger makes quick work of the fronds. I press the blade to the ropes around his wrists. Glinting silver threads woven through it makes my progress slow. I would bet they are made of night-forged silver, which would explain why he couldn't break them.

Finally, the rope snaps. Alaric jolts, but his legs are still tangled. I grab a fist full and slice. Our eyes meet. And then he races toward the surface.

I kick my legs to follow. Pressure squeezes around my middle then tows me deeper and deeper with a vicious jerk.

The unexpected force causes me to lose my grip on the dagger. It sinks fast, disappearing into the cloud of displaced silt.

The demon holds me down, pressing me into the shingle. They hover above me. Their voice penetrates the water as easily as air. "Yourrrr vammmpire can do nottthhing to saaave yooou thisss timmme."

This time?

An image of racing through the forest on a horse. Demons on our heel. Flying through the air. Searing pain. Arms carrying me to safety.

Stabbing pain pierces my side as they drag a talon across my waist where my top has ridden up, exposing a band of skin. They scratch, leaving angry welts, and on the next pass, they press down harder, deep enough to slice open skin. Blood darkens the water, making it harder to see.

Or perhaps it is unconsciousness swallowing the light.

Desperation is the only thing keeping me from giving in. My fingers claw uselessly at the lakebed. Air bubbles escape my lips.

The demon lowers its maw toward my neck. Razor-sharp teeth scrape against my skin. They are taking their time, drawing out fear as they find the spot where they will cause the most damage.

I feel the brush of smooth, silken warmth against my cold hand. The demon tenses, readying for the killing blow. Wrapping my hand around my last hope,

I drive my fist up, aiming for the soft spot right behind their jaw. The blade sinks in. Using the last of my energy, I twist and wrench the dagger, slicing several inches down the demon's neck.

My grip goes slack, and my hand falls away. The weight of the demon is gone.

But it's too late now. I don't have the strength to escape this watery grave.

Varin?

There is only silence from the demon.

CHAPTER TWENTY-ONE

CLARA

Dying feels a lot like floating.

Pressure squeezes my jaw until it hurts.

I peel open my eyes and see Alaric hovering over me. He glowers and releases my face. Banding an arm around my ribs, he holds me against his side. Then we are rising.

I can't keep my eyes open.

My back crashes against something hard. The jolt rouses me… but it's too late.

The air is sharp. It pierces my soaked clothes and singes my skin. Pressure comes down on my chest over and over until my lungs spasm, forcing the water out. I cough and gasp. Every breath is like shards of glass scraping along my throat and lungs.

Two hands help me roll to my side, then rub soothing circles over my back until I'm no longer struggling.

My thoughts are sluggish. At first, I don't understand. Lifting my head is a monumental effort, but as I look into Alaric's face, everything becomes clear.

"You saved me," I rasp.

His carefully neutral expression returns to a scowl. After a long moment, he says, "I should have let you drown." Only there is no bite to his words.

"Thank you."

At that, Alaric goes perfectly still, as if he doesn't quite know what to do with my gratitude.

I try to sit up, but my entire body is shaking uncontrollably. Everything hurts, and I'm exhausted.

Moving around to my back, he lifts me, helping me to stand then drapes my left arm over his shoulder. I do what I can to assist him. He's so warm, and I'm so cold it feels like I'm being held against heated metal. My feet drag over the ground with every step. Alaric makes a derisive sound and hauls me over his shoulder.

I must pass out because the next thing I know, I come to, propped against a rock wall like a rag doll. Alaric kneels with his back to me, building a fire.

Varin? I call to the demon in my head.

If you had hoped to be rid of me by nearly dying, I regret to inform you that it did not work, they bite out, tone seething.

I press my lips into a tight line from the unexpected wave of emotion upon hearing their voice. *I am glad.*

Varin doesn't speak anymore but I feel a flash of some emotion, but it's gone before I can identify it.

Once the flames are strong enough to cast their

heat to where I sit, Alaric straightens and comes to crouch in front of me.

"You called the demons down on us all." He narrows his gaze, studying me. "They spoke to you—they *recognized* you." It's not a question.

Better a harmony of demons than a cruelty of saints, Varin says derisively. *Those demons were corrupted.*

"That is impossible." Varin's comment is so shocking I speak aloud by mistake.

Alaric lists his head to the side. "You are a confounding creature. It is as if you cannot decide if you want to kill me or not."

Corrupted? How could that happen?

Like any human, there are many things that can corrupt my kind, though cruelty is the surest way. I was already imprisoned before they escaped the Otherworld.

Then... are saints real too?

Varin's laugh causes me to wince. *What do you think saints are? Demons and saints,* Varin says in a mocking sing-song voice. *They are but two sides of the same coin.*

I thought exactly what everyone believes them to be. The spirits of those who have passed on from this world and into the Otherworld.

Alaric's hands cup my face, deep blue eyes searching mine. "Are you dying, little nightmare?"

My lips part, but my throat is dry, and I need to swallow before I can find my voice. "No... I am fine."

He releases me and sits back on his heels. "That demon knew you."

"I... it didn't," I say. "How?"

Was that the same one who chased me when I returned to Windbury after Kitty's wedding?

Alaric regards me, waiting for me to speak coherently. I can't stop shaking, but it must be shock because the air is warm. Almost uncomfortably so. When I don't, he wordlessly gets up and walks away.

I think over what happened, trying to piece things together. Everything comes in fractured images. My thoughts catch on the moment the demon and I faced off and how Varin wrenched control away from me. Even though I suspect they used much of their power to keep us alive in the water, there is a part of me that feels violated. In this weakened state, what little control I have over my heightened emotions slips, and I can't stop my frustration from surfacing.

Do not ever attempt to control my body again without my permission. I seethe.

We would have died because of your foolish actions, Varin snaps back.

I had a plan. Do you honestly think I would have tried something like that if I didn't know what I was doing?

Varin's emotions are a tempest against my own. *I have traded one prison for another.*

I let my head fall back against the rock and close my eyes. My anger is justified… but so is theirs. We were forced into this before we were ready by circumstance. There wasn't time for us to understand each other or work out how to do this.

Feeling guilty for only thinking of myself, I say, *I am sorry.* Then add, *You're not alone anymore. I am with you now.*

Varin's presence stills, almost as if they vanished.

Once we find the wolves again, you and I will find a way to compromise. Still, the demon doesn't react.

The pull of sleep settles like a heavy blanket and I lower myself to the ground, unable to resist.

Varin? I say. *Why didn't you turn into an animal like Cherno? And why am I still human? I thought bonding with you would have turned me into a vampire.*

I tuck my arm under my head and curl away from the fire on my uninjured side. The heat is strong, but I am too weak to move further. My fingers brush something smooth and cool. The night-forged dagger is there. I don't know if I was clutching it when Alaric pulled me from the water or if he brought it with me.

Their quiet response comes a moment later. *Our bond is temporary. We will need to find another solution soon.... And you did not want to be changed.*

I am nearly asleep when I think I hear them whisper, *I am sorry, too.*

My eyes snap open at the pain along my side. Fingers prod at my tender flesh, sending bolts of electricity through my entire body.

"Why didn't you tell me you were injured?" Alaric growls from above.

I fall to my back, reeling from the rude awakening. He tugs at my shirt to show me the red stain, exposing my midsection. The cut inflicted by the demon has stitched itself back together, leaving the skin a bright pink. Alaric swipes at the dried blood. I hiss through my teeth at his rough treatment against the still-tender injury.

I could not fully heal you before. I needed time to regain my energy. It's good it was not too deep. Varin's explanation comes faintly. *Your bond with him helped.*

My gaze drifts from the new pile of wood to the throat of the vampire holding his body inches over mine.

"There is something unnatural about you, little nightmare," he says slowly. "I should kill you right here and return to Nightwich." His breaths grow ragged, and when I meet his gaze, there is something feral and hungry flashing within his eyes.

"When was the last time you fed?"

He snarls. "That is none of your business." As he speaks, he leans forward, almost like he isn't aware of what he's doing.

He never needed to feed often, but since Elizabeth cursed him, it seems as if he has gone months between rather than days.

I think back to that night in the library, to the curse spreading…

Could it be draining him?

As if to prove my theory, those black veins slither up the side of his neck, then across his cheek. Now that he is away from Nightwich, Elizabeth's hold on him will weaken.

"Feed," I say. I tilt my head to the side.

Alaric stares at me, utterly bewildered. "And what of your vampire master?"

"My blood is no one's but my own to offer."

He hesitates. "And if I tell you that I have killed others I have fed on, would you still offer it up so freely?"

The question is intended to frighten me, but even cursed, he cannot hide the flinch of guilt at the admission.

"Things turned out well last time." I reach up and push a lock of hair back. "You will not hurt me now, either."

His chest rises and falls with shallow breaths. The hold on his control is threadbare, with desire and the need to feed straining against it. Then Alaric lowers himself on top of me. His lips skim over my shoulder, and he inhales the scent of my skin, but he doesn't bite me right away. Instead, he presses a kiss to my collarbone, then another at the hollow of my throat.

I close my eyes as he continues all the way up and along my jaw until he finally reaches my mouth. He starts out tentative and soft. When he nips on my bottom lip, desire wins out. I moan and his tongue meets mine, as he deepens the kiss.

Alaric settles his hips between my legs, the press of his arousal against my thigh. My hands travel over his back as his warm palm slides up over the exposed skin of my stomach to cup my breast. His fingers massage and tease my flesh. We move against each other, both wanting more. Craving.

He breaks away for breath. "You are poison and my undoing," he says with a sigh against me. "But I will taste from your lips until I am immune, and then, little nightmare, I will consume you."

That promise sends heat through my veins,

pooling between my thighs. I arch into him, the desperate need to feel him is almost overwhelming. So, I show him, pulling him closer, hooking my heels around the backs of his legs. Shadows dance around us, rising from him like wisps toward me.

He needs no more urging than that. Alaric shifts, and then there's the slight press of his fangs on my neck a moment before he bites down. Our connection sparks with his first drink, growing stronger with each swallow.

Alaric moans against me, the sound prying a whimper from me. He lifts his hips. I tug on his shirt, detesting the material that separates us—wanting the press of his weight and the warmth of his skin against mine.

Soon, I find I don't mind as much as I thought when he reaches my waistband and undoes the fastens, giving him access to my most intimate parts. His touch is a delicious torment, teasing lower and lower. I cry out as he drags a finger along the length of my core. I lift my hips, seeking him, but he refuses to let me rush.

"Please," I plead. The word is breathless.

Alaric chuckles against my neck. Then his tongue slides over the puncture marks until they heal. "Yes, little nightmare." He lifts himself up on one arm and watches how easily he can control me. "Beg me. Tell me what you want."

I can barely think with the demanding way my body craves him muddling my thoughts. "You..." I groan as his finger grazes my aching flesh again and again. "I want to feel your skin against mine, please, Alaric."

With agonizing slowness, he increases his pressure, entering me. We can both feel just how ready I am for all of him. Still, he takes his time with every touch and stroke. Then he adds another, his pace remaining languid.

I moan because, *this. Is. Torture.*

Alaric lowers his head to my shoulder, and as his fangs pierce me again as the pace of his hand picks up. I buck against him.

"The trail leads in here!" a distant shout grates against the deliciously wicked sensation that has wrapped itself around us.

Alaric stills then removes his hand. I can't stop the plaintive noise that escapes me. I grip his collar, keeping him from moving away.

A low growl rumbles from his chest, vibrating against mine. He makes no move to separate himself from me.

"Remove your fangs, vampire, and get up slowly," a man says. "If you try anything, you will find my arrow through your heart before you can blink."

I don't need to see the man's face to know I hate him.

Alaric withdraws his fangs. The skin already tingling as it heals, though a few beads of blood escape first.

Then Alaric clears his throat, and I realize I'm still holding on. Reluctantly, I release my hold.

He adjusts my clothes as he slowly lifts himself up. The expression on Alaric's face as he sits back on his heels is a mix between a smirk and irritation. I sit up, pulling my knees to my chest.

Four more wolves have surrounded us. It's embarrassing enough as it is without the whole pack bearing witness to such an intimate moment.

"You ought to learn control," Hunt says.

"And you ought to learn how to knock," Alaric mutters to the beta at his back.

Everyone's attention is on Alaric, which makes it easier for me to hide the heat searing my cheeks.

"Is she unharmed?" Oliver asks, making his way forward, leading Nyx by the reins.

"We stopped him in time," Adalynd calls over her shoulder. She kneels behind Alaric to retie his hands.

Oliver stops short, both brows rising as he takes in the way Alaric kneels between my legs, the way I wrap my arms around my middle, and fail to hide the heat stinging my cheeks.

"Do you have any other injuries?" she demands of me. "You still have good color to your complexion, so he couldn't have been feeding long."

I wince. She misunderstands and offers a pitying look.

Oliver leans against Nyx and pinches the bridge of his nose, doing a terrible job of hiding his amusement. I glower at him until his shoulders stop shaking. I am torn between hating that the rest of our audience misunderstands the situation because they think Alaric is dangerous and trying to hurt me and being grateful that they aren't openly gaping because of our intimacy.

When Oliver regains his composure, he lowers the hand covering his face.

"All right, we found them." Oliver waves a hand. "Miss Valmont and I will meet you all back at the rendezvous point."

The pack files out one by one. Hunt lingers, leaving only when Oliver sends him a stern look.

Once the last of them have left, I rise, turning my back to compose myself. When I'm ready, I face Oliver again.

He is leaning casually against the rocky wall, arms folded over his chest, ankles crossed, and an infuriating grin. Nyx bobs her head, which just seems like she's laughing with him.

"He wouldn't have hurt me," I hiss.

"Oh, I could scent as much," he says with a sharp laugh. "I don't know how no one else noticed."

"He doesn't need to be tied up like a criminal," I say, intentionally ignoring his comment.

Oliver pushes off the cave wall and strides over to the fire, kicking dirt into it, extinguishing the flames. "It isn't only for your protection."

I drop any further protests because I can't argue with him putting the safety of his people above the word of someone who isn't part of the pack when it isn't actually hurting Alaric.

"There is something I must ask," he says. Oliver's gaze flicks to my hand. "That demon…"

"Is not the one that attacked," I finished.

He nods then throws an arm over my shoulder. "I truly am glad we found both of you alive and well,"

Oliver says gently. "Come, it is already night, and we still have a ways to go before reaching the Keep."

CHAPTER TWENTY-TWO

CLARA

Now that my mind has had a chance to clear, I can already see Elizabeth's hold on him beginning to weaken. Within the castle walls, he seemed to feel the pull of our bond. But it was never as strong as it was in the cave. The realization stuns me. I find myself curious how much of that is due to our connection or his distance from Nightwich.

As we travel on, the weight of tension settles heavily on us all. Silence has replaced the whispered conversations and quiet laughter. A somber mood has descended like night, giving our band the air of a funeral procession.

With two pack members killed in the fight, I suppose it is.

We fashioned a makeshift sled to carry their bodies.

The guards around Alaric have doubled, and rather than walking at the back as before, they march him at the front. They all believe he attacked me, but part of me doubts the truth will do any good. There have already been a few murmurings that I must have been under his thrall without realizing it and that he probably intended to kill me.

I hate that they think even worse of him now than they did before.

At least Oliver knows the truth. I can take some small comfort in that. Now, all I must do is convince him that Alaric doesn't pose a threat. But that will have to wait for later.

"Oliver… where are we going?" I ask. It's not the most pressing topic on my mind, but I want to feel him out before attempting to talk through my theory.

"To the Keep," he says.

"I mean, why? Why take Alaric?" I press my lips together as I figure out how to word the question without it coming out too much like an accusation. "What are you planning to do with him?"

A long moment passes before he answers. "You know the answer to that."

Irritation simmers below the surface, and I need to work to keep it at bay. I cannot expect him to give me his full trust when I don't know if I can give him mine. We might be friends, but it is still a far cry from what I have with Cassius, Della, and Lawrence.

Oliver won't hurt me. At least not intentionally. However, I wonder how far that extends to Alaric. The two of them worked together to keep the demons at bay in the forest near Windbury, so there is some level of trust between them, which would mean He knows Alaric isn't a mindless monster—despite Elizabeth's curse. He might be the only one in the pack that does.

Although, I can't assume that will keep Oliver from killing him if he decides it's too much of a risk to keep Alaric alive.

"Does your offer to help break the curse still stand?"

"Of course," Oliver speaks with his typical airy manner yet offers nothing more than that.

I grab his sleeve, hating this game we are playing. "Did you find something?" My voice is strained.

He sighs, then grimly shakes his head. "I searched every lead I could find. There isn't much, and the curse has always ended in death. I am sorry."

My heart sinks. I plant my feet and tug on his arm again, stopping him. "What do you plan on doing with him?" There is no disguising the accusation in my question this time.

He meets my gaze, but there's nothing in it to give me an answer one way or the other.

"I told you about him because I trusted you," I say. "Was I wrong to do so?"

Oliver pries my fingers loose, then tucks my arm in the crook of his elbow, leading me on. "His fate has yet to be decided. That depends on the queen's next move, as well as his."

It was not a definite answer. However, it does tell me that whatever protection he offers extends only to me. Oliver and his pack might think they will decide what to do with Alaric, but they are in for a shock if they believe I will sit back and do nothing to stop them.

It is not for them to decide Alaric's fate.

An ache twists in my heart because every time I was treated like an object—as if I was something to be owned, traded, and bartered with, I resented it. Watching it happen to another, especially to someone I love, makes me furious.

He doesn't belong to anyone.

Not even me.

"I won't let you kill him," I say, pitched to him alone.

"We will not make a decision in haste." Oliver cuts a glance toward those ahead of us, the message clear. This is not the time or place for this discussion. I can respect that, but this is not the end of it.

Turning my thoughts inward, I focus on a problem that can be solved.

Varin? I try. The demon has been silent since we aired our frustrations. *I don't know how difficult it will be to work together... however, I think it's worth trying to find a compromise.*

I feel Varin's hesitation.

Explain. Their response is careful. Suspicious. Though unable to hide their curiosity.

I don't want either of us to feel powerless. Perhaps if we understood each other better.

I am listening...

When you took over to ride Nyx, it was... unsettling to have someone else command my every movement. I felt trapped... I trail off before continuing, *Would I be correct in thinking that is similar to what you are experiencing—only in an unfamiliar body?*

Varin's presence is restless as they consider. *That is a close enough approximation.*

I bite down on my bottom lip. It would be a lie to say their answer didn't make me uncomfortable. I have been so preoccupied with remaining in complete control I never stopped to think about how Varin might feel. Before I end up dwelling on my guilt, I push on, wanting to make things right between us.

Do you think it is possible to share control? Not taking turns, but a constant sharing?

Explain.

If I can give over control, then why not partial? Since most movements are the result of what is happening around us and basic needs, they are somewhat automatic and wouldn't require cooperation. For instance, now—we are doing little more than walking. All we have to do is sync our movements. I think it could work with a bit of practice.

What of the other times when things are not so simple?

Those will require more communication. What I want hasn't changed—I want to save Alaric in any way I can. We'll be fine as long as you don't attempt to stop me. If one of us needs control, we can say so—like you did to ride Nyx.

We practice moving in tandem. As we do, the warmth of Varin's happiness blooms within my chest. It's not a perfect solution, and it takes extra effort in the beginning.

Over the next hour, it gradually becomes easier. They give my steps a grace I never had. I even find that my stamina has improved by using less of my own energy, combined with the rapid healing through my connections to Alaric and Varin.

I don't notice the fog rolling in until it rises from wisps over the forest floor to thick clouds knee-high. An eerie sensation crawls down my spine. The entourage continues into the mist without pausing.

Intending to look at Oliver, I'm startled when I bump into him and Varin's confusion matches my own. Only he didn't move to block my path—I'd changed direction without realizing it.

"What is this?" I whisper to Oliver.

"This is the parameter of the Keep." He catches me by the elbow as my feet try to take me back the way we came. At the alarm on my face, he explains, "It is a barrier meant to keep those on the outside from entering and those brought in from leaving."

I glance at the last wolf disappearing into the thick mist, leaving us to catch up.

"Except for us," he adds as an afterthought.

He takes my hand and leads me in. I can barely make out anything in front of me. Oliver takes me on a path that seems to meander, doubling back and twisting in on itself. The more I try to move in a straight line, the more erratic the route becomes.

"Please stop, you're going to make me sick," I plead. "isn't there a straight path you can take?"

"It is the magic distorting your sense of direction. Without aid, anyone without wolf blood who tries to enter will be doomed to wander until they die." His voice sounds slightly strained. "Focus on me. The more you fight my lead, the more effort it will take to bring you through."

I press the side of my head to his shoulder and keep my gaze locked on my hand tucked into the crook of his arm.

Gradually, the haze thins, and we step through. The disorientation fades the further away we get from the spelled fog.

The last of the pack is dispersing by the time Oliver and I made it through the border of trees to a clearing. The guards in charge of Alaric have already disappeared with him. Dozens of men, women, and children emerge to welcome back their loved ones and assist with the injured and the dead.

We stop beside a large pavilion attached to an elongated building, and I take in the small hamlet that is nothing like I expected. Instead of a stone wall surrounding a space cleared of natural vegetation and leveled, I'm greeted by the sight of something straight out of a fairytale.

Lanterns hang, stretching between branches, over the open space. From the western edge comes the sound of a gentle stream trickling over rocks.

Makeshift huts, built close together within the line of trees, form a horseshoe three rows deep. The shapes of the small dwellings are irregular, fitting into the landscape rather than intruding. Moss and vines grow up the outer walls, adding a sort of camouflage. Pale stone paths for walkways are between each, making it easy to see even in the dark of night.

"I can give you a proper tour after we've all had a chance to rest," Oliver offers. "Behind the pavilion are the kitchens." He directs my line of sight to the largest building in the direct center of the homes. "That building is our pack hall, where we hold council meetings, and mine is the one leaning against the right side. If you need me for any reason and can't find me, Hunt and Adalynd live in the two on the left."

He doesn't mention having family members. Whether something happened or not, it's clear by the set of his jaw that it's not a discussion he's willing to entertain. Much as he had with introductions, he tells me where everyone lives, whether I've been introduced to them or not.

"For your privacy, you will stay in the house beside mine," Oliver says. "Unless you would be more comfortable staying with someone? There are several members who would be happy to open their homes to you."

"You're letting me choose?"

He lists his head, then says, "Of course. You are our guest, not a prisoner."

I consider for a moment. "Where are you keeping Alaric?"

Someone more skilled in social niceties might ask where he was staying, but I don't see the point in pretending he isn't their hostage.

He is extending a great kindness to me, and while I am thankful, I cannot allow myself to forget that we are not on the same side. His duty is to his pack, and mine is to Alaric. Our objectives could align, but there is no guarantee. If I cannot persuade Oliver to ally with me, there is every possibility this fight will have three sides.

He sighs. If he were hoping I would forget about bringing it up, then he should have known better. "He will remain in the holding cells until we come to a decision."

I lift both brows. "And where are the holding cells?"

"The building behind the hall," Oliver gestures to the manor. "I figured you would want to be near him."

I nod. "I would like to see him."

"While you are free to come and go as you please, there are rules when it comes to prisoners," he adds quickly.

Of course there are rules. There are always rules. It would be remiss otherwise. Besides, I don't *plan* on breaking Alaric out. I have every intention of negotiating with them first.

"Then I accept your offer."

It's peculiar to hover in a gray area of trust. Knowing the person you're working with doesn't want to hurt you unnecessarily, but will if it's the only way to achieve their goal.

Oliver escorts me to where I'll be staying. It's a modest home, but sturdy and clean. Inside is a table with two chairs in front of the window that faces out on the clearing, with drapes made of undyed linen, pulled to the side with a cord.

Through the door, directly halfway in, is a full-sized bed. Across from that is a fireplace already burning away the chill, with two chairs and a settee on either side. Along the back wall is a dresser with a mirror with a pitcher and basin on top.

"The bathing room is through there. The water

reservoir should already be heating." He rubs the back of his neck and jerks his chin toward a door at the furthest corner. "It isn't much. I know you are accustomed to more luxurious accommodations—"

"No," I cut him off. "It's perfect." I take his hand in both of mine and squeeze. "This is far more than I could have asked for," I say, meaning it.

He visibly relaxes. "I will send someone with food and fresh clothes over within the hour. I'll be right next door should you need anything. You're welcome to knock, no matter the time."

"Thank you."

"Then I will leave you to rest." Oliver backs out of the door.

When I am alone, I sit on the edge of the bed, then fall back, stretching my arms over my head. These accommodations may not be opulent, but the mattress is soft, and the blankets are thick and warm.

For so much of my life, I never knew the luxury of safety when I slept. I'm thankful for it now. And it means more to me than any gilded adornment or several wardrobes filled with gowns made of the most expensive materials ever could.

I reach into my pocket and pull out the small vial, then tuck it under the mattress.

My stomach is growling by the time there's a knock on the door. I'm surprised to see Calla and her brother, who appears to be around ten years old. They each come bearing a basket. One with clothes and the other with meat and cheese wrapped in wax paper, a large heel of bread, a bottle of cider, and a plate and napkin.

As I eat, I think over the scraps of information I managed to wring from Oliver. He said they wouldn't make any hasty decisions regarding Alaric, but he also didn't make any promises to include me in any discussion, either.

At least I know where the holding cells are. I will go there every day, or every hour if I must, to make sure Alaric is treated well and remains unharmed.

CHAPTER TWENTY-THREE

ALARIC

"WHAT MAKES YOU THINK I WOULD WILLINGLY swallow your poison?" I cross my arms and lean against the wall, out of the young guard's reach.

That pain rises up like a noxious beast crawling and writhing under my skin.

"It's not poison. Now drink it," the young wolf says, shoving the vial into my cell. He can't be more than seventeen or eighteen years old.

Careless of him. With little effort, I could snap his bones before he could react.

"We will gladly chain you up if that is what it takes."

Whoever trained him did a poor job. I don't know if I should be insulted or amused that my abductors chose to put a veritable child on guard duty.

In a blink, I am standing before him, pulling his arm through the bars as far as it will go. The wolf's eyes go wide as he realizes his mistake too late. The fear makes him look years younger than I first judged him to be. He is lucky I've decided to only give him a warning.

"You dragged me to this demon-forsaken place, trussed up in night-forged silver binds—and you think such paltry threats will intimidate me?"

I squeeze his wrist until his grip loosens and releases the vial. I snatch it and let go of him. The young wolf retreats several steps and stares at me, mouth gaping.

"What is your name?"

"E-Emmett. Emmett Germaine."

"Never give your opponent the opportunity to draw you out, Mr. Germaine. Make them come to you."

"How?" The question seems to slip out unintentionally. Emmett throws a glance toward the stairs.

I turn away as I feel the venomous black veins slithering under my skin, across my back and abdomen. I pretend to study the liquid in the vial, hiding a grimace.

"What is this?" I hold it up to the weak light. It's milky against the green glass. Emmett says nothing. I lower my hand and send him a withering look. "The least you can do is tell me what this is, after I let you keep both arms intact," I add.

"It's only a simple nightshade tonic," he mumbles, dropping his chin.

A sleeping draught. My attempts at hiding my affliction have not been sufficient. I pop the cork with a flick of my thumb and down the contents. It's bitter, lingering on the tongue.

"Learn their weaknesses so you can use them against them, and never reveal yours." I toss the empty vial to him and turn my back on the young guard.

His footsteps are almost silent as he departs. I wait until the door closes behind him before sitting on the narrow wooden bench with a thin, lumpy mattress I was so generously given to serve as a bed. The dirt floor is a more appealing option.

From what I can gather from the changing of the guard routine, they've kept me here for almost a full day. They have offered me food and water—everything except what I need.

Already I feel the tonic working. Forced unconsciousness will make me vulnerable to these wolves, yet the relief from the pain will be a blessing.

A temporary solution. If they can't come up with something more permanent, there is a good possibility these drab walls will be the last thing I see.

I am pulled from the vestiges of slumber by a sound that has haunted me, even in my unnatural sleep, since I first laid eyes on her

"Let me pass," a woman's voice carries from the top of the stairs.

"I have strict orders not to allow anyone in."

A lengthy silence follows. I listen for what my little nightmare will say or do to the unfortunate guard.

I flex my fingers to get my blood to move again. The cold that has stiffened my muscles indicates I was unconscious longer than anticipated. A full day, at least. Possibly two.

"Miss Valmont," the alpha's voice croons with an obnoxious amount of cheer. "What a pleasant surprise running into you." There's a pause followed by his laugh. "What are you doing?"

"Checking to see if you have a fever."

"Nonsense. I am as healthy as ever."

"Then what other reason could you have for saying something so idiotic?" my nightmare snaps.

I snort. If I didn't know better, I would say she was a demon in the form of a woman.

They lower their voices, and I am unable to make out the rest of their conversation. A moment later, the door opens and then closes.

"I don't think it's a good idea," he says placatingly.

"Demon shit," she spits. "How long do you plan on keeping him locked up?"

Eavesdropping is for thieves and spies, yet I have little choice with so few resources to draw from. She has haunted me since I first laid eyes on her. I don't know what she wants from me, but if she thinks to gain my confidence under false pretenses, then she will be disheartened to know it won't work.

"We can't trust him."

"Trust goes both ways, and you haven't even tried," she says. "He isn't dangerous."

Even I wonder if her sanity is intact. Vampires are, by definition, dangerous. I remain perfectly still so as to not draw their attention.

"Give me a chance to earn his trust."

"He is *cursed,* Clara, of course he is dangerous," the alpha hisses. "We had to subdue him yesterday, because of what it was doing to him. It might be a while still before he wakes."

Cursed? That is impossible. Signs would have shown within the first months after I turned, not well over one hundred and fifty years later.

Clara sniffles. "How could she do that to someone she loves?"

"Elizabeth doesn't love him," he says. "She only wants his love to fill the void of heartbreak another caused long ago… Well, that's what many believe."

Just when I think she has given up, she speaks again. "Please, Oliver. If he's sleeping, I'll turn around and leave, but I need to see him."

"Very well. I will be right outside if you need anything."

She doesn't make a sound until he is gone. I keep my body still as her footsteps near. I'm on my side, with my back to her, yet I can still sense her approach the bars.

She sighs. I listen to her steady breathing for several minutes until she shifts her weight and begins walking away.

"That is a pathetic attempt, little nightmare." I don't know why I speak at all. I had no intention of entertaining any of her attempts at manipulation.

I hear her sharp intake of breath, then I sit up and face her. She is a better liar than I would have given her credit for.

"Did you really come here to stare at my back?" I ask mockingly.

She cocks her head and gives me an unamused look. "How long were you pretending to be asleep?"

The way she speaks to me as though we were equals is as jarring as ever. I glare, not deigning to answer her. "Why are you here?"

Clara wraps her hands around the iron bars and rests her forehead against them. "I wanted to make sure you were well," she says, as if it were obvious.

"Is anyone kept in a cramped cage ever truly doing well?" I gesture to the cramped cell. "You have seen. Now you can put your mortal mind at ease and go about your day playing with those dogs."

No matter my tone, she never takes offense. In fact, she appears amused as she lowers herself to sit on the ground, sitting back on her heels, hands resting in her lap. She watches me. Studying. I can't fight the whisper of sensation that feels as though the way she looks at me means so much more than she lets on.

"I'm glad you are awake." My little nightmare grins, cuts a glance toward the door, then whispers, "I was tempted to wake you so we could talk."

The corners of my mouth twitch before I force them back into a scowl. "Why are you here?" I repeat.

She pouts, then says, "I told them I would earn your trust—believe it or not, I *am* trying to get you out of here..." Her brows furrow, then she shoves an arm through the bars. "Do you need to feed? There probably isn't much time—"

"Little nightmare, whatever game you are playing,

I will not be so easily manipulated into being used as a pawn."

She heaves a sigh, retracting her arm. "Alaric Devereaux, I am not using you," she admonishes.

I scoff and lean forward. "Liar—everything you say and do is a lie."

"How can I prove—"

"You can't," I cut her off.

She throws her hands up and growls in a very human-like manner. Her frustration is almost endearing. "If I can't earn your trust, they will keep you locked up. Is that what you want?"

I fold my arms over my chest. How long will it take for her to stop dancing around everything she is hiding? "It's fascinating how you can be so dishonest without speaking a blatant lie."

"Then ask me whatever you want, and I will tell you everything."

As I rise, she mirrors the movement. I approach the bars, and rather than retreating, she inches closer. My hand is around her throat between one heartbeat and the next. She stiffens at the sudden movement but doesn't struggle.

"You should have seen that coming," I snarl. My grip is firm but careful. This confounding creature is entirely too relaxed for her own good. The slight flexing of my fingers is all it would take to snuff out her life.

She simply shrugs. "I took a calculated risk. Besides, I know you're just trying to frighten me, you won't hurt me."

"There is something unnatural about you, little

nightmare."

"Clara," she says. At my arched brow, she clarifies, "You can call me by my name if you'd like."

Gold flecks are scattered within her warm brown eyes. My thumb strokes the column of her throat. I can practically taste the blood flowing under her skin. It calls to me like a siren's song. Hypnotizing. I release her and take a step back.

Her eyes are glassy, and she bites her bottom lip and nods as if in answer to some unspoken question. "This isn't how, or where, I wanted to tell you, but there is something you need to know," Clara begins. She looks off to the side, wrings her hands, then takes a deep breath. "We are oath bonded."

I stop breathing.

I'd expected her to use this supposed curse to manipulate me into doing her bidding or attempt some elaborate twisting of the truth...

Nothing could have prepared me for those four words.

It cannot be true.

"*Liar.*" I am to be bound to Elizabeth... she would know if I were already bound to another. *I would know.* "I would never tie myself to a mortal—let alone one my queen detests," I snarl.

My nightmare flinches but keeps her head held high. Her calm demeanor is unnerving. "Your queen is the one who cursed you."

"No." My denial is weak. I back up, needing space between me and this... *demon.* This woman must be a demon—there is nothing else she can be, nothing else that makes sense. "If that were true, she would have killed you for the insult alone. And yet, you live."

She nods. "When Cherno told me what happened, part of me thought she would kill me the first chance she could." A frown settles on her features. "I think… the only reason she hasn't is because of a deal you made with her. At least, that's the only thing I've been able to come up with."

"What would she want that I have not already freely given?"

Clara blinks. "You never wanted to sit on the throne."

My blood chills. Elizabeth has had my undying loyalty since I was first turned. I would do anything she wanted, be anything she wanted.

Not for a second had I ever sought to wear the crown or possess the power that comes with it. I accepted only to please her.

I have kept this secret closely guarded, never speaking it aloud or showing any hint of its truth. This nightmare should never have been able to guess.

"You agreed to be her consort in exchange for my protection. But when she realized we were oath bonded, that is when she cursed you." She reaches for me through the bars.

"The oath bond is no light matter. In all my days of being a vampire, I have never wanted to be connected in such a permanent way to anyone. I doubt a mortal woman could so easily trick me into doing so."

She flinches. "It wasn't a trick. I would never—"

"Leave."

"Let me explain everything from the beginning, then you will understand."

"Leave!" My back presses into the cold stone wall. "Get out!"

Her fingers curl into her palm. She hesitates. "If you change your mind, I will tell you."

At the top of the stairs, the door hinges screech. She stares at me with a mix of hurt and determination, then turns and walks away.

I slide down the wall to the ground.

No.

Nothing she claimed can be anything but a deception.

I refuse to be so easily turned against my queen.

Elizabeth loves me.

Then my throat goes dry when I realize she has called me "my love," but I cannot recall a moment when she ever said that she loved me.

After Clara is gone, a guard comes to check on me. Hours later, another comes with a bowl of food and water. I ignore them, focusing on untangling the turmoil my nightmare has caused.

A small voice in the back of my head whispers words that chip away at my reality.

Since I have agreed to become Elizabeth's consort, an incessant hunger gnaws away at my insides. Never ceasing. And though I am loath to admit it, this mortal's blood has been the only thing that has provided a respite from that demand.

Her whispered words with that wolf could have been a clever ruse to make her deceit seem more believable. Yet I can't help feeling as though she hadn't intended for me to overhear. The surprise when she realized I was awake seemed genuine.

Her simple lies should be easy to unravel, yet they only make it harder to hold onto what I know is true.

What I wouldn't give for another vial of that bitter draught to drown me in the darkness of unconsciousness just to escape these thoughts.

I lie down on the uncomfortable mattress and try not to think of truth and lies. Like a true nightmare, she plagues me.

It's impossible to stop thinking of her and how she bends my power to her will... precisely the way my shadows reached out for her against the side of that barn and again in the cave.

CHAPTER TWENTY-FOUR

CLARA

LAUGHTER RINGS THROUGH THE DINING ROOM AMONG the chatter of multiple conversations at once. After Alaric refused to see me again today, I hadn't felt like being around others. So, when Oliver knocked on my door with an invitation to have lunch with him and a few other pack members, I tried to refuse. But that stubborn wolf wouldn't take anything other than a yes for an answer.

Not wanting to put a damper on everyone's mood, I keep myself occupied with the food on my plate. I answer questions in between bites but otherwise say very little.

A few have thrown warm, furtive smiles in my direction when they noticed my somewhat distant demeanor. I appreciate everyone respecting my feelings rather than pointing them out or making a scene.

Stop moping, Varin chides.

I stuff another bite of food into my mouth. *I'm not moping.*

Varin harrumphs, and I chomp down on the tip of my tongue. I pull in a long, calming breath and take a sip of water, choosing to ignore their petty antics.

Do you think it was a mistake to tell him?

The demon hums, considering, before finally answering. *It was never going to be easy for your vampire to accept while he is under the influence of the curse. There is no telling what he would have done had he been free this past week. Unpleasant as it is to be locked away, these wolves will not harm him for now. They seem to have good intentions, but I know they are hiding something.*

For days now, Alaric has instructed the guards to refuse me when I try to see him. At first, they simply shrugged and told me to try again later or the next day. Soon, their looks turn to pity.

As a consolation, they update me on how he's doing.

They say after my visit, Alaric became docile. Quiet. He no longer flings sharp comments or argues with any orders. He eats their offered food and drinks the cups of my blood sent to him when their tonic isn't enough to push down the effects of the curse. Though he hasn't asked, he must know where it comes from.

Elizabeth's control is weaker away from Nightwich. He is more himself, though he still doesn't remember anything. I thought—hoped—it would have broken by now.

Curses do not work that way—least of all, this particular kind. No one has ever come close to breaking it.

"Clara?" Oliver's voice cuts through the din of

conversation. My head jerks up, and I raise my brows, not wanting to talk with a mouth full of food. "Will you be joining us for the celebration tonight?"

I furrow my brow. "Tonight?"

"Of course she is," Calla cuts in. "I've already had a dress taken to her room." Then at the baffled expression I continue to give them, she turns on Oliver. "Did you bother to say anything to her?"

"It must have slipped my mind," he admits, grinning sheepishly, and dodges her attempt to swat his arm.

The two of them bicker playfully while laughing.

Adalynd shakes her head and turns to me. "It's the night where we call back the moon and welcome new beginnings. There will be food and—" she smirks in Oliver's direction. "—and a lot of mead."

For as long as I can remember, night has always been a time to take shelter in the home, safe from the outside world. No one in Littlemire would risk being caught outside after sunset.

Of course, within the bounds of the Keep, it is entirely void of demons. Well, all but one. So even if the wolves couldn't fight them, there would be no need to fear them.

Oliver leans over the table. "Come, even for an hour."

I look around the table at everyone waiting to hear my answer. My dark mood makes me hesitate, though something tells me that refusing isn't any more of an option than this meal.

Still, there are more reasons to go than not.

"I would love to," I say.

For the remainder of the meal, they all take turns regaling me with stories from years past.

From what I can tell, the entire pack is crammed into the clearing. Bodies crowd the outer edge, a mix of wolf and human forms. Inside the ring of spectators, they dance. Some in pairs, and others are alone, jumping in and out of the circle, clapping and singing, while others shift to howl at the dark sky.

The night air is fragrant with the scents of burned sugar and honeyed wine. Lanterns hang from twine strung through tree branches, crisscrossing over the clearing. It's livelier than any party or celebration I've ever been to, and I find it almost overwhelming.

I weave in and out of the throng in search of Oliver. My goal is for him to see that I came. Then, the first chance I get, I will sneak away to the quiet of my room. I spot him engrossed in conversation with a small group. When I catch his eye, I smile and wave.

There. Mission accomplished.

Now to find my way out of this labyrinth of bodies.

It takes a lot of dodging and side stepping to inch toward the edge of the crowd. I am nearly out when a movement off to the side catches my attention. I scramble to get out of the way and accidentally bump into someone.

Before I can apologize, a ruddy blur plows into

me, knocking me on my ass. The beast lands on top of me, sending me sprawling onto the grass.

Two large amber eyes blink down at me from the ruddy wolf pinning me. A large pink tongue lolls out of the beast's maw as it makes a sound that is a mix between panting and... *laughter?*

The wolf changes into a man. Oliver props his chin on one hand, and plays with my hair with the other, twirling a strand around a finger. "You weren't thinking of leaving already, were you? The night has just begun." His breath smells of sweet wine.

"Oliver," I say slowly. He hums, grinning wider. "Get off of me."

At that, he pouts. Just when I think I will have to forcibly remove him, he leaps to his feet, pulling me with him. I've barely caught my balance before he's dragging me to a table. Oliver shoves a glass with sparkling golden liquid in my hand.

I start to protest but he pops a slice of caramelized peach into my mouth as I inhale. Thoroughly unprepared, I end up half choking on the bite-sized piece of food and it takes the entire glass of mead to recover. He gets rid of the empty glass, and in the next moment he is leading me into the mass of dancing couples.

"Are you hoping I will send you into the Otherworld tonight?" I ask with false sweetness.

Oliver sighs wistfully as if I hadn't just threatened him. I wonder how much he has had to drink. I try to pull away, but he holds firm.

"I do not feel like dancing," I grind out.

"This is a night for joy. For a few hours, set worry

and sorrow to the side," he says, then tips me back so far, that the ends of my hair brush the ground. "I have a gift for you."

We straighten, continuing to whirl to the music.

"I don't want or need anything." I stop fighting. It's not doing any good, and Varin is no help.

Oliver smiles. "I promise you will want this one."

I cannot tell if he is too drunk to hide how pleased he is with himself or if he's teasing me. We stop at the crowd's edge, out of the way. Oliver tilts his head to the side, gesturing, and I turn to look.

"He is free, at least for tonight," he whispers in my ear as my gaze lands on Alaric.

My breath catches in my throat. Our eyes snag. Alaric glares, then quickly looks away.

"Of course, there are guards everywhere, should he try anything he ought not to…."

I move to go to him, but Oliver pulls me back. "Give him time to regain his bearings. He will find his way to you." He lifts my chin with a knuckle. "In the meantime, why don't you try to enjoy yourself?"

I nod and let him pull me into another dance. As much as I hate to admit it, he's right. Alaric and I are not of the same mind yet. And I wouldn't want to be rushed if I were in his place, so I must be patient.

"Congratulations on your bond, Miss Valmont. Forgive me for not saying so earlier."

Caught off guard, I feel warmth rise to my face. "Oh, umm… is that something people are usually congratulated for?"

Oliver gives me a bemused grin. "I don't see why not. It is something rarely seen."

Before I can thank him, the music changes and all the couples split up. The dance transforms, and I'm pulled in the opposite direction. At nearly every turn, we have a new partner. I take Oliver's advice, and soon, I lose myself in the music and the joy of those around me.

Between songs and glasses of honeyed wine, it's all too easy for time to slip away. Eventually, the rhythm changes again, and everyone pairs off. Oliver finds me and sweeps me into another dance. This one is slower than the last several.

I finally have a chance to catch my breath. My head swims pleasantly. When I look around, we are on the outer fringes of the crowd. Somehow, he guided me out of the throng without my noticing. Those drinks must be stronger than I realized.

Oliver pulls me in close, his arms wrapping around me intimately. "I am glad you decided to stay and enjoy yourself, after all."

"What are you up to now?" I ask, narrowing my eyes.

Oliver lowers his mouth to my ear, cupping the back of my neck with one hand. "He hasn't taken his eyes off you for a moment." He laughs softly. "I thought perhaps a little jealousy might spur him into action."

I groan at his antics.

"You should do that again, it might hurry him up."

Demons take me. "You shouldn't tease him," I admonish. "He's been through enough already."

Oliver pulls his head back. "It is unavoidable that we must all deal with unpleasant things to get the reward we seek." He turns us and winks, mouthing, "It's working."

The song ends, and he releases me. Bowing, he brings my hand close to his as if to kiss my knuckles. Instead, he whispers against my skin. "You can thank me later."

And then he's walking away.

CHAPTER TWENTY-FIVE

CLARA

Now that I am no longer moving or surrounded by a host of other bodies, the night air chills me, sending a shiver skittering over my skin. My fingers trace over a beaded detail of my skirt as I try to keep from searching for Alaric. Though I can only keep my hands busy like that for so long before it will look conspicuous.

Minutes pass, and uncertainty creeps in. When Oliver rushed off, it made me think Alaric was already on his way over.

Not wanting to give myself time to wonder if he changed his mind, I meander toward the pavilion to grab a drink, then sit on a bench where I can watch the revelers from a distance.

I sigh and drop my head back to gaze at the moonless sky through the opening in the canopy. Two pools of midnight ringed in crimson peer down at me.

My heart flutters, trapped in my throat. Alaric

shifts, moving to the side. I set my glass down as my gaze follows him. He clasps his hands behind his back and watches the celebration for a long moment. When he looks at me again, his expression is impossible to read.

"Your willingness to move on, despite your claim of being oath bonded, is quite *singular*." His tone is barbed and stings. "I shouldn't be surprised, and yet I am."

Heart sinking, I lower my head, unable to find the words to respond. What did I expect when we parted on bad terms the last time we spoke? It was naïve to believe things would be better between us simply because *he* approached *me*.

"I… apologize," Alaric says haltingly. "I shouldn't have said that."

My head jerks up. "What?"

"I can't put my finger on it, but there is something about that man that strokes my ire." He gestures in the general direction Oliver had walked in. Alaric's midnight eyes flick to my face, looking like he wants to say something more, but hesitates. Clearing his throat, he shoves his hands into his pockets.

He's probably waiting for me to respond. Or breathe. But I am frozen with warring uncertainty. The biting comment wasn't directed at me but rather toward Oliver.

Alaric sighs in concession, then lifts his arm, holding his hand out. "Shall we call a truce?" he asks almost grudgingly.

This moment feels important, and the words poised on the tip of my tongue are of how much I love him. My fingers itch to slide over his shoulders and embrace him. I still lack control over my heightened emotions.

After a painfully long moment, the tentative hope glittering in his eyes fades, and his arm slowly lowers.

Saying anything at this point would be an improvement. Are you able to handle this, or must I take over? Varin's sarcastic tone jostles me into action.

"A truce," I finally blurt, nearly stumbling to grab his hand. "I-I would like that."

One corner of his mouth curls. I let go, but his fingers remain curled around mine. His hold is firm yet gentle enough for me to pull away. I don't. Neither of us does. Not until the moment has stretched out longer than the situation warrants.

"Would you care to dance?" he asks.

"Yes… I would like that." My voice has gone breathy, but I don't care because the man I gave my heart to has found a way to reach out through the cracks forming in the curse.

A smirk plays across his lips at my lacking vocabulary. The music is a faster number, meant for switching partners after almost every turn. We don't acknowledge it, too lost in a world of our own. A spell as delicate as spider silk wound around us from the moment we touched.

Slowly. Very slowly, Alaric moves my hand to his other and steps in until barely more than a breath separates us. His palm alights on my hip, fingers flexing over the curve.

As he begins to lead, I follow. I cannot take my eyes off him. It's almost unfair how beautiful he is.

Strong jaw, full mouth, expressive eyes that can are both warm and sharp, framed by thick, black lashes, high cheekbones, and everything I know about him—all the reasons I came to love him—make each of his features more striking, as though his appearance is the physical manifestation of who he is at his core.

"You are a better dancer than I expected," he says, then cringes, belatedly realizing I could take it as an insult. If it wasn't for Varin's shared ability to see better in the dark, I would miss the way Alaric's cheeks slightly pinken.

"Is my upbringing that obvious?" I say with a light laugh. "It's all right. I am not ashamed of my less-than-noble upbringing. What skill I possess I owe to my lessons with you."

His posture stiffens, lips drawn into a thin line, and I worry my comment was insensitive.

"It is a peculiar feeling…" he says, looking off into the distance over my head. He frowns slightly. "This familiarity with you, to know we have a history together, while I lack any memories to draw from."

"The curse took your memories. If I can break it, then perhaps…."

"It is unbreakable." Though he speaks matter-of-factly, he cannot disguise the crestfallen pain his words cause him.

I refuse to believe that of this man, who has sacrificed his freedom for his sister and me, over and over… I can think of no greater injustice than to sit back and accept his inevitable demise.

"Isn't that the nature of curses—to be broken?"

"Perhaps some, not this one."

"There must be a way," I insist.

We have stopped dancing now, but our bodies remain close.

Alaric shakes his head. "If there is, it is a price no one is willing to pay."

"I will." Two simple words, yet it is a heavy vow. "Whatever the price—I will."

Alaric arches a brow. "If you can manage to pull off the impossible, but my memories never return— what then?" The question is uttered quietly as if he is afraid to hope.

"Then I will tell you all I can, and so will Cherno… and Lawrence and Della, and even Cassius." His expression makes my heart ache. "It won't be everything, but maybe it will be enough." I curse myself for each word that falls out of my mouth because my attempts to make things better seem to do the opposite.

Alaric doesn't respond, only continues to lead me. After a few steps, he stops beneath a tree and leans against it, and as he does, his hands remain where they are, bringing me with him so the front of my body is pressed to his.

"Why?" he asks. "Why follow me here? Why fight for me? Why attempt something so hopeless for my sake?" The genuine lack of understanding is stark. Unguarded. Painful.

"No one deserves to be treated like an object to be bartered for another's gain," I tell him. "I do it because you deserve to be saved."

I hadn't noticed the way we gradually leaned in, pulled by the gravity of each other's gaze, until now.

"Am I so weak as to need saving?"

"We cannot always be the one to save others. Everyone needs to be saved sometimes. That doesn't make you weak—it makes you real."

"Is that the only reason?" Alaric's breath is warm against my lips.

I can't help the warmth that tugs the corners of my lips into the beginnings of a smile. "Don't you know?"

He starts to shake his head, then stops. "Perhaps I need to hear it spoken aloud."

"Because I love you." The response is immediate, without a breath of hesitation.

Alaric sucks in a breath and holds it. The way he looks at me with awe and surprise flitting across his features as if he thought I wouldn't say it. The intensity in his eyes has heat rising up my neck.

"It is a bit terrifying to think I might never regain what I have lost... but I find you infinitely more terrifying. Because only when I am with you do I feel as if I am more than a monster."

"You are no monster." I flatten my hands against his stomach, the hard plains of his body tense beneath my touch. "I chose you and would do so again because I love you, every side of you, every version of you— your every strength and flaw because they are all part of you."

Alaric takes my chin between his thumb and forefinger. "You should forget about me. If I can never go back to being the man I used to be, I may never be able to return your love with my own... not in the same way."

I freeze. It's hard to breathe. My throat tightens

with emotion. I lower my gaze to the knot of his cravat. Before my thoughts can turn sharp and cutting, I force myself to speak. "It would not be love if I thought you owed me your heart, or anything else, in return."

Strong arms encircle my waist, and I cling to Alaric, inhaling the comforting scent that lingers on his skin. I lean my head against his shoulder, and his cheek rests atop mine.

He rubs my back absentmindedly. Small circles become longer, then wander to my hips, my waist, then ribs, pausing when he grazes the bottom of my breast.

I turn my gaze up to look at him. His fingers slide to the center of my back, then up my spine. His touch is warm, brushing over the bare skin of my shoulder and tracing a path up my neck. Alaric cups my face, his eyes searching. Studying.

I am hypnotized by the way he looks at me—touches me. The pad of his thumb traces my bottom lip, and my eyes slide closed at the caress.

His lips skim across mine. Tentative and uncertain. He stills for a moment, giving me a chance to pull away, and when I don't, he kisses me again. His mouth moves over mine and I respond, matching his fervor. Each time he claims me with his lips is more confident than the last.

When I sigh, he loses the last thread of uncertainty. His tongue sweeps over mine. I slide my hands up his chest and around the back of his neck, curling my fingers in his hair. He shudders against me when my nails lightly scratch his skin.

It is so easy to get lost in him.

Alaric tightens his hold on me, moving the hand cupping my face, around to the back of my neck. He holds me tight as if he might refuse to let me go. His other hand inches to my low back, ridding even the smallest space between us. Need for him ignites my blood. And pressed against him as I am, I can feel he is equally affected.

He breaks the kiss but lingers, tongue dragging across my bottom lip. "You taste of peaches and honeyed wine."

A moan escapes me. "Yes," I say. Though it makes no sense. All the wine in the world couldn't do what this man does to me. Our chests press together with each of our ragged breaths.

"Would that I had another hour or three alone with you in that cave." His voice is low and gravelly.

Suddenly, my clothes feel restricting and cumbersome. I let out a shaky breath. "What is stopping you now?"

He groans. "If you continue to test my restraint? Nothing."

I nip at his bottom lip. "Damn your restraint to the Otherworld."

I'm about to lean into him again when a howl breaks through the fog. An unpleasant reminder that we are not as alone as either of us would like.

Surveying the revel, I note that no one is paying us any attention, too busy in the celebration's chaos or finding their own hidden corner of the world. No one stands in the way between here and my tiny cabin. I waste no time and tug him along.

After a few steps, he tugs my hand to get my attention. "I was told to stay where I can be watched," he says grudgingly.

"Then my watch will have to suffice," I say.

That is enough for him to relent. His hands skim around my waist, flattening against my stomach, and his mouth dances over my neck and shoulder as we walk. We end up stopping several times in the shadows, pressing against walls as his tongue traces the vein in my neck. The distance to our destination is too far to go without the feel of each other.

Finally, we make it, fumbling our way inside. The latch clicks into place, and we are alone. Truly alone.

Alaric whirls me, pinning me between him and the door. Without a fire in the hearth, the room is dark, lit only by the dim light of lanterns piercing the linen curtains over the window.

He looks at me. Traces his fingers over the features of my face. "You are beautiful. Though I suppose I must have told you that countless times, I cannot help but say it again."

I go still.

He lowers his hand, his guard slamming into place. "What is it?"

"I think you might have… once?" I say uncertainly.

He frowns, but the tension leaches out of him, and he shrugs. "Nevertheless, you are beautiful. And I look forward to discovering what it is that made me fall so madly in love that I would bind myself so irrevocably to you." He dips his head and trails kisses along my jaw, inching lower between words, making my nerve endings come alive and my skin more sensitive to his ministrations. "I wonder… could it have been the way you taste? Or was it the sounds you make? Perhaps it was the feel of your body…."

The heat in his voice, more than the words, exposes me more than if he stripped me bare before the world. Alaric trails a series of kisses down the column of my throat and over my shoulder. By the time he reaches the neckline of my dress, he's already loosened the lacing, so it easily heeds him.

"No…" he murmurs. "It wouldn't have been something so simple. Such things would only make it impossible to resist your claim on my heart." He takes his time, revealing me inch by inch, tasting my skin as his hands lift my skirt, allowing him to grip the backs of my thighs and pulls my hips against his.

He has never made me feel as if my worth to him was tied to the way I look, not even now. I wrap my arms around his neck as he takes the peak of a breast into his mouth. The sharp points of his fangs scrape over my flesh.

A moan slides from my throat. I am glad he is holding me upright because I do not think I could stand on my own if I tried.

He moves to the left and pauses long enough that I whimper. When his fingers brush over the scar above my heart, I freeze. It takes an effort to open my eyes and meet his gaze.

"What happened here?" he asks so quietly I barely catch it.

That is a whole other conversation I am not sure either of us is ready to have just yet. It would be easy to say it was nothing or that it happened a lifetime ago. Still, I cannot bring myself to diminish or lie about the reasons or costs of my actions.

So, I pull myself against him and bring my mouth to his, kissing him as if I am drowning and he is air. He yields to me, walking backward until he bumps into the bed and falls back.

CHAPTER TWENTY-SIX

CLARA

I land on top of him, straddling his hips, and reach for his shirt. As I work the first button open, Alaric captures my wrists, his eyes shining.

"No," he rasps.

We stare at each other for what feels like a lifetime. I frown, not quite understanding. I shift to move off him. "We don't need—"

Alaric rolls us, pinning my hands above my head. His chest rises and falls with quick breaths, body seeking mine even as he goes to stop this. "It's not that. I have every intention of taking you tonight," he tells me. Slowly, he releases my hands and sits back, turning his face away. "I do not want you to see… how monstrous I am."

The confession costs him. The way he feels about his scars is a wound all its own, invisible to the eye, yet bone deep. It's something he's carried with him for so long that not even Elizabeth's curse could erase it. When he'd given me the second mark, I hadn't known him well enough to see his insecurity, and he had no intention of bringing it to my attention.

I slide off the bed and stand. Alaric watches me cautiously as I slip my arms from the sleeves. The dress pools at my feet. "And my scars?"

Pain is written across his features as his gaze drifts from the web of scars at the crook of my shoulder, the still pink mark above my heart, gliding over to the slashing lines on my forearms and down to the four pale stripes over my abdomen. Then, lower still to the three jagged marks below the knee on my left leg.

"It is not the same." He shakes his head. "You are beautiful… and human."

"It is the same—whether you are human or vampire or demon," I say, stepping up to him. He reaches for me as if he can't help but grip my waist. "Your scars are the reminder that you fought to survive and won."

Alaric closes his eyes and swallows. And I know no one has ever told him that before because he has never allowed himself to share this vulnerability.

"You are perfect, inside and out."

When he opens his eyes again, he stands and curls a hand around the back of my neck, then rests his forehead against mine.

This time, when I go to unbutton his shirt, his midnight eyes lock intently on every movement of my fingers, breaths coming in quick, shallow bursts. But he doesn't stop me from sliding it over his shoulders and down his arms. I drag a finger over one of the raised lines.

He shudders and closes his eyes as I go from one

to the next, all the way down his abdomen. I lean forward and press a kiss along his jaw as I trace a scar below his waistband. That touch sets something off in him. His eyes flash, and the next thing I know, he lifts me up and lays me down on the bed.

Alaric prowls up my body. His mouth crashes down on mine in a bruising kiss. A fang nicks my lip enough to draw a bead of blood before it heals. As he nips, skimming his lips along my jaw, fangs dragging over skin, then lower still as a hand kneads my breasts. Every caress sets my blood aflame.

By the time I realize he doesn't intend to make his way back up, Alaric already has my hips pinned down. He waits for me to meet his gaze, then presses a kiss right below my navel.

I try to wriggle away, but I am shaking from need, and my attempts are weak and clumsy.

He kneels and settles between my thighs, draping my legs over his shoulders. His warm breath makes me ache for his touch. With a malicious grin, he slowly makes his way up and down the inner thigh of one leg and then the other.

"Please," I beg, not exactly sure what I am asking for. Just that I need him.

He chuckles against my skin, a light vibration. And when he finally reaches my core, I moan loud enough that I clap a hand over my mouth, afraid someone outside might overhear.

Then he moves against me, kissing and nipping. Every time his tongue darts out, my hips jerk involuntarily. A pleased, low rumble vibrates from him right before he drags his tongue up the length of my center. I grasp at the coverlet, trying to anchor myself.

His lips grow more and more demanding until I'm writhing beneath him. A palm slides up my stomach, pinning me down, and his other hand cups my ass, angling me to devour me deeper. The unrestrained fervor has pleasure coiling low, overwhelming, climbing higher and higher until I cry out.

Cool air replaces the warmth of his mouth. I prop myself up on my elbows. Alaric continues watching me from exactly where he's at, then slowly angles his head to the left, and my pulse kicks up. The sight of him there, knowing what he will do, leaves me breathless.

The points of his fangs pierce the skin of my inner thigh, and he drinks. Every time he fed since our oath bonding, it created an all-consuming desire, but none of them could begin to compare with this moment because it started with us.

My arms go boneless, and I collapse back. He slides a finger inside me, and I gasp for air, back arching. As he drinks, my body rocks against his hand. He moans against me and adds a second finger, increasing his pace as he works me. The sensations build faster and faster until my release rips through me. It is so much more intense than the first. I cry out, writhing against him as he draws out every ounce of pleasure.

Gradually, he slows. I don't realize he stopped feeding until the warmth of him is no longer there. He stands and stares down at me, grinning when I whimper. My gaze follows his movements as he undoes the stays at his waist and removes the rest of his clothing.

I take in the sight of him as he rejoins me on the bed, draping his body over me. He settles between my legs, his hard arousal trapped between us.

Alaric kisses me, slow and gentle, swallowing my needy whimpers as he drags his swollen length over me. I grasp at him, my hands trying to pull him closer to me.

He draws his head back and watches me with such intensity that my heart stutters as he positions himself against my entrance. The tip of his cock teases my core for an agonizingly long moment that threatens to drive me mad from need. He pins me with his gaze as he shifts, pressing his hips forward, achingly slow.

I gasp as I'm stretched to fit, never once looking away as he slides in and out, again and again, sinking deeper and deeper until he is fully sheathed. Alaric's expression is painfully tender. He brushes back a wayward lock of hair clinging to my damp skin.

Suddenly, I am overwhelmed by emotion. I don't know if I can contain it. Every look from him, the way he fills me, and the contrast of everything we've gone through. This moment is something we never had the time or freedom to share before. When we bound ourselves, it was a need we sated, with the knowledge that we could not linger. And now that we have time—it hurts because the curse has taken something vital from him.

"Clara…" He says my name as though he's afraid to breathe. "What's wrong? Did I hurt you?"

"No—" I shake my head and sniffle. "This is—" After forcing myself to take a calming breath, I try again. "I was afraid I might never be with you like this again."

Above me, I feel the tension melt from his muscles. He kisses my forehead.

"I'm okay now," I say. Then I bring his mouth to mine and kiss him fiercely.

He brings his hips back, then drives into me again. I shudder around him, and he groans, then continues stroking me, sliding languidly in and out as if trying to memorize how to pull every reaction and every sound from me.

Alaric kisses his way up my neck to my mouth, claiming the cry I make as he moves faster and harder. He nips along my jaw, tugging on my earlobe with his teeth. "If I had you like this every day for a thousand years, it still wouldn't be enough."

I smile at that. "I am yours. I'll always be yours. For a thousand years or as long as you want me."

The world tilts as he repositions himself under me, and my body adjusts on instinct, chasing the conclusion we both desperately crave. I rock against him as he drives himself even deeper than before. He grips my waist, controlling the pace, savoring every exquisite sensation, drawing out our mutual satisfaction.

"Let me see you come undone around me," he says, thrusting up. Alaric slides a hand lower, down to my core, drawing circles against the bundle of swollen nerves with his thumb.

My body moves without thought. Liquid heat

pools where our bodies are joined, pleasure so intense it aches. Alaric's thrusts grow harder, more demanding, meeting me move for move.

My release lashes through me. I cry out and shatter. He continues to move in and out, in and out. I am still reeling from my orgasm when Alaric is on top of me again, clutching my body tightly against his. The sharp points of his fangs pierce my shoulder as he drives into me rougher, deeper, more demanding, as if he needs as much of my skin against his as possible.

Moaning against me, he is relentless, prolonging every decadent sensation. I feel him thicken inside me right before he finds his release, riding it out on the crest of my own.

We continue to cling to each other as our movements turn languid, our legs tangled together, breaths mingling in the small spaces between us. Alaric kisses me on every inch of skin within reach. My shoulders, breasts, neck, mouth. Each one worshiping.

Eventually, we separate and crawl under the blankets. Alaric's arm curls around my middle, pulling my back against his chest.

"All those days in that cell, I tried to deny you and the things you said. But every day, every cup of blood you sent to me quieted my mind. I can remember nothing but being loyal to her, yet my body and my soul longed for you," he whispers into my shoulder.

I am unsure how to respond to that in a way that wouldn't sound arrogant. And I don't want to put added pressure on him as he struggles to find his own way. So, I say nothing.

"I cannot deny you any longer, even if I wanted to."

I take his hand and kiss his palm before pressing it against my cheek. He sighs and relaxes into me. Neither of us breaks the silence for a long time. The celebration's music continues beyond the walls of this small cabin, muffled and distant.

"Sometimes," Alaric says quietly. I am not sure if he knows if I'm awake or thinks I'm sleeping. "I feel as though I am fracturing, and at any moment, I might break into a thousand pieces."

My eyes prickle instantly. I do not know if he intends for me to hear, but I cannot bear to stay silent. I twist in his arms and cup his face. The tears fall when I blink, and I make no move to hide them. "If you fall apart, then I will help piece you back together."

He gazes at me with such raw emotion that this small moment is the most intimate thing I have ever experienced with anyone, even after the last hour. Every barrier we possessed has shattered, including the ones we never knew existed. What I said before—loving every side and every part of him—is true. I hadn't realized just how true until now.

"I will end this curse," I say again. "Or I will find a way for you to. Either way, I will be with you, and I will see you safe." I am not entirely sure why I say this to him again. I suppose I feel the need to give him something to hold on to—some comfort or sliver of hope.

He dips his head and kisses me in a way I can only describe as reverent. "I think I am beginning to understand why I fell in love with you in the first place," he whispers, eyes drifting closed.

He says it with all the importance of a passing thought, with no more consequence than a comment on the weather. I wonder if he is aware of what he said or what it means to me.

I am drifting off to sleep when the music stops. Rather than the gradual fade of festivities coming to an end, it's a jarring halt mid-song. Alaric stirs, his arms holding me a fraction tighter.

Good things tend to end far too soon, and it is because of their fleeting nature that we spend our lives chasing them. Wordlessly, we untangle ourselves and redress. Once we step outside, this private world we hid in will be gone. I'm not ready to let it go yet, but time doesn't care for the wants of the living.

Alaric follows a step behind as we make our way to the center of town. Pack members pass us, hurrying to return to their huts, some rushing with heads down, others helping those unsteady on their feet.

In the center of the clearing, Oliver is with Adalynd and Hunt, huddled close around a young, dark-haired scout I do not know. He is tall with a young face.

The scout looks up as we near, drawing the attention of the others to our approach.

"*You,*" Hunt seethes.

I draw up short, taken aback by the viciousness in his voice. He was always so mild-mannered before.

Hunt storms over. Oliver and Adalynd are not far behind. It's then I see what they were all looking at. In his fist, the scout has a tight grip on a small gray bat.

"Cherno?" I reach for the demon, but the scout yanks his arm back with a scowl.

"It's all right, that is my—our demon," I say. The only thing stopping me from further argument is the struggle behind me.

I whirl to find that the betas are restraining Alaric. Adalynd ties his wrists behind his back while Hunt holds a knife to his throat. I take a half step toward him, but Alaric flashes me a warning look.

"I will go with you willingly," Alaric says calmly.

Hunt leads him away, motioning for Adalynd to remain behind.

CHAPTER TWENTY-SEVEN

CLARA

"I caught this demon trying to get past the wards," the scout says. "I don't know how they tracked us, but I think it was trying to lead Elizabeth's army here."

"That's not true!" I snap. "Cherno would never do anything like that."

"It's a demon—of course they would," he retorts.

Oliver groans. "Give her the bat, Emmett."

Reluctantly, he opens his hand. Cherno leaps into the air, floundering slightly as they fly to me, tangling themselves in my hair. They peek out and chirp angrily at the young wolf for the rough treatment.

Adalynd looks from Emmett to Cherno, then over her shoulder to the tree line. She presses her lips into a thin line as she contemplates the situation.

Oliver remains silent.

"We should destroy the demon," she says finally. "If what Emmett suspects is true, there's no telling how close Elizabeth's army is."

I step back, reaching up protectively to block them. "You can't."

What would happen if they killed Cherno? I ask Varin.

It is difficult to say for sure, they begin slowly, *but it would destroy his powers at the very least. A demon will die if their vampire is killed, so I suspect it works the same the other way around. Though there is no guarantee.*

"We can—and we should, even if there is a small chance they were followed," Hunt grunts his agreement, rejoining the group and startling me. "For the good of the pack."

I level a glare at him before turning to Oliver.

"I told Cherno where to find me." That gets everyone's attention. "What about your wall? You said no one could get through without your help."

Adalynd folds her arms across her chest. "It might protect us, but what good is it if our enemies lie in wait on the other side? We'd be trapped here."

I take several steps back. "Oliver, you can't allow this to happen."

He is unfazed by the expectant looks his betas give. Then he shrugs. The casual gesture is out of place in this situation.

"Why don't you ask them if they were followed?"

Their wings flap against me. "No one followed," Cherno chirps.

"See?" I say, gesturing.

The three of them look at me as if I am insane while Oliver covers his mouth with a hand, trying— poorly—to hide a smile. "Would you mind translating for us?"

"She has your family," Cherno says at the same

time. "She will kill them in three nights if Alaric has not returned to her."

Blood roars in my ears, and my chest feels so tight I can't breathe. The world spins and quakes.

"Clara?" Oliver calls my name, but his voice is distant.

No....

I stumble. My legs give out from under me, and I drop onto my ass. Faces hover near me. They are speaking, but their voices are muffled, and I can't understand them. I can barely hear.

Use Alaric to free my family or sentence my family to death. How can I choose? How could anyone choose when it means death for someone they love?

"Let me through," I demand of the two guards standing between me and the room I desperately need to get into.

They shift into their wolf forms, blocking the double doors of the conference room. I try to slip past, but the one on the left leaps to bar the way. He snarls and snaps his teeth at me.

They won't actually hurt me, I remind myself. I flick his nose before thinking better. The guard sneezes uncontrollably for a minute.

The larger one growls, transforming back. "There's a pack meeting—and you're not pack," he grinds out, puffing out his chest. Though he is already an imposing figure, the posture makes him look even more intimidating.

"Considering the topic of discussion, I have every right to be in there." I try not to think what this wolf is capable of doing to stop me as I try again, pounding my fist on the door.

Two massive arms wrap around my waist and lift me into the air.

"Put me down!" I kick out my legs but find no foothold.

His growl vibrates in his chest against my back and rumbles in my ear. "A few hours in a cell might calm you down."

He carries me like I am a child. My attempts to free myself are in vain. The other guard, still in wolf form, snaps at my feet.

"I won't let you hurt him. I won't let you hurt either of them," I yell, knowing they can hear me inside.

We are halfway down the hall when the doors on the far end finally open, and Oliver steps out and glares. We all freeze.

He takes in the spectacle and sighs, pinching the bridge of his nose. He's been doing that a lot lately. "What in the Otherworld are you lot doing?"

"She's trying—"

"You have no right to decide their fate without me," I interrupt, struggling in the guard's hold.

The man at my back growls low in warning. Sick of it, I twist my head and bare my teeth at him, growling right back. I am sure it is the opposite of intimidating, but if he wants to bully me, I am not about to take it. He can use his words.

"Put her down, Liam," Oliver says wearily.

He sets me down gently, though I half expected to be dropped on my ass.

Oliver glowers at me, but I hold my ground, refusing to look away. At first, I don't think he will budge, but then he relents.

I follow when he motions with a jerk of his head. Stepping inside the meeting room, I find several faces scowling. Better they are irritated than think they can decide if someone else should decide without a single voice to defend them.

Oliver takes his place at the head of the table, his betas on either side. I am only slightly surprised when he arranges for me to sit beside Adalynd. It is a position that would normally grant someone more power than those further away. Yet this is not about giving me authority so much as keeping me close to those able to subdue me if I act out.

Several wolves throw sharp glances my way, not even disguising their displeasure at my intrusion.

Once the doors are shut, a man with a scholarly appearance stands and clears his throat. "The majority believe it would be best to kill both the vampire and his demon now. We could easily leave them on the border of her territory and avoid any... *unnecessary* conflict."

Unnecessary—I gape at him as I process his words, then at Oliver, who remains infuriatingly silent. Seconds tick by, and he doesn't object. And my blood begins to simmer.

I slam my hands down against the table. The impact sends pins and needles over my palms. Every set of eyes in the room turns to me.

"You were the ones that attacked Nightwich. You were the ones who abducted Alaric—and now you want to kill him to avoid *unnecessary conflict*?" I am relieved my voice comes out measured and unwavering. Because I feel anything but that.

"It is for the good of the pack!" he half growls the words.

"We are in this situation because of the pack's decisions. Or do you not care who pays the price for your actions?" I don't wait for his response. I lean past Adalynd to address Oliver directly. "You cannot allow this. Elizabeth has my family—if you harm him, she will kill them, and their blood will be on your hands."

"It is not my decision alone to make," Oliver says evenly. "If Elizabeth learns it was us, there is no telling what she will do."

"If you end up trapped here because of the fight you started, then so be it. At least you will all still have your lives. But you would condemn—"

"Elizabeth is the one who created the wall to keep the lands separate," Oliver interrupts. "If she followed that demon here, she'd stop at nothing to get what she wants. We can't risk her destroying it."

That sets me back. Knowing Elizabeth is strong enough to do something like that strikes a chord of fear in me. I lower myself to my seat.

"She doesn't just want him to soothe her ego," he continues. "She needs his power. If we allow her to crown him, it is a matter of when—not if—she moves against us whether she finds out we were behind the attack or not. We'll be lucky if the worst she does is trap us as well."

As well?

I do not know who else she has trapped, and I do not care to ask. That is a matter for another time. Right now, my only priority is finding a way to keep Alaric and my family alive. After learning about this meeting, I only had a moment to speak with Alaric to update him on the situation. He wore a grim expression that told me nothing of how he felt. Then he hadn't said anything, only nodded.

It was unfair of me, but I hoped he would give me some clue as to what to do.

"Your plan didn't work," I say. "You need to let him go." I cannot bring myself to say return him to her—because I don't want that. And I will not allow them to take away my only chance to save Kitty and Father.

They will never relent if I can't offer an alternative. As I take in each face in the room, I realize they are satisfied with their decision. It is up to me alone to find a solution.

I wrack my brain. In the halls of Nightwich, Hunt grinned at me and called Alaric bait....

An idea brews, slowly taking shape. There is a slim possibility that it will work, but I don't see any other option.

"We will make Elizabeth believe that we'll turn Alaric over to her, long enough to see my family free."

Without waiting for further explanation, everyone talks all at once, pointing out the flaws of the idea to negate any merits it has.

A man at the far end scoffs. "He is the queen's lapdog. If we give him half a chance, he will find his way back to her, begging to lick her boots while telling her everything. It will only put us at risk."

"You don't know him. And killing him or holding him prisoner won't serve your goals."

"You know nothing of our goals," a woman on the far side of the table says. "You are merely an interloper here."

Cutting a glance her way, I ask, "Do you think Elizabeth will simply let the matter go if he is nothing but a corpse?" I shake my head. "She will not stop until she finds whoever is responsible."

I know I should avoid stepping on toes. Yet there is no time to waste pandering to their feelings or expectations of diplomacy. I am not above issuing a threat if it will stay their hand. Every minute that passes is one less I have to put a plan in motion.

"Elizabeth needs him alive," I say. The room falls silent. The scholarly man sneers, but I continue before he can speak. "I don't know how long he has until the curse consumes him. And unless anyone knows of another way to break it, she is the only one who can."

The scholarly wolf snorts. "She won't need him alive once she oath bonds him to her long enough to take his power."

I pull in a shuddering breath. I want to believe she wouldn't leave him cursed, though I know better. Once Elizabeth gets what she wants, he will have served his purpose.

Except I am standing in her way.

I know little about magic, though it is too real that she could find another way to seize his power without an oath bond.

"Even if she regains control over Alaric, she cannot oath bind him because he is already bound to me." I send a pointed glare at everyone, squashing any lingering doubt about my right to be present at this meeting.

A few wolves attempt to stand, retaking their seats when Oliver waves his hand. "What exactly are you proposing, Miss Valmont?"

My idea is half-formed at best. With more time, perhaps I could come up with something that could offer us a better chance of outmaneuvering her. "Make her think she won."

"I'm listening," Oliver says, cocking his head to the side.

"When you attacked Nightwich, you went after Elizabeth. And when you couldn't get to her, you took Alaric hostage to use as bait."

Hunt makes a choking noise. Adalynd levels him with a glare, prodding him in the ribs with her elbow.

"What I propose is this: We use him as bait. I will go under the pretense of returning him. She will expect me to bring whatever show of force I can cobble together—but if I show up alone, it will take suspicion off the pack." I take a breath. "Once my family is safe… I'll release Alaric, giving him a chance to get her to break the curse."

"Why would she believe a human could carry out such a feat?" the scholarly man laughs.

"If she asks, then I will say I used the attack as a distraction and drugged him with nightshade."

Murmurs fill the room. Many of the wolves wear smirks that make it clear they have no issue with me risking my neck. That ends when Oliver rises from his chair. A low warning rumbles from his chest.

"We led the attack and took her prince captive, so we cannot expect you to clean up our mess," he says, looking around the room and making eye contact with each member. "Especially when it is you who stands to pay the price for it."

I shake my head and open my mouth to speak.

"We will remain out of sight. But we will be there to aid you and your family," he says, tone resolute.

CHAPTER TWENTY-EIGHT

CLARA

The trees begin to thin as we near the forest's edge. Cherno sleeps in one of the saddlebags, hiding from the sun that weakens them. Our return to Nightwich has come far too soon for my liking.

I don't know if I'm ready. But we don't have the luxury of time. Alaric and I ride Nyx while a small group of reinforcements travel beside us in wolf form.

"You don't have to do this," I say. Though my entire plan depends on his willing participation, I do not want to use him… and that is exactly what this feels like. "We can think of some other way."

After the meeting, I went straight to see Alaric and filled him in on everything. And I have been trying to talk him out of it since he agreed to go along with it.

Alaric leans forward in the saddle, his chest warm against my back. The hand resting at my hip slides across my stomach, fingers splaying, pressing me tighter against his body.

"You said yourself there is not enough time to come up with anything else. And if Elizabeth is the one who cursed me, then only she can remove it." When he speaks, his lips brush the shell of my ear. The heat of his breath reminds me of how it felt against other sensitive places of mine.

He is trying to distract me. And it is nearly working.

Several yards ahead, Oliver comes to a stop and shifts into human form, then the rest of the pack follows suit. Alaric dismounts, then hands me down.

I cling to him, soaking up as much comfort from his firm grip as I can. "I will come back for you. I promise," I say. "Get her to break the curse—whatever it takes."

Adalynd pulls something from a bag strapped across her shoulders and hands it to Hunt, then reaches for another.

They each hold a round, clear glass bottle wrapped in gilded filigree with an atomizer pump filled with a cobalt blue liquid. They go around spraying each pack member before coming over to us.

Adalynd lifts her hands, ready to spray, and pauses. "It's exactly what it looks like," she says. Then narrows her eyes at Alaric and adds, "Nothing more than a simple perfume I found in a human market, but it will disguise our scent."

Between the two betas, they have Alaric and me, and even Nyx sprayed in no time. I inhale, wanting to identify anything about the perfume that could explain how it could keep vampires from recognizing the wolves through scent. It's slightly floral and woodsy with a smoky incense underneath. The fragrance is faint, especially considering the amount used.

There must be something my human nose can't pick up that is the source of its magic. Despite what Adalynd claimed, I doubt it is something so simple.

The wolves break off into three groups. One to the north, another to the south, the last remains here—they will follow us at a distance.

For a few minutes, we are alone. This feels like a moment for no longer holding back the things I have been wanting to say. For last confessions. For all those words that people always wish they said before it was too late.

But I don't say any of them. Doing so would seem too much like surrendering before the fight even began.

Alaric leans over and kisses my forehead, then holds out his hands for me to tie. My efforts at binding him are halfhearted until he lightly chastises me for making them too loose. When I'm done, I check to ensure they don't chafe his wrists.

I look up and meet his gaze. His expression is hard, and there are shadows in his eyes. Deep down, Alaric is still the man I've known him to be. It's in the way he moves, thinks, acts...

As much as I want to believe he is wholly loyal to me, that there is no question in his mind that everything I told him is the truth—deep down, I am afraid the curse has too tight a hold on him. That once he is with Elizabeth again, she will make him believe he is the hollow version of himself that she crafted… and I am terrified that the night we spent together was nothing more than a dream.

"You look uncharacteristically frightened," he says.

I release a shuddering breath and nod. "I wish I could say I wasn't." He arches a thick, dark brow in question. "I've asked a lot of you recently."

"I told you—"

"Not just this plan," I say. "*Everything*. Who we were—are to each other, our oath bond, the curse…." My words trail off.

Oliver clears his throat. He nods to me from several yards away, signaling that it's time. There's only a short window of opportunity. Alaric and I need to be out in the open while there is still plenty of daylight to make sure the guard sees us, but not so much that we'd be waiting long enough for Elizabeth to question why he hasn't tried to escape.

"It's a lot to ask you to believe," I add quietly, hating that the fears and doubts I have about him are stark, even without voicing each one.

"It is," he says. The admission is slow and measured. "Yet I cannot deny the evidence, and the longer I thought about it, the more everything supported what you said, and Elizabeth's claims fell apart under the weight of it."

The best I can do is offer a weak smile. I reach into a saddlebag for a borrowed dagger. With the weapon in one hand, I grab the tail of the rope with the other, then lead him forward.

I pause when we are beside Oliver. "No matter what, stay out of sight unless I signal. We are not here to fight."

He still looks displeased but doesn't argue.

From here, Alaric and I go alone. Neither of us speaks. He has his reasons. As for me, my nerves are wound so tight I might get sick. What horrible things have Kitty and Father been forced to endure at Elizabeth's hands?

This has to work.

I have to believe it will.

Varin has been quiet, though still present. I can feel their partial control in every movement.

In the space between bare branches, the forbidding silhouette of Nightwich looms. Its towers are sharp spikes that pierce the sky.

We step out from under the cover of trees. I hold the rope taut and hold the point of the dagger against his ribs. He hisses through his teeth at the prodding.

"Sorry—"

"Leave it," he says, cutting me off when I start to pull back.

Without knowing how far Elizabeth will push me, I didn't want to take the chance that I might have to use my weapon on Alaric. So, I left the night-forged silver dagger with Oliver and borrowed one made of steel.

Alaric and I are not out in the open for long before I spot the queen and her entourage emerge from the castle. My breathing is coming too fast. Among them, I see a guard walking with Father, and after another moment, Kitty comes into view. I had half feared she would bring them out, already cold and lifeless.

"We must choose to trust each other now," Alaric says under his breath.

Not daring to speak, I hum in agreement.

Days-old snow crunches beneath our footsteps. The sky is a solid cover of turbid gray clouds, and a light dusting of fat, white flakes drifts down.

Our groups meet halfway between the trees and Nightwich, with as much distance between us as possible while still within speaking range.

Elizabeth brought minimal force. And why would she need more against a single human?

It is only her, the Voice, a soldier for each hostage, and one other—who I expect she brought along to do her dirty work.

Kitty's dress is torn and frayed around the hem. The once soft pink is now a mix of filthy shades of dirt and soot. The white, full-length gloves are not in any better condition. One has had most of its length ripped off. The other is bunched around the elbow.

I can now see that what I first took for dirt on the bare skin of her arms are actually deep bruises. My protective side rises up. I want to run to her. To take her far away from everything she has been through. It is only through Varin's firm control I keep from moving or showing my emotions.

Father's clothes, though wrinkled and dirtied, were recently new. His face has days of stubble, and his left cheek is discolored by a repeated injury in different stages of healing. Probably struck for not obeying.

After leaving Littlemire, I shoved him into my past, content to forget about him. He stares at me with clear eyes filled with shock. I cannot recall the last time he seemed so present.

For the most part, they both seem well enough. I can only hope that whatever they've been through is not so terrible that they won't recover, given enough time.

Elizabeth wears a column dress. When she was farther away, I thought it was a flat gray, but now I see it is a shade of silver, with intricate and heavy beadwork that would shimmer in harsher light. A heavy, black mantle flutters out behind her. Obsidian shards cut to look like feathers are stitched on her shoulders with more to form a collar that rises in the back.

Her pale blonde hair is piled high, with a cascade of long curls flowing over both shoulders. And atop it all sits that awful bone-like crown with its sharp points and rubies that glitter like fresh blood.

I wait for Elizabeth to speak. There is no need to push my luck—I will challenge her enough as it is during this exchange.

"I was not entirely sure you would come," she says. The sidelong glance she sends toward my family, her nose wrinkling, expresses what she leaves out—that she considers them worthless. That a hundred humans do not come close to the worth of Alaric's life.

To her, everyone is worth only what she can get by bartering. But she is wrong. Nothing so simple or inconsequential can measure the worth of any living person. Life is not a currency for the powerful to spend on a whim.

When I don't respond, her lips purse. Annoyance

skitters over her face before she dons her mask once more.

"Release him," Elizabeth commands. "And I will allow you and your pathetic family to go live the rest of your short lives back in your dirty little town."

Not for a second do I believe she means a single word of it. "How do I know you won't come after us?"

"My generosity will not last long, so I suggest you take this deal before my patience ends," she adds through clenched teeth.

I flex my wrist to draw attention to the dagger pressed into Alaric's side. "To level the stakes, first release one of them, and then we will release our hostages together."

Kitty begins sobbing uncontrollably. The guard holding her snaps at her to stop, but it only makes her cry harder. He backhands her across the face, snarling. The hit rings out, sharp and vicious. Her head snaps to the side and when she straightens, her skin is red and already swelling.

I clench my jaw so hard my teeth ache. The only thing keeping me in place is the determination that no blood will be spilled today. Perhaps when I return for Alaric, I will kill him, too.

"Run, Clara! Don't trust her!" Father shouts. He struggles against the vampire holding him back.

My heart squeezes in my chest. Once this is all over—

But I don't have the chance to finish the thought before Elizabeth rounds on him. Her movements are almost too fast for me to follow. She grips the sides of his head and twists in a single, violent move.

A sickening sound echoes through the field and fades. Father's body crumples to the ground with a dull thud.

It must only be a second, though it feels like a small eternity passes before Kitty's scream rents the air.

"Shut your fucking mouth, or I will do it for you," Kitty's guard spits the threat, looking as if he would like nothing more than to follow through.

Father....

Shock keeps me frozen in place. The possibilities of my tiny family reuniting and any slender chance we stood of mending the fissures that formed between us flash before my eyes. Gone. All of it gone before I even had a chance. A sob works its way up my throat, choking me.

There is still time to save your sister, Varin reminds me.

"All right," I call out. "I will let him go." My hands tremble as I take the dagger and slice through the rope woven with false strands of night-forged silver.

Kitty runs toward me, sobbing before Alaric's binds fall to the frozen ground. I don't notice when he steps away, only that cold air replaces the warmth at my side. My full attention is on my sister. I open my arms to her, ready to protect her from further pain. She stumbles when she's only a few feet away. Her face contorts.

Then she is falling. I lunge forward and catch her.

A silver bloom unfurls into crimson in the center of her chest. I don't understand what I am seeing until I lower us to the ground. My mind doesn't want to accept it because if I do, if I know, then it might break me.

A gleaming arrowhead protrudes from her chest.

No… no, no, no, no, no! I cradle her against me.

Not Kitty.

She was supposed to be safe.

She was supposed to be happy.

"I'm sorry. I'm so, so sorry." It's the only thing I can say. Kitty's face blurs. Hot tears track down my cheeks with every blink.

She shudders in my arms. Coughs. A trickle of blood pools in the corner of her mouth. Kitty parts her pale, cracked lips to speak. Blood stains her teeth an awful red.

"I told you to kill him." She coughs again, wheezing for breath. "You should have killed *him*."

Those words are a jagged, rusted knife hacking at my already wounded heart. I know she doesn't mean them—she can't. She never knew the truth of what he did for her. Still, I can't blame her.

"I'm sorry. I'm sorry. I'm sorry." I am stuck… trapped in this moment. Even when Kitty's body goes limp in my arms and her gasping breaths fade, I cannot escape. "I'm sorry. I'm sorry. I'm sorry. I'm sorry."

A shadow falls over us, bringing with it a harsh cold that pierces down to my marrow.

"This is the least of what you deserve," Elizabeth hisses from above. "Did you honestly think *you* could win against *me*?"

Her hand snakes out and grabs me by the hair. She wrenches my head back at a painful angle. I am forced to release my sister's body as Elizabeth pulls me to my feet. "Even if you brought an army, you would have only accomplished giving them an early death as well."

I grit my teeth.

Alaric growls. "Let us end this, my queen."

Elizabeth's gaze snaps to him. She reaches out and takes something from his outstretched hand. When she turns back to me, a poisonous smile turns the corners of her lips up.

Leaning forward, she whispers, "No one could ever truly love someone as pathetic as you." She laughs, but it is cold and cruel. "She blamed you for the consequences of your insolence. You were why I came for them—why they suffered. You were the reason for their deaths. She knew that—and she hated you for it."

Searing pain pierces my side. It twists. Scraping against bone. I try to scream, but I cannot find the air.

As she rips her hand away, my body jerks. Crimson dapples her dress in an angry slash.

I drop, my knees hitting the frozen ground. And then I crumple, unable to move... unable to breathe. My head hits the hard earth, and stars explode across my vision.

CHAPTER TWENTY-NINE

ALARIC

THE SIGHT OF THE LIFELESS GIRL IN CLARA'S ARMS twists my insides. She reminds me of Rosalie, not in her appearance but rather in her fragile nature. A flower easily stripped of its delicate petals by rain. Clara is more like a rose hidden within a cage of thorns to protect it.

Elizabeth steps up to Clara, a look of disgust and ire twisting her delicate features. No human has ever gotten under her skin the way Clara has managed… as far as I know, with the memories I possess.

I almost do not recognize my queen.

My queen… she is still that, even if she is the one who cursed me.

I bend down and pick up the dagger. It is only steel, yet with each step, the tip dug into my side like a barb caught in the fabric of my shirt.

"This is the least of what you deserve. Did you honestly think you could win against *me*?" Elizabeth hisses. Her eyes shine with power in the dimming light. The glow casts a reddish hue across her cheeks.

Her hand lashes out and grabs Clara by the hair, forcing her to her feet. Clara gasps but does not scream or cry. She is forced to release her hold, and her sister's lifeless body tumbles to the ground.

I take a step forward. A growl is on my lips before I can hold back.

Nothing can be done for her now... she is not Rosalie.

Lavender and red eyes snap to mine.

"Let us end this, my queen," I say.

The sneer on her face transforms into one made of ice. She leans to whisper in Clara's ear. "No one could ever truly love someone as pathetic as you." She laughs, but it is a cold and harsh sound. "She blamed you for the consequences of your insolence. You were the reason I came for them—the reason they suffered. You were the reason for their deaths. She knew that— and she hated you for it."

The cruelty of her words takes me aback. Elizabeth's hand snakes out to take the dagger from my hand. I realize Elizabeth's intention too late. The weapon is already buried in Clara's side—the same place she'd held against my ribs. Slowly, Elizabeth twists the blade, savoring her agony, before ripping the blade free. The vicious jerk causes blood to splatter across her dress in an angry slash.

A single drop lands on the back of my hand. I stumble a step to the side as if struck by some unseen force. White hot agony crashes over me like a wave. I double over and gasp for breath. It pierces like shards of glass. Searing my every nerve ending.

My vision wavers. I collapse to my hands and knees. No matter how hard I try, I cannot find my voice. Cannot breathe. I think I will be sick.

The dagger slips from Elizabeth's hand and lands with a dull thud. Fresh, bright blood glistens on the shining metal, contrasting against the white dusting of snow. I try to say her name, but the sound does not come. Her gaze remains intent on Clara.

I wrap an arm around my abdomen, pressing against the talons of the curse and the teeth of the oath bond as they claw and scrape against me. Each cut presses in deeper. Pulling and shredding me into pieces from the inside for an eternity.

Just as I think it will cleave me in two, the pain gradually recedes, condensing beneath my sternum and bearing down on my lungs. The pressure builds… then releases as one magic prevails and the other vanishes like fog in the heat of day.

Air flows into my lungs. The winter chill is harsh at first, easing with each breath. I squeeze my eyes shut. When I open them again, the world is no longer shaking, and the roaring in my ears has silenced.

It takes immense effort to raise my head. A hand stretches out over the ground. My gaze travels up the arm to warm, brown eyes watching me. They shine impossibly bright, brimming with tears that overflow when she blinks. Clara's chest rises and falls with an unsteady rhythm. It slows.

Her eyes lock onto mine. Beseeching. And she is pale. Too pale. Clara's fingers twitch, straining to reach.

For me.

She should know better than to look to me for comfort. I am the queen's pawn.

The broken spell vanishes as if it never existed, taking its pain with it.

But which spell was it? I cannot sense what magic still lives in me yet. It lies dormant, waiting, resting. I suppose time will tell.

Rising to my feet, I force myself to turn away from the dying human and face Elizabeth. She is the woman I've always known her to be, yet the sight of her is unnerving as her expression of joy contrasts with the macabre slash of blood.

"Come," she says, in a tone sweeter than honey. "It is time to put such trivial matters behind us. There is more important business we must attend to."

A raven circles overhead, and then it dives. Wings beat the air as it alights on Elizabeth's shoulder. It bellows a screeching croak once, then bounds back into the air.

I obey. At her side, Elizabeth slips her hand into the crook of my elbow. We walk toward the castle, and the queen's guards follow far enough behind to allow us privacy but not so much as to be ineffective.

The Voice remains behind. Though I did not see Elizabeth give a command, she must have. If not, it doesn't seem to bother her in the least.

In moments, we are within the walls of Nightwich. I am alone with Elizabeth, my thoughts hazy. I seem to have lost a bit of time. That or the curse consumed more memories. Devoured parts of my mind as it fought for control.

We stop before the closed doors of my quarters. With my hand hovering over the doorknob, I turn to Elizabeth. "What… happened?" I ask.

I glance over my shoulder as if I could see through the walls of Nightwich to the field. Back to the moment that some magic splintered and broke away from within.

Elizabeth turns her face up, her lips a bright red. "Everything was finally made right." Her hands press against my chest, and she pushes up on her toes, bringing her mouth to my ear. "Rest, then feed."

She pulls back and looks me over, evaluating.

I frown, then shake my head. "I don't understand."

"That human was responsible for everything that you have suffered. She is the reason for your curse. Do not doubt that." The last comes out like a command.

Kharis circles above our heads. Their wings mimic the beating of a heavy drum.

I bow my head and give her the only answer I can. "Thank you, my queen. I am in your debt."

"That will be settled soon enough." Elizabeth turns to leave, pausing after a few steps.

My mouth goes dry and I cannot figure out if I hope she leaves or turns around and decides to stay.

"The coronation will be here before you know it. Once you are crowned, you will never again have to worry about being cursed because of some insignificant mortal."

I dip my chin. It seems to be the correct response. And then she is gone. Disappointment shakes me at the core. The reasons for it are as hazy as everything else since leaving that field. Is it from Elizabeth's lack of concern? Or the turn of events?

A fire roars in the hearth, chasing away the cold and stale air that settled in my absence. The wood crackles and shifts as the dancing flames consume it.

Inside the quiet parlor, I lean against the door. Impossibly, it feels less welcoming than the cramped underground cell the wolves kept me in. I press my palm to my chest and rub. I can still feel the resonance from the snap of magic within.

Was Clara so skilled at lying that she could rewrite the truths of reality to suit her purposes? Skilled enough to make me believe her over my queen, even for a moment? There was something inhuman about her, though she is nothing more than mortal.

Elizabeth said Clara was the one who cursed me. Except a human cannot curse a vampire. They would need the power of a demon—and that would make them something else entirely.

What I felt that night couldn't have been manufactured by an enchantment or manipulation… and the way she looked at me as she lay there bleeding to death. Her fingers reaching for me… it was not help or comfort she sought for herself. She was offering it to me.

Was…

Already, I have begun to think of her as one of the dead. With the oath bond, I thought I would be able to sense it either way.

No human could have survived those injuries long enough for help to arrive. I wonder if that wolf reached her in time to hold her hand as she slipped into the Otherworld.

I took a chance and gambled. Yet, all I accomplished was creating a hollow pit where some spell once clung to my marrow. I have gained many questions but no answers.

CHAPTER THIRTY

CLARA

THOUSANDS OF STARS EXPLODE ACROSS MY VISION, blotting out the world and fading into an endless night.

I hear a sound.

A voice… familiar, but I can't make out what they are saying or who the voice belongs to.

I blink. Squeeze my eyes tight, then open them again.

A cruel face scowls down at me. My gaze tracks down over the bright slash of red on Elizabeth's dress to the blade in her hand, soaked with blood…. my blood. A fat droplet falls to the earth.

And I remember.

I remember the pain. The scrape of steel on bone, twisting. Elizabeth stabbed me.

I try to get up, but Varin has taken control, keeping me from moving. My lungs struggle to draw in shallow breaths.

Keep still, the demon warns. *It is lucky you did not bring the night-forged dagger with you.*

Alaric grunts—a horrible sound of agony—and drops to his hands and knees. Lolling my head to the side, I try to look for the reason but find nothing. He wraps an arm around his middle.

Cold seeps through me, making the blood spilling from my sliced flesh feel like scalding water as it spreads out in a puddle beneath me. I reach for Alaric, but he is not close enough.

What's happening? Is he dying?

Varin does not answer. Their power slides along my veins, crashing over my bones like a wild river. It tugs and concentrates on the wound, slowing the flow of blood.

The dagger drops to the ground between Alaric and me, just out of reach.

In the back of my mind, I knew this outcome was a possibility. But I wanted to believe I could do this. Wanted to believe Elizabeth cared more about getting what she wanted, that killing my family wouldn't be worth the effort.

I should have known better. Pressure builds up behind my eyes before spilling over in rivulets of hot tears.

I couldn't save them.

I couldn't save anyone.

Elizabeth shifts, stepping into the edges of my vision. Her gaze is pinned on me even as Alaric gasps. She ignores him, doing nothing to help him.

Why? She needs him alive...

Or have I been wrong about that, too?

The moment stretches on and on. I make a weak sound in the back of my throat when Alaric's breathing evens out.

He straightens, standing against a backdrop of ashen sky, and his eyes meet mine. The expression he wears is a little amazed, with the barest hint of a smile on his lips. I don't know what it means.

A high-pitched ringing fills my ears. Elizabeth speaks, drawing Alaric's attention to her. She hooks her hand in the crook of his elbow and leads him away. There is nothing I can do but watch as he turns his back on me. The guards trail after them.

They disappear as snow begins to fall.

Varin's hold partially relents. I cover my mouth with my hand, muffling the sob I can no longer hold back. I don't understand how everything went so wrong.

You need help, or you will die here, Varin hisses. *The injury is too deep for me alone to heal.* Whether it is the demon's will to live or mine or a combination of both, I don't know. I roll onto my uninjured side and work the small, polished piece of metal no bigger than my palm free from my pocket. Angling it toward the trees, I signal to Oliver.

Each shift is a strain that sends bolts of sharp torment all down my side. It makes blood seep through the wound faster. Nausea washes over me in a wave, too fast and strong to escape. My vision wavers. I can barely find the energy to lift my head.

Night is almost upon us, but there is still enough light to make out the movement of figures racing from the trees.

Snow crunches under slow footsteps at my back. They stop, and a hand with a vice-like grip grabs my shoulder and rolls me onto my back.

A woman made of ice and snow stares down at me. "Stop being weak," the Voice says, her annoyance evident. She sighs and reaches for something. It's small enough that her fist conceals all but the cork.

I scowl, knowing precisely what it is. For creatures who possess speed and strength far beyond the ability of any human, they seem to love their poisons. I wonder what it is why some find pleasure in watching their victims squirm as they suffer a slow, painful death.

"Do you still have the queen's vial?" she demands. Her long fingers pinch my jaw and jerk my head to look her in the eye.

I press my lips together and don't answer. Elizabeth said it was rare. That could have been another of her countless lies, but in case she spoke the truth, the last thing I will do is allow it to find its way back into her possession.

The Voice takes my silence for what it is, a refusal to answer, and lets the subject drop. She brings her fist to her mouth, biting the cork and spitting it out.

The pounding of feet grows louder as Oliver and the other reinforcements draw near, though I don't think they will make it in time.

Her long fingers press painfully into my cheeks, forcing my lips to part enough for her to pour the contents into my mouth. I cough and sputter on the syrupy liquid. It does little good because she covers my nose and mouth with her hand, tossing the empty vial over her shoulder with the other.

"Drink it, or suffocate," she hisses through her teeth.

I fight it for as long as I can, but in the end, I am betrayed by my body's reflex, swallowing twice before she releases me.

I suck in deep lungfuls of air as I choke on the cloying aftertaste. Other than a trace amount that spilled from the corner of my mouth and the sticky remnants on my lips, I drank it all.

One set of feet, swiftly joined by several others, comes into view as I go limp. Bone-chilling snarls surround us.

"What did you give to her?" Oliver demands. But then the Voice straightens, and the growls cease abruptly. "You…"

She walks around me, making way for two wolves kneeling on either side of me. They get to work. I don't have the strength to tell them it's pointless. One shifts me, the other ripping at my clothes to get to the wound.

"It has been a long time, Mr. Wolvrik."

Fingers press against my side. I can barely feel it— I can barely feel any part of my body anymore. It seems they really were too late. A giggle escapes my lips, a half-mad sound, though there is nothing humorous about this situation.

"So it has," Oliver says.

My sanity is unraveling. My ally and the woman who remained behind to finish me off are speaking like old friends.

Fresh-cut grass and something else, something I can't identify, fills the air. At first, it's light and almost warm against the winter air, then it quickly morphs, turning thick and cloying.

Several conversations are happening all at once, but I can't focus on any of them.

The wolf holding me up straddles my legs, pinning my arms off to the side. I grunt at the uncomfortable new position. Though, I don't have to wonder at the reason behind his actions for long. A needle pierces my flesh, tugging over and over.

Varin seizes full control, and I gladly allow it. *They are mending you.*

Their explanation is little comfort. I'd gathered as much.

Each stab of the needle is another small torture added on top of all the others. Heat washes over my skin, pushing away the frigid air and harsh cold of the ground beneath me. Beads of sweat break out across my forehead, my neck, and down my spine, dampening my clothes so they cling to me. I am not as numb as I thought.

"Unless you want to see her dead, I suggest you get her away from here," the Voice says coolly.

Bile rises, and I think I might be sick. The stitching stops, replaced by a slimy mixture, the consistency of paste made of ground leaves and mud.

"What did you give her?" Oliver repeats his earlier question.

"Blood bane."

A growl that could almost be mistaken for thunder

rumbles over my head. "She is bleeding to death, and you still give her poison?"

The wolf holding me down relaxes his grip, shifts, then returns to keeping me balanced with my injured side up.

Seemingly unaware of Oliver's ire, the Voice crouches down. She brushes my hair from my face. It's difficult to know what she's thinking. I can't read that stoic expression.

"She will not die from such an injury." Her hand remains pressed to my head as she looks up at Oliver. "It is poison only to your kind. Miss Valmont may have claws, but she is no wolf. It will help her sleep and stave off the risk of infection."

I cannot begin to guess why she would help me.

The Voice rises gracefully, then walks away. She hasn't gone more than a few yards before she pauses. "You would do well to make sure it does not fall into the wrong hands."

When I blink, she has vanished. Logically, I know she used her vampire speed, but in my delirium, I'm left with the strange impression that she was a specter, vanishing like the smoke from a match.

Then Oliver is before me. Gentle hands, only slightly calloused, cradle my face and check me over.

"Lift her up so I can wrap her," a soft voice orders.

I am surprised that the wolf who sewed me up with such stern motions owns a voice so gentle.

If Oliver takes exception to one of his pack members daring to give him an order, he does nothing to show it. His hands slide under me and he gingerly lifts me into his arms. My fingers curl into his jacket, and I bury my face against his shoulder. He strokes my head and murmurs soothing words.

Was I poisoned? I ask Varin silently.

Even when they do not speak, I'm able to sense them with me. Their constant presence is a comfort I never expected.

The moment stretches before their answer comes. *No. Trust in these wolves. You will heal before we reach the Keep.*

With that, I relax. I still don't understand why the Voice would help keep me alive. Part of me wants to believe it's a trick. Elizabeth wants me dead, so the only reason that makes sense for her to keep me alive is if I still serve some purpose to her queen.

Someone tugs on my clothes, tearing my top further, and more poultice is pressed against the wound, then the wolves who have been tending to me work together to secure a wrap around my middle.

The effects of whatever the Voice forced me to drink is beginning to work. My limbs grow heavy and my body numb. No matter how hard I try, I can't keep my eyes open any longer.

The sounds of activity are all around me. Hoof steps clomp over, bringing the scent of warm apples and grass.

Oliver hooks his arm under my legs and lifts me up. I am cocooned in warmth as he carries me. He shifts, and then I'm rocking from the gentle sway of Nyx's gait.

"Clara?" Oliver speaks my name.

"Hmmm?" It's the closest I can come to forming an answer.

"What happened back there?" The question is tentative.

"Mmm... a trick... she never...." I try to explain, but I am exhausted, and I am not yet ready to talk about what happened.

The pull of sleep is irresistible, so I quit fighting it.

"Clara," a man's voice calls, breaking through the dark fog of unconsciousness.

It's warm and comfortable here. I feel like I'm floating. And I'm not ready to leave. I try to sink deeper into unconsciousness.

"Clara." That same voice continues to follow me, tugging and pulling. "Clara, you need to wake up now."

The more he calls to me, the faster I am forced out of the peaceful dark.

Someone pats my cheek. After a pause, he does it again.

I groan. Shifting slightly is enough to make me aware of every ache and pain. My entire body is stiff with cold, even though I'm being held against a warm body and blanketed.

An ache in my side causes me to hiss through my teeth. I peel open my eyes to see a dense forest of trees. It is dark. I wonder if it's been hours or only minutes since I passed out.

Soft murmurs of conversation float around me as

several members of the pack go about setting up a fire and collecting water.

"Clara," Oliver repeats my name. "Time to wake up."

Lifting my face, I look at him. The worry in his scrunched brow eases, then the rest of him relaxes.

"Thank the saints, I was beginning to worry."

I try to ask why, but my throat is parched, and my lips are so dry it feels like the skin will crack from the movement.

"You have been getting colder over the last hour," he explains. "I thought..." Oliver shakes his head, not finishing the thought. "We're a little over halfway to the Keep, but we need to get you warmed up."

Not knowing what else to do, I nod and surrender to his orders.

CHAPTER THIRTY-ONE

CLARA

Oliver swings his leg over Nyx and dismounts with little effort, with me still in his arms. He walks a short distance and stops before a fire.

"Do you think you can sit up by yourself?" he asks.

Again, I nod. I am surprised to find how quickly I've healed. My side is tender, and the skin feels a little tight. Beyond that, I am exhausted, as though all my strength has been depleted, and there is almost no pain. It's as though the wound is over a week old.

Thank you, I whisper silently to Varin. They don't respond with words, sending a flare of warmth blooming within my chest instead.

Oliver places me on a felled log, keeping an arm around my back. He hands me a water skin once he's sure I won't topple over. I take it gladly, lifting it to my lips and letting it soothe my throat. As I drink, he drapes a heavy cloak over my shoulders and wraps it around my arms and legs like a blanket.

He takes the water away, telling me not to drink too much at once as he sits down beside me. A thought flitters in the back of my mind, wondering if I should worry with the way Oliver is fussing over me.

Several wolves head off in pairs to hunt for small game, while one stays behind to start a fire and build a spit to cook meat while waiting for a pot of water to heat. The first pair of hunters bring back a wild hare. By the time it's finished cooking, a few more have dropped off three more rabbits, two squirrels, and seven birds of various kinds.

I am in a fog, barely noticing anything that isn't directly in front of me. The voices of those around me are a distant, gentle hum. My fingers are stiff from the cold as I clutch the edges of the cloak, so I lean forward, holding them out to soak up the warmth of the fire.

Oliver holds a small cup out before my face. I must have been dazed by the dancing flames because I hadn't noticed him getting up. "Drink this. It should help warm you."

I take it, curling my fingers around the smooth, carved wood. Dandelion petals float in the steaming amber liquid. The tea has a light earthy fragrance. I take a sip and notice it's lightly sweetened with nectar. After finishing, Oliver refills the cup and watches me silently until I'm done.

The woman in charge of cooking tears a leg off the rabbit and brings it to Oliver.

"Thank you, Agatha." He takes it with a smile and then hands it to me.

I try to refuse. She clearly intended it to be for him.

"Eat," Agatha calls, back at her place across the fire. "He's waiting for the squirrel."

Oliver sends her a scowl. She smirks, which causes him to chuckle and shake his head. "I'm waiting for squirrel," he repeats, unable to disguise a wince.

The aroma makes my jaw ache from watering. Though I mean to insist that he take the first piece, my stomach has other ideas and chooses this exact moment to growl.

"You need to regain your strength," he adds.

I relent, accepting the offering, and bite into it. Rabbit has never been my favorite, but right now, I can't recall ever eating anything so delicious. I suppose hunger will do that.

I remember thinking the same thing about the first loaf of bread I ever made. It was unevenly cooked, charred in places, undercooked in others, and so dense we had to dip it in tea before it was edible.

Once I finish, I cannot escape the somber expression that slips over Oliver's face. The food settles in my stomach like a boulder because I'm not ready for what he wants to talk about.

"Clara," he begins gently. Too gently. "What happened back there? You should have signaled earlier."

My throat is suddenly thick with emotion, and heat rises, building pressure at the back of my eyes. No matter how hard I fight to push it down, the tears well up.

Oliver scoots closer and settles an arm over my

shoulder, pulling me into his side. I take a shuddering breath. The warmth that I've gathered seeps out of me.

"She..." I struggle to find the words. "It's all my fault." I cover my mouth with my hands as if I could hold back every emotion that is clawing its way to the surface.

I shake my head, yet it's no use. Horrible images of the way Father and Kitty were murdered are the only thing I see. Unshed tears burn, building and building, until they finally spill over. I squeeze my eyes tight against the visions, but it doesn't stop them from replaying over and over again.

Oliver hugs me, my face pressed against his lapels. He stands with me then begins to walk. I follow, not seeing or caring where we're going.

We stop where it's quiet and the air is much colder. I shiver even though crying has made my face feel uncomfortably hot. No matter how hard I try, I just can't seem to halt or even slow my tears. For a long time, Oliver murmurs soft words while rubbing circles over my back.

When my sobs eventually ebb, he hands me a handkerchief to wipe my face. It's hard to tell how much time has passed. Several more minutes go by before I can speak again. My head throbs and my face feels swollen and puffy.

"Thank you," I mumble, pulling back, only to realize his shirt is damp. Uselessly, I attempt to dry the spot with my sleeve. "I ruined your shirt."

Oliver stills my movements and angles my face up to look him in the eye. "What happened was not your fault, Clara," Oliver says quietly. I open my mouth to disagree, but he continues before I get the chance. "There was nothing you could have done. Elizabeth was never going to let them live. If you hadn't met her, they might have suffered at her hands for days or weeks longer."

You were why I came for them—why they suffered. You were the reason for their deaths. She knew that—and she hated you for it.

Kitty loved me—I know she did. However, that didn't stop Elizabeth's words from hitting their mark, piercing a vulnerability I never realized I had. Cutting deep, a sharp knife slicing at my heart.

"She killed my father when I didn't let Alaric go immediately." I shake my head, swallowing a few times so I can get the rest of it out. "She released Kitty... but then... then Elizabeth had a guard shoot her with an arrow. She died in my arms..."

I'm crying again, but not as uncontrollably as before. After a while, each new hurt becomes lost among the others, and I can no longer feel the contrast of them against the lack of pain before the first cut.

"If I'd only—"

"You did everything you could," he says firmly. "If there was any way to have saved them, *that* would have been it. Regardless of what she said, their blood is on *her* hands, not yours. Grieve for them, but do not blame yourself for Elizabeth's actions."

Eventually, my tears run out, leaving behind a hollow chasm in my chest.

Enough.

This must be enough for now.

I must lock the pain down—numb everything. I can't afford to fall apart, can't afford to feel or succumb to the heartache.

I can't fall to pieces.

Not yet.

Not until there is a conclusion to all this. Not until this is all over and either Elizabeth, or I, or both of us are dead.

I splash my face with water from a nearby stream, then Oliver and I return to the temporary camp.

Numbly, I notice the food is gone, and the pack keeps themselves occupied with busy work. The fire is low but still burns, though there's a pile of dirt next to it, ready to smother the flames on Oliver's command. Guilt tightens its grip for making everyone wait.

Oliver insists on having me sit by the fire for a while longer. It's well into the night when he issues the order to continue on. He rides behind me on Nyx while the others shift into wolf form. The remainder of the trek is passed in silence. I am thankful for it. There is a lot I need to sort out in my mind.

The branches overhead creak as they sway in the light breeze, but it doesn't seem to touch us as we move through the forest.

Since I woke, I haven't been able to shake a nagging thought. Elizabeth has wanted me dead for a while now. So, I am not entirely surprised that she stabbed me.

We must choose to trust each other.

Those were Alaric's last words to me. It is

something one would say when they need another to trust them, no matter what. But it is also something one would say to make their intended betrayal that much sharper. If he planned to turn on me from the beginning and leave me for dead, then why say anything at all but not for added cruelty?

But I chose to trust him, and he knew that. Had he intended to betray me the entire time?

Mist begins to move in, first, little more than wisps over tree roots and loam. My head turns, looking in every direction, before I realized we are in the thick of it. Nyx doesn't seem to be affected by the fog, following the pack without the slightest direction from Oliver.

"It might help if you close your eyes," he whispers, almost as if he's afraid to break the quiet, and tightens his hold to keep me from falling.

I do, and it does help... mostly.

The mist creates an eerie silence that swallows the world. For several minutes, my thoughts roll and repeat. So loud without the company of voices or paws padding around us.

"Oliver," I say.

"Hmm?"

"I am going to stop Elizabeth."

His posture goes ridged against my back. After a brief hesitation, he says, "It's pointless to try saving him now, and I will not risk the lives of my people for a traitor."

I promised Alaric I would go back for him. I don't even know if he can be saved... or if he wants to be.

But he is not the only reason to return to Nightwich one final time.

"She killed my family and left me to die." I twist within his hold and face him, craning my neck. "With him back under her control, she won't be satisfied until he is crowned, and his powers are hers."

Oliver is quiet as he considers.

I know he is thinking about the pack. The risk, the consequences of leaving things as they are, and of acting against her. They attacked Nightwich once, attempting to get to her because there's no telling what she will do if she succeeds in taking Alaric's power. We have to try again.

A thought comes to me. Twists my stomach into knots.

"Something happened when she stabbed me," I say slowly. "If I was close enough to death to break the oath bond, she will get exactly what she wants."

Oliver's arm around me tightens, making it harder to breathe. "How can you be sure that is what happened?"

The truth is, I can't. I prod Varin to ask, but their presence is like a cat curled up on a high shelf, out of reach. I wonder how much of their power they used to heal me. This cannot go on much longer, but it seems we may have less time than I thought. Yet another reason why this must come to an end once and for all.

"There is only one reason I didn't die back there," I say. Varin kept me alive. Without their power, most likely, I would have been dead before Oliver and the others reached me.

Once more, I go over everything Elizabeth said and did, doing my best to avoid getting caught up in the worst of it. There is something important about what happened. A detail, small but vital. If only I could put my finger on it.

"What can you tell me about that perfume?" I ask.

"Why?" The question is slow. Cautious.

"Because I think it's the key to everything." I twist in his hold to face him. "During the attack, Elizabeth ordered all humans within the castle killed because she believed it was a human uprising. And in the field, Elizabeth mentioned something about *if* I had brought an army—she thought Alaric and I came alone."

"If she doesn't already know the truth, she will know soon enough when your vampire spills our secrets," he says bitterly.

My chest squeezes in my chest. I cannot deny that Alaric handed her the dagger.

Memories of the new moon festival flash. Whispered words. Caresses filled with desperate need. Was any of it real, or was it all a deception to get back to Elizabeth? The possibility that all of it could have been an act for him when it was real for me pierces like an arrow.

I won't think of what it means if he chose to deceive me, intending for me to die. The frayed string of hope is all that is keeping my heart from breaking into a million jagged splinters.

We must choose to trust each other.

Despite the evidence to the contrary, I cannot believe he is capable of such a heartless betrayal.

"I don't think he will."

Oliver scoffs derisively. "He handed you over to Elizabeth and didn't lift a finger to save you."

The wall of mist thins, and the horrible disorientation releases its hold. Nyx steps out at the edge of the Keep.

"Even under the influence of her curse, he isn't the type to cause unnecessary bloodshed," I say, feeling the need to defend him.

Then I wince, remembering what happened with Elise. Although she'd been about to kill me, my connection to Alaric through the oath bond sparked at that moment.

I know I should make my next move under the assumption his treachery was real… though some foolish part of me is desperate to find a different meaning for his actions.

"What if there was a reason—"

"Don't do this to yourself," Oliver says.

I sigh. "All right… Let's say he tells her everything. She will know it was your pack behind the attack. Even so, I think we could use the spray to our advantage."

A bone-chilling snarl near the back of my neck sends a shudder through me. "Fuck."

Anger radiates off him. Though I know he won't hurt me, it triggers a deeply buried instinct of fear. Even Nyx senses it, her steps faltering before returning to the steady clomping.

"How much of that perfume do you have left?"

"There should be enough for one use on most of the pack… Why?"

"How does it work?" I ask again.

A rumble rises from his chest. "It's not that I don't trust you, so please do not take this the wrong way. But it is a closely guarded secret, and you are not part of the pack."

The *how* is a matter of curiosity rather than a need. Disappointing? Yes. But I can accept that answer.

"Can you get more?"

"I suppose…" he says slowly, suspicion thick in his tone. "It would take a few days."

"Good." A plan forms in my mind. "Get as much of it as you can."

Oliver leans to the side and eyes me with suspicion. "What are you plotting?"

"Exactly how I will kill the queen."

A ruddy brow arches.

I take a breath and explain. I go over every detail that comes to mind, sharing everything I've learned about Elizabeth through experience or observation.

He hums. Considers.

"I will need to discuss this with the pack." An arm wraps around my shoulders, and Oliver presses the side of his face to mine as he hugs me. "Regardless, you will always have a home with us."

A few hours later, I pace back and forth in the hall. The same two guards from before bar the entrance. Both eye me with clear, unfiltered irritation.

With part of the plan solidified, I put yards between myself and the guards and turn my back on them. I lift Cherno from my shoulder and go over a few details again. "Have them meet me at the eastern edge of the city the morning of the day before—and tell them to find something gold to wear so the wolves will know them."

The doors open, and Oliver emerges—the pack has come to a decision. I rush over as he walks toward me.

"The dissolution of the oath bond made the choice easy. Without it, there is no stopping Elizabeth from gaining the power she desires."

I release a breath, the tension in my shoulders melting. I wasn't entirely sure they would agree.

Oliver takes my arm in his and walks with me. A handful of others join us as we make our way out to the wall of fog.

"Several have expressed doubt in your promised allies," he continues. "A single court member is hard to believe… let alone two."

"They will help destroy the court if necessary."

"They are *part* of that court." He heaves a sigh and looks away, mouth pressing into a tight line.

"Yes. And they have seen what she is capable of firsthand."

"The lives of the entire pack will hinge on them not revealing everything to Elizabeth."

"You can trust them. Come up with a plan to get everyone out of there in case it's necessary to retreat. We will only tell each other the necessary details to coordinate our efforts. It will also serve as a failsafe in case anyone is captured."

Oliver scratches the stubble on his cheek as he mulls it over. He nods. "That will have to do."

He signals, and five scouts shift, disappearing into the misty forest like ghosts. A sixth wolf clasps Cherno between their hands, then follows after.

This time, we will succeed.

CHAPTER THIRTY-TWO

CLARA

My fingers tighten around the thin, wrapped bundle in my hand, not wanting to drop it while riding through the mist. Even without looking, I can sense the moment we are out of it. The pull on my senses urging me to go in another direction dissolves altogether.

I let out a relieved breath and peel open my eyes. Behind me, Oliver dismounts and comes to stand next to Nyx's head. He absentmindedly scratches her between the ears while studying me.

"I can go with you," he says. Again.

I shake my head. "You're needed here."

"Then let me send someone else with you. I don't like the idea of you traveling alone." He holds a placating hand up, stopping me from interrupting. "I know you're capable, but it would make me feel better. I would never forgive myself if something were to happen to you."

We've had so many similar conversations now I've

lost count. "I appreciate the offer," I say honestly, reaching forward to stroke the mare's neck. "Nyx will take good care of me, and we'll see each other again in a few days."

He nods and steps back—a silent signal of his surrender.

"I have a favor to ask." I hold the bundle out to him and hope the theory that Varin and I came up with is right.

Make sure they don't aim for the bird. We don't know if killing Kharis will work.

Oliver's brows go up. He takes it from me and opens it. He looks at the singular arrow with a thin green stripe painted near the arrowhead. Lifting it up to his face, he turns it this way and that, not understanding.

"Give this to your best archer. If there's an opening, have them aim for Elizabeth."

Carefully, he rewraps it, securing the leather tie. "Why only one? Why this one specifically? The tip is steel. Unless it hits something vital, it won't kill a vampire."

I bite the inside of my cheek. Perhaps I should have tried to get one made of it, just to be safe. I sigh. It's too late now. "Have them aim to hit her anywhere they can—even if it's not a mortal wound. If they miss, it won't matter because I doubt we'll get another chance."

He waits for me to continue, but I don't. "I'll give it to—"

"Don't tell me," I say before he can finish.

Oliver looks Nyx straight on and feeds her a few slices of apple. "Run fast and be safe."

The only farewell he offers me is a nod.

I urge Nyx forward. After a few yards, I glance back, smiling weakly, and wave. My nerves are already on edge. Then, as Nyx speeds up, Varin takes control, keeping the ride smooth as we gallop into the forest.

An hour passes before we slow.

We must find a more permanent solution soon. A single body was never meant to house the consciousness of two beings, Varin says.

What will happen?

Your body will begin rejecting both of us until one of us surrenders or we both die.

I shiver.

I do not ask which of us will surrender if it comes to that, nor do they offer an answer.

The trek through the forest is long and takes the majority of the night. Nyx pushes herself as if she understands the urgency of the situation.

Durring the first half of the journey, I am on alert for demons. I may have killed the higher demon during the fight, but some lesser demons escaped. Varin assures me there is no sign of any—within a harmony or alone—in the vicinity. Any who survived have fled, or at least have the sense to be wary of me and my connections to the Shade pack.

We break through the tree line as the sun crests the horizon ahead of us. I am thankful the sky is clear, allowing the sun's meager warmth to reach us.

I turn Nyx south, and we run until the castle is little more than a shadowy shape in the distance. It adds time to our ride, but that is better than being spotted. We circle around to the easternmost edge of the city.

Cherno meets us a few miles out, guiding us to the meeting place. I trusted they made it back safely, but it's a relief to see it with my own eyes. They perch on my shoulder and nestle against my neck, using my hair to shield them from the rising sun.

Della and Lawrence wait beside a carriage. No sooner do I have both feet on the ground than Della has me wrapped up in a hug, one hand stroking the back of my head.

"We heard what happened," she says with a sniffle. Her hold tightens until I can barely breathe. At the faint whimper of pain, she pulls back, looking at me. "Did I hurt you? I wasn't sure you'd be well enough to ride. Why did no one accompany you?" She bombards me with questions, not giving me a chance to respond.

Lawrence approaches. "You can talk later," he says gruffly.

Della looks me up and down before reaching for the reins. Nyx shies away, then again when Della tries a second time.

The two vampires and I gape at the small horse.

Nyx shakes her head and moves backward several paces. I motion for them to stay put and inch forward.

"You don't need to be afraid. They won't hurt you," I say soothingly.

When I reach out, Nyx does the same thing. I frown. She turns her head to the east, then looks back at me.

"Are you trying to tell me something?" I ask, half sure I'm losing my mind.

You are being ridiculous, Varin chides.

I would agree, but once again, Nyx bobs her head as if in answer, throwing another look behind her.

"You want to leave?"

Another nod.

"All right…" I say uncertainly and gesture toward the saddle. "Would you like me to remove that for you?"

Nyx turns to the side, and when I approach her this time, she doesn't back away. I remove the satchel and sling it over my shoulder, then remove everything else. When I finish, Nyx nudges me with her muzzle.

"Thank you for everything," I say.

She blinks at me with large, warm brown eyes for a moment, then she turns and gallops away.

"What a peculiar little mare," Della murmurs, then climbs into the carriage.

Lawrence nods toward the carriage. "If you're done here, we should get going." There's a hint of impatience in his tone.

My muscles are stiff as I walk, though he doesn't rush me, his pace matching mine. I'm taken aback when he offers to hand me up. The kindness is at odds with his stern demeanor.

The carriage sways as we travel through the cobblestone streets. Hooves clomping fills the silence for most of the drive.

"You seem to have healed remarkably well," he says with a note of suspicion. After a short pause, he adds, "I'm glad."

The genuine warmth in those two words fills me with more emotion than I expect. I smile, unable to know how to respond. Della seems stunned into silence as well.

My friendship with Lawrence only exists because of a similar goal. I doubt he would have suffered my presence after the day we met were it not for that. Still, I know I can trust him without a second thought. I think he is warming up to me.

Lawrence clears his throat as if sensing the direction of my thoughts. "I take it you will let us all in on whatever it is you've schemed up once we reach the manor?" His voice is flat and has an air of disinterest.

I nod.

He blows out a huff of breath through his nose. A moment later, he reaches under the seat for a small basket and then hands it to me as he mutters, "Food."

Taking it, I fight to keep the smile from reaching my lips, earning a faux sneer, and Della sends a dubious look my way.

He is definitely warming up to me.

The food is simple but thoughtful. Two sweet rolls the size of my hand and a bottle of cider. Though I had stopped on the way to eat and let Nyx rest, the dried meat and hard bread don't compare.

I finish just as we arrive at Cassius's manor. The carriage comes to a stop, and the driver climbs down to open the gates. Metal clinks, and a moment later, we're moving again.

Della exits first, then once more, Lawrence offers me his hand. His arm curls around my lower back as he escorts me up the front steps.

Cassius throws open the door the moment we reach the stoop. He surrounds me in an encompassing hug while simultaneously dragging me inside, unwilling to let go yet.

"Between the two of you, she'll suffocate before she can tell us anything," Lawrence says flatly, immediately followed by an oomph, which I suspect is from Della prodding him again.

The remark does its job, and Cassius releases me. "You must be hungry," he says, guiding me into the sitting room.

I laugh. The physically affectionate nature of vampires still takes me by surprise. The notion that a dangerous predator could have such a soft side is an unexpected and strange amalgamation of traits. Though, the more I am around them, the more it fits who they are.

"I ate in the carriage."

Cassius arches a brow, looking over my head at Lawrence as if to say he's been found out.

There is already a tray with tea and a cup for each of us waiting on the glass and wrought iron coffee table. Curls of steam rise from the spout, filling the room with the gentle scent of chamomile.

Being in the arms of safety allows the exhaustion I've ignored with the help of adrenaline to sink into my body and mind. All three hold tension along their spine and lean forward, waiting for me to start.

If I asked, they would let me sleep and bathe first. And even though the morning is still young, the coronation is tomorrow night, and there is so much we need to do and organize before then.

I tell them everything. Understanding settles on their faces as I fill in the gaps from the little Cherno knew before they returned. I even explain which parts of our plan we will keep from the wolves and that they will do the same with parts of theirs.

As soon as I finish, the three vampires divide the remaining tasks between themselves, adding several small errands to the list that I hadn't thought of. Della and Lawrence leave right away, promising to return soon. I rise from my seat because if I don't, I might fall asleep right here.

Cassius is before me in a blink. He cups my face in his hands and looks into my eyes. "You have no idea how worried I was."

He leans in and lowers his face to press a kiss against my forehead. I pull in a sharp gasp as he lifts me, and my arms go around his neck on reflex.

"I can walk. You don't need to carry me," I protest. It doesn't help my case that each word feels weaker than the one before.

Cassius strides through the hall toward the stairs. "I know I don't have to, little bird—I *want* to."

He only sets me down once we are outside the bathing room attached to his bedroom. He enters first, filling the tub with hot water and scented oils.

I lean against the doorframe, watching him. Once, I would have felt uneasy about his motivations. Now, my heart twinges slightly. He's doing this as my friend, expecting nothing from me in return, but behind every gesture, I feel his love.

I wonder if I would love him the way I love Alaric if we had met first. Maybe… but maybe not, if what he told me was true because things would have gone very differently.

Then I shove that thought down. We didn't. And allowing my mind to wander down that path will bring nothing but guilt and questions without answers.

Cassius pauses before me after he's finished. "Take your time bathing, then sleep. One of us will come by to check on you every few hours to make sure you're all right and see if you need anything."

I open and close my mouth a few times before I can respond. "I'll rest for a bit, but I should be helping."

He shakes his head. "Your part will come later. Right now, it's time for us to do ours. Rest and regain your strength. Something tells me you haven't given yourself the time you need to fully heal."

I want to deny it, but Varin's unintelligible grumbling only confirms what Cassius is saying.

My eyes snap open, and I inhale sharply. I'm disoriented. It takes several seconds to remember where I'm at. I keep perfectly still, listening for whatever sound yanked me from deep sleep.

The fire in the hearth has burned down, giving off a soft glow. The window drapes are drawn tight, making it impossible to know what time it is or how long I've been asleep. It feels too long.

Another sound. Two sets of footsteps. Downstairs, a door opens and closes, then a long silence. None of it seems like the noises of someone moving about their own home.

Slowly, I sit up, pushing the downy blankets away, and lower my legs off the side of the mattress. I am careful to be quiet as I gather the clothes laid out on the bench at the foot of the bed and get dressed.

I slip from the room and make my way down the hall. I pause at the top of the stairs to listen. At first, I don't hear anything. Then I catch two deep, unfamiliar voices. My fingers wrap around the hilt of my dagger and pull it from the side of my boot.

With the wall at my back, I gradually shift my weight to prevent any floorboards from creaking as I make my way down.

I have no idea if Cassius, Della, or Lawrence have come back and left again or if they've returned at all.

More whispered speaking is cut off by a harsh

shushing. It's coming from the kitchen. There's a clank followed by a warning growl. My pulse thunders. I focus on keeping my breaths steady and quiet.

If I ran, I could get away, but it's likely whoever is here would follow. They probably know the town more than I do, so it's better to face these intruders in a place more familiar to me than to them.

Beside the kitchen door, I take a few seconds to calm myself. I reach for the doorknob just as it swings open. A man I've never seen before strides through. The stranger's golden brown eyes grow wide.

I react, aiming to strike. But my wrist is halted mid-motion, inches from my target's chest.

"Do try not to stab our guests, little bird," Cassius drawls.

CHAPTER THIRTY-THREE

CLARA

I meet Cassius's gaze, green eyes sparkling with amusement. The corners of his lips curl slightly as he releases his hold on my wrist.

I back up several steps, hiding the dagger behind me. The gesture feels childish and causes my face to warm. However, it's more to show that I don't intend to make another attempt on his life than to pretend I'm not holding a weapon.

"Sorry," I say. "I heard noises and…"

Cassius sweeps past him and out into the hall. He stands beside me, casually throwing an arm around my shoulders. "Worry not. No harm was done."

I'm relieved when an amused smirk replaces the shock on the stranger's face. He and his companion join us in the hall.

"We could really use our own murderous human," the second says. His eyes are a similar dark honey color, but where the first man has striations of gold, his are a richer brown. "I've been meaning to increase security."

"Bram," my almost victim hisses in admonishment, then sends me a dubious look.

Before either man can speak further, Cassius says, "Clara, this is Lewis and Bram López. Lewis and Bram, this is Clara Valmont." Then, with a wink in my direction, he adds, "She isn't usually this feral. I think we just startled her."

"You shouldn't lie," I say, leaning into the well-deserved teasing, wanting to dispel the last of the uncertainty. "I'm usually far more feral."

Cassius ushers us into the sitting room. Lawrence arrives just as he's explaining that Lewis and Bram are the alphas of a neighboring pack west of Progsdale. He lingers just inside the doorway, reclining against the wall as he listens.

Not long after that, Della returns, and there is another round of introductions, cut short by the loud growl coming from my stomach. Everyone falls silent, turning toward me in unison.

Lewis and Della gape at me while Bram covers his mouth and fakes a cough to hide his laughter. Lawrence guffaws, openly enjoying my embarrassment.

Cassius takes me by the shoulders with a smirk and leads me toward the kitchen. "Why don't the four of you continue to get acquainted while I find something for Miss Valmont to eat?"

Cassius sets a plate before me at the island counter in the middle of the room, then goes about gathering a wedge of cheese, some meats, two apples, and bread from the pantry.

I slice portions of the food, popping the occasional piece into my mouth as I go, too hungry to wait. He fills a kettle with water and lights the stove.

"You don't have staff to do this?" I ask when I finish chewing a bite.

He smiles wryly, rolling up his sleeves, and begins arranging a beautiful porcelain tea set for six on a tray. "I used to. I dismissed them when I moved into my rooms at the castle."

Pausing mid-motion, my gaze flicks from him to the food in question.

"When Cherno told us to expect you, I picked up a few things from the market." He frowns disapprovingly at the plate I made. "There wasn't enough time to bring on a cook to prepare something better."

I reach out and place my hand on his. "This is more than enough. Thank you, I'm truly grateful." I stop as something occurs to me. "You can understand Cherno?"

The question seems to catch Cassius off guard for a moment. He shakes his head and resumes preparing tea. It's strange to see a noble doing this kind of work, but he seems entirely at ease with it.

"No. I don't have a connection with them. Fortunately, our demons can communicate with each other to pass on messages."

Ah.

Cassius jerks his chin. "Eat."

I dig into the food. After a few bites I realize how

hungry I really am. Cassius busies his hands with whatever he can think of doing, keeping me company. I am finished with my meal well before the water for tea boils.

He reaches for my empty plate, but instead of taking it away, he stands across the table, just watching me. "After you left, we were half sure we'd never see you again."

I swallow thickly, not sure how to respond at first. I hadn't thought about returning on the day of the attack when I left or while I was at the Keep. The only thing on my mind was making sure Alaric was safe and unharmed. It never crossed my mind that I might have never seen my friends again... or that they would wonder. I took it for granted that we'd reunite eventually. But so much has happened since, and if anything had ended differently, they would have never known.

"I should have found a way to get a message to you."

Cassius leans across the table and pats my cheek. "I didn't say that to make you feel bad. You were missed, that's all. We're glad to have you back."

He must see something in my expression because he sighs and looks at me with gentle disapproval.

"There's no need to make that face. We've been over this already, little bird." The kettle whistles, and he removes it from the stove and adds a mixture of dried leaves to steep. "I lost my humanity a long time ago," he says quietly. "You reminded me what it was like to care for someone other than myself. Now that

I have that back, it would be all for nothing if you let yourself fall in love with me."

I stare, slack-jawed. While I do care for Cassius, I could no more stop loving Alaric with every fiber of my being than I could sprout wings and fly.

Yet somehow, between the last time we spoke and now, it feels as if so much still remains unsaid. Though, I don't know if there are words for any of it.

"Cassius—"

"Little bird," he says, turning serious. "I am your friend. What I did for you is equal to what you've done for me. You need to put away any lingering guilt you've been telling yourself you should feel and focus on tonight. Come tomorrow, the world will be entirely different."

I nod, knowing he has no intention of letting me get another word in on the subject.

We rejoin the others, setting the trays on the coffee table. Della sits across from the wolves, leaning forward as Bram finishes recounting a story of his childhood antics. She laughs, swiping a tear from one eye. Lawrence is perched on the arm of the couch beside her, not nearly as amused.

Reaching for a pocket watch chained to his waistcoat, Lawrence checks the time. "The coronation will begin in just over eight hours from now," he announces, effectively altering the mood to a more serious tone. "We've already managed to sneak a few of the higher-ranking members of various packs in already. The rest will have to wait until nightfall when the majority of the guests arrive, or someone will notice there are more servants than there should be.

With all the new faces, no one is likely to differentiate which of the newcomers do not belong." He swallows, his lip curling in disgust. "It is one thing out of that tragedy that we can use to our advantage."

My stomach churns. The massacre the night the Shade pack attacked was a side effect so bloody and terrible no one could have anticipated it.

It's common knowledge that Elizabeth holds little love for humans, seeing them as a ready food source that also serves the needs of vampires. But even that act shocked some of the oldest court members.

Such a heavy silence settles over our group that I jump when there's a knock on the door.

Cassius rises from his chair to answer, returning a minute later with two sealed letters and a small package. There's nothing written on the outside of either envelope. He hands one to Lawrence and the box to Della. Lewis, Bram, and I sit patiently while they each open their missives.

Cassius remains expressionless as he reads his letter, but Lawrence glowers at him. I wonder if they say the same thing or something different since it didn't seem to matter which one either of them opened.

Lawrence stands, crumpling up the parchment, then tosses it into the fire, scowling while it burns. Then, when Cassius is finished, he does the same, although he looks far less irritated.

"Well?" Della asks when neither of them offers an explanation.

Without turning, Lawrence says, "The fucking sewers."

I have no idea what that means, but after a beat, Della bursts into laughter, leaning back and clutching her stomach. I throw her a questioning glance when she regains her composure.

"The bulk of our forces need to be guided through one of two entrances," she explains. "It seems Cassius got the servants' side entrance, which leaves poor Lawrence with the sewers leading into the lower levels."

My face contorts from the effort of holding in my laughter at his reaction. I feel guilty until I see the wolves looking away as they try to hide their amusement.

A low growl rumbles. "I will have to take several baths to get that stench off me. How would it look if a court member came reeking of shit and piss? I would be a disgrace," Lawrence grumbles to himself. "Will you open the box already?" he snaps.

Della huffs as she unties the twine. "Don't take it out on me. I'm not responsible for your assignment."

Inside are three gold items. A pair of cufflinks, a delicate chain necklace, and a raven skull cravat pin. She takes the necklace and then offers Lawrence the first choice of the remaining two items.

Cassius retakes his seat, a signal to get back to the matter at hand. "We will leave in two hours," he says, then pauses to give the wolves a pointed stare. "The two of you can decide among yourselves who will go with each of us. We will need your help guiding everyone through."

The two wolves eye each other.

"I'll go—" Bram starts.

"We will draw lots," Lewis interrupts.

More discussion follows for the next two hours. From where everyone should be, when to act, what signals to watch for, what to do in case something should go wrong, and every eventuality in between that any of us can think to plan for.

That is, everything other than one crucial detail.

When there's finally a lull, I take the opportunity to speak. "How will I get inside?"

Cassius looks at me, head cocked to the side. "Through the front, of course."

CHAPTER THIRTY-FOUR

CLARA

Sighing heavily, I sink deeper into the warm bath until I'm submerged up to my chin. The mixture of scents I'm too unfamiliar with to name wafts into the air with every ripple along the smooth surface of the water. Here, I am forced into inaction.

Waiting for something to happen is always the worst part.

Each minute passes agonizingly slow. I've gone over the plan countless times, imagined so many ways things could go wrong, and planned for how to bring things back on course.

Yet none of it has eased my tattered nerves. The closer the time comes to put the plan into action, the tighter my insides twist.

"I have never heard so much discontent from someone lucky enough to use such rare oils," Della calls from the other side of the door.

"I've been in here for hours," I return.

Della sticks her head in and shoots me an unimpressed look. "It's been less than one hour."

"What if I don't get there in time?" My voice comes out small and frayed by worry.

"Your hair needs a little more time for the color to set. Even with the mask, Elizabeth might recognize you before you get close." Then, with the promise that I must only endure this for a few more minutes, she leaves.

She's right. We cannot afford to take any chances. Still, it leaves me with nothing to do other than continue to ruminate over Alaric's actions and the numerous questions to which there are no answers.

I skim my fingers over my ribs. Over the spot where Elizabeth stabbed me. Thanks to Varin's power, no sign of the wound remains. But if I think on it for too long, my bones ache with the remembered scrape of metal.

Della knocks to let me know I can finally wash my hair. I let my head fall back and rinse the dark paste from the strands, massaging the scented water into my scalp.

A dress of midnight blue hangs in the window to let out any wrinkles. There are layers of contrasting fabrics wrapping diagonally across the bodice and flowing over the satiny skirt. The delicate gold details, scattered in varying clusters, sparkle like the night sky in the flickering firelight.

Della sits me down on a chair in front of a mirror and begins working on my hair. She works out the tangles first, then adds cream to make it shine. Her face remains serene as fingers move deftly and efficiently, twisting and pinning my hair.

The silence between us is strained.

"I'm sorry I made you worry."

Della lowers her hands and looks at me through the mirror. There's no mistaking the hurt in her eyes.

I pull her around so I can apologize to her directly. "I've been a terrible friend." She opens her mouth to speak, but I don't give her a chance. "Let me finish. I'm not saying this because I want you to excuse my thoughtlessness. I *have* been a terrible friend, and you all deserved better than that. I am truly sorry."

Della's demeanor softens.

"I'm still not used to others worrying about my safety, but that's no excuse. From this moment on, I will do better."

She nods and resumes styling my hair. After a moment, she says, "Thank you."

When she finishes, there's no time to admire her skill. These last few hours started out in a crawl and somehow managed to race by. Della leaves so we can both finish getting ready.

I run my fingers over the skirt. It might be the most beautiful gown I've ever laid eyes on.

The asymmetric neckline covers the scars on my chest and neck. On the high side is a simple petal sleeve made of diaphanous material and an off-the-shoulder loop of the same fabric on the other. The bodice accentuates my figure, with the back cut so low, it borders on indecent before the skirt flares out at the hips.

Layers of tulle bunched are strategically in places

to make it appear to float above the main skirt. The effect gives the dress the illusion of more bulk than it has in reality.

I test out how well I can move around, and I am pleased that rather than being cumbersome, it is light, making it easy to move around. The cloth is delicate enough to rip if necessary, and there is even a hidden pocket at the waist.

Satisfied, I strap the night-forged dagger to my upper thigh. I retrieve the amber vial from where I stashed it at the bottom of the leather satchel and roll it over in my palm, trying to decide what to do with it.

A knock on the door interrupts me, and I shove it in my pocket. The weight of the glass against my hip makes it feel visible to the world.

"Come in," I call, slipping a pair of midnight blue silk gloves on. They are long, coming up almost the entire length of my arm, hiding the last of my visible scars.

"Is it too late to take back what I said about not wanting you to fall in love with me?"

I whirl to find a grinning Cassius with Asmod draped over his shoulders. The demon blinks their crimson eyes, watching me.

My gaze flits to the bed, then to the door, searching for Cherno before I remember that they have returned to Nightwich to be near Alaric. Their absence there would only raise Elizabeth's suspicions that I am still alive.

"You are a vision in that gown." He clears his throat and strides over. "I wanted to give you this before we left."

He holds out a box, urging me to open it when I hesitate. Inside is a choker made of pale gold, fashioned into thorn-covered vines.

"It's beautiful."

Cassius takes it out and fastens it around my neck, then steps back to examine me. A mischievous glint flashes in his green eyes. "I still don't like him, but when this is over, if Alaric doesn't prove himself worthy of you every day, he will have to answer to me."

Before I can respond, Della enters. She's smiling, but her expression is tight around the edges. "The carriage is waiting."

Those four words, though spoken lightly, fill my stomach with butterflies.

"That is my cue to take my leave." Cassius kisses me on the cheek, and in the next moment, he's gone with a soft rush of air swirling in his wake.

I take a deep breath and blow it out, then follow Della. The sun has nearly set, and the gray sky seems to grow heavier by the second.

We climb into the carriage. Suddenly, it is too difficult to speak. I can't tell if Della feels the same or if she's giving me space to sit silently if I need it.

The curtains over the windows remain drawn. We only travel for a short time before we come to an abrupt stop. We've only just left the cobbled streets of the city, and it is far too quiet outside, so I know we haven't arrived yet.

I pull back the corner of the curtain, chancing a peek out, but see only darkness beyond. Then I catch the rumble of men's voices. Just as I send a questioning glance toward Della, Lawrence, and Bram climb in, joining us.

The driver sets the horses back into motion the moment the door is closed. Looking at both men now, it's impossible to tell what they've been up to or that they could be involved with anything outside attending the coronation.

"Where is Cassius?" I ask.

"He is taking another carriage with my sister," Bram explains.

Lawrence relaxes back into his seat, a bored expression sliding across his features as he smooths his fingers down his lapels and sleeves, erasing nonexistent wrinkles.

"Many vampires will bring their own humans. As the three of us are not officially attached to anyone else, it will not appear odd for us to bestow the honor on someone to witness such an event or act as a source of sustenance, should we require it."

Della tenses beside me.

If Lawrence notices as well, he makes no sign of it. He reaches into his jacket and pulls out a small perfume bottle, offering it to Della. She sprays herself, then me, before offering it to Bram. When he's finished, he passes it back to Lawrence to use the remainder of the lightly scented liquid.

The hollow sound of hooves on wood signals that we are now crossing the drawbridge over the crescent chasm bordering the southern edge of Nightwich.

Lawrence lowers the window, letting in a biting wind that steels my breath. He tosses the empty bottle with a flick of his wrist. There's something about the lack of glass shattering that's unsettling. I don't take another breath until we are on solid ground again.

We proceed in a series of halts and jolting starts. I clasp my clammy palms in my lap to keep from fidgeting.

The two vampires don their masks, signaling for Bram and me to do the same. Everyone appears so calm compared to how I feel inside. It makes me wonder if I will be able to do what is needed....

Do they have more faith in me than I deserve?

You are more than capable. Varin's voice says softly against my mind. It's the first they've spoken since the bath. *Remember, I am with you.*

Everyone remains seated until a footman opens the carriage door. The men exit first, each reaching in to hand us down. Lights are set in nearly every visible window of the castle. Bleached white branches, made to look like bones and antlers twisted together with thin silver wire, decorate the outside walls.

I suppress a shiver at the stray thought that some might be precisely what they appear to be. I keep my head up and my eyes downcast, not wanting to examine it close enough to find out.

Lawrence's arm tightens against my hand hooked into the crook of his arm as we reach the entrance. He lifts his mask and gives his and Della's names. The sentinel's cold glare cuts from me to Bram, but Lawrence doesn't provide ours. His silence must communicate enough because the man nods and lets us through.

It is strange to be within the walls of Nightwich

again, feeling both familiar and alien. The din of voices carries out through the arched doors and into the great hall. More sconces have been mounted to the walls and lit, chasing away the shadows from every corner.

The throne room is even brighter, with crystal chandeliers and polished metal branch-like garlands wrapping around every pillar. The air is thick with the scent of honey and is too warm even with half the balcony doors open.

Musicians play near the balcony, the song is upbeat and loud enough for dancing yet not drowning out conversations. Silk and velvet garments of every dark hue swirl in time with the music.

Dancers move in perfect synchronization, not a single misstep, as they whirl in tight circles that make up larger intersecting ones.

There are several long tables draped in burgundy and black lace cloth stacked with platters of food. At the center of each is a different roasted animal, still whole. Bowls with different colored liquids ranging from amber to dark red. Some have slices of fruit, others flower petals, or nothing at all.

Human servants bustle in and out of side passages, adding more and more to the tables until every inch holds some decadent dish.

Several vampires feed on their mortal guests, tucked away in corners, against pillars, and even as they dance.

Upon the dais, Elizabeth sits back on her throne, watching the revelers, fingers tapping to the beat of the music on the arms. Beside her is another throne, slightly smaller and empty.

Atop her head sits the heavy, bone-white crown studded with rubies on its sharp points and along the base of the band. It looks like fangs covered in blood, protruding from red lips. Several strands of pale blonde hair are twisted into knots and cascade over her shoulders in immaculate curls.

Her dress is peacock green, shimmering with hues of cobalt when she moves. The neckline plunges down, nearly to her waist. Feather-like stitching covers her bodice to match the mask covering the upper half of her face. Filigreed silver talons, connected to matching bracelets with thin chains, cap the tips of her fingers.

Alaric enters from a door at the back and stops before her. Under his black jacket trimmed with silver threading along the collar, lapels, and cuffs, he wears a white shirt. Even his mask is simple black leather. The only color is the large ruby pinned at the throat of his white cravat.

Lawrence nudges me. I immediately lower my head, keeping my gaze averted.

Della and Bram go off together in another direction, and Lawrence draws me into a dance along the edges of the crowd. He keeps his face angled toward me with an easy smile while his gaze casts about.

As the others move into place, Lawrence and I need to find a way for me to get close to Elizabeth. It would be better to get her alone, but that might not be possible. She may be more powerful, but I am counting on the element of surprise and my training to make up for the difference.

"May I cut in?" Cassius's voice has our dance coming to an early end.

Lawrence glares. "What are you doing?" he hisses through a feigned smile.

At first, I think he will ignore the request, but then Cassius says, "I will keep your guest company while you greet our queen."

Cassius picks up the dance seamlessly. His movements are unusually stiff, and I don't think it's from nerves. On the next step, he grimaces.

Something is wrong.

"What happened?" I mouth the question.

He doesn't answer right away. Instead, he leads me to one of the many long tables along the outskirts of the room, far enough from anyone else so we can speak without being overheard. Cassius fills a cup with a dark liquid from a large glass bowl with pieces of cut fruit that float in a mimic of dancing courtiers.

I repeat my question in a harsh whisper.

"Only a minor scuffle," he says airily.

If that were true, it would have healed already. "Clearly, it is more than that," I say with false sweetness and step closer, furtively placing a gentle hand against the side he favors.

He hisses through his teeth. Beneath my fingers, I feel the slight unevenness of a bandage wrapped around his middle.

Cassius takes my wrist and lowers my hand. "It has been tended to. I will be fine soon enough." I glare until he offers at least some explanation. "We were surprised by an unexpected guest. But we managed to rise to the occasion."

This veiled way of speaking is frustrating, but we can't risk talking openly.

I take a breath and turn to look at the dancing while I pretend to sip my drink. My gaze snags on Alaric's face, and something inside my chest squeezes at the sight of him.

Too late, I realize I am staring as his eyes meet mine. He does not look away.

Demon shit.

Fear jolts up my spine.

I cannot breathe, cannot move, cannot think.

CHAPTER THIRTY-FIVE

CLARA

The sharp recognition in his gaze sets my heart hammering against its cage of ribs. Between the mask that covers all but my mouth, the darkened shade of my hair, and having been left for dead—our bond severed, Alaric should not be able to recognize me.

The rest of the world drops away, the music turns distant and muffled, and everyone else in the room becomes as insignificant as leaves swirling in an autumn breeze.

Partially turning toward Elizabeth, Alaric bends to whisper something in her ear. She waves a dismissive hand, not bothering to look away from the constant procession of vampires who come to greet her as they arrive.

Alaric descends the dais steps and casually makes his way through the crowd. His course appears meandering as he stops to speak to court members and the gentry. However, I can't help but notice that his path will bring him to me. Cassius's hand tightens around my upper arm with bruising force when he comes to the same conclusion.

"I think it's time for another dance," he grinds out under his breath. Then proceeds to drag me onto the floor and away from Alaric. But with his injury, we are not fast enough to lose ourselves in the sea of dancers.

"Mr. Wellington." Alaric's voice is dark and rich. "You look in need of feeding. I will keep your guest occupied until you get back."

There is a chance Alaric approached us, not because he recognized me but mistook Cassius's pallor caused by his injury for hunger.

Cassius hesitates for only a fraction of a moment. Yet there is only one thing he can do in this situation. He cannot refuse without giving our ruse away.

He releases me and dips his head in a bow—our dance ended before it could begin. "Thank you, your highness. I will not be long."

I am frozen in place, not daring to face the man at my side as Cassius walks away. Either unaware or unconcerned by my unease, Alaric takes my hand and guides me into position.

No good will come of being in his presence before I can act. But there isn't a single way to refuse him that wouldn't blatantly give me away.

Protocol dictates I say something about this being an honor. And yet, if I speak, he will have no lingering doubts about my identity. Pulse erratic, I keep my stare pinned on a fold in his cravat. It is the best I can do to remain hidden behind this mask.

Alaric's gloved fingers press against the bare skin

of my lower back. He doesn't press me to speak, and his touch is as gentle as ever, holding no irritation or anger at my lack of respect.

After a while, when there still isn't any indication he recognizes me, my shoulders relax. The moment only lasts a breath before he leans in and whispers in my ear. "I never thought to see you again."

He catches me as I stumble, disguising the misstep fluidly. My head snaps up. When I meet his gaze, I find his expression unreadable. Candlelight glitters in his deep blue eyes, like stars in the night sky through his mask.

There is no point in lying. "Will you tell her I am alive? That I am here?"

"No." His answer is immediate.

I do not know what to say to that, because I am unsure what game he's playing.

There are too many things to consider, too many things to predict, too many things it could mean if he is lying. The string of hope keeping my heart from breaking into a million jagged splinters, frays a little more.

"Why did you do it—tell her to kill me?" I ask, my voice is barely above a whisper.

Alaric's brows furrow, as if he has no recollection of that day. "I—" he starts, then shakes his head. "Why are you here?"

"Because you are here." The words are out before I can stop them.

"You have said that once before," he says. The knot of his throat bobs. "I didn't—"

Whatever he is about to say is cut short by the abrupt cessation of music.

I jerk my hands from his grasp and move back, pressing into the throng, keeping my head bowed and gaze locked on the polished floor.

Unnatural silence fills the room. Though the air is warm, a chill washes over me, and I am barely able to keep my body from trembling. Fabric rustles as the crowd parts. The slow clack of a single set of footsteps nears.

Despite what Alaric said, had I missed him sending her a signal? Or were we betrayed by someone else… someone pretending to be an ally?

I squeeze my eyes tight, begging the saints to let me go unnoticed but when I open them again, the hem of her blue-green dress stops within my line of sight. And I know the saints have not heard my pleas, or they have chosen to turn their backs on me.

I gather my fury and rage around me like armor, using it to strengthen my spine and keep the crushing weight of all Elizabeth stole from breaking me. Then I lift my head and face her.

Her lip curls. "I should have expected it, but I am surprised to see you alive." Her conversational tone turns venomous, "It would have been so much better if you'd died."

Now is the time to be careful. I cannot fail. I must weigh each word and action, but I cannot bring myself to cower at her feet.

A large hand grabs me, twisting my arm behind my back, and shoves me forward.

Demon shit. There's no way to reach the dagger fast enough to act without Elizabeth killing me first.

Nearby revilers shift away, not wanting to get between their queen and the human unfortunate enough to stoke her ire.

Keeping my head held high, I remain silent.

"Defiant until the end." Elizabeth scoffs. Then she looks around, seeming to remember that we have an audience. A wicked twist curls her lips. "To show you how magnanimous I can be before I end your miserable life, I will allow you the honor of witnessing a moment foretold to me almost three hundred years ago." She steps close enough to whisper so only I can hear. "All you have ever done was cause harm to anyone unfortunate enough to be near you. Have you learned nothing from the death of your family? How heartless to care so little about the end you wrought upon them."

I struggle against my captor, ignoring the cruel words. Varin reins in my strength, rendering my efforts useless. The man at my back tightens his grip, fingers pressing into my skin as if he's feeling for my bones below the muscle.

"You would do well to be on your best behavior." The warning is mild, yet there is an undeniable threat underneath.

There's no time to wonder at her meaning. Elizabeth lifts her hand, and at the snap of her fingers, the door behind the thrones is flung open. The echo of marching soldiers precedes their arrival.

Seven guards emerge. Each holds a chain attached to a metal collar around the neck of a prisoner. The bands have the unmistakable gleam of night-forged silver.

Bruises cover their faces, with smears of blood marking their lips and noses. Yet, it does not stop them from standing tall and scowling at the crowd. I scan the line of captives and am relieved that none of them are ones I recognize. But I am no less furious that anyone is subjected to her abuse and humiliation.

"You should not have involved your wolven friends in your pathetic plots," Elizabeth says, coming to stand beside me and admire her line of hostages. "Should you disobey me, my men will kill them. Should they attempt to shift, they will kill themselves."

Elizabeth has relied on her power for too long. I am under no illusion that she has any intention of letting them live.

I hold my tongue. If I can just get free…

"Soon, you will have even more blood on your hands than I do." She laughs at her own mocking words.

I will not allow her cruelty to crawl under my skin and eat away at me. Every death she has ordered or carried out is of her own doing.

It was all her.

She believes she has the right to decide the fate of others. The right to use whoever she pleases if it means getting what she wants. The right to kill anyone it takes to exert her control over whoever she wants under her thumb.

But I will not bear the burden of those deaths in her place.

Elizabeth tilts her chin up. The Voice, understanding the signal, steps to the edge of the dais from where she has silently been observing, nearly unnoticed against the background of white and silver.

Demons curse her—she was the betrayer.

It was the Voice who told Elizabeth I lived, stripping us of our advantage. They both knew I would come. Knew I would try to stop her—

And Alaric… she knew I would wrest him from her control.

I hurl every ounce of hate I possess that is not already bestowed on Elizabeth toward her with my gaze. If she can sense it, then she hides it well.

Why bother to help me at all? Why not kill me before Oliver and his pack could reach me? Does she believe I deserve to suffer more at Elizabeth's whims before she finally kills me?

Fine. If I must die, then I will drag them both into the Otherworld with me.

The entire room slides their attention over to the Voice, pulled by the spell granted by her position.

"Midnight draws near. It is time to crown our prince and welcome him as our queen's consort."

Alaric approaches, never taking his eyes off Elizabeth. She removes her mask, letting it fall from her slender fingers and clatter to the marble floor.

Lifting up on her toes, she presses her body against his. Her hands slide over his chest and curl around the back of his neck in a deliberate show, claiming him. She wants to prove that she can have anything and anyone she wants. Elizabeth pulls his head down and kisses him deeply as her fingers untie the ribbon of his mask.

It churns my stomach to watch, especially because he doesn't fight it. But to turn my face away would give her the first of many victories she seeks tonight.

Blurring my vision, I slide my gaze to the back of her head, and the shining pin stabbed through her hair.

Varin, I plead, though I do not know what to ask for.

The demon rumbles, a sound of anger directed at her. Their emotions are as easy to read now as my own. Varin takes control of my face, removing every trace of emotion.

Finally, Elizabeth pulls away, and Alaric offers her his elbow. As she accepts, she can't resist sending a cold flash of teeth back over her shoulder before they climb the stairs.

They reach the top of the dais and then face the room. Light reflects off the surface of her crown, polished to look like it's encased in a thin layer of glass.

The guard at my back intentionally pins down the hem of my dress with his boot and shoves me. I stumble. Tittering from several nearby revelers is his reward for the humiliation.

He can have his fun. If it puts them at ease and solidifies my weak humanity in their eyes, then all the better for me.

"Tonight, we will usher in a new power. A strengthening of our force that none could dare deny. As a reward for unwavering loyalty, our queen will command the heavens themselves and grant upon us an unending night. We will no longer be weakened by the garish light of the sun but will thrive in eternal shadow."

As the Voice continues droning on about the changing world, a page emerges from the same entrance the prisoners had. She is young, young enough that I wonder if she is still human, or a vampire turned far too soon.

In her hands is a bone-white crown on a black velvet pillow with silver tassels that chime as they sway. It is identical to Elizabeth's, though the claw-like spines are shorter. It looks like a wide open maw filled with sharp teeth, meant to shred prey in a single bite.

The page stops between Elizabeth and Alaric, who now turn toward each other.

"Alaric Devereaux, if you accept the honor of Queen's Consort, then kneel," the Voice says. Each syllable seems to boom through the massive room.

He does, bracing his arm over his bent knee and bows his head.

Frantically, I cast about, looking for any sign of hope.

Were the others captured as well? Are they chained up in the lower levels… or worse?

Elizabeth takes the crown and holds it over Alaric. Kharis swoops in, croaking with each toll. The demon circles them again and again. The bell tower in the city rings out. Each chime is a countdown to everything that we needed to prevent.

On the final peal, Elizabeth lowers the crown

upon his head. A pulse of power flares out through the chamber, passing through all. It sends a rush of icy air, powerful enough to throw every door open wide.

Gasps arise all around, accompanied by the shifting of feet and frantic whispers. Even the guard holding me is taken by surprise. His hands fall away as he tries to keep his balance.

Elizabeth takes a step back and spreads her arms out to the side.

The snap of a bow cuts through the air. An arrow flies. My gaze snags on the movement, following it through the air.

Kharis screeches in warning. Elizabeth twists. The arrow slices through the material of her bodice, then strikes the floor and skids away.

Shit. Shit. Shit.

From this far, I cannot see if it struck her at all or just came close.

Dozens of bowstrings snap from the shadowy rafters above.

I feel the swipe of a hand on my arm. Another arrow sails past my head, entirely too close. Shrill screams rent the air. A heavy body collapses against me, but I am already running forward as my guard collapses, dead.

Arrows rain down, and everything descends into chaos.

CHAPTER THIRTY-SIX

CLARA

Everything happens at once. The crowd scatters in all directions, pushing and shoving, even lashing out at anyone nearby. Arrows clatter and break against the marble floor. Most miss, but some find their targets, sinking into their flesh.

Alaric scans the room, taking it all in, searching for the source of the attack. Then his sharp eyes alight on mine. The set of his jaw is harsh. Whatever he's thinking is hidden behind a darkened gaze. Time moves agonizingly slow, and my mind and body cannot react fast enough to do anything.

When the volley from above subsides, the wolves take form. They chase most of the vampires from the room, fighting only those who stay instead of fleeing.

A couple clings to each other as they race past. The man holds onto his crying partner. A large black wolf cuts them off, lunging—maw snapping. He swings the woman around, directly into the wolf's path.

The beast's large fangs sink into her neck and shoulder. Bone cracks. Blood flows from the wound like a river, and she collapses to the floor, twitching. The man who was with her is long gone before she finally goes still.

Elizabeth's pretty face is distorted in fury. She grabs Alaric's arm, leaning against him as she shouts. It's impossible to make out the words through the din. He rips his gaze away and guides her from the room.

Kharis lets out an ear-splitting screech. I clap my hands over my ears, pressing them to my head as hard as possible, falling to my knees. Humans closest to the dais collapse, blood leaking from their ears, ruby tears streaking their cheeks.

The guards turn on the hostages. I pull in a breath to shout a warning, only to swallow it down when the captives shift.

Their arms and necks elongate and their legs shorten. White feathers burst out, covering their bodies. The night-forged silver collars slip from their elegantly curved necks.

Swans.

The soldiers seem more surprised than I am. They do not react until the birds are already attacking, using their beaks to distract as their wings beat hard enough to break bone. The guards fall to them in no time, writhing in agony. A few change back into their human form to wrest the weapons from their captors and dispatch them.

Decoys—they were decoys.

I exhale my bated breath and push myself into

action, running toward the dais. I need to go after Elizabeth—I need to stop her.

Halfway up the steps, I stop. Many arrows litter the floor, but it's the one with a green band near the tip that catches my eye. I change direction and weave through the pandemonium.

I snatch up the arrow and snap the shaft so it will fit in my hand. But when I turn, a mob of warring bodies has already coalesced into a wall between me and the door I need to reach.

The flash of Elizabeth's skirts vanishes through the dark opening, with Kharis following close behind.

I won't let her get away.

Pushing the material of my skirt back, I unsheathe the dagger strapped to my thigh. As I stand, I feel the strength of Varin's power flows through me. I strike and slice at any vampire who crosses my path.

Though I am nearly on par with their abilities, progress is slow. For as soon as one enemy falls, another takes their place. I grit my teeth in frustration.

Then, there's an opening, but I don't get a chance to take it. A large furry body crashes into me, sending me sprawling. The wolf scrambles up and leaps back into the fray. The impact forces all the air from my lungs. I push up on my hands.

Through a gap between brawling bodies, my gaze lands on Cassius. He's several yards away, pulling a vampire off a tri-colored wolf. Behind him, a woman reaches for him, fingers skimming his jacket collar.

Razor-sharp teeth sink into the first vampire's leg, keeping him from wrapping his hands around

Cassius's neck for him. The wolf tears into the man until he can no longer fight back.

But the touch draws Cassius's attention. He looks over his shoulder. A movement—caught too late, like the strike of lightning—nails are over Cassius's side. They cut through his clothes, sending a spray of blood as they rip into his flesh.

I am in motion before he hits the floor. Blood pooling at his side. I barely register driving my dagger into the vampire's neck, dragging it down her spine, then shoving her away.

I drop to my knees at his side. All around, the fighting is slowing. Most vampires have fled. Several wolves shift to bind the remaining court members and all others who are quickly surrendering, while others battle against the last few continuing to resist.

I drive my blade into my skirt, cutting off a wide swath, and press it to his side, trying to stanch the bleeding with shaking hands.

The gashes are deep. She tore through the bandage, and down through the wound that was already there. Making it worse. So much worse.

Cassius cringes away from my less-than-delicate touch. I refuse to let up. Pain is preferable to the alternative.

My hands are coated in his blood… and there's so much of it. "Why aren't you healing?" I snap, panic making my words harsh.

Cassius blinks through the haze of pain. "Clara," he says, surprised to see me. He tries to push himself up but can't quite manage it. "Help me sit."

Keeping a hand pressed against the wound, I shift

to his other side, hooking his arm over my shoulders, and prop him against a pillar.

"I will be fine," he says, voice thick and watery. "There is no need to waste your tears."

I swipe at my face. The back of my glove comes away damp, the front soaked through with blood. With a frustrated growl, I force his hand to hold the scraps of my skirt while I yank my gloves from my arms.

"You're not healing," I say. It comes out as an accusation. As if he is doing it on purpose. As if I blame him.

Cassius gives me a flirtatious smile. His hand alights on mine, still desperately holding the glistening wet material to his side. His breathing grows more labored with each inhale.

I shake my head, not understanding. He is a vampire. A powerful one at that. He should be healing.

"Why?" I ask, a waver in my throat. I can't let him die. Not because of me. Not when too many have already died trying to help me.

Cassius coughs then winces. "I am sorry, little bird," he says. "I did not want you to worry about me on top of everything else."

"What are you saying?" I bite out. With every blink, another tear slides free, burning a briny trail down my face.

He lets his arm go limp at his side and sighs, his eyes falling shut. It seems to take great effort to open them again, and when he does, the green shimmers beneath the glassy surface. "There is always a price to magic, especially where life and death are concerned."

My stomach churns with the need to be sick, but I force the sensation down. I will not turn from him. Comprehension hovers along the edges of my mind—a conversation left hanging, unfinished, between us.

"No…"

"I was glad to do this for you." The way he says it feels like a surrender and a goodbye.

"Stop it. Don't you dare give up. We will stop the bleeding and you—" my voice cracks and a sob breaks free of my chest.

The look of heartbreak and pity on his face cuts me off. "Even without injury, at best, I would only have a few days left."

"How is that possible? I don't understand." I bite down hard on the inside of my bottom lip.

He sighs. Shifts. "But you do."

I shake my head, refusing to listen. Refusing to accept. But I can't stop the threads from tying together and forcing the truth on me.

Back at the oracle's cabin.

You should have told her.

She will find out after she heals.

This is how we were bound. He hadn't simply given me a few years of his life as he claimed—he traded it in exchange for mine.

Days…

And now the magic has come to collect its due.

Is that why I was able to beat him when we trained? Was this the secret darkening his expressions?

"Go, Clara, stop Elizabeth, save your oath bonded. Do not let this be in vain." Cassius hisses in a sharp breath and holds it as he tenses. After the wave of pain passes, he reaches up to caress my face, thumb swiping away a tear. "I am relieved Asmod will have you."

As if summoned by their very name, the demon slithers up to us, brushing against his side. Cassius strokes the demon snake's head lovingly. When he lifts his head again, there's a fiery gleam in his green eyes. "Now, go."

I am frozen. Everything inside me is warring. I have to stop Elizabeth and get Alaric away from her. But how can I leave Cassius like this?

Lawrence kneels beside me. His cool hand settles atop mine. "I will take care of him. We've all done our part, now it is time for you to do yours."

"Clara…" his voice is a rasp. "You need to go."

My hand trembles as I remove it. Then I lean forward and press a kiss to the corner of Cassius's mouth. "Fight for me," I whisper. "I am not ready to lose you, too."

"I will do my best." It is a promise. Not a simple platitude without conviction behind it.

Selfishly, I steal one more moment before rising. Some part of my heart splinters and falls away to remain behind.

CHAPTER THIRTY-SEVEN

CLARA

Varin aids my movements as I weave through the waning fight. Asmod catches up as I reach the top of the dais. We slip through the doorway and into a darkened corridor, lit only by the light leaking in from the throne room.

The passage is narrow and smells of damp minerals. Farther up ahead is a solid wall of shadow. I keep my hand against the wall as I venture deeper in. My vision adjusts, but the shadows are so thick it's still difficult to see.

Then the wall curves and the sound of battle fades in the distance. I am surrounded by an eerie quiet. Around the bend, it continues on for several yards before leading to a winding stairwell. At the top, sallow light flickers as if disturbed by a slight breeze right where the steps turn out of sight.

I race up. After what must be several levels, I realize there must be only a single exit. When we make it to the top, there is a single door left ajar. It sways from a breeze coming through the room beyond.

"I will make sure the way is clear." Asmod slithers through the opening. It can't be more than a few seconds before they return, but it feels like minutes. Their head pokes into view. "The queen's chambers—it is safe."

Despite the demon snake's warning, coming out into the excessively opulent parlor is disorienting. Directly ahead is the table where Elizabeth sat and asked me in veiled words to end my life for her pride's sake. But between that and the fireplace is something I had not noticed the last time I was here.

The faint crease of an outline in the damask wallpaper, the size and shape of the door we just passed through, and a small divot in the wainscoting. I hook a finger into the cavity and pull. It gives easily. Beyond is the landing of yet another narrow stairwell.

I hesitate, unsure if I should go up or down. Without knowing how close we are to catching up, I cannot risk speaking.

Asmod slithers forward, facing down. Their tongue flickers out, then they turn and taste the air in the other direction. The demon looks to me, motioning with their head for me to follow.

We climb—slower this time. I am careful to keep my footsteps as silent as possible. It isn't long before we make it to the top. Elizabeth must have been in a hurry because she did a poor job covering her tracks.

Then again, there's always the possibility that this is a trap, and I am walking right into it.

Rattling chains and harsh whispered commands

come from the other side of the door. I inch closer and peek through the cracks between the slats of wood, warped by time.

A frigid breeze pierces through, carrying the scent of winter air. Sconces are lit every few feet along the wall of the circular room.

There is a workbench covered with glass bottles and vials of all shapes, sizes, and colors, spread out in no discernible order. They hold an array of liquids, crushed plants, and an assortment of objects, including small animal bones. Bunches of herbs hung with twine, dry above the workspace. I wonder if this is where Elizabeth has her poisons created.

My heart leaps into my throat. Near the edge, Cherno is trapped beneath a bell-shaped glass dome. Their wings beat uselessly against it.

The Voice walks over to stand before it, gathering what she needs, mixing and measuring. She turns, holding a cup in her hands. Her wide sleeves fall back, exposing one thick bracelet on each wrist. I frown at the strangeness of it.

But my attention is stolen by Alaric. He stands against the wall with an expression somewhere between confusion and anger. A window, built into the vaulted ceiling, is propped open, letting the frigid night air inside.

"Now," Elizabeth commands with a snap of her fingers. The Voice hurries over and holds out the vial with a small amount of blue, syrupy liquid. She snatches it impatiently and presses it against Alaric's mouth. "Drink."

Whatever it is, it can't be good.

When he doesn't immediately comply, she forces it past his lips, and with her other hand, she grabs his jaw and forces his head up. That is when I finally see the night-forged silver collar around his neck. Both his arms are bound behind his back. Alaric coughs and sputters on the potion. I am not sure what she's doing to him, but I will put a stop to it.

I adjust my weapons and motion to Asmod to stay put, then carefully guide the door open and slip through.

Elizabeth turns as I step inside. Her nostrils flare with her temper.

"Why does it not surprise me that you have found your way here? You are like a cockroach. Difficult to kill—" The corners of her mouth curl up. "—but not impossible."

It only takes two strides for her to reach me. She lifts a silver-taloned hand and swipes at my jugular. Varin jerks my body to the side, dodging.

The sharp caps on her fingertips glance off the choker of metal thorns and grate against my shoulder and down my upper arm. I suck in a hiss of air through my teeth.

She glowers, chest heaving, and poises to strike again.

I leap out of the way, but this time I am not her target.

Elizabeth's fingers curl into wicked claws, pressing against the thin band of exposed skin at Alaric's neck above the metal collar.

He doesn't move or react, and his eyes hold a vacant stare.

"What have you done to him?" I demand.

"Make one more move, and I will rip his throat out." Elizabeth's metal-tipped fingers press in, causing thin rivulets of blood to trickle down his neck. She smirks when I am frozen into inaction. "Good. Now, drop your little weapon."

I hesitate.

She growls low and her nails press in hard enough to cause more blood to run down, staining Alaric's white color.

The dagger slips from my grip. It clatters against the floor. Two cold hands connect with my back, shoving me forward to the middle of the room. The Voice kicks my dagger, sending it spinning out of reach. It comes to a stop as the hilt collides with Alaric's foot.

Elizabeth's fingers flex.

"Don't hurt him!" The demand leaps from my tongue.

Fury blazes in Elizabeth's eyes. Desperation makes me quick. I pull the amber bottle from my pocket and hold it between us.

Her eyes narrow, the anger dying out. Replaced by something colder than a winter storm.

Elizabeth lowers her arm and saunters closer. For the first time, I see where the arrow sliced her bodice. Pale skin shows through the tear in the fabric. There is only the thinnest line of blood from a scratch, already healed. Patches of flakey white sores mottle the area. A shiver crawls down my spine at the sight.

"I was wondering what you did with that." She reaches out for it, but I jerk my hand away.

"I will break it if you come any closer."

Elizabeth throws her head back and lets out a sharp laugh. "Do that, and I will grind your bones into dust—right after I make you watch as I rip Alaric's heart out with my bare hands."

We are at a standstill. My gaze darts around, never leaving her for more than a fraction of a second.

Demon shit.

I will make you suffer for all the trouble you have caused." Maliciousness glints in her eyes, but she keeps her distance.

Whatever she put in the vial... she wants it.

My heart hammers against the cage of my ribs. "Let him go, and I will give it to you."

Red splotches break out across her pale skin, rising from her chest and moving up her neck to her cheeks. The idea that I would dare command her in any way makes her seethe.

I am balancing on a fine line. Anger will make her careless, but if I am not careful and push her too far, she could lash out faster than I can react.

"I will enjoy every second as I take you apart until there is no doubt that you are well and truly dead."

The beat of wings pulses through the air. Elizabeth's demon soars through the opening overhead, coming to perch on her shoulder. Kharis watches me with glowing red eyes. The wing that was hit earlier is missing a few feathers, a small patch of white tarnishing the oil-slick black.

A slow smile slides over her face. "I will release him."

Suspicion laces its fingers around my heart. "In

exchange for what?" I prod when she doesn't continue.

"All you have to do is drink what is in your hand." Elizabeth glances over her shoulder at Alaric. "Break your bond with him, and I might just let you live."

A heavy weight settles in me.

She knew when we bonded ourselves to each other, and even though I didn't die in that field, the bond was broken that day. So, she should be able to sense that it's no longer there. Which means my hunch was correct—it was never what she claimed, but poison.

When I hesitate too long, she spins, strides back over to Alaric, and rips his jacket open, pressing her nails against the spot over his heart. The metal tips dig in, causing red to bloom over his white shirt.

"Fine," I gasp, panic stealing the strength from my voice. "I'll do it."

She watches me.

Popping the cork with my thumb, I bring the vial to my lips and swallow it in a single gulp. It's bitter on my tongue, leaving behind a strong, earthy aftertaste.

A golden brow arches, demanding proof. I hold out my hand, showing the empty bottle. It slides over my fingers, cracking against the gray stone floor with a hollow clink.

Varin, I call down to the demon within me.

Their power seeps into every muscle and bone. Their presence is feather light, stretching out as they take partial control of my body.

We face Elizabeth down. This is the moment everything we have done has been leading to.

With a jerk, she pulls her fingers from Alaric's chest. Elizabeth closes in and toes the glass. She lifts her cold lavender eyes to mine. "I am impressed."

In the space of a heartbeat, she shoves me against the back wall. My head cracks against the unforgiving surface, and stars explode across my vision. When they clear, her hand is tangled in my hair.

She forces me to my knees. "You should feel it working already, numbing your limbs… slowing your heart." Elizabeth leans in, close enough for me to feel her metallic breath on my face. "In the end, you killed yourself."

Varin rises within me. My vision grows sharper, and the world more vivid. I feel the bright gleam of their power circling my irises. But unlike the crimson vampires, this is different, golden, tinting the world in a warm glow.

Elizabeth's eyes flash with something wild. Fear. Recognition of the demon in my eyes, right below the surface.

"No… that cannot be—that's impossible," she rasps, the slightest bit of red coating her teeth. Each breath is shorter than the last, rasping. Her face contorts. "Wh-what have you done?"

She releases her grip on my hair and stumbles back. Elizabeth lowers a trembling hand to her side, feeling the white sores. At the contact, they rupture. Sickly yellow pus oozes from them. Her lip curls up as understanding sets in.

My fingers curl around the broken arrow shaft in the folds of my skirt. I drive the arrow into the center of her chest with every ounce of strength I can muster.

Her hands flutter over the broken shaft embedded in her chest.

I straighten and step forward. "Slayer. That's the name you gave me for defending myself against the vampires you sent to kill me even though I'd done nothing to you." Another step. "But you still wanted me dead."

Elizabeth tried to kill me once already with her demon's blood. I wasn't about to believe her claims that a potion could break my bond with Alaric. Varin and I thought it safer to assume it was intended to kill —after all that *would* break the bond.

I let the arrowhead soak for days, carefully disposing of it. I rinsed the bottle, even boiling it, to eliminate any trace of the poison. Then, I refilled it with over-steeped tea to get a similar color.

I don't bother explaining all the reasons I have for acting against her, for deciding to end her life, because she is incapable of empathy for all the pain and suffering she's inflicted on others. She thought to use my crimes to frighten me into submission, but now I have used the status she forced on me to show her that *she* should have feared *me* all along.

Varin curls my lips into a cold smile, listing my head to the side. "So a slayer I will be."

At first, I don't know if it is the demon or Elizabeth that makes the horrible noise that rents the air, only to realize it is both.

Elizabeth gasps and flounders woodenly for a moment, then pitches back with wooden movements, fingers clawing, scratching angry lines into her chest. Her eyes roll back, and she collapses. The crown slips from her head, tangling in the mess of wild golden hair.

Kharis lands on her chest, claws digging deep gashes and tearing at her skin in an effort to remove the arrow. The sight of torn flesh is horrific. Dark, viscous blood oozes out from the edges of her wounds.

The raven rears back as if struck and takes to the air. Their flight is erratic, rising into the sky. Then, they plummet like a stone.

Gone.

I lower my gaze to Elizabeth's unmoving body. White patches of rot break out from the wound, spreading in mottled patches identical to the ones on her side. The stench of rot is immediate and overpowering.

The bone crown cracks. Piece by piece, it flakes away until it reveals another underneath—night-forged silver, shining like liquid moonlight, surrounded by a pile of ash.

CHAPTER THIRTY-EIGHT

CLARA

Varin releases all control, sinking deeper and deeper, retreating within me. Their strength wanes, and with it, I can feel just how much I've been relying on them. Every muscle in my body aches and trembles with weakness.

A vicious wave of dizziness rocks the ground beneath my feet. I gasp, staggering back into the wall. I can barely hold myself upright with the violent tremors wracking my body.

Elizabeth lies in the middle of the room.

Unmoving.

Not breathing.

Something deep down inside my gut doesn't trust this—doesn't trust her.

I can't seem to make myself turn away. It's a fear whispering that if I do—if I get too close—she will reach out and kill me. Despite the unnatural way, she didn't react as Kharis clawed at her. That the torn flesh around the arrow lodged in her chest and the sores spreading over her body, blistering, consuming, won't stop her.

But I cannot remain standing against the wall, frozen. I have to move, have to check on Alaric... on my friends.

There is a shuddering gasp to my right, but it's a quiet weeping that breaks the spell. I drag my gaze from the strange and grotesque scene before me over to the Voice. She kneels, bowed over, staring at her hands. Tears fall into her open palms.

Not her hands—her bare wrists. Two metal cuffs lay open in front of her. Shackles. The silver bands I mistook for bracelets earlier.

Staying pressed against the wall, I inch away from her and toward Alaric. I'm not sure if she can be trusted or what her role in all of this was.

I bend down to pick up the dagger, and another, stronger wave of dizziness hits. Unnatural cold encases my skin, and beads of sweat break out across my forehead, over the back of my neck, and slither down my spine.

I stagger.

Varin, what is happening? I ask, but the demon is unnervingly silent.

"Is she—" My head spins, feeling heavy. "Is she dead?" I demand, putting as much force behind it as I can.

Logically, I know Elizabeth and Kharis are dead— but I have to know. Have to hear it spoken aloud. I *need* that confirmation.

There's a crash of glass and leathery wings taking to the air as Asmod frees Cherno.

The Voice gasps, startled. She lifts her head, staring at me with wide, wild eyes that show too much white around her vibrant pink irises as if she forgot I was in the room.

Surprise slips into clarity. She assesses me for a long moment before turning her attention to Elizabeth's body. Snow frost lashes flutter, fanning her cheeks as she contemplates.

Alaric still hasn't moved—his expression slack, gaze unfocused, but he is breathing, and the wounds on his chest have stopped bleeding. It's like he is in a trance.

"She was the first of her kind... the only one. I never dared hope, not for a single second. I..." she says, her voice frail and distant. Her cheeks are wet, but her expression is entirely blank. "I should hate her... I should feel..."

I don't know if she heard me or if she is simply ignoring me. I squeeze my eyes shut, gritting my teeth in frustration. "Is she dead?"

"Yes," she says flatly. "She is dead."

"What did she do to him?" I point to Alaric with the dagger.

If she notices my irritation, she doesn't show it. "He will be fine once the sun rises. It was only a potion to keep him docile until daybreak."

"Why?" I struggle to keep my rapidly waning strength from showing.

Rising gracefully to her feet, the Voice edges forward. Her head lists from side to side, reminding me of an animal, curious and uncertain about the potential prey in its sights. "So, she might attempt the very thing you were trying to stop. She wanted his power—needed it—to make up for what hers lacked. It's what she has been after since the beginning."

I lift the dagger, pointing it at her. A warning not to come any closer. Her eyes flick from my face, down to the weapon, and back up. Then she stops, waiting.

"Unchain him."

Without protest or hesitation, she obeys, gently easing Alaric down onto his back.

My vision wavers until the world doubles, shivering and vibrating, weaving in and out like a kaleidoscope. I squint, willing my eyes to focus again. Slowly, everything shudders, trembles, then goes motionless again, but everything has taken on a soft haze.

Varin! I shout down to the demon again, but still, they do not answer.

I shake my head, trying to clear it and lower my arm to my side. Tired. Too tired and weak to hold the dagger up anymore. "What do you mean 'she wanted his power'?"

"It wasn't the spell she thought it was that broke that day in the field," the Voice says, once more inching closer. "When Mr. Devereaux went to you on the dance floor, she realized her mistake. If her curse still had him in its grasp, he never would have done so." A cold smile spreads over her lips. "He hid it well."

The curse....

I shake my head again, trying to clear the soft buzzing that makes my thoughts blurry, sluggish, and nearly impossible to hold on to. They break off in fragments before they have a chance to fully form.

It's broken....

I forget everything before she finishes a sentence. What she's saying... what she's telling me... it's important.

Something... is broken?

I furrow my brow, frustrated that I can't hold on to any thought, that I can't focus.

What is...

Something is wrong. Very wrong.

And it terrifies me.

"He gave her the ability to curse him for as long as she didn't harm you. She broke her word when she tried to kill you and thus relinquished any hold she had over him."

Her voice is half obscured by a droning buzz, a ringing clogging my ears, making it hard to understand what she is saying.

My knees give out, and I slide down the wall to the floor, chest rising and falling with the strain of continuing to function.

I drag my gaze over to Alaric, still ensnared by a spell. But images flash. Images of him standing against an ashen sky. "He left me to die... He betrayed me."

I slump, toppling onto my side.

Varin?

I am sorry, Clara... I thought we had more time. Varin's voice inside my mind is almost too soft to make out.

A warm palm alights on my forehead. I blink up into a pale face with delicate features and the Voice kneeling beside me. Her eyes are different. Changed. No longer pink and red, but pink and gold.

When *I possessed you, I must have broken off more of my power than I realized. It would have been too much and forced you into the Otherworld.*

I am too weak to worry whether or not her intentions or if she is a friend or foe. Too stunned by the things Varin is saying. They diminished their power—part of themselves—to keep me alive.

Thank you... because of you, I was able to see the night sky one last time, they say.

"The demon is dying," the Voice says. "And their death will be yours if you do not get it out."

How could she possibly know about Varin? It seems like such a silly, unimportant question when it won't matter in a few minutes. We are out of time.

"No single body is meant to bear such a burden," she continues.

I barely notice as she shifts me, her leg pillowed under my head. The way she strokes my head offers a small comfort.

"You freed me from a bargain I made long ago, when I was young, and gave my trust too freely. So, now I will repay you."

Throat too dry to speak, all I manage is a weak groan.

"First, I must rid you of this demon." She glares as though she can see through my flesh and bone to that unseen place where Varin has settled over the last few weeks.

We didn't plan this far yet. We thought we had more time. I don't know how this works. I am not sure what options are open to me. Though it doesn't matter because we made a deal.

Varin followed through with their end, letting me use their power to save Alaric. And now, Elizabeth can't hurt him or anyone else again, which is more than I had asked for.

Now, it's my turn to follow through. Things were not always easy between Varin and me. They are temperamental and stubborn. Then again, so am I. Even without a bargain, I would make the same choice. We have come so far together in such a short amount of time in the grand scheme of things. I care about them too much to let them die now after everything we went through—after everything they sacrificed without my knowing.

My throat is as dry as sand, and I am fading fast. But I need to say something before it's too late. A simple shake of my head could cause a fatal misunderstanding.

"Save them." Those two syllables take a monumental effort to get out.

Her head jerks back. Varin's surprise is a distant jolt within my chest that mirrors the shock on her face. They struggle to let go, but I hold on to them, refusing to let them fade away.

The Voice recovers quickly. "It will be painful." She lowers me to the cold stone floor and stands. "I will give you a draught to keep you unconscious until it's over."

My eyelids are too heavy to keep open any longer. There's a pounding, growing louder, resounding in my head. Closer and louder. Voices, familiar and unknown, join in, then replace it.

I can't make out the words they're saying. Only that everything is too loud. Too cold. Too heavy. The world shifts, and I am drowning, choking on bitter water.

Varin... please... don't leave me...

With no other option than to trust everyone around me, I let go. Unfeeling darkness crashes around, pulling me into fathomless depths.

The first thing I am aware of is an ache. Deep and unwavering. I want to get away from it and return to the peaceful nothing it is forcefully dragging me from.

But the harder I try to cling to the void, the more I move, the more I stay still, the more insistent the pain becomes.

A groan rises up my throat. The sound burns as it claws its way up my raw and stinging throat. Moments pass, and consciousness reforms, taking hold in my mind and bringing awareness of the world with it.

Blood flowing through my veins. The sound of quiet breathing—mine, surrounded by other, smaller breaths. Snapping and crackling of flames. Warmth. The weight of a blanket.

Something soft and leathery pressed into the space between my neck and shoulder on one side. On the opposite, the smooth, almost metallic slide of scales wrapped around my arm.

I peer through my lashes at first, adjusting to the low light. Though dim, it still makes my eyes ache, as if I have been in the dark a long, long time.

I do not recognize the ceiling above me or the scent of freshly cut wood mingling with the musty air that has permeated each inch of the room. Heavy drapes cover the window, blocking the view and time of day.

Varin? I call down to them. They do not answer, and the space they once resided, where I could sense them, is empty. I am alone in my body, as I've been for most of my life. But for the first time… it feels lonely.

When I shift to look at Cherno and Asmod, I am confused by the weight of something else pinning my hair to the pillow. My movements rouse the two demons, their heads popping up in unison.

"You're awake," Cherno says, climbing onto my chest. They wrap their wings around my cheek and chin in what I think is a hug.

With a light tug of hair, whatever is pinning me down moves, freeing my head. A tiny black rabbit with ruby eyes flecked with gold comes into view, their limbs moving awkwardly, getting in the way. They tumble down the pillow and roll, landing with a fluffy tail in the air, and back feet dangling over their head.

I bolt upright, sending Cherno tumbling into my lap. An instant headache forms from sitting up too quickly. I press a hand to my temples to quell the pounding inside my skull. Cherno takes to the air and wings their way through the door like a puff of smoke while Asmod unwraps themselves from my arm and slithers after them.

"Wh—" My question is cut off by a coughing fit.

On the night table is a filled cup and a pitcher just out of reach. The water is tepid, but I drink it all down. It eases my parched throat, though not entirely.

Carefully, not wanting to hope, I lean in close to the animal—more fur than body, with tall ears too big for their body. Each paw is tipped in an ashy gray.

"Varin?" I whisper, too afraid to let myself hope. They are a demon—but is this my demon, or the demon of some unknown vampire?

The rabbit takes a single hop closer. Their legs are not quite in sync, and the awkward movement instantly brings a smile to my lips.

"What other demon did you expect?"

And it is Varin's voice. Hearing them speak, knowing they are alive, brings a wave of emotions crashing within the walls of my chest. Tears well in my eyes. I scoop them up and cradle them against me.

Tiny paws push against my face while their back feet tap against my chest in a halfhearted struggle against my embrace. I am laughing and crying at the same time, unable to express how I feel in any coherent way.

"This is undignified," they mutter. Varin resists the hug a moment longer, then gives in to it.

I sniffle into their soft fur. "I am so glad you're all right."

Varin is quiet for a few seconds. "I, too, am happy

to see you awake and well," they say, with more affection than I expected, only to ruin the moment when they continue, "But if you do not stop leaking all over me, I will bite you."

I relent and hold them in front of my face. They swipe their tiny front paws over my eyes, drying my tears. It's a touching gesture, but I don't point it out.

An abrupt thought intrudes on my relief. "If you're... this," I say. "Then, does that mean I'm a... vampire?"

Varin rolls their eyes, which is a little unsettling to see on a rabbit. "Are you asking because you crave blood or because you did not think to check for fangs?"

I pull a face to show my lack of appreciation for their tone. "A simple 'no' would have sufficed." Then I lower them to my lap, furtively running my tongue over the tips of my teeth.

Nothing *feels* different.

I suspect their remarks often hold a bite to them as a defense. In the time they possessed me, I have come to understand that their captivity and the cruelty they suffered has left more scars than the ones made by their night-forced silver chains. There is no telling how long it's been since they knew kindness, but from now on, I will make sure that is all they know.

Varin bumps my hand with their nose. Their long whiskers brush over my skin, tickling. "You are not a vampire because you did not ask me for anything."

I frown. "I wanted your power...."

"You asked for my help in exchange for my

freedom. And you asked for me to be saved when you could have easily let me die."

Even the suggestion that it was an option has unease twisting up my insides. Varin may be a demon, but after everything, and I would like to think somewhere along the way, our tenuous trust took hold in a solid foundation.

Help me, and I will free you. Those were my exact words when we struck our bargain. Though I did want the strength and magic they possessed, it never crossed my mind to want it longer than that. Had they realized all of that from the beginning?

"For the most part, you are as you were," they add.

My jaw goes slack, pulse roaring in my ears, and all previous questions evaporate. "For... the most part?"

"You cannot remain fully human while being bonded to a vampire and a demon."

The breath halfway down my throat catches, and my mouth goes dry.

CHAPTER THIRTY-NINE

CLARA

It takes a long moment before I remember how to make my lungs work again, to regain the feeling of my tongue and lips, to form the simple question I need the answer to. Even if I'm not entirely sure if I'm ready to hear it.

I swallow. Inhale.

When I find my voice again, it is almost entirely all breath. "Then… what am I?"

"A dhampir." At my bewildered expression, Varin continues, "Technically. Your body will require nothing more than it always has. Only now you will have the abilities of a vampire and the power of your demon."

It takes a few moments for that to sink in and wrap my mind around what it means. I am relieved I have not changed, at least not more than I was ever willing to be, but I'm also curious if there is more to it than that. Perhaps it is just that simple. Either way, that explanation is enough to ease any anxieties.

"Is it terrible being in this form?" I ask quietly, needing to know what Varin went through and that they all right before anything else is said or done.

They tilt their head and use a back foot to scratch at the base of the ear. "It is not so bad."

"Were you hurt? Why a rabbit?"

Varin eyes me. "It was bearable," they admit grudgingly, then rush on. "And I am *this* because it was the animal that would serve you... and me, best."

"Well, I think you are adorable." I scratch the top of Varin's head between their ears. They narrow their eyes at me as if insulted, even as they lean into it. Their large round eyes gradually close.

"I'm sorry you spent so long in chains," I whisper.

Varin twitches their nose. "I am free now."

"How did you end up down there?" The question is out before I can think to stop it.

They don't answer at first, then the demon's ears lower, lying flat. I wait, giving them time to gather their thoughts and not push them into answer if it's not something they are ready to talk about.

"Before Elizabeth bonded with Kharis, she summoned me first. She wanted to use my power to strip another of their free will. But she was too weak, and it would have cursed us both, so I refused her. Even without the threat of corruption, I had no desire to be connected to someone with such an unfeeling heart."

I take careful breaths as Varin speaks, fearing to break the spell. Instinctively, I sense it is no small thing for them to confide in me. To possibly be the first to know of their story.

"Eventually, she found Kharis. They were not strong enough to do what she wanted, but managed something close. If that was not terrible enough, they betrayed our kind by helping Elizabeth imprison me.

"She kept me locked and chained, stationing guards to patrol the empty cells as a reminder that I would never be part of the world outside my prison. Once every ten years for the first century, she would come and offer me freedom in exchange for my power. But I am no fool—better I die than to allow that."

My chest aches for this demon—for all they have suffered to keep Elizabeth from unleashing worse cruelties into the world.

I am glad they lured me down to that dank cell, glad I bargained with them, glad to have risked my life to free them.

The door swings open, and a servant enters, stepping to the side with his head bowed, letting a line of familiar faces into the room. Each of them belongs to someone dear to my heart, with Cherno and Asmod leading the way. The two demons waste no time reclaiming their spots on the bed, curling up into the plush, down comforter.

Della rushes over and begins fussing with my pillows and checking my forehead while the others quietly find a space to occupy. Alaric comes to stand between the bed and windows as Oliver takes a seat on the foot of the bed beside Della. Lawrence leans against the wall on the opposite side of the night table. I think he's trying to appear casual, but he keeps shifting in an uncomfortable sort of way.

I pause petting Varin, and peer through the door into the hallway, waiting for one last face to appear.

Seconds pass, but then the servant backs into the hall and closes the door. The sound of the mechanism clicking into place seems to draw the air from my lungs.

Time seems to freeze. The moment stretches on and on, but nothing happens. Oliver shifts uncomfortably, and Lawrence adjusts his cravat. But no one speaks a word.

It is Della who cuts through the tension. She directs an exasperated sigh at the men, then sits on the edge of the bed.

My chest aches. I know the answer to my unspoken question when she takes my hand and squeezes it, the way people do when they are about to deliver bad news.

"I am sorry, Clara." Della's voice is low and raspy.

Pressure builds behind my eyes, filling my skull. The *thump, thump, thump, thump, thump* of my pulse hammers between my ears, then turns into a roar.

No.... No, no, no, no, no! I shake my head, refusing to accept it. But the harder I cling to denial, the heavier the weight of truth presses down on it, cracking the already fragile thing.

My throat tightens, and I cannot breathe through the sharp agony as a fissure forms, spreading until yet another piece of my heart breaks away and shatters. It cries out, angry with him, shouting, *he promised, he promised....*

It doesn't matter if he didn't use absolutes. He said he would do his best, and although it's not the same as saying he would live, that is what the promise I held him to.

But life does not bend to the will of one's word, but the heart is foolish and expects impossible things.

Cassius knew he would die there. It would have been easy to say what I wanted to hear. Instead, he gave me the only truth he could. As if he didn't want his final words to be a lie.

"I am sorry, Clara," Della says again.

Meeting her gaze is a mistake. Seeing her eyes brimming with tears is all it takes for a sob of my own to rip free of my chest, breaking the lock that has kept all the pain I shoved down at bay.

It all comes crashing down in a single, earth shattering wave. Unstoppable. Overwhelming. Suffocating from the force of my heart cracking open. It is so much more than any physical pain I have felt that I don't know if it's possible to survive so much heartache at one time. Della wraps me in her arms, holding tight as if she could keep me from shattering.

Pieces of me crack and break away. For Cassius. For Kitty. For the mother I never had the chance to fight with until I could forgive her. For my father and the opportunity to mend our relationship—all of it... lost forever.

I cover my mouth against a scream, but the agony is so deep it is a sound no physical form can make, and all that comes out is a long, excruciating, silent exhale.

So many people I loved...

Gone.

Taken by acts of cruelty and hate without reason.

She holds me until I have run out of tears and am worn out. Lawrence thrusts a handkerchief toward me, looking away. There is not a single stitch of color on it. The embroidery is unembellished along the edges, with a simple 'H' in one corner.

I bite my lip to keep from blubbering over the gesture and use it to wipe away the dampness on my face, offering it back with another sniffle when I'm done. He gives me a flat look, holding up a hand to refuse.

Della refills the empty cup from a pitcher on the far end of the night table. She wraps my hands around it. I sip on the cool water. She once again takes charge, telling me what happened. Though she is careful not to mention the fighting or any fatalities I don't yet know about, only recounting how worried they were for me and their relief when I woke. The three men all nod and interject a few mumbled words here and there.

I twist and untwist the square cloth around my fingers. Guilt gnawing at my insides. My tears have dampened the mood and brought an awkward air to the room. But everyone has stayed, comforting me and offering their love and support, letting me know I am not alone in my sorrow. The conversation dwindles until a weighted silence settles over the room.

Alaric clears his throat. "We should let her rest… and I would like a moment to speak with Clara. Alone," he says, then he turns to me. "If that's all right with you?"

I nod. Though there is probably more for us to discuss than could fit in a week, let alone a moment.

Oliver comes over and smooths a hand over my hair, kissing my cheek. He glances behind me, then straightens and backs away. Lawrence snorts, and I send a sideways glance back at Alaric. His face is a little too carefully set into a neutral mask.

Della suppresses a smile and shakes her head. When her attention returns to me, she pats my shoulder, dark eyes moving back and forth, scanning my face before she slides from the bed.

I get the sense she almost doesn't believe I am fine. Which leaves me wondering how much worse things were than they are letting on.

"I'm sorry I made things uncomfortable," I speak to her, but the apology is for everyone.

"Crying is not a weakness. It is a virtue to bear your heart openly, exposing your vulnerabilities, and only those who are capable of putting themselves back together, stronger than before," she says.

Oliver continues to inch away until his arm brushes Della's, only to be forced to the side when Lawrence moves to stand between them.

"It is not something you ever need to apologize for," Della says, ignoring the men and their odd behavior. "You must be hungry. I'll have food brought up."

Then Lawrence takes her by the arm, and the two of them take their leave, with Oliver not far behind.

"That includes you three," Alaric says to the three demons burrowed under the covers. He gives them a stern expression when they hesitate, and after a brief standoff, they obey. Even Varin, much to my surprise. I expected them to refuse out of pure stubbornness.

When bat, snake, and rabbit pass through the wall in puffs of smoke, Alaric turns his deep blue gaze on me. My pulse speeds up, a wild staccato in my veins. After everything, he can still change the beat of my heart with a single glance or word.

"Your... curse?" It's hardly a graceful way to ask, but I have to know for sure if he is all right or if we are still racing against the clock.

Alaric's spine stiffens minutely. A deep agony shadows his eyes. His throat bobs. "Broken."

I continue to twist the handkerchief around my fingers and quickly change the subject. "Where are we?"

"Nightwich." He nods in the general direction of the door as he brings the chair from the writing desk in the corner to sit beside the bed. "This is one of the spare rooms intended for distinguished guests."

He lays a hand over mine, lingering for a few heartbeats, before taking the handkerchief from me and setting it aside. It's hard to tell if he finds my fidgeting distracting or thinks I don't know what to do with it.

Accustomed to how we used to be around each other, this feels... strangely formal. I smooth the coverlet over my legs, giving myself something to do with my hands. He must read the uncertainty on my face.

"Do not look so worried, little nightmare." He leans forward, resting his elbow on his knees. "You just woke up, and I didn't want you to feel overwhelmed."

Tension seeps from my shoulders. I can't fight the gravity he possesses. It tugs like a siren's song, angling my body toward his. He's half an arm's length away, close enough for me to catch the lingering scent of soap and musk with every inhale.

Alaric leans over and adjusts my pillows, then retakes his seat. But from the set of his jaw, it is clear the reason he gave for sending everyone out of the room is not the whole of it.

I swallow thickly. "How long have I been asleep?"

"Two days." He fidgets, nervous about something. Then he stands and walks over to the padded bench at the foot of the bed, picking up a box I couldn't see from where I sit. It's a black stained wooden box with decorative silver caps on the corners and thorny vines and roses embossed on the sides.

I'm not sure I can handle any more bad news just yet. Instead, I settle on a topic that centers on him. "What is it like, being a king?"

"There's—" he starts at the same time. Stops. Blinks a few times. "I actually wanted to talk with you about that."

I frown.

Seeing my dubious expression, he hurries to add, "It's nothing to worry about, only a matter of formality."

An apprehensive flutter takes hold in my chest as I dissect his words. I can't imagine what discussion he wants to have about his new status that might concern me. I motion for him to proceed.

"I am not king." Alaric watches me closely as that sinks in.

There are only a few reasons I can think of why that might be. Either Alaric rejected the crown, or in the time I slept, he did away with the need for a ruler among vampires.

Neither of which seems like something he would do. It would be too risky to leave the existing vampires without some rule or government to hold them accountable. Unless....

Unless the court rejected him as sovereign. But even that doesn't seem likely as we are still in the castle, and it wouldn't explain how there's a matter of formality concerning me.

"I think I'm going to need a little more information," I start slowly. Disquiet takes flight in my stomach like a swarm of moths. "If you're not king, then..."

Alaric unlatches the wooden box in his hands, all the while keeping his sharp gaze trained on me. "You killed Elizabeth," he says quietly, lifting the lid.

Inside is a crown, delicate and sharp. It has the telltale sign of night-forged silver, impossibly sleek as if it was made from liquid moonlight.

"You, Clara Valmont, are queen."

CHAPTER FORTY

CLARA

The ability to think, let alone respond, eludes me entirely. I can only gape. I press the back of my hand to my forehead, checking to see if I am hallucinating from fever.

He's saying something, but I can't hear him over the roaring that fills my ears and the scrape of air as it flows in and out of my lungs in short bursts.

"What?" I say when I finally manage to drag my eyes up to his face.

"Because you killed Elizabeth, you are now the vampire queen."

"No… I… that—that doesn't make sense. She crowned *you*. And… and I'm not even a vampire." My chest rises and falls with quick, shallow breaths that make my head swim. I shake my head over and over. The world tilts on its axis, making me dizzy. I cannot imagine any circumstance when waking up to find that you are queen would be considered *only a formality*.

Alaric sets the box off to the side and half crawls onto the bed, gripping my face in both hands. "Breathe, Clara."

He inhales and exhales in slow exaggeration, nodding when I match his breathing. When I've calmed down as much as I'm going to, he releases my face and sits back.

"No vampire would bow to a ruler who inherited the throne. You killed her. That makes you queen." Alaric reaches for my hand. His is warm and dry against my cold, clammy skin. "You don't need to do this on your own. Your friends and allies will be there to help you—whatever you decide."

I swallow thickly. "What about you?" I ask, needing to hear it, needing to know if he considers himself one of those people... to know if there is anything left between us.

His shoulders relax. "I will be there, too." Alaric hooks his finger around a strand of hair clinging to my cheek and tucks it behind my ear. "It would be dangerous to leave a void of power." His words echo my earlier thought.

There are likely a million details that will need to be ironed out. At least I have the comfort of knowing I won't need to find my way through this mess on my own.

If I accept this... I will spend the rest of my life looking over my shoulder for anyone who wishes to depose me. I've never wanted that kind of authority, let alone imagined something like this was possible. I don't even know where to begin.

"Clara..." The way he says my name brings me

back from the overwhelming implications of what such control would mean.

"I am not sure I can do this," I admit. "I'm not cut out to rule over anyone."

"As queen, you will be in the undeniable position to help forge new laws. Things need to change in ways no one else but you can set in motion. I think you will agree that it is long overdue." He smiles, but there is a bone deep weariness in it. "Though if you want to abdicate, then we will find a solution, and it will only be until necessary arrangements are made."

He's right. We cannot allow things to go on as they have, and this is a rare opportunity to set things right. Those with power must be kept in check. Because no one deserves to live in constant fear or have their lives and families torn apart.

Demons and saints... Am I seriously considering this?

"Would we have to stay here—forever? I don't know if I could bear that," I say. A shudder rolls through me. "There are too many memories, too much pain in these walls."

"No," he says gently. "You can go anywhere you want—you can go home."

Home. Images of his manor spring to mind at the word. It might not be the home he meant for me, but it's the first place I truly felt safe—despite the dangers that found me. Thinking of being there again is comforting. The way it feels, the way it smells. *Him.*

"If it will make things easier, there is a way I can help...." He grimaces, shifting uncomfortably. "I can become your consort." Alaric suddenly stands and begins pacing the length of the bed. "You would not be obliged to any part of the role and could dissolve that position whenever you wish."

My heart stutters. Most would consider such an offer to be a proposal. Albeit a backward one... it is a request for a proposal. I am rendered speechless and confused.

On the one hand, it would be safer, but on the other... I can't deny that it carries a slight sting that Alaric would make such a suggestion for purely practical reasons.

To his credit, as discomforted as he seems by the ever-widening silence, he grants me time to gather my wits and find my voice.

"I am unsure what to make of such a romantic proposal."

Though I mean to say it lightly, he goes perfectly still mid-stride. I stare at his back for several heartbeats before Alaric faces me again. Panic widens his deep blue eyes. The crimson ring around his irises shimmers a vivid hue.

He straightens, running a hand down his face. "Demons shit, I have made a mess of this."

As his nerves fray, mine begin to ease. I shrug. "I have known you to be more charming on occasion...."

He sits on the edge of the bed and takes my hand in both of his. "What I am so inelegantly trying to say is that while I am still uncertain what it is that's between us, do not think your choice has any bearing on what will become of it. I will respect whatever decision you make."

I study him. Nothing in his tone or features hints

at the answer he's looking for. "My decision on accepting the crown… or how I feel about you?"

Alaric exhales. "Either. Both. You will need to make a final decision regarding the crown sooner rather than later. As far as anything else is concerned, if you refuse me, I will still do everything in my power to help you until you send me away." There is a flash of something in his eyes.

And all at once, I understand what he is really asking me. Disguised beneath the practical suggestion, the doubt and fear that I might not need him—might not want him—was an attempt to feel me out.

That small uncertainty is almost too much. Everything is all twisted and knotted inside my chest, made heavier by exhaustion. Impossibly, my eyes haven't run dry yet. Though sorrow colors it all, it is mostly the release of far too heavy a load for one heart to carry.

"I'll do it… I accept your offer." As hard as I try to keep my voice even, my words are halting, interrupted by ragged breaths.

His confusion quickly switches to apprehension as my tears begin to fall. Alaric looks around helplessly. If I could stop crying, I might laugh.

"I—" he flounders. "Tell me what to do, what to say." His hands hover over my shoulders and arms, unable to settle. "I didn't mean to upset you."

I don't think he's ever looked so lost before. I almost feel bad. "I am not upset," I say between sniffles.

He doesn't look convinced.

I shake my head and hold a hand up as I calm myself enough to speak. "You can doubt anything in this world, but never doubt that I love you…." I trail off when his palm slides over my damp skin, wiping the tears away. It isn't an answer to his question, but it is the one he was looking for.

The relief in his expression is immediate. "I thought your words in that cabin might have been colored by wine and desire, but how could anyone be expected to resist giving you their heart when you make such pretty vows and devotions?" Alaric leans in, only leaving a small space between his lips and mine. Our breaths mingle. A seductive grin that shows his fangs curls his mouth. It should make him look menacing, but I find the opposite to be true.

I frown, pulling away. "Please don't tease me."

"I am not teasing you," he says, his hold bringing me back. "Without all of my memories, it is difficult to gauge how to act or what to say. My heart and my past are in two different places. It is a constant push and pull between them, but even so, I always find myself searching for you, reaching for you. It is a need that won't be denied."

It is not a simple vow of love. It is complicated and twisting and deep and… real.

"I think I could be queen," I say slowly. "If you were at my side."

Alaric lifts my hand and kisses the inside of my wrist, pinning me in place with his midnight blue gaze. "You are like air to me. If I were a fish, I would grow wings to always feel you and learn to live without water just to breathe you."

His words make mine feel inadequate. My tongue darts out to lick my suddenly dry lips, and his eyes follow the movement.

Alaric leans forward, brushing his mouth over mine in a whisper of a kiss, then shifts to sit beside me in a way we did what seems like a lifetime ago at his manor. Hip to hip, he drapes an arm over my shoulders and pulls me into his side. His long legs stretch out over the top of the bed. I curl into him. I have missed his warmth, his touch, his presence.

Even if I did not love him, I couldn't live with myself if I left him to suffer at Elizabeth's hands. He showed me kindness and friendship and love when he had every reason not to, and he did so without conditions or expectations. He sacrificed his freedom for the chance to keep me safe.

Alaric might not have known what she would do to him, but knowing him as I do, it wouldn't have changed things if he had. Even without his memories, the core of who he is remains intact.

Alaric strokes my head, smoothing my hair back, lulling me. "If your offer still stands to help me remember, then I would like to take you up on it."

"Yes." I sigh, my eyes fluttering shut. "I will tell you everything, as many times as it takes, until you remember or until we have made more than enough new memories."

CHAPTER FORTY-ONE

CLARA

A LARIC AND I TRAVERSE THE BACK HALLS TOWARD THE meeting room, where we will convene with the remaining living court members. My nerves are on edge. I don't know if I can do this. It is one thing to fight and run when I can act on my instincts. But this will take a type of calculating I am not used to, from every word I speak to every movement I make.

My hair is pulled back in a long, simple braid, with the night-forged silver crown pinned in place. The design is sharp and delicate, but in my mind, the weight of it presses down as if demanding I bow to its power.

Today, it is imperative that no cracks or weaknesses show. I will prove that I don't need fangs for them to fear me. That I am not someone to be trifled with.

Rather than wearing an elegant gown or having my hair styled into curls and knots atop my head.

Appearing pretty and regal will not send that message.

Instead, I wear a blood-red, long-tailed jacket with a high collar. Silver embroidered button loops, made to resemble daggers, run from my collarbone to my hips, where the tail flairs. More silver stitching borders the collar and sleeves.

Under that are simple, unadorned black leggings with black leather, and knee-high boots. The dagger strapped to my thigh glints with every step. And at my throat is the choker of thorn-covered vines Cassius gave to me.

We enter through a door hidden by hanging tapestries shrouded in shadow along the back wall. Only the sconces at the front of the room where the courtiers will enter are lit.

At the head of the table are the two high-back chairs, identical to the thrones, only smaller in scale. The one on the outside is slightly smaller than Elizabeth's chair—now mine. Behind them, the fireplace is lit, chasing the chill from the room. Cushioned chairs for each remaining member are situated around the crescent table.

It looks exactly as it did when I was dragged here for that farce of a trial. Now, it feels different. It feels terrifying in a whole other way. I tamp down that fear, shedding it like an old skin, and walk up to the head of the table and move to sit.

Alaric stops me with a hand on my elbow, tipping his head to the larger one. "*That* one is yours," he says. Then, when I hesitate, he smiles reassuringly.

I lower onto the mock throne, wanting to get a

sense for it. It's cold and not particularly comfortable. I shift, fidgeting, as I adjust my position to find one that feels right.

Beside me, Alaric watches me quietly. After a while, the warmth of his hand alights atop mine. I drag my gaze up, meeting his. Those dark depths allow me to take a deep breath.

"You will do fine," he says, his voice pitched in low, soothing tones. "I will be right next to you the entire time."

I don't think I can do this. The words are on the tip of my tongue, urging to be set free. But I swallow them back down, refusing to say them aloud—refusing to believe them any longer.

I have already said them a hundred times over in private. Saying them one more time would be pointless. It's too late now, anyway. The last of the living council, the vampires Elizabeth created, are already on their way.

As if reading my thoughts, Alaric stands and holds out a hand to help me up. "We should take our places."

I slide my palm into his. The caress of his skin against mine quells the nerves rattling beneath the surface. It gives me the courage to stand with my spine straight and head held high. Courage to do what must be done. Not just for me or for him, but for everyone.

Though I still don't want this any more than when Alaric first informed me of my new title, it doesn't change the fact that I am in a unique position. And it would be inexcusable to squander the opportunity to help others who deserve so much better than what they've been given.

To run from this now would mean abandoning so many who need things to change. Abandoning everyone who has died because of the old laws. Abandoning my younger self, who wished more than anything that the world was less cruel.

This is the first step. Today is about ridding the court of anyone tempted to undermine me. The coronation that will come later is a formality because I inherited the crown the moment I ended Elizabeth's life.

I set my jaw and nod. Alaric holds the tapestry back, allowing me to slip into the alcove of the hidden door. Our eyes lock, and something more significant than words passes between us.

"Wait for my signal," he says, then lowers his hand, letting the tapestry fall back in place.

His footsteps echo in the empty room, stopping after a few paces. I peer out through a small gap between the fabric and the wall. He is halfway between our seats and where I wait.

Soon, the main doors open. My throat constricts, trapping air in my lungs as the first of the court enters. Lawrence walks in, taking his place next to mine, on the opposite side of where Alaric will sit. The procession continues until each seat is filled, save for the two at the head of the table.

A few members whisper among themselves as everyone settles in. Some wear neutral expressions, while others have smirks curling up the corners of their lips, hoping for amusement.

Two, however, sneer, not bothering to hide their disdain. It's them we will have to observe carefully, quelling any discord before it can gain a foothold.

The doors close with a resounding thud that hasn't even entirely died out when the higher ranking of the two scowling men rises, looking down his nose at Alaric. Blatant disrespect smattered over his face.

"Let me be clear. We did not come here today on your order but to inform you that we will not bow to a lowly former consort who held the position for mere minutes." Lips twisting into a thin line, he pauses and takes a long, slow look around the room.

It did not take long for him to voice his objections. I expected to get further in before we had to deal with hostilities. I can already tell he came here today with an agenda and will no doubt make a bid to claim the throne for himself if we don't stop him early.

"There has been a misunderstanding," Alaric says before the man can continue. "I was not the one who called this council."

Murmurs quickly morph into exclamations and questions and demands for clarity.

Alaric doesn't wait for things to quiet down. His voice resonates over the din as he answers. "It was your queen."

Gasps, frantic talking, and cries of outrage mix, creating a cacophony of voices. One rises above the rest.

"The queen is dead. If one of us had dared to kill Elizabeth, they would have stepped up immediately." The objector opens his arms to the room as if the fact that no one has stood up to say just that somehow proves his point.

Now, Alaric holds up a hand for silence. My heartbeat kicks up, and I must force myself to calm down. "It was not a member of the court who claimed the crown. But it is not for us to question our Her Majesty's reasons for waiting to announce herself."

He holds an arm out, gesturing toward the tapestry where I hide. I take a fortifying breath, then step into the open. The room is silent as I stride from the shadows and stop beside Alaric. I lay my arm on his and let him escort me to my seat.

One by one, recognition settles over the room. I am careful to keep my features neutral as we settle at the head of the table.

"What are you playing at, Mr. Devereaux?"

"Whosoever kills the queen is the rightful heir." Alaric tilts his head toward me. "Miss Valmont did exactly that."

"Demon shit! If you think any of us will stand by and allow this—*this farce*," he spits the words, "to continue uncontested, you are gravely mistaken. We will not allow you to use a worthless, claimed mortal to seize control of the position you held for mere minutes. The very idea is laughable." His face has turned ruddy with indignation.

"You would do well to show her respect," he warns. Then, in a mild tone, he adds, "I watched her kill Elizabeth, but I am not the only witness."

On cue, the doors open again. Every eye in the room turns toward the new arrival.

The Voice holds her head high. Her stride is

assured. Calm. Confident. Powerful. Everything royalty should be. Nothing like the specter that moved about the halls of Nightwich doing Elizabeth's bidding. It makes me wonder who she really is.

She takes her usual place. No one speaks, whether out of habit or respect, I'm not sure.

"I was present when Elizabeth Fairfax was killed." She angles her body and gestures toward me. "By this slayer's hand."

The second scowling man stands, mouth agape. "I —we urge you to reconsider." He looks around, but no one else joins him, remaining silent as they consider their options. He lowers his head in forced deference. "The gentry will not take kindly to a lowly human as our queen."

I narrow my gaze. At least he has the sense to temper his tone.

The Voice looks at him with placid patience, in the way one might a stubborn child, still too young to understand the unfairness of the world. "When our previous queen created that law, it never stated the vampire queen must *be* a vampire—only that whoever took Elizabeth's life would be her rightful successor. By rights, the throne and the crown belong to Miss Valmont."

Elizabeth had set that law believing that it would never happen, that nothing like that *could* happen. It was arrogance, a dare to attempt a feat she deemed impossible.

"This is absurd! If she is a slayer then she must die for her crimes!" Anger radiates off him in waves.

An unnatural stillness descends. All eyes are on

me. Watching. Waiting to see how I will deal with this display of disrespect. If I will cower and bow to him, or if I will hold my own.

I rise from my seat, commanding the room's attention. "What is your name?" I ask as if we are all having a pleasant conversation. As if he is so beneath me that his fury is of no concern.

His eyes bulge, and though it galls him to do so, he answers, "Arthur Greene."

"Ah," I say and smile sweetly, not pointing out his blatant disrespect by not using my title. "Mr. Greene, I know how difficult it can be to adjust to unexpected change." Then I drop all pleasantries and look each vampire in the eye. "But hear this—I am your queen now, and from this moment on, things will change. Elizabeth's laws died with her. Humans will no longer live under the rule of vampires—punished and used with impunity. If anyone thinks to act against me or the new decrees set forth—" I pin Mr. Greene down with my stare, making sure he takes in every word. "—they will not live to do it a second time."

Though he remains pinned under my glare, everyone else seems to speak at once, looking at each other with uncertainty and worry. I allow them a moment to process the information. This is only the beginning.

A woman seated near the center of the table stands. She sends the courtiers on either side of her a beseeching look. They only offer a nod and the wave of a hand to go on. "Won't some humans see that as free rein to slay vampires?"

I barely hold back my shock to hear a concern that

isn't about deposing me. "Vampires can defend themselves but should take measures to subdue and not harm if it is avoidable."

She nods and lowers back down, looking at those nearest her with a nervous smile.

"Measures will be put in place to ward against any retaliation on all sides," I add. "We will do away with the uneven distribution of power, allowing everyone to live without fear.

"As part of this change," I continue. "The Claiming will end. "No human is to be hunted, forced, threatened, or compelled into offering their blood or anything else. A vampire wishing to feed must find a willing human—who is to remain unharmed and fairly compensated for their services."

"What if none are willing?" Mr. Greene sputters.

"Then I suggest you learn to be more personable," I say flatly. What I imply seems to break the last of his restraints. The corner of my mouth ticks up.

He bares his teeth and hisses. But before he can launch himself over the table and run at me, Alaric has already crossed the room, his hand around the man's throat, fingers pressing into the tender skin of his neck.

CHAPTER FORTY-TWO

CLARA

Lawrence and the Voice have positioned themselves to block anyone else from approaching—their alliance made clear.

"She is your queen, and my oath bonded. If you, or anyone else, so much as attempts to harm a single hair on her head, they will find their heart removed from their chest before they can lift a finger."

Every gaze in the room snaps to Alaric's face at the mention of the oath bond. Gasps and murmured questions rise like the tide, falling silent as he continues to stare the man down.

I cross to the far end with long strides. Alaric has the other vampire pulled forward. Mr. Greene braces his palms on the table to steady himself. I draw my dagger from the sheath strapped to my thigh and drive it into the center of his hand—the metal slices through muscle and bone with ease. Arthur Greene's eyes bulge, his pallor turning waxy and gray. "Consider this my warning," I say. "Next time, it will be your life." Then I rip the blade out and turn away.

Alaric releases him with a shove. "Clean yourself up."

We return to our seats as if what just happened was of little consequence.

Mr. Greene cradles his bleeding hand inside his jacket, rubbing his neck with the other and trying to disguise it as fixing his collar. Already, the skin is discoloring from the force of Alaric's grip.

Not a single vampire in the room failed to understand Alaric's message or mine. He will kill them without hesitation, even if I didn't wear the crown, and I will kill any who pose a threat.

"We are here to discuss the future of the court, not to ask for the court's approval of our queen," Alaric says.

The Voice makes the most subtle movement, commanding the floor. A spell all its own. It's easy to see why Elizabeth wanted her.

She has a rare power, understated and valuable. Anyone not looking closely would miss it.

When I woke up the second time, the Voice came into my room. She said she was in my service. Though she made it sound like a debt for freeing her, I understood that whatever bound her here had not ended with Elizabeth's death.

Without hesitation, I freed her. As beneficial as it would be to have someone like her, I will not follow in Elizabeth's footsteps. As repayment, she agreed to stay and help me with the transition.

"Before we go any further." The Voice lets her gaze

sweep the room. "Each of you will stand and pledge loyalty if you wish to retain your position. Or should you refuse, you will be dismissed. No one will face retribution for their decision…. Those who decline will have their powers fettered."

One by one, each vampire stands and offers an unwavering loyalty to the crown… to me. I am surprised that so many have readily accepted my sovereignty.

I suppose it shouldn't be entirely unexpected for those with power to welcome inconvenient changes in order to keep it.

With each pledge, there is a subtle pulse of magic, like a dandelion seed brushing over skin, binding them to their oaths. From one to the next, everything goes smoothly.

That is until only three remain.

It doesn't come as a surprise when Mr. Greene does not make the same decision as those before him.

"I will act in accordance with the laws of this rule, but I cannot remain as part of this court if it means I must participate in whatever changes a *human—*" Voice raspy, he spears me with a look of open hostility. "—should decide for all vampires."

The man beside him stands and repeats the refusal, word for word, though with far less venom in his voice.

Neither retake their seat when they finish, turning expectantly to the last remaining court member.

She gets to her feet and exchanges a long look with them before turning to address me. "I have always been loyal to the crown. Your Majesty has made it clear that your own loyalties do not lie solely with humans but with all." She pauses and sends a sly smile at the men who tried to urge her to go along with them. "And because of that, I look forward to helping bring about a much needed change."

The objectors don't even attempt to hide their irritation as those around them make their feelings known. Some lean away, distancing themselves. While others turn their heads, attempting to appear inconspicuous, looking at the walls or anything other than him. It seems they hoped for their influence to be stronger than my own.

"The two of you are dismissed," I say.

Their spines straighten as they indignantly shove back from the table and storm toward the doors.

"While you are no longer members of this court," Alaric says. His tone causes them to halt at the threshold and turn back. "You are still expected to attend the coronation in one month's time. You will not want to find out what will happen if you fail to make an appearance."

The men each offer a terse dip of their heads, then exit.

I take a slow and measured breath, relieved that the worst part is over.

In the week leading up to this meeting, Alaric and I spent long nights with our closest friends detailing the new laws. Copies were made, then sent far and wide to every city a vampire has ever set foot in.

Now, it is time to announce what will become of the court.

The bite of winter is still in the air, but it is not nearly as sharp as it was days ago. I breathe deep and tilt my head back to gaze up at the stars. "That was nerve-wracking," I say.

Alaric chuckles. I drop my chin to glare at him, but he only shrugs.

"You hid it well. Even beside you, I couldn't sense any trace of fear," he says.

A very unladylike snort escapes me before I can stop it. "We're alone. You don't need to flatter me," I retort, continuing our stroll.

Alaric stops walking, reaching out to catch my wrist. I turn to face him. We stand on the edge of the winding garden path near the high stone wall that blocks the worst of the chill. For several heartbeats, the only sound around is the rustling of dried vines in the breeze.

"Your presence did more than you realize." All teasing, now replaced by weighted sincerity. "No other human could have stood there as unwavering as you did."

I raise a brow. "How many humans in this world are bonded to a demon?"

Pulling me to a stop beside a statue, Alaric forces me to meet his gaze. "You cannot keep attributing all your strength to a demon."

I sigh. He's right. I know he is. But that doesn't

mean I have to admit it. It feels wrong. Like taking credit for something that isn't my doing. I was only able to be strong because of the strength that came from him and Varin—it wasn't something I was born with or worked to achieve.

Rather than repeating a discussion we've already had and will probably have again many more times, I change the subject. "You told them I was your oath bonded."

Alaric is silent for so long I start to worry that I made it sound like a negative thing.

"I should have talked to you before announcing that. I shouldn't have assumed—"

"No, it was necessary," I cut him off.

There are times when we are utterly at ease with one another. Then there are times like this when neither of us can seem to break through the unknown lingering from everything that still remains unsaid.

It will take time. Our journey to the way things used to be is a tangled path, weaving in on itself. Alaric still needs time and space to recover what he's lost, and I don't wish to rush him.

"It surprised me—that's all." I toe a stray pebble on the pathway with my boot.

"I have made you doubt—"

A shrill screech pierces the air. I flinch, covering my ears as I search for the source of the vnoise. But my reaction made me slow.

It isn't until the mix of black and ash white is nearly upon me that I realize *I* am the target.

Alaric shields me with his body. The bird collides with his arm, emitting another unearthly sound.

Wings flap wildly as sharp claws rip through his sleeve, slicing his skin.

I don't know how it is possible, but... *Kharis is alive.*

Alaric snatches the bird with his other hand and flings it at the stone wall, hollow bones cracking on impact.

He turns to me. "Are you hurt?"

"I should be asking you that," I say, reaching for him so I can assess the damage.

"Do not trouble yourself over mere scratches," he says with a grin. But his chest rises and falls with labored breaths, belying his words. Alaric sways. Stumbles.

Then he falls.

I drop to my knees at his side and roll him onto his back to search for the wounds. Black webbing sprawling and stretching out from every scratch on his hand and forearm. The lines twist and writhe beneath his skin, spreading rapidly.

Shit. Shit.

Cursed.

He's been cursed. Again. But it is no slow infection as it was last time. Kharis intends to end his life within the hour.

I glance around franticly, scanning the area where the demon fell. Panic spikes through my temples when I don't see them. They must have landed in the tangle of dormant plants. I scramble to my feet, searching.

A twitch among a pile of dark, rotted leaves catches my attention. Drawing my dagger as I kneel down, I take aim, then plunge the blade into their chest.

They convulse, and their beak opens wide as if to make another horrible sound, but all that escapes is a hiss.

I yank my arm back, ripping out the dagger. A sizzling sound rises from the wound, bubbling up and out. The shining black feathers change to a dull gray, expanding until Kharis is nothing but a form made of ash. My foot stirs the leaves as I stand, creating a domino effect. The demon's form crumbles, collapsing into nothing but a pile of dust scattering into the wind.

Returning to Alaric's side, I check his wounds, watching for the curse to recede.

Only it doesn't.

The lines continue to grow.

"No… no, no." I gather him in my arms and rest his head in my lap. I search, grasping desperately for something… anything, anyone, to help, but we are alone, and there is nothing.

The night-forged silver dagger winks in the moonlight as if telling me to use it. I didn't fight to get this far just to watch him die or end his life to spare him pain.

A thought or memory itches in my mind. It's important. If only I could grab onto it, capture the broken pieces, and put them together. They are too knotted up in hazy moments of darkness and pain and death for me to understand. Only, there is no time.

The bond….

As I think of the connection we shared, it sets off a spark deep in my chest. *Yes… It was… something about the bond. But what?*

A sob wrenches free. Panic overwhelms me, and I can't think. The poisonous lines of the curse slither up one side of his neck and face.

I close my eyes and take a deep breath, and when I open them again, I stop trying to think, stop trying to remember, and let instinct guide me.

I pick up the dagger and drag the flat of the blade over the side of my leg, wiping away any trace of Kharis that might remain. The shining metal reflects a beam of moonlight, casting it like a beacon on my hand pressed against Alaric's chest.

Once I settle him on the ground, I kneel beside him, holding my palm in front of me, remembering the feel of the slice he carved into my skin, remembering the exact path.

Then, I drag the tip of the blade along the invisible line. My entire body is numb from fear, and I hardly feel it. Blood wells up, dripping like thick crimson tears. I take his hand and drag the dagger in a line to mirror my own.

Pressing my palm to his, I lock our fingers together. Hot tears burn, tracking down my face as I wait and wait for a spark of magic to ignite.

"Please… please… please, please, please, please, please," I beg, crushing our hands together as tight as I can.

The black veins don't stop. They spread and spread and spread.

Warmth seeps into my hand. And at first, I can't

tell if it's my imagination, but as it begins, I know it's not.

The dark marks of the curse shift, not pulling back entirely but changing direction. They coalesce around Alaric's wounds, then flare, moving from his skin to mine, slithering up my arm, and searing their way through my body.

I collapse, unable to move as it fills me with its acid touch. But I don't let go.

Blinding pain erupts until I swear an all too real fire ignites within, charring my flesh… melting my bones. Its presence is mindless. Famished. Wanting to consume everything in its path. Vicious in its ravenous need.

It pulls and pulls and pulls.

Then I drown beneath its pit of darkness.

CHAPTER FORTY-THREE

ALARIC

The soft tap of my leather soles echoes with every step as if I am striding through a massive barren throne room. Fog, thick and endless and unnatural, surrounds me on all sides. Though there is no light, I can see the ground for about a yard in any direction before it's swallowed by the mist.

I do not know how long I have been walking nor how far I have gone. And no matter what direction I turn—how fast or slow I walk—it is always the same. Continuing this aimless wandering is pointless, yet I cannot seem to stop.

A distant wind howls, gradually picking up, and it takes longer than it should for me to notice. I pause and listen, slowly turning in a full circle, squinting into the mist. The sound seems to come from every direction.

Louder and louder.

Closer and closer.

Until, finally, it becomes unmistakable, scraping along my bones.

Demons.

Lightning flashes, cutting through the haze. Seconds later, a deafening crack follows. The boom rattles chips of loose rock, making them shiver across the surface of the ground.

Only it isn't thunder. It's too loud, too close, and rather than trailing the flashes of light, this one came from a distinctly different direction.

I whirl to face the source I can't yet make out.

Another crack erupts. Then another and another and another, with no rhyme or reason to it. Near and far, encircling me. With each resounding boom, the ground shakes.

I peer into the mist, scanning for any sign of movement. I think I see something, the barest movement.

Not daring to breathe, I wait. At first, it almost seems like a trick of the mist, but then it quickly morphs into reality. Dark, obscured shapes rise up, shifting. Moving so quick, it is impossible to track.

Half a stride ahead, a protrusion bulges up over the flat ground. Fissures form as the rock begins to crack and break under the stress of the force. In a burst of rubble, a taloned hand punches through, a long arm stretching up. Then it comes crashing down, sinking pointed fingers into the earth. Clawing for purchase as a second limb breaks through. The hands scrape and dig, cracking the rock, until a twisted and gnarled form breaks free.

Eyes like embers pierce the fog, searching. The

demon's charred bone face turns, narrowing their focus on me, and releases a low rumble from deep within their chest.

I keep perfectly still as they lower their face within inches of mine. Hot, reeking breath washes over my face. Their jaw unhinges with several painful clicks, revealing flashing, jagged rows of teeth that jut out at every angle. And then they roar.

Carefully. Carefully and slowly, I inch one foot back, but that movement draws the creature's notice. In response, they crouch, thin yet powerful muscles bunching as they ready to attack.

Not a single twitch of muscle betrays my intention. I call down to the power residing within my veins to banish this beast. Yet, with every attempt, it eludes me. Slipping from my fingers, as water from a tightening fist, only to sink further from reach.

Fuck.

Pivoting on my heel, I turn and run.

More demons erupt from the ground, forcing me to change direction every few yards. Even then, I must dodge and leap to avoid colliding with countless others. All the while, the one hunting me follows entirely too close. Jaws snapping. Claws pounding in a steady beat.

Without warning, my strength ebbs. My power siphoning it away as it vanishes. I stumble over the newly uneven terrain, staggering, barely catching myself in several graceless strides.

Searing hot pain rips down my back. Spine arching, my pace falters. One strike is quickly followed by another. Again and again and again and again. Shredding my skin into ribbons, then my arms and chest. The overwhelming agony steals the breath from my lungs. Inch by inch, my flesh is sliced away.

My knees buckle and hit the ground with bone-cracking force. Talons assault my arms and chest, the scrape of their sharp points leaving behind trails of caustic poison until I cannot see or hear or think. Until there is nothing other than unimaginable pain.

I wait for the demon to finish killing me. And wait.

And wait.

Gradually, my senses return.

I lull my head to the side. Vaguely, I notice the demons are nowhere in sight. The destruction they wrought as they broke through the rocky ground has been undone as if it never happened.

Distantly, I am aware I must stanch the flow of blood before I bleed out. Somehow, I find the strength to lift my hand to my chest. Delirium oozes in, corrupting reality.

I find my clothes dry and untorn, but my palm comes away stained and dripping red. I cannot seem to drag my gaze away, and the longer I stare at it, the more familiar this moment feels.

This…. this pain, this torture… it's familiar.

The ghost of a dream that fades upon waking, leaving only slivers behind to tell you it was ever there at all. It is worse than anything I've felt before… not since… since—

This has happened before.

This is my death—or what would have been—had I chosen differently.

If I had not chosen…

"*Rosalie.*" Her name is little more than a whisper on my lips. And with it comes flashes of memory. Sharp and fast, in a whirling torrent of confusion.

Howling.

Blood.

So much blood. Too much.

I am trapped in my own body. The cold fingers of death seep into my limbs, and I welcome it. Because I am ready to die… for someone.

A woman's screams—*her* screams.

Rosalie.

My sister falls to the forest floor, stirring up a whirl of leaves. Pale hair, tangled and stained dark from open wounds. Her bloodless lips move, opening and closing, gasping for breath. Tears spill from the sapphire depths of eyes identical to my own. I drag my hand over the damp loam until my fingers brush hers.

Rosalie…

She shouldn't be here. Why is she here?

I press my hands to my temples, trying to slow the images, to separate the sounds as they repeat, mixing together.

A sultry voice like smoke and treacle. An offer of power—power I can use to save her—to save Rosalie.

For that, I would give anything.

I will give everything.

Warm breath whispers in my ear. "But first, you must change. Only when you are immortal will you be able to save your beloved sister… I can show you how."

There is no time to question, no time to wonder what it means, only time to answer.

"Yes."

I squeeze my eyes tight, willing the images away.

"Why in the Otherworld are you on the ground, Alaric?" There is a lilt of gentle laughter in the question.

A delicate hand alights on my shoulder. The touch chases away the pain and memories.

I lower my arms and look up into Rosalie's smiling face. It seems impossible that she's here. She is gone... *was...* gone?

When I don't speak or move, her grin fades, and she kneels beside me, brows furrowed with concern. "What's wrong?"

I take her face in my hands—she is solid and... *real.* "I—I thought I lost you."

Why had I thought that?

It must have been a nightmare. The kind that lingers, trying to grasp onto a foothold of the mind to keep from fading with the sunrise, as if it could drag itself into the waking world by sheer will.

The worry eases from her features, and Rosalie lowers my hands with infinite patience. It has always been the other way around. She must think I lost my senses.

Am I drunk?

"No," she says in the same tone our mother used when we were very young, assuring us no demons could pass over a threshold unless invited. And nobody in the right mind would ever invite a demon inside. "You *saved* me, Alaric."

I shake my head.

"I lived far longer than I was ever meant to."

My temples throb with the steady pounding of a drum. "What are you saying?"

"And even though it was a cursed half-life, you gave up everything and more to make me happy. And I was." Rosalie ruffles my hair. "I was happy for a long time."

The awful truth seeps through with every word she speaks. *Lived... was...* A sharp ache twists beneath my chest, squeezing my heart painfully.

"You... died," I rasp, barely able to get the words out.

She nods, confirming the fear I desperately need to be wrong. "I didn't feel a thing."

"That doesn't—"

"I knew how she felt about vampires, and I knew how you would react." She pauses, and there is heartbreaking sorrow in her smile.

"Who?"

"I didn't want you to be alone. She was strong and stubborn enough to handle your moods and brooding—"

"I don't brood," I object.

Rosalie only laughs as she continues, "—and drive you mad with frustration." She sighs, then stands, taking me by the elbow, urging me to get up.

I let her pull me to my feet and look around. Despite what she told me, I still half expect to be in my room at our parents' house—to find that Rosalie woke me from a nightmare caused by too much liquor.

But there is only that strange fog of nothing, for as far as the eye can see. Then, it changes before my eyes, fading to reveal two endless paths forking out from where we stand, stretching out in different directions, growing farther apart with every inch.

Facing her again, I ask, "Where are we?"

Rosalie tucks a lock of hair behind her ear. "You are in the space between the Otherworld and life."

Most might dismiss such a claim as childish imagination or madness, but I feel the truth of her words as they strike with the force of a hammer.

"You have changed, Alaric."

"No." I shake my head. "I am the same. I'll prove it."

Again, Rosalie laughs as if I said something utterly ridiculous, but there is no mockery behind it. "I did not mean that as a bad thing. Do you remember what Mother used to say?" She sends an apprehensive glance over her shoulder. "For better or worse, love has the power to change us."

From someplace far away, someone calls my name.

"You finally allowed yourself to claim happiness. I just never thought you'd be quite so literal about it."

"Alaric?" The distant voice causes my heartbeat to stutter, though I can't pinpoint why. Rosalie and I turn toward it.

A woman appears, walking along one path. Her head moves side to side, searching as if she can't see the two of us standing directly ahead of her. Over and over, she calls out. Then she stops as her gaze finally lands on me. She bites down on her bottom lip.

Clara.

Her name is as clear and bright as the summer sun. It's filled with meaning and emotion. Then she is running, racing toward me.

"You have a decision to make, Alaric. It's not one many are fortunate enough to get."

"Decision?" My head whips toward Rosalie. "What do you mean?"

But Rosalie is backing up, going down the second path. As I wait for her to explain, she is farther and farther out of reach. The distance between us increases. Still, she doesn't answer.

"Rosalie! What choice?" I ask again.

She stretches her arm out for me to take. "You must choose."

"Alaric!" Clara calls.

I am rooted in place, not understanding. I am caught between them, looking from Rosalie and the warm smile she always wore to Clara with tears streaking down her cheeks. Each one is a hot needle piercing my chest.

"Clara?" Her name falls from my tongue.

I look at my sister. She continues to walk away, holding her hand out, still waiting for me.

The choice I am supposed to make is obvious now, and I know what I must do—what I *want* to do. Though I will always love my sister, my heart is so deeply entrenched inside the woman running deeper into the Otherworld.

I take Clara's hand, opening my arms to her, and she falls against me with a sob.

Thousands of stars wink down from an inky black sky. Winter air scrapes down my throat, frigid enough to form ice crystals in my lungs.

The warm hand clasping mine is an anchor to the earth, to life. I flex my fingers and squeeze gently. I turn my head to the side. Fingers entwined with mine, Clara lays beside me. Tears have stained her cheeks and clumped her lashes. I watch her for a moment.

The final piece of something powerful slips into place.

Her eyes flutter open. For a while, neither of us moves.

"Alaric?" The way she says my name is tinged with uncertainty and pain.

This moment is like a dream, the last hallucination of a dying man's mind. Strange and unreal.

"Am I… are we… dead?"

She presses her lips into a tight line and shakes her head.

"Is this real?"

She swallows down a heavy emotion lodged in her throat and nods. "Yes."

Her free hand reaches up, fingertips grazing the edge of my jaw. I pull her on top of my chest. Her arms encircle my neck, clinging so fiercely that not even a harmony of demons could pry their way between us. I kiss the top of her head and hold her just as tightly, rubbing soothing circles over her back.

My palm stings. I lift my hand and examine the cut with a frown. Then I spot the night-forged silver dagger discarded off to the side. I catch the lightest scent of human blood on the cool air. I'd missed it before now.

I was dying… caught between worlds.

When Elizabeth tried to kill her, I couldn't be sure if it was the curse or our oath bond that broke. Not until I saw her on the dance floor. I had wanted to tell her then, but we were interrupted before I could.

Did she realize we were still bonded and somehow used that connection to drag me back from the Otherworld? Nothing like that has ever been done. It seems impossible.

If I never figure it out, then so be it—the how is not what is important. What is important is the breath in my lungs and the woman on top of me, whose heart beats against my own as she weeps silently.

I hold her because she needs it. I hold her as though I will be dragged into the Otherworld if I let go—because I very well might. I hold her because even though I cannot recall our history together, my heart was always drawn to her, as if *it* remembered what was stolen from my mind. I hold her because it is the only thing that feels right.

CHAPTER FORTY-FOUR

CLARA

"You don't need to do this," I say again as Della puts the finishing touches on my hair. "There are others…" I trail off at the glare she levels on me.

It's pinned in an elegant style that waterfalls down my back and over my shoulders, morphing into something wild.

"We are friends," she says as if it explains things. Though I haven't had many friendships in my life to tell either way, so perhaps it does, and I have more to learn than I realized. "You would do the same for me."

I look at her through the mirror, brow arched. "Would you really want me to?"

There's a hesitation in her movements. "Mmmm." She hums thoughtfully. "Perhaps not, but you would insist on helping me in—" Della attempts to hide her wince when she realizes she shouldn't have kept going. We are both aware that I lack most skills noble women begin learning from birth. "—whatever way you could," she finishes haltingly.

It has been a month since the meeting with the court, and we are still at Nightwich. We've stayed longer than I first thought we would. Much longer than I wanted to.

I am still wary when I walk these halls, expecting something to happen. It's like holding your breath, waiting for the final note of a symphony. Waiting, waiting, waiting… but it never does. And despite everything that has changed, it is no more inviting than it ever was.

My dashed expectations are my own fault. I hadn't realized the time everything would take. After I woke up, we poured all our energy into making new laws and preparing to deal with the court. The subject of time didn't come up until our plan was already in motion.

We began sending missives right away, but then there was the time it took for them to arrive, for the recipients to respond to the invitation, and send them back. And time for our guests to travel, for the injured to heal, and time to mourn the dead.

Soon, Della has me in my dress. Another midnight blue with fabric that shimmers when I move. I run my fingers over the front of the skirt, a smile playing over my lips, knowing it's not a coincidence that the color matches Alaric's eyes.

Unlike any I've worn in the past, this one isn't designed to hide my scars. It has a low-cut neckline and off-the-shoulder capped sleeves. It leaves me more exposed than I have in a long time—but not vulnerable.

Silver embroidered filigree embellishments curve

over the bodice and spill down the roundness of my hips, with more sewn along the hem of the skirt, rising up like glittering stalagmites. It is a work of art, but it leaves me feeling like I am pretending to be someone else.

There's a knock at the door. A maid hurries over and answers, quickly scurrying out of the way, bowing deep as Alaric enters.

Within moments, we are alone. He wears black trousers and a matching jacket over a white shirt. The material of his cravat matches my dress, with a silver ornament pinned at the throat.

"You are beautiful." He crosses halfway into the room.

I cannot help noticing that every inch of him doesn't *just* look like a king—it proves he is. From his posture to the way he moves, to the way he wears the crown. And though he claims to hate it as much as I do, there is no denying he fills the role perfectly.

I may have killed Elizabeth, but he was born to rule. He is the kind of king this land needs. Fair and just, someone who will protect the people. I worry my wanting to leave will somehow take that from him. From everyone.

"If you want to change your mind and stay, then I will stay with you," I blurt in place of a greeting.

The soft curve of his lips flattens, and he's quiet for a long moment. In two of his long strides, he is before me, taking my hand in his. He brushes the back of his white-gloved knuckles over my cheek.

I hope I am successful at hiding my fear that he will accept the offer.

"No," he says softly. "I will be glad to never see this place again." Alaric steps around my skirts and crosses to the windows, gazing out over the landscape bathed in moonlight. "These halls are haunted by the countless deaths spanning the centuries. Elizabeth built it to separate herself from the rest of the world, to show that she was above them all. That she alone held power over everyone, whether or not they were hers to rule. This place is a symbol of everything we are trying to change."

It is everything he says, but when he faces me, I see that there is more he left unsaid. It is the pain he endured by her hand. It is my loathing for this place. It is a reminder of all that was taken from him.

"Are you ready?" he asks quietly.

I bite down on the inside of my bottom lip and nod. "As ready as I will ever be."

Alaric cups my cheek, and I lean into the touch.

"The hardest parts are done. This is all that remains." He dips his head and presses a chaste kiss to my lips. "I will see you soon."

Guards accompany me through the halls, but I barely notice the walk, lost in my thoughts.

Standing before the double doors to the throne room reminds me of another time I stood in this spot and how things have changed since then. I am not waiting to be reclaimed by someone who would happily spill my blood for sport.

This time, I will stand before a crowded room to establish my authority.

I nod, and the guards open the doors. The room is packed, split down the middle with a thick, black velvet runner leading to the dais where Alaric waits. On either side of the aisle is a sea of bodies—every living vampire summoned here today, and far more than I imagined there would be. Not just nobles and gentry, but all. I intend for things to be different, and this is one way I plan to make that clear.

Stretching out along the bottom of the steps is the new court. The vampires who pledged loyalty, an equal number of wolves and swans. Though they are all in human form, their clothes are embroidered to resemble symbols of their animal shape—claws, teeth, wings, and feathers.

Standing before the thrones, Alaric waits for me. I walk forward, keeping my gaze locked with his because if I look at the sea of bodies surrounding me, my legs might not make it to the end.

Gasps and hushed whispers rise in my wake. Because I am human, and a sharp crown of night-forged silver rests upon my head.

I climb the stairs and take his hand, and he gives me a smile that says, *"Didn't I say this would be easy?"*

Then, we turn to face our audience. Most are strangers, but all along the back, mixed between the vampire guards who swore fealty, are more wolves and swans, though their presence is temporary.

The Voice steps up and speaks. Looks of uncertainty pass over the throng. It will take time for them to feel comfortable with a human as the vampire queen. But much of that is eased at my announcement to crown Alaric, not as consort, but as king. Two rulers holding equal power is unheard of.

The backs of my eyes prickle with heat. I do not

care about our titles. Only the steady echo of his heartbeat I feel inside my chest.

I thought it had been severed when Elizabeth tried to kill me, but somehow, when I held my sliced palm to Alaric's, it reignited. Neither of us understands why or how any of it happened. I am only glad it's restored.

I barely pay attention to the words the Voice speaks. Before I know it, a crown identical to my own sits atop Alaric's head. The night-forged silver shimmers like liquid starlight.

"Bow to your queen and king, and pledge yourselves," the Voice commands.

A few kneel immediately, then more and more. Only a handful vampires remain standing. I sense Varin's presence from somewhere in the shadows.

A wave of magic pulses out, much as it did before. The strength of it makes the air shiver, flickering and crackling with its charge, binding every vampire to their choice. The strength of their powers is tied to their word. As long as they obey our rule, it will remain as it always has. But should anyone decide they want to return to Elizabeth's laws, it will be tethered, diminished.

We conclude by introducing the new court, letting all know from now on, it will represent those it governs over. The power of this world is shifting, and we want it to suit all who inhabit it.

Alaric and I stand just outside the grand entrance, watching the last carriage depart. Bram pulls the curtain back and waves out the window with a wide grin, bright teeth flashing. His face disappears for a second, then Lewis joins him with notably less enthusiasm and a simple nod. This past week following the coronation has been full of goodbyes.

"How does it feel to be a queen?" Alaric asks, echoing the question I asked him weeks ago.

Queen. I shake my head. "It is only a title. I can play the part when necessary, but… I do not think I will ever see myself as one."

He nods, accepting what I say rather than trying to convince me to feel otherwise. "It is the same for me. I will be glad to return to Windbury."

I glance up at him, surprised. He hasn't said or acted in a way to indicate any of it didn't suit him. My heart flutters from the effortless way he confided in me.

We are oath bonded, and the curse is broken, but still, his memories remain trapped in a dark abyss. There's no telling if they will ever return or if the curse fed on them when the bond prevented it from devouring him.

The curse changed him. There is something wild and fierce around his edges now. But at his core is everything I fell in love with. Perfectly *him.* I love every side of him. The pieces I know, the pieces he lost, the pieces that are new, and the pieces we have yet to discover.

From the edge of the courtyard, the Voice stands beside a man—one of our new allies. The swans were the first to leave, except for one. He is tall and quiet, never straying far from her. Even now, he watches her closely as she turns from him and walks over.

She bows, first to me, then to Alaric. If I didn't know better, I would think he prefers it, if for no other reason than it makes me squirm.

Deferring to me first is something few do, most likely because I am human in their eyes—the truth of which I have only told Alaric. And neither of us intends to correct that assumption.

"I wanted to thank you both for everything." Her pink gaze flicks to Alaric, then back to me, taking my hands in hers. "You, especially. I am sorry I couldn't do more...."

Not many would stay where they were held captive for centuries after regaining their freedom.

"You have done more than most," I say. Then, the prickle of curiosity alights on my tongue. "Now that you are no longer the Voice, will you tell us your name?"

She blinks, lists her head to the side, but doesn't answer.

I glance at Alaric uncertainly. He shrugs with one shoulder, offering no help. "The Voice cannot be your name," I say with a grimace.

She laughs. "No. It most certainly is not." She

sighs, a blend of wistfulness and sorrow. "My name… was lost a long time ago."

Lost. Not forgotten. I am uncertain how that is possible, but nevertheless, I let the subject drop.

She looks between us, a furtive curl to the corners of her mouth. "I see you managed to restore the bond."

Alaric and I exchange a wary look. "What do you mean?" I ask.

"Don't you remember?"

I shake my head.

"After you killed Elizabeth, I told you that the bond had never been broken. The elixir I gave you was more than a tonic to prevent infection and help you sleep."

Alaric tenses, shifts. I reach for his hand, keeping him from reacting.

"It muted your connection, making it dormant. A pinch of bitter thorn was all it took." She turns to address Alaric. "Elizabeth needed to believe she succeeded in breaking the bond," she says kindly but without apology.

Neither Alaric nor I speak. It's hard to be upset when her actions benefited us. Still, it would have been nice to know earlier.

The tension eases from his muscles. He stretches his fingers, then coils them with mine. I squeeze his hand gently.

A ruddy wolf lopes toward us, but I don't notice until he is about to barrel into me. I flinch, preparing myself for the impact.

When the collision doesn't come, I slowly peel

open my eyes to find Oliver inches from my face. His grin makes it clear he wanted me to think he was about to knock me on my ass again. I level him with a scowl, but it's the soft growl behind me warning him to move back that he heeds.

Oliver clears his throat and pointedly ignores Alaric. "I have come to say goodbye. It's time I returned to my pack." His eyes darken with something I cannot read. "I've received word that the mist is beginning to dissipate and will continue to do so until it is gone."

I catch what he doesn't say aloud. Without the wall, the Keep will no longer be their safe haven.

"What will you do now?" I ask.

Oliver shrugs, never once losing his bright smile. "Now that you are queen, there is no longer any need for it."

In the distance, a howl resonates, stretching from the edges of the forest across the plains. We all turn toward the sound, listening. Oliver cocks his head, understanding the message.

"There are things beyond its borders that are waking for the first time in centuries, and there's no telling what will come of it."

"Thank you, Oliver. For everything."

"Will you still not call me Oli?" he asks with a false pout.

I smile and shake my head.

He shrugs and takes my hand as he bows, kissing my knuckles. Then, without warning, he wraps me up in a tight hug.

"I suggest you remove yourself from her person before you regret it," Alaric says, low and dark.

I laugh at his reaction, swatting Oliver's shoulder. "You shouldn't tease him like that."

He releases me and steps back. "If you are ever in need of my services, my pack will return to the Shade forest in a month's time."

I reach out and grab his sleeve before he can leave. "We wanted to thank you both for staying as long as you have and agreeing to be part of the court."

Alaric slips an arm around my waist, tucking me into his side, putting more space between Oliver and me.

"We were honored," the Voice says.

Oliver snuffs. "You should learn not to speak for others."

She raises a brow. "Oh, were you inconvenienced by the position? My apologies."

"Of course not," he says indignantly, then rolls his eyes when she and Alaric cannot hide their laughter.

The swan who has stood back has inched closer since Oliver's arrival. The Voice follows the direction of my gaze. We share a furtive smile, then she bows to us once more before turning and descending the steps.

He follows without hesitation. I can't tell if he's taken it upon himself to be her personal guard or if he is smitten with her. Halfway down the stairs, she shifts. Her long, delicate arms transform into wings with feathers as white as snow. A few heartbeats later, he slips into his swan form and joins her, and together, they disappear into the clouds.

EPILOGUE

CLARA

THE DARK SPIRES OF NIGHTWICH NO LONGER SCRAPE their claws against the sky. Nothing more remains of the castle but rubble filling the ravine bordering the eastern side.

I wanted it gone for many reasons. But most of all, for Alaric and Varin. There will be no trace of her legacy left, nothing for the world to remember her by. And slowly, year by year, until all memory of her fades entirely.

There was too much pain trapped within the walls, haunting the darkened corners, and waiting in the shadows, ready to rear up. Too many suffered and died within its cold stone walls.

We took the silver and gold and melted it down to pay for the railway already being built. It will span over the land, giving rise to new cities and towns while allowing smaller, poorer villages like Littlemire to flourish. Humans will be able to travel greater distances faster and without fear of being attacked by wild demons.

Issues and problems are inevitable. Adjustments will be required as situations arise that we weren't able to anticipate. The court has agreed to meet twice a year until things are settled, and it's no longer necessary to convene quite so often.

"Clara?" Alaric's hand alights on my shoulder. The way he says my name makes me think it wasn't the first time.

I turn my face up, blinking. He smiles, but it does not reach his eyes.

"Are you ready?" he asks, with a gesture toward the waiting carriage.

Ready… ready to put this place behind us, to heal, to make new memories, to stop being afraid, to find happiness.

But most of all, I am ready to live.

"Yes," I say.

He tucks my hand into the crook of his elbow, and together we turn and walk away, never looking back.

The past is full of shadows, but like the dawn, we will fill whatever lies ahead of us with light. I have never desired power or a crown. It can be blinding when looking in from the outside. The truth is, such things come with invisible shackles weighing you down.

We climb into the carriage and begin the journey back to Windbury, where we will make a quiet life and wake beside each other every evening.

One year later

The sky is a kaleidoscope. Bright ribbons of oranges, reds, and violets weave into darker shades of night as the sun slips below the horizon. Though the day's warmth lingers, a sign that spring has chased away the biting chill of winter.

I make my way up the knoll beyond the manor. Alaric stands before the mausoleum, hands in his pockets, lost in thought.

Inside the white stone monument rests the loved ones we have lost. Shortly after returning to Windbury, we had them brought here to give them the respect they deserve. Though they are in the Otherworld, we will never forget them.

I stop beside Alaric and join him in silence. Sometimes he comes up here by himself. He doesn't say what he does, and I don't ask. But I think he comes to work through the mess of scars left behind by the curse.

"That day in the field," he says after a while. "Elizabeth broke her own curse."

Several heartbeats pass. I am speechless.

"It was something you said—she cursed me when I agreed to become her consort in exchange for your protection."

Of course. I assumed, it broke when she died but

the answer was there all along. It's the reason she held back as long as she did. If I died as she wanted, she still would have got what she wanted. Satisfaction curls in my chest that I ruined her plans simply by staying alive.

"I picked up the dagger because I thought she would order me to kill you. I never intended to offer her the means to do it. I never expected she'd go as far as she did." He glances at me from the corner of his eyes. "I am sorry. You suffered—you almost died—because of me."

"It wasn't your fault. You did the best with the options you had. Elizabeth took away your memories and free will. She used her power so you would only see what she wanted you to see—not the truth."

Alaric hasn't spoken about it since the day I woke up, and I never pushed him to. Trusting that he would come to me when he was ready. Whether he tells me everything now, or in pieces over the years ahead of us, I will be here. Waiting.

A lazy breeze sweeps through the graveyard, ruffing the ends of his black hair. Alaric slips his hand from his pocket and waves his fingers through mine. The gentle squeeze expresses so much. Gratitude. Seeking comfort as well as giving it.

I am not entirely sure how much of that is how well I know him or what I sense through our bond. Perhaps a little of each. It doesn't matter how I know, only that I do.

"I should have told you sooner...." His voice is barely audible.

"No. I've always known you will tell me what you

can in time." He finally turns his face to mine. "I will always be here, waiting, whenever you are ready."

I hate the shadows that pass over his eyes, haunting him. I cannot chase them away or shield him from them. But I can be with him. I can be there, listening, holding him, distracting him, being and doing anything he needs until the worst of it passes. I will be his safe place, offering refuge and my love.

"You can tell me every detail about the curse, or never speak a word about it."

Squeezing his eyes shut, Alaric exhales a long, shaky breath. A steeling, a letting go.

"Every second was agony," he says quietly. "My thoughts were not my own. Everything I did or believed was based on lies." A shiver vibrates through him. "I think the worst part was the constant feeling —*knowing*—that something important was missing and not being able to identify what it was."

He falls silent, and I wait for him to continue or to signal that he is done for now.

Healing is not something that should be rushed. Two people can endure the same injury, but the time they need and the path they take to recover will always differ. And sometimes, it is the emotional and mental wounds left behind that are the slowest to mend. They cannot be bandaged or stitched.

"I was nothing more than a shell of myself." His gaze hones in on mine with such intensity it renders me breathless for several long seconds. "Except when I was with you. You frightened me at times. It was like coming up from the water and gasping for air, but unable to catch my breath."

I step into his side and wrap my arms around his waist. He curls himself around me, and we stay like that until the pain eases. Just a little. And then a little longer, until we are able to smile again.

He leans down and kisses me on the corner of my jaw, below my ear. "Thank you, little nightmare," he murmurs against my skin.

Every once in a while, he will still call me by that name. He says it's because I am the nightmare that keeps the things that would otherwise break him at bay.

It makes the space between my ribs ache for him. But I will be the nightmare for as long as he needs until his wounds have healed and scarred over.

The clatter of hooves on the drive alerts us to the arrival of our guests. Alaric's mouth curls into a mischievous grin that sends heat pooling low in my belly.

I take a half step back, but his arms are around me, pressing our bodies together. He kisses me deeply, making my suspicions evaporate.

At first, it starts off light, testing, barely a brush of his lips across mine. I feel the pull of the mark, then something deeper in our bond, but beneath that, there is so much more. It's quiet in the way it snuck up on me, but no less demanding than all the other ways we are connected.

He has captured my heart in a way I never thought possible. And no matter what we have gone through, no matter what trials we have yet to face. I could no sooner give him up than I could command my heart to stop beating. I wouldn't want to.

Then, between one breath and the next, his arms crush me to him, and the kiss has transformed into need. A fang scrapes over my bottom lip… and then he lifts me in his arms and runs, racing back to the manor. I cry out in surprise and cling to his neck, pressing my face into his collar to hide from the dizzying effects of the speed.

We arrive at the entryway as Mr. Steward opens the door. Lawrence steps out of his carriage first, holding up a lanky, black rabbit by the scruff. "I believe this is yours," he says dryly, bringing the demon to eye level to glare his disapproval. "I found them out terrorizing the birds. Again."

"I was hunting," they grumble. Then Varin swings their back legs, connecting with his face. Stunned, Lawrence drops them. They twist in the air and land on their feet, scurrying inside.

Asmod joins Varin halfway down the hall, with Arinah scurrying after them. Then the four demons pass through a wall, disappearing in puffs of smoke— no doubt on their way to cause mischief.

Alaric clears his throat, and I press my mouth into a tight line, trying to hide my amusement.

Lawrence scowls and starts up the steps just as Oliver does. They stop when they realize neither plans to yield to the other.

Della shakes her head, pushing between them. She sweeps me up in a hug, then throws an admonishing look back at the men.

"Shall we wait in the drawing room while they figure out how to act civilized?" she asks loudly. She doesn't give me a chance to respond before leading me inside.

Ms. Westfield did a beautiful job decorating the room with vases filled with bright flowers on almost every available surface. Black cloth covers the windows and mirrors. The grandfather clock has been stopped and covered as well.

Portraits of Rosalie, Mother and Father, Kitty, and Cassius, are in line atop an altar in the center of the room. In front of each is a single coin made of night-forged silver beside a long tallow candle that we light as the last ray of light fades from the sky. They will burn through the night, finally sputtering out at dawn.

After dinner, the five of us walk up the hill and sit around a small fire outside the mausoleum, sharing stories to keep their memories alive in our hearts. With each bottle of wine, we offer the first and last drink to the dead.

Between the laughter and tears, the hours slip by. The fire is nothing but embers among ash. Once the sky lightens with the first blush of day smearing across the horizon, we make our way back to the warmth of the manor to share a simple breakfast before our friends depart.

When Alaric and I are alone again, there is a hollow space of time that lingers, the quiet is broken only by the crackling flames in the hearth.

By the time we bathe and get ready for bed, and the sun's glow gilds the edge of the windows, the world feels solid beneath our feet again.

We climb under the blankets and draw the bed

curtains. Alaric reaches for me, warm hands sliding over my skin. Then he pulls me to him, our limbs tangling.

"There are times when I'm wonder if I am not still lost in the space between life and the Otherworld," he whispers softly into the dark.

"This is real," I say.

He presses his palm to the skin above my heart, fingers splayed as he feels for the steady rhythm of my heartbeat. "And you will still be here when I wake?"

"Yes," I say. And then I kiss him to chase away any last sliver of doubt, to show him that this is real, that he is alive. That he is safe and loved, and to assure him the nightmares won't last forever.

Want more in the Shadow World?
Go grab your copy of The Vampire Trap
A stand alone novella!

Thank you for reading The Vampire Crown. It's always so much fun to explore new worlds and old, and to watch my characters come to life on the page.

If you enjoyed reading The Vampire Crown, then please consider leaving an honest review on Amazon, Bookbub, or Goodreads.

Reviews are so, so important for helping other readers decide whether or not to read a certain book. They don't need to be long or super descriptive. A single sentence or a few words is all that's needed. Positive, neutral, or negative feelings are all valid. All I ask is that you be mindful not to spoil the story or the ending for your fellow readers.

Stay in touch and be among the first to learn about new releases, cover reveals, character art, special offers, exclusive content (first few chapters, bonus scenes, and spontaneous shorts), and more by signing up for my newsletter!

www.aliwinters.com/newsletter

SHADOW WORLD: STAND ALONES:

WICKED PRINCE OF FROST: an epic gothic romantasy

He promised to heal her broken heart, but if she's not careful, he may just end up taking it for himself.
Learn more: **www.aliwinters.com/shadowworld**

THE VAMPIRE TRAP: A Shadow World novella

When a series of murders breaks out across the city of Sangate, all evidence points to the most powerful vampire in the city.

Learn more: **www.aliwinters.com/shadowworld**

STAND ALONES:

HIGH STAKES: A stand alone Urban Romantasy novella

Elle Darling takes a bounty on an item retrieval

job that sounds simple enough, but soon becomes deadly when the secret surrounding it is one many would kill to possess. She could end up losing her job or worse… her life.

Learn more: **www.aliwinters.com/standalones**

YOUNG ADULT TITLES

THE HUNTED SERIES:

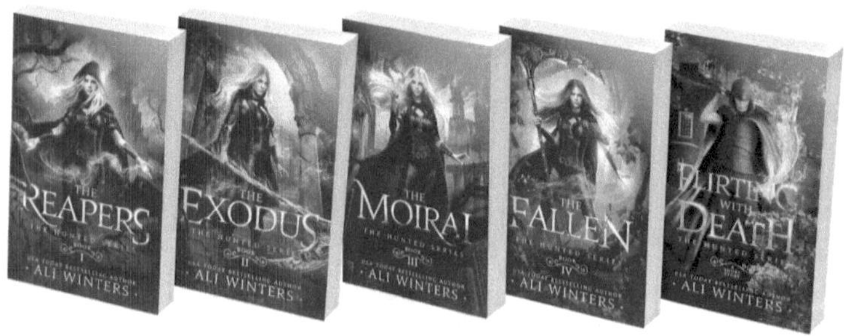

A Reaper and her mortal enemy must team up to save the balance of life and death before all is lost. Unfortunately, to succeed, one of them must die.

Learn more: **www.aliwinters.com/the-hunted-series**

IN THE END DUOLOGY:

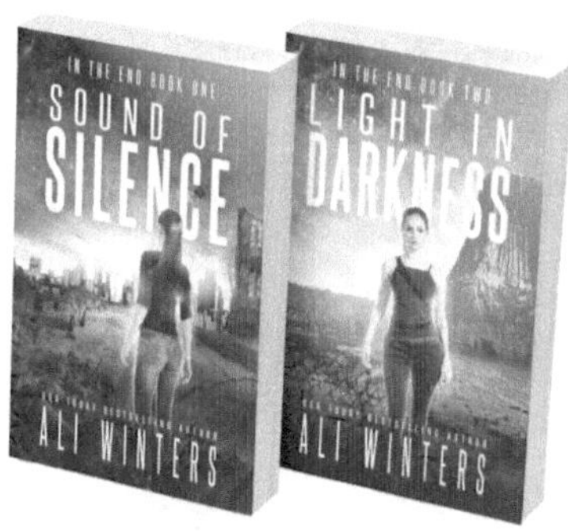

We thought we were alone in the universe. Turns out we were wrong. Dead wrong. —This book is a Romeo and Juliet retelling and contains insta-love, aliens, a virus, and zombies.

Learn more: **www.aliwinters.com/sos**

FAVOR OF THE GODS: a short story

"Like Icarus, you flew too close to the sun. Someone had to bring you back down to reality. You don't belong with princesses, heroes, or demigods."

Learn more: **www.aliwinters.com/standalones**

CAST IN MOONLIGHT

Welcome to Havenwood Falls, a small town where nobody is what you think, where truths pose as lies, and where myths blend with reality.

Cast in Moonlight is a stand alone novella in the shared world of Havenwood Falls, a multi-author collaboration.

Learn more: **www.aliwinters.com/standalones**

ABOUT THE AUTHOR

Ali Winters is the USA TODAY Bestselling author of several series filled with romance, magic, and adventure. She enjoys breaking down characters to build them up so they find their true strengths.

Her first love will always be fantasy, but she fully admits to being obsessed with coffee and T-Rex, and has a weakness for love interests that walk the line between gray and villainy.

Connect with Ali online
www.aliwinters.com

facebook.com/authoraliwinters

instagram.com/authoraliwinters

bookbub.com/authors/ali-winters

tiktok.com/@authoraliwinters